BANKING *the* BILLIONAIRE

BILLIONAIRE *Bad Boys*

BOOK TWO

max monroe

Banking the Billionaire (Billionaire Bad Boys, #2)
Published by Max Monroe LLC © 2016, Max Monroe

ISBN-13: 978-1535434003
ISBN-10: 1535434007

Editing by Indie Solutions by Murphy Rae
Formatting by Champagne Formats
Cover Design by Perfect Pear Creative
Proofreading by Silently Correcting Your Grammar

DEDICATION

To Cassie and Thatch: You guys are assholes.

Disclaimer: We're assholes too. Love you.

Thatch

I'm Thatcher Kelly.
Harvard graduate.
Financial Consultant for Brooks Media and its subsidiaries and several other Fortune 500 companies.

What? It sounds familiar? Fuck that.
I can't help it if Kline went first and stole all of my shit.

Net worth: $1.2 billion. Yeah, perfect Kline is worth more than me. But I have my hands on a lot more things. *Important things.*

Okay, maybe not important. But they're…pussies. I have my hands on pussies.

Relax, I'm kidding. Well, mostly.

A man of many talents, I have more interests and jobs than you would expect.

Adrenaline Junkie. Jumps and falls, dives or climbs—*orgasms.*

If it makes the bottom fall out of your stomach and end up in your throat with a wave of pleasure for your whole body to surf afterward, I'm *in*.

I'm built like a tree, but I'd rather do anything than *just stand there*.

Get out, get wild, fucking live life.

It's also probably not a surprise I'm known for going through a laundry list of women. Quite frankly, I won't fucking apologize for it. They've all meant something to me, regardless of the amount of time they've been in my life, long or short, and they've all taught me something about life or myself that I won't give back.

But I've also longed for the kind of monogamy my friend Kline has for most of my life. A person who does their best to know you in and out and looks out for you when you can't look out for yourself. The kind of person who wants to live life to its very fullest—but wants to do it *with you*.

Bottom line, **I'm eclectic.** A confusing mix of inappropriate jokes and heartfelt sentiment, you can dig and dig, and you'll still be miles from the bottom of me.

At least, that had always been the case **until Cassie Phillips**.

She's crazy and needy and borderline inappropriate at all times.

But she's got the softest untamed heart when you're someone she cares about, and fuck if that hasn't become my singularly most important goal—mean something to the woman who already means all the things to me.

Because for the guy who wants wild and commitment in the same fucking breath, you better believe it's going to be **one bumpy ride**.

Fasten that seat belt tight, ladies and gentleman.

This is us.

CHAPTER 1

Cassie

As the sun started to descend below the optical edge of the ocean and the Key West sky turned pink and orange with the last rays of the day, I snapped a few final photos before pulling my camera away from my face. Twelve crazy-hot male models frolicked in the sand, their muscles wet from the water and their tight bodies clad in nothing but next summer's swim line for an up-and-coming New York designer by the name of Fredrick La Hue.

Yeah, it was a really tough life I was living.

"All right, boys, I think we can call it a night," I announced as I got to my feet and dusted the sand from my knees. "Great work today, everyone. If you're thirsty, which I know most of you lushes are, meet me at Sloppy Joe's. Drinks are on me."

The models and staff cheered, and I grinned.

"Consider this motherfucking shoot finished!" I exclaimed to a chorus of resounding hoots and *Here, here*s as I headed toward the tent and hooked my camera up to my laptop.

Hundreds of photos loaded on to the screen, and their tiny thumbnails begged to be clicked. Doing as their teeny beckoning bid,

I clicked to select all and opened them up in my editor. I could hardly contain my excitement as I caught sight of some of the raw shots I had managed to capture. It had been a long day, toiling from sunup until sundown, but after I worked my editing magic, I knew Fredrick would get a big ol' fashion boner over the plethora of sexy photos he'd have to pick from.

I grabbed a bottle of water from the makeshift snack table and, upon my return, found my assistant, Olivia, scrolling through the photos on my laptop. She glanced up from the screen and grinned. "These are fantastic, Cass."

"Thanks. I think Frederick is going to be really happy with them. He loves a good bareskinned man huddle. But who doesn't?"

Olivia smirked and continued clicking from one photo to the next.

She had been my assistant for a few years now, and I'd grown fond of our working relationship. Not only was she a good friend but I'd felt compelled to take her under my wing and teach her everything I knew about photography. She had the raw interest, and with my help on the technicalities and work ethic, I hoped that one day I'd eventually help her make the big jump from assistant to photographer.

Joshua, one of my favorite makeup artists and a pathological flirt, peeked over Olivia's shoulder and then nudged her out of the way with his hip. It didn't take his nosy ass long to start scrolling through my personal collection. "*Wait*…what is this? I don't remember this shoot."

An entire album of Kline, Thatch, and Wes's rugby team filled the screen and glinted like horny glitter off the apex of Joshua's eye. I smiled at the memory of taking those photos a few weeks before Kline and Georgia's wedding. We had stopped by the boys' practice before grabbing dinner, and needless to say, hot men playing rugby made me thankful I'd had my camera with me that day.

Joshua pointed to a picture of Thatcher. The Jolly Green Giant's tall frame was unmistakable, perfectly defined lines and toned muscles taking up so much space in the shot they almost jumped right off the screen, and the only thing covering that fuck-hot body was a pair of black knit shorts. Hair wet with sweat, he was just standing there, hands on his hips, grinning like a cocky son of a bitch.

"Seriously," Joshua insisted. "What is *that?*"

"That's a Thatch."

"A thatch? Is that one of those new cool words like *fleek* or *rachet?*"

I shook my head and laughed. "Thatch is his name, Thatcher Kelly," I explained before muttering under my breath, "Or an action. God, yeah." I stared at his photo. "I'd thatch that for sure."

He sighed. "Is he single?"

The question felt strange for a fraction of a second, and then the fleeting uncertainty was gone. I grinned. "Oh, yes, he's very single."

I mean, he *was* single. So technically, I wasn't lying. I was just leaving out the little detail of him not being into cock.

Joshua stared at the photo for a disturbing amount of time before asking, "Can I have his number?"

I didn't think twice about it. This was Thatch we were talking about, and I would gladly take any opportunity to fuck with him. "Give me your phone."

He handed it over, and I happily added Thatchsquatch's number to his contacts. I chose not to think about why I had it memorized.

"Dayum, I need this man in my life," Joshua said, staring down at the picture on my computer screen before glancing at the number in his phone.

I tilted my head to the side. "I thought you were dating someone."

Joshua grimaced. "I was, but apparently, I'm too clingy."

"Well, fuck that guy. He sounds like an asshole."

"Yeah," he muttered. "An asshole I was in love with. Hell, I'm still in love with him. I wish my heart would get the memo and forget he ever existed."

I shook my head in sympathy. But empathy? That was undeniably missing. "Man, oh man, love sure is a bossy bitch, isn't she?"

Joshua chuckled. "Wise words from the girl who never settles down."

I smirked. "Maybe I'm a bigger bitch than love."

He glanced down at his phone again, and then his eyes lit up. "Fuck it, I'm about to yolo and call this sexy motherfucker."

Before I had the chance to stop him—which probably wouldn't have mattered because, yeah, I wasn't going to miss this—he was tapping Thatch's number on the screen and putting his phone on speaker.

Three rings later and the deep voice my pussy would gladly flock toward filled the room. "Thatch."

"Is this Thatcher Kelly?" Joshua asked with a smirk, his eyes meeting mine.

I probably should've felt bad about throwing Josh to the proverbial wolves, but man, it was hard not to get a sick amount of enjoyment out of what was about to go down.

"You got him," Thatch responded, business and bossy and hot as fuck. My pussy made a bid to crawl out of my pants.

Oh, shit. Do not get excited, you flirty little bitch, I told her. *This phone call is about laughing, not boning.*

"Hi, Thatcher," my makeup artist turned sexual siren purred into the phone. "My name is Joshua, and we have a mutual friend."

"And who might that mutual friend be?" Thatch asked, open but wary. I knew he was a fairly private person despite his boisterous personality.

"Cassie Phillips."

Thatch chuckled, deep and throaty, and my nipples pebbled. "Yeah, I know Cassie." Apparently, based on their general non-reaction, I was the only one feeling like he meant *know* in the biblical sense. And I was the only one who knew he *didn't* know me like that.

"She happened to show me some pictures she had taken of you, and I gotta—"

"Cassie has a picture of me on her camera?"

"Oh, yeah, baby, she sure does. You're shirtless, and I can't deny I'm interested."

"You're interested?" Thatch's voice was laced with confusion.

"Yes. I'm very interested. And Cass happened to mention you were single. And well, I'm single. I think we'd hit it off. So, I was wondering if you'd like to grab a drink sometime?"

"And Cassie told you this was something I'd be interested in?"

Joshua's gaze shot to mine, but he kept his composure on the phone. "Not in so many words, but, yeah."

A soft chuckle filled the receiver. "Well, Joshua, it's a pleasure to talk with you, truly, but I've got a bit of a problem with this scenario."

"Oh." His voice was dejected. "And what would that be?"

"I'm kind of in love with a set of talking tits. And the owner of said mystic wonders is pretty fucking head over heels for my cock."

"I'm not in love with your cock, T-bag," I responded, and Josh's and Olivia's eyes aimed right at me.

Joshua stared at me for a few seconds and then flipped me off.

"You *are* a bigger bitch than love," he told me with an amused grin, handing me his phone and whispering into my ear, "You totally want to get Thatched, you little floozy. And don't think I'll forget about this anytime soon. You owe me, Phillips. You owe me big."

I laughed and shook my head. "Nah, I just like fucking with him. And how big are we talking here?"

"A new boyfriend with a ten-inch snake coiled inside his pants."

"Ten inches?" My eyes went wide. "You can take that much?"

"Oh, yeah. My deep throat game is strong." Joshua winked. "And you're a liar, by the way. You want that big, bad man between your thighs," he added in a whisper before heading toward the other tent to clean up.

I switched the phone off speaker mode, and Thatcher's deep voice filled my ear. "You know you don't have to create these elaborate pranks just to hear my voice, honey. The subscription messages and now this. Seems like a lot of extraneous effort when you can call me any fucking time."

"Bye, Thatcher," I said in dismissal, feigning annoyance even though I was anything but annoyed. Thanks to the photo and Thatch's throaty fucking chuckle, I was too busy picturing him driving his big train through my tunnel.

"Be good, Cassie."

"I'm always good."

He laughed. "I'm having a hard time believing that. Tell Joshua I appreciated the call and the offer. And if I wasn't into pussy, I would've taken him out for a nice dinner, some drinks, and then back to my place so I could fuck his brains out."

"You paint such a pretty picture. Are you sure you don't want to give him a shot? Who knows? Maybe you'll love the D?"

"You think?" he asked, audibly playing along even though we both knew when Thatcher Kelly pounded something, it was pussy.

"I let you kiss me, so stranger things have happened."

His voice dropped a few octaves. "You wearing a bra right now?"

"What does that have to do with anything?"

"You wearing a bra or not wearing a bra always has everything to do with everything. It's literally never off topic."

I shook my head but glanced down at my T-shirt. "This shouldn't surprise you, but no, I'm not."

If there was one thing Thatcher Kelly loved, it was my boobs. For all I knew, he had a fan club dedicated to the mounds on my chest.

"Yeah, I'm hard at that visual. It's safe to say I'm straight as an arrow."

"Put your boner away, Thatcher."

"Come help me," he dared.

"That's a lovely offer, but I'm not in New York. "

"Where are you?"

"Key West."

"And when are you coming home?"

"Not for another couple of days," I answered honestly.

"You should call me when you're back in town."

"Oh, I should? And why would I do that?"

"Because you can't stop thinking about me."

I stared out toward the darkening blue sea. I couldn't deny he was slightly correct on that front. Almost two months ago, we had spent an ungodly amount of time together while watching Kline and Georgia's cat, while they banged like bunnies in Bora Bora on their honeymoon.

The cat watching had turned to cat searching when Walter had gone missing for a few days, and somehow during that debacle, Thatcher Kelly had started to grow on me. I'd even found myself occasionally calling him or sending him random text messages just to see what he was up to.

It was all very unlike me, and I was starting to wonder if I just needed to fuck him out of my system.

"I don't know about that," I answered with a skeptical tone. "I mean, I just saw the new Superman movie, and I've been using up a lot of brainpower on Henry Cavill fantasies."

"I'm down for role-playing, honey. I'll even put a cape on my cock if that's what you're into."

Well, that was a hot visual.

"But how would I blow you?"

"You wouldn't. I'd be too busy with my mouth on your pussy. We'll save the blow job for our second date."

God, he was the king of one-upping. It probably should've annoyed me, but it didn't. I got far too much enjoyment out of bantering back and forth with him.

"Have you been Googling pickup lines again?" I teased.

"With great penis comes great responsibility, honey."

I laughed at that. "God, that's awful."

"Fuck me if I'm wrong, but I know you want me to kiss you again."

Yeah, so he had kissed me. *Once.* I was pretty sure it was used to shut me up, but it didn't leave a bad taste in my mouth. Though, it'd pissed me off when he acted like that kiss was a game. I wasn't normally sensitive to that shit, but I'd been fully invested in the moment until he'd taken me out of it. The bastard.

"I'm hanging up now."

He laughed. "Fine, fine. Call me when you're back in town."

"I'll consider it."

"You'll consider it?" he repeated. "Well, fuck, that's a hell of a lot better than the last time I told you to do that."

My eyebrow quirked up. "What'd I say the last time?"

"That you'd slap me in the dick."

"Don't worry, T. I'll find a way to accomplish both."

His deep chuckles were the last thing I heard before hanging up the phone.

Only then did I realize I'd expressed my intent to see him. Because no matter how I planned it, dick slapping was an in-person kind of thing.

CHAPTER 2

Thatch

Forty years of my parents' marriage and thirty-five years of my own life history had brought me here, back to my hometown, Frogsneck, New York. My parents were the picture of everything I wanted in a marriage when it came to commitment, and celebrating so many years of their love for one another tonight had been a seriously special experience. They were the best kind of people—loving and loyal and fucking honest to a fault.

But I hated being back here in my hometown, the looks people gave me *and* my parents never having faded even after this many years.

Perception is the ultimate example of "it is what you make it." Unfortunately, what people "made it" sometimes lacked basis in the truth.

I knew I shouldn't have come here to the local watering hole after the party. I should have remembered the past and toasted to the future in the privacy of my childhood home instead, but I hadn't.

And now, as the door opened to reveal one of my most negative high school memories, I had to face the consequences.

"Hey, Ryan, you see who's here?" Johnny Townsend asked his friend, Ryan Fondlan.

I'd spent so many of my younger years despising Johnny that even the sound of his name made my blood pump faster. That was probably the half-baked reason John from BAD rugby and I couldn't seem to get along. BAD was the rugby team Kline, Wes, and I played on during the week and the basis of our ridiculous nickname, the Billionaire BAD Boys. The team was aptly sponsored by and named after Wes's restaurant, BAD. It was a terrible fucking name for a restaurant, but hell if Wes wasn't profiting. It probably helped that he owned an NFL team and drew in the professional athlete crowd.

John was on that team, and I couldn't deny we spent far too much time tossing jabs at one another. *Shit*. I probably needed to try not to be such a prick next practice.

"Johnny—" Ryan attempted to interrupt, but it was no use.

Ryan had always been the well-meaning sidekick to Johnny's insensitive ways, and it pained the fuck out of me to see them both singing the same tune after this many years. It's one thing for boys to be boys, but it's quite another for men to act like them.

"I almost couldn't believe my eyes. A big shot like Thatcher Kelly at the Sticky Pickle? Seems odd to me," Johnny prodded, trying to incite a rise out of me. He'd been pushing my buttons since I was an overweight freshman just trying to survive high school. I'd never been insecure, but he'd been all too happy to try to make me that way. The tables had only turned when two years, a foot of height, and fifty extra pounds of muscle on my frame made them.

"Cool it, John," Ryan suggested, directing, "Have a seat and get a drink," before turning to me.

"Hey, Thatch." Ryan greeted me with a grimace, settling onto the stool next to mine and keeping himself between Johnny and me—a smart move—but that didn't stop Johnny from looking over me closely as Ryan spoke. "How are things?"

"Pretty good," I told Ryan honestly, but I kept it short in an attempt to make this interaction as painless as possible. I took a pull of my beer. I wasn't normally that big a fan of Coors, but tonight it seemed to be going down smoothly.

"Been a while since you've been around," he went on.

"Yep."

"And you're okay with that?" he asked, and Johnny scoffed.

"Of course, he fucking is. Too good for places like this."

My jaw ticked, but I did my best to ignore Johnny and focus on getting through the conversation with Ryan.

"Yeah. I see everyone I want to regularly. My parents come up, and Frankie's in the city." I shrugged.

"Frankie," Johnny said derisively under his breath, and I started to get really fucking annoyed for the first time tonight.

"Fucking watch it," I warned as I pushed off my stool. The sound of it scraping across the wood floor pulled the attention of several nearby patrons.

Ryan immediately stood up between us. "He's just having a bad night, Thatch. Recently divorced and his wife won custody today," he whispered.

Forcing my pounding heart to slow, I sat back down on my stool and flagged the bartender to close out my tab. Safe to say going out for a relaxing drink was no longer anything but stressful.

"How *is* Frankie these days?" Johnny asked, undeterred. I tried my best to take Ryan's information to heart and ignore him—and get the goddamn bartender to hurry up. The faster I got out of here, the better.

"Fucking shut up, dude," Ryan advised as I towered over them. I'd never been meek, but now I was the exact opposite of meager. At six-five and two hundred and fifty pounds, I was practically double their size.

"He stays away too," Johnny continued. "But I guess I wouldn't come home if I were him either. A fucking scumbag pig in his own shit, clinging to the coattails of the guy who killed his fucking sister just to keep his crappy business afloat."

Johnny stood up from his stool as my blood boiled, and he rounded Ryan to get in my face, a slimy smile on his.

His smarmy voice dropped to a knifelike whisper. "Tell me,
Thatch. How does it feel to get away with murder?"

I watched as a drop of blood ran from the raw split in my knuckles and dripped to the concrete floor. One and done, I'd knocked ol'
Johnny clean out with a halfhearted swing of my fist, and now, here I
was—in the cold concrete confines of an eight-by-ten cell.

As far as the eyes of the law were concerned, the one hit wasn't
that much of a problem, but the bar brawl that ensued between everyone else sure was. I guess in an old quiet town like this, entertainment
value could be found nearly anywhere—even in an unlikely and un-
founded opportunity for a fight.

"Kelly!" Sheriff Miller yelled, startling me from my focus on the
ground. "One phone call!"

I nodded with a polite "Yes, sir," and got up from the bench in the
holding tank to exit the cell. Sheriff Miller looked on while one of his
young deputies opened the sliding door. His eyes held disdain, and I,
frankly, couldn't blame him. I'd caused him more than enough prob-
lems in the years before leaving Frogsneck, and now, my first night
back after half a decade, I was his problem again.

Still, he respected my parents, something I couldn't say for a lot
of the small-minded people here, so I did my best to appeal to that.
"I'm sorry about this, Sheriff."

"Right," he said through a chuckle. "I'm sure you are. I can't imagine expensive suits are comfortable jail attire."

I filed that away and kept my cool. His eyes changed when mine
didn't. A flicker of begrudging respect, perhaps. "No, sir. I'm just sorry I'm in here, keeping you busy in the middle of the night. No matter

what somebody says, I should be able to keep my cool at thirty-five years old. That's why I'm apologizing."

"Margo's a pretty big sore spot, I imagine," he murmured, showing he knew the real reasons behind everything, no matter how much he actually witnessed. That's what made him a good sheriff.

My high school girlfriend, Margaret—Margo to most—died on a weekend away with me. I'd been the only one there to witness the whole horrible thing. Honestly, I'd moved on from it. Not her death, and not what I'd witnessed, but the whole life-changing aspect of it. I didn't carry it with me into everything I did, and I certainly didn't spend my time worrying over something I knew I wasn't responsible for. Small-minded people apparently had a lot more time on their hands.

But being accused of something so horrendous never becomes routine, and I still hadn't figured out exactly how to keep it from besting my patience. That was why I usually stayed away.

I hated that my first trip back in years had ended so predictably.

"Yes, sir," I answered honestly.

"Make your phone call," he ordered, gesturing toward the lone pay phone.

Fuck. It was safe to say technology wasn't helping me now. I didn't know anyone's number by heart other than my parents'. Well, I knew one. I laughed to myself at the reason I knew it.

"The last four digits spell out Cass now," my memory of a single late-night phone call with a tipsy Cassie Phillips said in my head. *"How fucking great is that?"* Fucking ridiculous is what it was. But, yeah, that wasn't happening.

"Sheriff—"

"What?" he snapped. Fucking great. We'd had our moment of mutual respect, and now I'd already ruined it. Fucking *fuck.*

"Would I be able to look through my phone to get a number? I only know one by heart—" I started on a lie.

"Then use it, Kelly," he interrupted.

I cringed as I pressed on. "I'm sorry, sir, but that number is for my parents, and quite frankly, I'd rather sit in here for eternity than ruin their fortieth wedding anniversary."

"Fine," he agreed, and I breathed a sigh of relief.

But it was short-lived. "No phone call. Go sit down."

Shiiiiit. The deputy opened the door again and waved me inside. As my ass met the cold bench, I leaned my head into the hard wall behind me with exasperation.

I was going to rot here. Sheriff Miller was going to make me stay here forever. *Way to fucking go, big mouth.* Johnny started to smirk at me from across the cell until he realized there weren't any bars between us.

"Townsend!" Sheriff Miller yelled. "You're up! Phone call."

Johnny pushed himself up off the bench and walked out, wandering down to the phone without one word. Five minutes ago, I'd have said I was the smarter of the two of us, but now, I wasn't so sure.

Closing my eyes, I tried to drift off to sleep or happiness, whichever came first. I thought I'd be thinking of a green-eyed girl, the one from my past who had given me so much grief tonight, but the eyes I saw were ninety degrees counterclockwise on the color wheel. Bright blue and fierce, I hadn't seen them anywhere but my fantasies for an entire month. There had, however, been an exorbitant amount of fantasies.

Oh, fuck. Jail was *not* the place to start thinking about fantasies.

With a deep breath, one thought bled into the next as I fell into a fitful sleep.

"Kelly!" being yelled by Sheriff Miller woke me from my catnap. I shook my head to clear the sleep and glanced around the otherwise empty cell. When my gaze landed on him, his expression was amused, and two beefy fingers were gesturing me toward him.

When I stood in front of him, he opened the door and waved me out and toward the phone.

"Hopefully, that nap helped you remember a number. You've got one minute to think and three to call. I'd suggest you make the best of all four of them."

Shit.

Still groggy from sleep and frustration, I didn't waste time, scooting out of the cell and heading straight for the phone. If I didn't go now, I had a feeling I wouldn't get a third chance. I mean, the practical side of my mind knew he couldn't actually keep me there forever just because I didn't know a phone number, but after the night from hell, it sure felt like it. I tried to use the brain in my head, man up enough to call my parents, but the effort was fruitless. Any time I spent avoiding this call was nothing but a delay in getting out of here, and today was the last day I could afford to spend on piss-scented vacation.

CHAPTER 3

Cassie

A shrill ringing in the distance echoed in my ears. I stirred in my sleep, turning over to blearily glance at the clock on my nightstand. The blood-red numbers revealed it was half past two in the morning.

"Fuckin' hell," I mumbled to no one in particular, pulling the comforter back over my head to form a cave of covers.

But the phone continued to ring, vibrating across the nightstand and mocking my sleep-deprived brain. I loved my sleep. *Loved. It.* While most women daydreamed about Henry Cavill sexing them into oblivion while his Superman cape slapped them in the face, I split my daydream time between Henry Cavill, Channing Tatum, and my bed—and the men weren't the majority of my fantasies.

I could only assume whoever was calling me must have lost a limb or literally been on fire because anyone who knew me understood *not* to interrupt my sleep time.

Two seconds away from screaming myself into a full-on tantrum, I wrenched the blankets off my body, and with eyes still closed and fumbling hands—knocking shit onto the floor in the process—I grabbed my phone, held it to my ear, and let fly with my best guess. "Georgia, I swear to God, if this is you, I will kick your husband's big dick so hard he won't be able to spend his nights banging you into the headboard."

A chuckle filled the receiver, but it wasn't of the female variety. It was deep and throaty and one hundred percent male.

When no words replaced his laughter, I sighed, pulling my comforter back over my head. "Seriously, dude. If you don't tell me who the fuck you are and why you're calling me, we are going to have some serious issues."

"What kind of issues?" he asked, amusement evident in his voice.

"My-foot-up-your-ass kind of issues," I snapped back.

He chuckled again. "Maybe I'm into that kind of kinky shit."

"All right, you deranged psychopath," I said, irritation highlighting my tone. "I don't care what kind of kinky shit you get off to. You could enjoy jerking off with cream cheese smeared on your schlong, and I wouldn't care. What I *do* care about is the fact that you're calling me at two in the morning."

"Cassie," he responded, still sounding irritatingly amused by fucking up my sleep. "It's Thatch."

"*Thatch?* I don't know a Thatch," I lied. I knew it was him, and more than that, I'd known before he told me. That voice had been rooting around inside my brain for a while now. Fucking *Thatcher Kelly*. He'd wiggled his way into my thoughts and hung around for-fucking-ever, seemingly quite the parasite.

Hopefully, if I continued to feign confusion, he'd let me go back to sleep.

He laughed again at that. "It's the guy you've been finger-fucking that perfect pussy to for the past month. Don't you remember? We were in a wedding together. I helped you find Walter after you lost him. You even called me from Key West because you missed me so much."

"None of this is ringing a bell."

And I didn't lose that goddamn cat. *He* did.

"I even let you feel my dick. Which you fucking loved, by the way."

"I did not fucking love feeling your dick," I retorted. "It was hardly memorable, if we're getting down to the *real* details."

"How big is it?"

I was *this* close to fucking answering.

"Why are you asking me so many goddamn questions?"

He chuckled *again.*

Yeah, the whole Jolly Green Giant nickname was right on the money, wasn't it?

But seriously, if he laughed again, I was adding "Kill Thatch" to my to-do list for Monday morning.

"Why are you calling me? Couldn't it have waited until, I don't know, the sun is up and I'm not sleeping?"

"Sorry," he responded, clearing his throat. His breathing was muffled as though he was moving around. "But this couldn't wait. I'm in a bit of a bind, and I could really use your help."

"My help?" I asked, sitting up on the bed. "Right now?"

"Yeah." He started to say more, but he was cut off when someone in the background shouted, "Your three minutes are up, Kelly!"

My eyebrows scrunched together of their own accord. "Where are you?" I questioned, highly suspicious. "And who was that?"

"Oh, that was just Sheriff Miller," he answered, his tone nonchalant. I could almost picture him shrugging as he said it.

"Sheriff Miller?" I repeated his words, having a pretty good idea where this conversation was headed. I mean, I was still kind of half asleep, but it didn't take a genius to deduce the basic details. "Tell me you're not calling me from where I think you're calling me from."

"Yeah, about that…" He trailed off, voice uncertain. "Have you ever been upstate before?"

"For fuck's sake, Thatch," I muttered, rubbing sleepy irritation from my eyes.

"Listen, Cass, I know I'm a pain in the ass."

"I'm gonna put a fucking pain in your ass, all right," I grumbled, voice thick with sleep and exasperation.

Thatch forged on, unfazed. "But I kind of got arrested tonight and I was hoping you'd be a sweetheart and come bail me out," he said, just as a robot-like voice warned that the allotted time for his call would be ending soon.

"Kind of got arrested?" I spouted back. "It sounds like you *are* arrested, motherfucker."

"So you'll do it?" he questioned, sounding far too hopeful.

"What about Kline? Or Wes? Or a fucking family member? How the fuck did I end up being your one fucking phone call?"

"I'm starting to realize fuck is your favorite word."

"What?" What was he even talking about?

He laughed again, and I wanted to reach inside the phone and strangle him.

Go ahead and mark the time as 2:35 a.m.
Kill Thatch is now number one on my to-do list for Monday.

"You say it a lot. Any variation."

"And?" I snapped when he didn't elaborate further.

"I *fucking* like it, honey." I could sense the smile in his voice.

"Are you hitting on me? In the same conversation where you just asked me to bail you out of jail?"

"That depends."

I sighed and leaned my head against the headboard. "On what?"

"If I say yes, are you going to hang up the phone?"

"I've been about four seconds away from hanging up the phone since I answered it."

"Thatcher!" A loud, booming voice called in the background. I could only assume it was Sheriff Miller. This was about the weirdest phone call I had ever received on a Saturday night. And that said a lot coming from me.

"So…you think you can help me out?"

"You're gonna owe me big time."

"Anything you want, honey."

"Where are you?" I put him on speakerphone and pulled up Google Maps, ready to GPS the convict's location.

"Upstate, in a little town called Frogsneck," he answered and proceeded to give me the address. He even told me to drive his Range Rover. All I had to do was go get it from his apartment.

"Oh, for the love of God," I muttered after seeing that it was going to be a ninety-minute drive. "Get ready, dickhead, because I'm about to get real fucking creative with payment for this favor."

I expected to hear laughter, but when I looked at the phone, his call had already dropped. I tossed it on my nightstand and hopped out of bed.

"What an idiot," I said to myself as I rummaged through my closet, trying to find something half decent and comfortable to wear for the drive.

I decided on flats, yoga pants, and a T-shirt that read "I just want to drink wine and pet my," with a picture of a cat at the bottom. Yeah, I didn't own a cat, but I had a pussy, and I loved to masturbate, so the shirt wasn't lying.

I threw my dark locks up into a messy bun and called it a day. I refused to waste time and energy on makeup because Numbnuts didn't deserve that kind of appearance after waking me up in the middle of the night.

As I strode into the kitchen and grabbed my purse, I decided I didn't want to pick him up in his car. No way, that'd be too generous on my part.

I almost called Georgia to see if Kline would let me borrow the Ford Focus she'd picked out for him, but I stopped when I thought about the fact that Thatch had called *me* over his best friend. Odd, for sure, but something in my gut told me there was a reason for it. Whatever the reason might be, I'd keep my mouth shut until Thatch said otherwise.

This left me with only one other option. *Zipcars.*

I didn't have a membership, but Tony, my neighbor across the hall, had one, and he also owed me a *huge* favor for doing a boudoir shoot for his five-year anniversary with his girlfriend, Francesca.

It was no secret I was a pretty successful photographer, and since I tended to have an open-door policy regarding anything sexual and perverted, it wasn't the first time someone had asked me to do a risqué type shoot. And if I'm being honest, my career had me in a lot of situations where I was snapping pics of half-naked men. It was definitely a perk, and I had met a lot of *fantastic* men doing what I did.

But the huge favor wasn't related to the actual logistics of the shoot.

The favor was because he hadn't given me a heads-up on the PDA situation between him and his girlfriend. Picture lots of dry humping and tongue fucking. Needless to say, I could've done without seeing his boner for the entire sixty minutes. And since I hadn't finished the final proofs for their shoot, I knew I had a really good chance of getting my hands on Tony's Zipcar membership.

After a quick phone call, I was at his door and having déjà vu from their horny boudoir shoot. Francesca was literally tits out with only a pair of boy shorts covering her curvy frame. Tony stood behind her, sleepily pawing her ass.

If I hadn't known I was in my apartment building, I would've thought I had just stumbled on to a soft-core porno shoot. Since I had no desire to be their fluffer, I grabbed the membership from Francesca and offered a heartfelt apology for waking them up in the middle of the night, strongly expressing that I was in a hurry.

Because I was. I needed to get the fuck out of their doorway before Tony started stroking his baloney pony.

"No worries, girlfriend. I'm just glad we could help," she said before they headed back inside their apartment probably to bone until someone passed out or went numb.

Once I hit the sidewalk, I hailed a cab and instructed the driver to head toward the Zipcar pickup that was about twenty blocks from my apartment. Thanks to the time of night, I was hopping out and tipping the cabbie within ten minutes.

Normally, I would've walked there, but I figured this whole bailing Thatch out of jail situation was a sooner rather than later type of situation. And unless you're looking to get mugged, women shouldn't be strolling around the city by themselves after last call.

Zipcars were a pretty easy concept. Anyone with a membership could head over to a Zipcar location, and with a simple swipe across the front windshield of a vehicle of their choosing, they were given instant access.

I glanced around the parking lot, taking in my options.

Jeep Cherokee…*No, too much room.*

Chevy Malibu…*Meh. I don't like the color green.*

Bright red paint glinted in the moonlight, and my eyes did the same as I landed on the final option. "Oh, yeah. That's the one," I muttered victoriously to myself.

Within minutes, I was heading toward Frogsneck with a grin the size of Texas smeared across my devious lips.

Yeah, he'd think twice the next time he decided to wake *me* up in the middle of the night to bail his ass out of jail.

CHAPTER 4

Thatch

Cassie had shown up at the Frogsneck Municipal Building just over two hours after I'd called her. Sheriff Miller had flirted with her shamelessly as she'd filled out the paperwork to bail me out on nothing more than good faith. *"Pretty ladies don't pay,"* he'd said, and of course, she'd eaten it right up.

What she hadn't done was say a word in my direction, choosing instead to wait outside while Sheriff Miller released me from the holding cell. He hadn't said much, but his eyes had said a lot, unspoken mirth pointing glaringly to the fact he'd found my whole ordeal more entertaining than anything else.

The direct sunshine moistened my eyes as it peeked over the eastern horizon, and her shadow stood leaning against one of the smallest cars ever created. I came to a stop at the end of the sidewalk and raised my voice across the three empty parking spaces between us. "You have *got* to be shitting me. I'm going to eat my knees in that fucking thing."

"I know," she said gleefully, spinning in a half circle to stare at the tiny red Fiat before turning to look over her shoulder at me. She wrinkled her nose as a smirk pulled one blue eye slightly higher than the other. "Let me know if you choke. I *might* pull over and try to clear your airway."

Scratching at my beard with both hands, I shook my head and laughed.

"So I guess you're not happy about the early morning phone call." She raised a pointed eyebrow as I walked toward her. "Or at least the accompanying drive and circumstances."

"Perceptive of you," she murmured as I got close enough to see, for the first time today, the tiny freckle that lived just under her right ear. It wasn't as big or obvious as a Cindy Crawford-style beauty mark, but I'd noticed it more than once. Maybe because I spent more time staring at her than anyone else.

As I analyzed her appearance for the benefit of more than my overeager cock, I realized she looked slightly disheveled, like she'd hopped right out of bed and come straight here. I hadn't thought about it before, but from a quick calculation of the drive time alone, I knew that's what she must've done.

Moving my gaze from the top of her wild-haired head down to meet her eyes, I tried to convey how thankful I was with two simple words. "I'm sorry."

Her wildly expressive brows activated again, and their message was doubt.

"I am. Really," I promised defensively. I hated to admit the embarrassing truth, but I owed her at least that much. "But a guy I know from high school said some things I should have ignored but didn't, and I didn't know who else to call. It's my parents' fortieth wedding anniversary, and even if it wasn't, there was no way I was calling them."

"Kline?" she suggested as she looked down and noticed my hand for the first time, her eyes widening at the open, raw knuckles.

I rolled my eyes and avoided confessing her number was the only one I could remember. Cassie Phillips's crazy ideas didn't need that kind of substantiation or power.

"The last time I called Kline in the middle of the night he told me he was going to amputate my most loved appendage. I've got five inches and at least fifty pounds on the guy, but he's clever, goddammit. He'd find a way."

"Wes," she pushed.

I shook my head. "On the West Coast. Some kind of recruiting trip."

Her whole body seemed to perk up, and for the first time, I noticed her shirt. A completely ridiculous creation by a company I owned a forty percent stake in. I smothered a smile as she asked, "Where?"

"What?" I asked, confused. She wasn't making sense, but if I was honest, I hadn't exactly been giving all of my attention to the conversation.

"Who, how, why," she rambled as she grew frustrated. "Where, as in what college, Numbnuts?"

It felt like a quiz, and I wasn't sure she'd let me in the car if I didn't come up with the right answer. And as much as I bitched, I wanted inside that fucking Fiat.

"Um, I don't know?" I ventured cautiously with a mindless scratch to my scalp. A shower definitely wouldn't be amiss at this point. "I think he was going a couple of places."

She huffed, yanked the driver's door open, climbed into the car, and slammed the door behind her, leaving me stunned in her wake.

Three seconds into the shock, I forced myself into motion, jumping toward and around the car, jerking open the door, and cramming my big body inside as quickly as possible like some form of origami. I had no doubt this crazy woman would drive all the way out here only to leave without me.

"What'd I do wrong?" I asked when she didn't even glance in my direction. I wasn't an expert, but I'd seen a woman pissed a time or two. Each time it happened I made an effort to log information so I could prevent it the next time. Unfortunately, I'd yet to establish a pattern.

"Called me in the middle of the night and talked me into driving to upstate New York!" she snapped.

"No," I clarified. "I got that memo loud and clear. I mean when we were talking about Wes."

"Would I have hit him?" she asked strangely.

I wasn't having any fucking luck following our conversation today. It was like we were constantly having two completely different ones.

"Who? Wes?"

"No! The fucker you hit! Would *I* have hit him?"

I couldn't help but laugh while I pictured it. Cassie was far from a heavyweight, but I imagined Johnny still would have ended up on the ground. "Long before I did."

She nodded, resolute. "Then you're forgiven for that." She backed out of the spot with ease and turned out of the parking lot in the direction from which she'd come.

A smile lifted the corners of my lips at the gift of her forgiveness. I didn't bother telling her I hadn't asked for it.

"Now I just want to get back to the city and climb into my bed. I'm about eight hours short on sleep."

"Um," I mumbled as I cringed. "I actually need you to take me to the bar."

"The bar?" The car swerved slightly as she took her eyes off the road to look at me. I fought the urge to grab on to the "Oh shit" handle.

"The scene of last night's crime," I explained with a slightly rough, self-deprecating laugh. "I've got a car there that needs to get returned to the Kelly residence."

She moaned, but she ultimately turned where I pointed and didn't say anything else. We rode in silence for two minutes before she took a hand off the wheel and ran it through her hair. Her mouth started to form a yawn, but she did her best to stop it. The result was a hideously unattractive facial contortion. My chest buzzed at the sight of it.

"Tired?"

She nodded for five straight seconds before speaking. "Yeah. You should know this by now, but in case you missed it, sleep and I are really fucking tight. Like, you know how people joke all the time about offering up their firstborn?"

I nodded and then realized it'd be hard for her to look at me. "Yeah."

"Well, when I have kids, they will be a legitimate sacrifice before sleep."

I laughed. "From what I hear, having kids is pretty much synonymous with no sleep."

"Fuck. So maybe I can't have kids."

"Nah. You just need to have them with someone who can stand to go without. It's all a trade-off."

Surprised eyes sought mine, and the car swerved again. I carefully avoided pointing it out. Instead, I offered the only thing I could right then.

"Want me to drive?"

She shook her head and yawned again. This time, the yawn won.

"Last night was your parents' fortieth wedding anniversary party?"

"Yep."

"A lot of lonely women in that crowd?" she teased.

A dot of dried blood stained the fabric of my pants, and I wiped at it even though I knew it wouldn't come out. My mind was sluggish as I processed her question, but the answer surprised me a little when it finally did. There might as well have been no women at the party for the amount I'd noticed them. "It wasn't exactly lively, but my parents enjoyed it, and that's all that matters to me."

"And I guess a phone call from their son at the local prison would put a damper on that."

I laughed because she had no fucking idea. "Yeah, I've already put them through enough for a lifetime."

As we approached the parking lot for the bar, I directed her to turn in. "This is it."

She leaned forward to get a better look out the windshield and let out a guffaw. "The Sticky Pickle?" A huge sign shot out of the earth and up about twenty feet, declaring it just that.

I smiled. "Yep."

"Good God, Thatcher. Not only can't you put your boner away, but now you've got it all sticky. Is this ever going to end?" she asked through humor-induced near-convulsions, two loose strands of hair falling down and around her frisky eyes. They seemed to turn up at the corners like an extension of her mouth. Moisture formed at the very center of her lips with an involuntary flick of her tongue.

My cock pulsed.

Oh, Jesus.

As I watched every single page of her flipbook of motion with utter fascination, all I could do was answer her honestly. Put my boner away around her?

"Not fucking likely."

After dropping my big-tire, 1964, sweet-as-*fuck* Chevy Nova SS off at my parents' house, we were back on the road. I'd wanted her to come inside, but all it took was one self-scrutinizing glance at her T-shirt and the connotation of an early morning visit to make her refuse. "*No way am I meeting your parents in a shirt that talks about petting my kitty before you have the pleasure,*" she'd said. I'd started to ask if that meant there was a chance of it happening soon, but thought better of it.

I'd rather have her fall into my trap without realizing it.

And in the end, she'd made the right choice. After a night of way more excitement than they were used to, my parents were still in bed.

A couple of quick kisses and apologetic good-byes from their bedside, and they were still none the wiser about my drama-filled night.

"Thank fuuuuuck," Cassie moaned again as we crossed the Hudson River by way of the Tappan Zee Bridge.

Any other time, any other place, and her moan probably would have had my titty-attuned tail wagging wildly. But not right now.

I had a serious cramp in my left thigh and my knees were about to become a permanent fixture in my chest, and still, as I glanced at my watch, I knew I had no other option but to trick my beautiful chauffeur into making another detour in this tiny fucking clown car.

After a night in the slammer, I could and would skip out on almost anything but this. There was a little girl with big eyes and a bigger heart waiting for me, and I'd have to be dead or dying to break a commitment with her.

"Um, Cass?"

"What?" she snapped. Her eyes looked like an exact embodiment of the root of all of the world's evil.

I sunk my teeth into my bottom lip to keep from laughing and looked out the passenger side window to conceal my smile. "I know you're not exactly happy with me right now—"

"Understatement," she emphasized.

"But I think I've got a cramp in my cock. Maybe you're not all that fond of mine, but you like them in general, right?"

Her eyes narrowed as she considered my lead-in. She wanted to ignore me completely, but Cassie couldn't deny her affinity for the D.

"What's your boner want now, Thatcher?" she asked suspiciously.

Laughter no longer concealed, I told her a version of the truth, but I wrapped it in a multitude of flirting in an attempt to distract her.

"Oh, honey, I can assure you, it wants many, many things, a great number of them from you. But I'm actually not coming on to you right now, not trying to insult your intelligence, and not asking your tits to keep my boner company."

"I don't get it. What else is there from you?" she teased, and I laughed. Because for the first time ever, from maybe the least expected person ever, she didn't sound serious when she said it. She sounded like she didn't actually think my intelligence stopped at the head of my dick. That my titty talk and boner references were just a coating for everything underneath. It seemed like she could *see* it—without prodding or encouragement—and that wasn't the norm. Most people never know more than a surface layer of each other's personalities. They take the bolder characteristics of a first impression at face value because they're lazy, and they carry those expectations and prejudices throughout the entire relationship. Maybe something about Cassie's appetite for new experiences made her dig deeper than the rest.

"Please," I begged, seeing the exit I needed approaching in the distance. "Just get off this exit and take me to the CVS a couple of blocks down."

"I don't know where I'm going—" she hedged, and I interrupted quickly so she didn't have time to overthink it.

"I do. I come up here all the time. I'll tell you where to go. Everybody wins. I'll get to stretch my legs, and I'll buy you a bag of Cheetos for your trouble."

"And a Diet Mountain Dew."

Bingo. I'd found a momentary weakness in her defenses.

"Yes," I agreed. "And a Mountain Dew."

"Diet!" she corrected.

"Yes. Diet. I promise. As long as the weight loss doesn't come from your tits."

She smiled and shook her head. "Sorry, bud. But the boobs are always the first to go."

Regular, I thought. *Definitely getting the regular.*

"Turn right," I instructed as we crested the hill of the exit ramp and approached the bottom.

As we got closer and closer, I kept expecting the car to slow, but it never did. Cruising at what had to be fifty, Cassie flew right out into traffic without even slowing amidst my screams.

"Jesus Christmas! Are you fucking nuts? Why the hell didn't you stop back there?" I yelled, looking back over my shoulder and grabbing the "Oh shit" handle without shame now.

"Oh. You wanted me to stop?" she asked, all mock-innocence. "You didn't say stop. You just said, 'Turn right.'"

Holy hell, she is insane!

"The stop was implied by the giant red sign!"

Her face took on a Gru-like air—as in, evil genius. "Maybe next time you'll be a little more specific and a lot more cordial."

"Fuck, you're a lunatic."

"Uh-uh-uh," she hummed. The red of her nail almost hypnotized me as it ticked back and forth in front of my face. Since my only choices seemed to be to concede or die, there was really no choice at all.

"Fuck, you're a lunatic, Fair Queen Cassie?" I ventured.

"Better."

"You scare me," I told her with a point of my index finger. "And that's saying something."

She shrugged. There were no fucks for her to give. Absolutely zero. I wouldn't have been surprised if she'd turned her pockets inside out just to prove it to me.

As the next turn approached, I carefully considered how to tell her. "Did you ever hear the story about Wei Wang?"

"No," she answered. Which was no surprise since I was making it up.

"Well, all the Wangs had a history of hanging right down the middle, if you know what I mean."

"Maybe you do only talk about cocks."

"But not Wei. He lived up to his name, hooking way to the left," I rushed on as we approached the fork in the road.

"Huh?"

"Stay to the left, hook left, this is your next direction, Luscious Cassie," I speed-replied as we barreled toward the divide.

"What the fuck?" she asked, but she did what I said. She did it at high speed and quite possibly on two wheels, but she did it.

"You wanted specific directions."

"Those weren't specific, they were fucking convoluted and ridiculous."

It was fair to say she was upset, but she had also been distracted, and in that moment, while trying to get her to do something she
wouldn't want to do, that was the more important of the two.

"Why the fuck are we in a neighborhood?" she asked, realizing
I'd taken her off course.

I could see the house I wanted, three down on the left, and appro-
priately timed my response. "Just pull over right here."

"Are you lost?" she accused and came to a screeching stop. "I
thought you said you knew where you were going."

I climbed out of the car carefully, sighing in relief when my back
cracked at the moment it reached full height. If it hadn't looked so
dirty, I might have considered kissing the pavement.

The glass storm door was the only one closed on the front of the
small, light blue, cape-style house, and my favorite little handprints
decorated the otherwise pristine pane.

"Come on," I said, leaning down into the car. "We're here."

"We're here?" Cassie shrieked. "What do you mean we're here?
What in the ever-loving fuck is going on?"

I rounded the car and opened Cassie's door, taking her by the
hips and pulling her out of the car and onto the sidewalk myself. "Sorry, honey, but I couldn't miss my best girl's party."

Her face dropped, and I swore she was a hot second away from
completely mutilating my nuts. It was stupid, but I never even considered moving my hands off her to protect the goods. There's a reason
natural selection is the way it is. When I was around her, I wasn't sure
I'd be the fittest in a survival scenario. But I didn't think other men
would be either. It had to be a biological deficiency.

"A girl?" she yelped. "You made me drive you to another girl's
party?"

It was dangerous, but I nodded anyway as Mila approached behind her. "Only girl I'd ever use you to get to is this one," I promised. And just because I wanted to, with a quick move forward, I pressed my lips to hers. The warmth of her mouth on mine spread immediately to my chest.

When I pulled back to look at her face and the shadow of a girl cast out in front of her, it was safe to say she was gearing up to tear into me for kissing her again without permission.

Until Mila's voice made her pull up short.

"Uncle Thatch!"

I felt like I could actually see her brain pump the brakes.

"There's my girl!" I greeted, dragging my eyes away from Cassie's slowly. The transition of my focus took just long enough that I caught the change on her face.

Mila's officially six-year-old little legs wrapped as far around my waist as they could go, and she grabbed me by the cheeks. "It's my birthday and you're here, la la la," she sang.

"You bet," I told her before swinging her around and back down to the ground. "I wouldn't miss your birthday for anything."

Cassie shifted beside me, and I hoped the movement was associated with her thawing. Mila, Frankie's daughter, noticed her for the first time.

"Who's this?" she asked. "Is she your girlfriend?"

Cass's eyes bugged out as I avoided the question. "This is Cassie."

"Hi, Cassie!" Mila greeted with an overeager wave. "I like your shirt!"

Cass's eyes shot to the *pussy*cat, and I stifled a laugh, stating, "I like it too," with a waggle of my eyebrows.

"Mila, come on!" Frankie yelled from the front door before he spotted me. "Oh, hey! Come on through, guys. Party's out back."

Mila took off, and Cassie slapped me on the back of the head. "That's for bringing me to a child's birthday party without any warning." Before I saw it coming, she slapped me right in the dick.

"Ow!"

"And that's for kissing me without my permission *again*."

I cringed internally because I'd taken the first warning during the cat-sitting debacle seriously. *"Don't ever kiss me again without permission,"* was a pretty easy command to follow. Or it should have been. From the seriousness of her scolding, I knew it meant something to her, but hell, I just hadn't been able to stop myself. She had some kind of pull I couldn't resist.

"All right," I agreed. "No more kissing without your permission."

"*No*, just no kissing," she expanded.

"See," I said. "That's the problem."

"Thatch—" she started seriously, turning to me. But I didn't let her finish.

"Come on. You can yell at me later. Right now we have to go to Mila's sixth birthday party."

She stomped back to the open door of the car and pulled out her giant purse, grumbling about castrating me the whole way, while I opened the back hatch and grabbed Mila's present out of my bag. Before I got arrested and changed everything, I'd planned to take a train early this morning. I'd actually thought it would be simpler than having to drive. Given the prison detour, it turned out to be a complication. When I glanced at my companion, I couldn't find the energy to get upset about it, though.

Herding Cassie inside was relatively easy, and as I introduced her to Frankie, she had a genuine smile on her face. I wasn't sure if it was for him or me, though; with his tan, tattooed skin and piercing light green eyes, he tended to have that effect on women.

Packed into the tight space of his kitchen, I stood between the two of them and waved a hand back and forth.

"Frankie, this is Cassie, Kline's wife's best friend."

"Hey, nice to meet you," Frankie said through a smile.

"And Cassie, this is Frankie. I own a tattoo shop with him."

"You own a tattoo shop?" she asked abruptly.

Frankie laughed. "I see you two know each other well."

I shook my head, laughed, and pushed on. "I also know Frankie from home."

"Home?" Cassie questioned.

"You just picked me up from there."

"Jail?" she joked, and Frankie drew his eyebrows together. I shook my head slightly to wave him off.

"Yes, exactly," I teased, but I could tell Frankie would be asking me questions later.

"Where's Claire?" I asked him.

"Out back with the kids." I glanced out the window and spotted her soft smile almost immediately. "Come on. We've got burgers and stuff."

We followed him out, and I set my gift on the designated table. Cassie watched as I set it down, and then rummaged through her bag, walking away from me and straight to Mila when she found what she was after.

Frankie and I both looked on as her hand appeared with a Barbie—still in the box—in tow.

"What the hell?" I murmured. "Did she just have that thing in there?"

Frankie laughed and crossed his heavily tattooed arms across his chest. He jerked his chin in her direction. "What's the deal there?"

"No deal."

"Right. I'm not blind. I read her shirt and noticed the swells underneath."

"Uh-oh," I teased. "I'm telling Claire."

"Telling me what?" she asked as she came up beside me and placed a hello kiss on my cheek. The sweet scent of her perfume filled my nostrils and made me smile. I'd been friends with the two of them for as long as I could remember. Our love for Margo linked the three of us together. She had been one of Claire's closest friends and Frankie's little sister.

"He was planning to tell you that I'd noticed his date's assets," Frankie admitted diplomatically.

Claire laughed and shrugged until the tips of her blond hair grazed her sleeveless shoulders. "I noticed too."

Empty burger dish in hand, she moved on quickly, carrying it to the kitchen to put it in the sink.

As soon as she disappeared, my eyes found Cassie again and watched as she rolled the ends of her yoga pants up to the top of her calves in preparation to play whatever game the kids had talked her into. Mila tried to mimic her by lifting the hem of her dress, but Cassie pushed it back down gently and laughed.

"She's the phone call from a couple of weeks ago, huh?" Frankie asked, and I just nodded. He'd seen me out the window of the shop laughing and smiling and swooning all over the goddamn place while Cassie flirted and flaunted her ability to converse while drunk, but my eyes refused to leave their perusal to acknowledge him with any more than that.

He laughed as Cassie stood in front of Mila, doing some kind of ridiculous dance for her and her friends, and I felt the sentiment of his humor way down deep in my chest.

"Man," Frankie muttered. "I can't wait to watch this unfold."

CHAPTER 5

Cassie

"So, how long have you known T?" Claire asked as she handed me a freshly washed serving bowl. We'd been at Mila's sixth birthday party for just over four hours, and while I was exhausted, I was also having the time of my life.

Hey, I don't have to pour beers from my tits to have a good time.

I took the dish and dried it, my eyes fixated on the scene through the kitchen window, watching Thatch hula-hoop with Mila in the backyard. "Not too long. He's best friends with my best friend Georgia's husband."

Claire smiled warmly at the tongue twister, and her eyes jumped as she followed the breadcrumbs all the way to the end of the trail. "Kline?"

"Yeah." I nodded, setting the dish on the clean rack. The fact that she knew Kline and at least of Georgia made me curious. "How long have you known Thatch?"

She grinned. "Since we were kids."

"So you know all of his dirty secrets?" I teased. Her grin fell slightly in response, and it was not the reaction I had expected. She grabbed another dish towel and wrung it in her hands.

"I've known him just as long as I've known my husband, and still, I don't know *everything*. He can be quite the mystery, but I'm not even sure he intends for it to be that way. Thatch is the kind of guy who's open and honest but doesn't exactly take it upon himself to open up, if you know what I mean."

"Yeah, I'm noticing that." I mean, I hadn't known about the tattoo parlor until today.

"But he's a good guy." She unclenched her hands, tossed the towel on the counter, and smiled as she looked out the window. "Underneath all of that charming swagger and big ego, he's got an even bigger heart."

My gaze followed hers back outside. I watched Thatch lift Mila up and throw her over his shoulder, running around the yard while all of her friends chased them, giggling and smiling as they ran. It didn't take a genius to see Claire was right. My chest ached from the overwhelming cuteness of it all.

Claire turned off the faucet with a muttered, "Oops," as though she'd forgotten to do it before. After a deep breath, she hitched a hip against the counter and faced me, eyes all-knowing. "He's basically a big teddy bear when you get to know him." She winked and put a kind hand to my arm. "Just go easy on him, okay? He hasn't necessarily had the easy road when it comes to relationships."

I shook my head, and my eyes made an attempt to bug out of my head. "Oh, we're not in a relationship."

"I know," she said, smirking. "But I also know Thatch enough to know he's fucking tenacious."

I grinned at the fact it was the first f-bomb I'd heard Claire drop since we got to her house, but I guessed little ears would do that.

"Tenacious?" I questioned, oddly amused.

She nodded and raised her eyebrows. "Especially when there's a hot chick with a fantastic rack involved."

That made me laugh. "Thanks."

"Thanks for helping me clean up. Everyone else is all about the eating, but when the dish soap comes out, they scatter like rats."

"No problem." What I didn't tell her was that I probably would have been with the other rats had I not been trying to make some sort of quasi-positive first impression. "Thanks for letting me crash Mila's party."

"You brought a present," she pointed out through a laugh. "I'd say you pretty much won my daughter over the second she saw the cat on your shirt and watched you pull a brand-new Barbie out of your purse…" She paused for a second, and then added, "Before I head back into the backyard, I have to know one thing."

I tilted my head to the side. "What's that?"

She nodded toward my chest. "They're real, right?"

Fuck, I loved Claire already. She was sweet and honest yet had no qualms about saying whatever was on her mind. I was hoping this wouldn't be the first and last time we hung out. This was a chick I could definitely get along with.

"Definitely real."

"I knew it!" she exclaimed as she walked toward the back door, opening it and shouting toward her husband, "You owe me twenty bucks, Frankie!"

He just laughed, and Thatch shot him a questioning glance. Frankie held out both hands in front of his chest, and Thatch immediately knew, chuckling in response. "I told you, dude."

"I want twenty bucks!" Mila yelled as she came barreling across the yard and through the door. She stopped once she reached the kitchen, hands on her little knees and lungs taking deep breaths. "Why does Daddy owe you monies?"

"Because he keeps forgetting that Mommy is always right," Claire answered and smiled in my direction.

"Girls are *always* right, Mila," I agreed. "Never forget that."

She put her hand on her hip and eyed me with a serious face. "But that's not what Patrick says."

"Who's Patrick, baby?" Claire asked, cupping a loving hand around Mila's sweet cheek.

"He's just some stupid boy in my class. He says boys are smarter than girls, and I'm the biggest dumb fathead of them all."

Oh, poor little asshole Patrick. He'd be in for a rude awakening when he got older. I had the urge to give him a come-to-Jesus moment now, but for some reason, society frowned on that kind of interaction with children.

"Sometimes boys say mean things when they like a girl." Claire sighed, visibly just as annoyed with a six-year-old boy as I was but trying to be diplomatic about it.

She shook her head. "Patrick doesn't like me. He pulls on my pigtails and chases me on the playground."

Claire and I exchanged a knowing look.

"You want to know a secret about boys, Mila?" I asked.

She nodded with enthusiasm.

"Come here, I have to whisper so your mommy doesn't hear."

Mila skipped over to me and put her hand on my shoulder, tugging me down to her level. "Tell me! Tell me! I *love* secrets!"

Claire just watched on with amusement as I whispered some very valuable advice into Mila's ear. When I was done, she covered her lips and giggled.

"Don't ever forget that, okay?"

She held out her pinkie finger and wrapped it around mine. "I pinkie promise, Aunt Cassie."

My heart squeezed.

"Oh, baby, she's not your aunt. She's just Uncle Thatch's friend," Claire interjected, flashing me an apologetic look.

"Yeah, but her and Uncle Thatch are gonna get married and have a baby and they's gonna take me and my new baby cousin to Disney World! We're gonna have so much fun!"

I wasn't sure how in the hell to respond to that, which was a first for me. I generally had a retort to every-fucking-thing.

"Mila!" Claire laughed in horror.

"What?" she asked, not the least bit concerned she'd just planned out my future. "Uncle Thatch said it was a really good idea!"

"Of course, he did," I muttered and met Claire's tickled gaze.

"Tenacious," she mouthed with a wink.

"Mila! It's time for presents, baby girl," Frankie called loudly enough that we heard him. Mila ran out the door at a dead sprint, straight for the picnic table covered in pink wrapping paper and sparkly ribbons.

As Claire and I followed her outside, she whispered in my direction, "What'd you tell Mila?"

I grinned. "Everything you probably wanted to say but didn't because you're a good mother."

"I hope you told her to kick that little asshole in the nuts."

I winked. "Oh, don't worry, it was definitely something along those lines."

She laughed, wrapping her arm around my shoulder. "Remind me to tell Thatch he's not allowed to come to our house unless you're with him."

"No doubt, I'll tell him while I'm buying our future child's and your daughter's plane tickets to Orlando."

For now, I'll give him a taste of his own medicine.

CHAPTER 6

Thatch

I watched as Cassie took off down the street, knowing her foot must have been nearly to the floor. She'd excused herself while I was saying my good-byes, her plan only evident when I heard the little hamster engine of the Fiat roar to life.

I shot out the front door at a jog, but she was already pulling away from the curb, my bag still inside.

"Looks like you're going to need a ride," Frankie said as he slowly came up beside me.

I forced a shrug as her fading taillights burned in my chest. "I probably should have warned her about coming here when I begged her to come bail me out this morning."

A woman like her only puts up with so much.

"Yeah, what's that about?" he asked.

"It's not important."

"Ah, okay. I'll take that to mean the opposite. Our friendly hometown is still giving you hell about my sister."

I nodded even though it wasn't a question, but I said nothing else. He didn't need to know it wasn't a remark about Margo that had upset me the most. It had been the comment about him that crawled under my skin. I turned to head into the house just as Mila came running out the front door. The sound of tires screeching to a stop filled the void behind me. Craning to look over my shoulder, I found Leadfoot Leann right back where she'd started.

"Thatcher!" Cassie yelled, apparently having circled the block. "Get over here and get in the car!"

Her smile was ear to ear, and there was nothing I could do to stop it from spreading to my own face. Cassie winked, but it wasn't at me. Curiosity made me turn around to find the source.

Mila stood there giggling and pointing at Cassie as Cassie pointed back at her.

"What did I say?" Cassie yelled through the open window of the car.

Mila's little voice was shrill as she shouted back. "Give boys hell!"

"Mila!" Claire admonished, but Frankie just laughed.

"Okay, now I really like her," he said, referring to my crazy driver. Safe to say he wasn't the only one.

I'd thrown her into the lion's den, for fuck's sake, but she'd flourished. Socializing and mingling without me and owning her yoga pants and T-shirt like a motherfucking gown. I still couldn't figure out the birthday gift she'd managed to pull from her purse.

She wasn't actually upset with me over my deceitful directions and unexpected stop; she was just checking in to the game.

With one final kiss to Mila's and Claire's cheeks and a fist bump for Frankie, I ran for the car and closed my hand around the door handle just as Cassie gassed it two feet and slammed on the brakes. Her laughter echoed throughout the neighborhood.

"Okay, Mary, let me in the car."

"Mary!" she shrieked and floored it again.

Frankie, Claire, and Mila looked on, laughing a little more with every exchange.

"You better remember my name, Thatcher. Some other women

might not care, but I'm liable to murder you."

"It's just a nickname," I said with a laugh as I finally got the door open.

"A nickname?" she laughed. "Well, I know you don't mean Mary of the Virgin variety, so you better explain."

"Poppins," I clarified, but only after my ass hit the seat and both feet were in. She was more likely to wait for me if she was also waiting on an answer. "Where the hell did you get that Barbie in your purse?"

She shrugged. "Stuff tends to build up in there."

"A Barbie? What else is in there? Tell me it's handcuffs and a short skirt."

She shrugged again like it was the most normal thing in the world. "You better tell me where to go. I'm not good with directions."

"You just backtrack."

"All I remember is that your wang hangs left."

"Not my wang," I contested through a laugh.

She smiled. "Take it up with the judge."

"Only if the judge is you," I teased back.

"Put your boner away, Thatcher. The ruling is final," she said with a wink and pretended to bang a gavel on the dash. My cock must have been a pretty shitty listener, though, because that fucker did the exact opposite. I shifted in my seat and pointed in the direction she should go.

"Just follow this back around to the right and turn right at the light."

"Right? Are you sure?"

"I'm sure," I said with a secret smile.

After she was done, I pointed out the next left, and that was when she really got suspicious.

"Wasn't the Saw Mill River Parkway back there? I thought I saw a sign."

"You have to go a different way to get back on," I lied.

Her eyes narrowed, but she kept driving for another mile before she questioned it.

"I think your wang is fucking busted, Thatcher. I'm not seeing the Parkway anywhere."

"Oh, you know what?" I said, playing along. "I think you're right. Just go right up here. You can turn around in this parking lot."

"Ughhhhhh," she moaned, and I had to stifle a laugh.

Gravel slid under the tires as she gunned it through the entrance and started to execute her turn. When she was about halfway through her U-turn, I yelled, "Wait! Stop!"

"What?" she shrieked back, slamming forcefully enough on the brakes that we skidded to a stop.

I pulled the door handle to open it and climbed from the car, watching as she did the same before answering. Her eyes were crazy again, and I felt the phantom lasers on my skin. Luckily, the burn of an imaginary laser was pretty mild. "Okay. Don't be mad, but I wanted a milkshake."

"Oh, you motherfucker," she seethed.

With a jaunty wave and a completely unapologetic smile, I turned to head into the ice cream shop, maniacal laughter rumbling my chest all the way to the door.

"Laugh it up now, but that's the only milkshake you're gonna see today. And you better fucking believe mine brings all the boys to the yard."

I'd see about that.

CHAPTER 7

Cassie

"**G**et out of the car, Cass," Thatch demanded, holding the door open with his bear claw of a hand. I stared at it with irrational anger as the size and strength and fucking veins of it did their best to tempt me into mental porn GIF territory.

Fuck you, traitorous tactile teases.

One activity after the next, the giant fucker had tricked me into chauffeuring him around all day. To the party and ice cream, of course, but also to the bank and several rental properties he apparently owned in Queens before taking over behind the wheel. Even then, I had a feeling he'd been tempted to take me to a bar or two, but I'd slurred several sleepy threats to his life and, evidently, one stuck.

Thank fuck.

We were currently sitting in front of his building, and I was more than ready to head back to my place so I could begin my sleep marathon. But he was trying like hell to cockblock me from my bed. After everything he'd put me through today, *now* he was convinced I was too tired to drive home.

I shook my head. "I know I'm a real joy to be around, but you've monopolized enough of my time today. So, move your ass, T-bag. I'm going home."

He stretched his big arms across the top of the door and the roof of the car and leaned forward, smirking down at me. "Honey, I know you have *many* talents, but I'm seeing a dilemma with trying to drive from there."

"What are you talking about?" I asked, fighting the gravity of my heavy eyelids. As much as I tried, they wouldn't open past a squint.

"Pretty sure you need the steering wheel and pedals to get this clown car to move." He nodded toward the opposite side of the dashboard. "Which just so happens to be over there."

I followed his eyes and realized I was still in the passenger seat.

Well, shit. I guess I really am tired.

"Thanks, Captain Obvious, but I already knew that," I lied, unbuckling my seat belt and making a move to climb over the console. Thatch stopped me before I could make another inch of progress by locking his big, meaty arms around my waist and pulling me out of the car.

"Goddammit! Put me down, you ogre!"

But Shrek ignored my demands, tossing me over his shoulder and striding toward his building. With impressive precision, he tossed the keys to the doorman and instructed him to park the Zipcar in an approved space.

"No! Do not park it! I'm using it!" I shouted as I slapped him across the back with an opened palm.

"Calm down," he said through a chuckle as his legs ate up the tile in long, fluid strides.

"*Thatch!*" I shouted even louder, my voice echoing against the marble walls of the swank lobby. Fucking hell, I hadn't been in control of one goddamn thing today.

One big hand landed against my ass in a smack, and I squealed in response.

"Cool it, Crazy, or else I'll just keep spanking."

I bored holes into his back, wishing like hell my feet were on the ground so I could slap the shit out of him. "If you touch my ass one more time, I will bite your dick off."

"You know, I'm not much on teeth, but for you, I'll find a way to enjoy it."

Fucking king of one-upping.

He gripped the backs of my thighs with his big hands and strode onto the elevator. I heard him tap a button as the doors slid shut and then we were moving, up, up, *way up,* to what I could only assume was the penthouse level.

Thatch didn't put me down until we were inside his apartment and my ass was hitting a plush leather couch. "Stay there," he demanded. "I'm going to heat us up some food, and hopefully, that will give you enough energy to ride the subway home."

"I'm not a dog," I retorted as I let my head fall back against the cushions. I didn't even allow myself the opportunity to browse his apartment. My eyes had already fallen shut from the luxurious feel of his couch, and I was too tired to think about anything else. The decor, the man—the weird way arguing with him made my blood hum—all of it would have taken a considerably larger amount of energy and cognitive function to explore.

"Comfortable, isn't it?"

I peeked out of one eye to see Thatch standing above me with an amused grin on his face.

"I thought you were making me something to eat?"

"I thought you weren't tired?"

The room went dark even as I flipped him the bird. "I'm just resting my eyes."

"You know, that's exactly what my mom says right before she takes a forty-hour nap."

My lips twitched. *Funny bastard.*

"Shut up and make me food," I retorted, but my voice wasn't very convincing. Sleep was trying like hell to make me her bitch.

All I got in response were a few soft chuckles and the sound of his footsteps fading away.

"Huh?" I mumbled at the feel of big arms cuddling my body against a rock-hard chest.

Am I having another Henry Cavill dream?

I lifted my hands to cover my eyes from the light and the possibility of getting hit by rogue debris. It always seemed to be dusty in my Superman fantasies. And if it wasn't a dirt thing, it was another. Last Cavill fantasy, I got a mouth full of cape instead of Supercock, and I had promised myself I'd never let that unfortunate dream sequence happen ever again.

"You fell asleep on the couch in about the most awkward position I've ever seen. I figured you'd be more comfortable in my bed," the voice said, soft yet husky, and undoubtedly turning me on.

"Henry?"

"Who the fuck is Henry?" The voice turned angry as we continued to move—*or maybe we were flying?*—to some unknown place.

I blinked my eyes open and came face-to-face with Thatch. His brown eyes were darker than normal, and his mouth was set in a firm line. I reached up and let my fingers run across the dark, scruffy, short beard covering his jaw. "You're not Henry Cavill."

"No," he said with a smirk. "I'm better."

"This dream is different, but hell if I'm not already into it."

The truth was, I'd been here before, but it had been more of a daydream, a completely conscious exploration of what it'd be like to be close enough to Thatch that I could feel him, smell him—fuck him until I couldn't walk. It made complete sense that I'd transitioned into thinking about it in my sleep too.

A soft chuckle left his lips. "This isn't a dream, honey."

My back was pressed into something soft, maybe a comforter...

or maybe we were about to bang on a cloud? I didn't know, but one thing I *did* know was that I was down for it. *All* of it.

Dream Thatch lay down beside me and pulled blankets over top of us, and that's when I realized we were in a bed, a huge motherfucker of a bed. Fantasy or not, it made sense the Jolly Green Giant would need a California King to accommodate his size.

He got comfortable beside me, stretching out and getting into what I assumed was his preferred sleeping position—on his back with one beefy arm stretched over his head. I turned on my side and perused his body, even lifting up the covers to find that he was only wearing boxer briefs. Lord, the muscles on this man. He was a buffet, and I was ready to get my money's worth.

"Cass? What are you doing?" He watched me rub my hands across his firm chest.

"I'm horny," I told him. Because, yeah, I was, and why did Dream Thatch have to be so damn irresistible? I had to squeeze my thighs together just to curb the pulsing sensation between them. But it wasn't enough. I needed more.

He laughed softly. "I think you're dreaming, honey. You should probably go back to sleep."

But he didn't make any attempts to stop my hands from taking inventory. And they kept exploring, sliding past his belly and down to his briefs. *Oh, yeah.* Dream Thatch was horny too.

I smirked down at him as I got to my knees and straddled his hips. A moan left my lips the instant I felt him hard and thick and pressed against my pussy. "Oh, fuck yes."

His eyebrows rose to his forehead. "Honey—"

"Shh." I pressed my fingers to his lips. "Just lie back and enjoy the ride, Thatch. I'm gonna make this *real fucking good* for both of us."

"*Shit,*" he groaned as I rotated my hips. "*Fuck.* What is happening?"

"I don't know, but I'm really liking it."

"Are you even awake right now?" He gripped my hips, stopping my movements. His eyes stared into mine, a heady mix of concern and raging lust.

I shook my head and laughed at Dream Thatch's attempts to trick me, and I bit into my bottom lip.

"*You're* awake." I rotated my hips again—despite his efforts to stop me—to punctuate my meaning. Thatch's dick was wide awake and raring to go. *Oh, yeah.*

"And I'm fucking loving the feel of you between my legs."

"Christ," he groaned again.

I leaned down and pressed my lips against his. I slipped my tongue inside his mouth and kissed him deep. He stopped questioning me then, and he tangled his hands into my hair as he took control of the kiss. Groping intensified, and the race to get as close as possible turned into an all-out wrestling match. We were both moaning into each other's mouths, our bodies instinctively moving and grinding in a perfect pleasure-inducing rhythm.

When it felt like a spark lit a fire between my legs, everything started to become a lot less fuzzy dream and more lust-fueled reality. Surprised, I sat up, breaking the kiss and staring down at him. This feeling and the rapid rise and fall of my chest were not the results of a dream. *Nope,* I was definitely awake and about two seconds away from fucking Thatch.

Well, this is unexpected.

I rubbed a hand over my eyes, blinking past the fog, and looked at the man beneath me. Thatch appeared utterly confused, but I could still see that layer of need beneath his pupils.

"Cass?" he asked, gauging my face.

I thought it over for a good thirty seconds. I could stop this before it went any further fairly easily. I knew he wouldn't push the issue. But the only problem was I didn't have any good reasoning to back that option up. I was now wide awake, Thatch's cock was still hard, and hell if my pussy wasn't begging for a ride.

And if we're really looking at the situation objectively, *he* woke *me* up. This meant Thatch had to take responsibility for his actions and help me fall back asleep.

Yeah, we're definitely going to finish this. I was going to ride the Jolly Green Giant until he lulled me into a mind-numbing orgasm and right back to motherfucking sleep.

"Guess what, Thatch?" I asked, smirking down at him. I'd paused for who knew how long, but he seemed perfectly content to rub his hands everywhere within reach to keep occupied.

"What?" He tilted his head to the side as said greedy hands rubbed across the tops of my thighs.

I leaned forward and pressed my mouth to his again, slipping my tongue between his lips and getting a taste of him before sucking on his tongue and spurring an intoxicating groan from his throat.

"I'm going to fuck you," I told him as I moved my mouth down his jaw to his neck and then, his tattoo-covered chest.

"You are?" he asked, shock and surprise and a whole lot of "what the fuck is happening right now?" evident in his voice.

"Oh, yeah. I'm about to get your boner out and have a fan-fuck-ing-tastic time." I grinned when I found something shiny and met-al for my tongue to play with. My lips caressed his pierced nipple, sucking the metal into my mouth and flicking it with my tongue. My mouth tortured a few "*fucks*" from his lips until I sat up on my knees.

Holy hell, Thatch's long body made for some kind of view.

"You owe me an orgasm after waking me up. And I *always* collect on payment."

"I—*what?*" he asked through a half laugh and moan. But I guess a girl grinding herself on you would get that kind of incredulous re-sponse.

"You. Owe. Me," I repeated as I took off my shirt and bra, tossing them to the side of the bed.

He stopped asking questions then, eyes too distracted by my chest. Gripping my breasts with both hands, I rolled my nipples be-tween my fingers and watched him watch me.

"Fuck, you're beautiful." He licked his bottom lip as he continued to watch, seemingly unable to look anywhere other than my tits.

"Do you want a taste?"

"I won't be satisfied with just a taste," he said, sitting up and taking my mouth in a toe-curling kiss. His tongue danced with mine as he gripped my ass, sliding me against his cock. "I want it all, honey," he whispered against my lips before leaning down and sucking a nipple into his mouth.

His tongue was devious, I knew that much as it flitted across my nipple with two short flicks and a deliciously long drag. My hips ground against him as I threaded my fingers into his hair, encouraging him to give the other nipple just as much attention. And he did. The man was nothing if not thorough.

But I could only take so much teasing before I started to get frustrated. I gripped his hair, pulling his eyes to mine. "Get naked. Get a condom. I need your cock inside me."

Thatch didn't think twice about my demands, flipping me onto my back and removing my yoga pants and panties like a goddamn magician. His briefs were gone, and he was sliding a condom on between one blink and the next.

Before he could take control, I pushed him back down onto the bed, straddling his hips and guiding him inside me.

"Well, *fuck*," I moaned the second his dick was buried to the hilt. "God, your cock feels so good," I said as I started a smooth up-and-down rhythm, my pussy clenching against him every time he was pressed deep. The heat of his chest seeped into the palms of my hands, and it felt like being zapped back to life by defibrillator paddles.

"I'm feeling all kinds of things about your pussy, honey. If you weren't sitting on my dick, I'd be worshiping this perfect cunt with my tongue." He grabbed my breasts again, his thumb flicking against my nipples and spurring tremors to roll down my spine.

"By all means," I said as I moved off of him and straddled his face. He started to disagree with the change in position until I gripped his hair in one hand and spread myself with the other. "Eat it, Thatch. Make me come on your face."

CHAPTER 8

Thatch

Surely I was having a stroke.

I mean…were these the symptoms of a stroke? Maybe not for everyone, but certainly for a guy like me, having a stroke would be something like this.

Cassie's creamy thighs rubbed against my cheeks, forcing my short beard to pull the other way and tug at the nerves.

God. Okay. Jesus, I needed to relax. My heart was beating unbearably fast, and there was no way I could maintain the pace for more than a minute.

But *fuck.* The smell of her pussy as she literally *rode* my face was goddamn indescribable. It didn't smell like anything else I'd ever smelled before—even other pussies—but whatever pheromones it housed must have been specially programmed for me. Like Miracle-Gro for my dick. I couldn't see it at the moment, because I couldn't see anything other than this wild woman's fucking perfect pussy, but it was bigger than it'd ever been. A wager of fifteen grand on that very fact wouldn't have even made me blink.

Not to mention, how the fuck had we gotten here? How in the

hell was I having sex with Cassie Phillips right now? My head was obviously too round and thick to wrap around the unexpected concept.

When she ground down harder on my mouth and whimpered, I recognized the need to forget all the details and just concentrate on what I knew. And I *knew* how to eat a fucking pussy.

The secret was simple.

It was never, *ever* the same.

It could be the same woman, the same day, the same fucking session, but a woman's pussy is a special kind of woman. She's picky but fucking generous, and she gets off on all kinds of wicked shit, but her biggest turn-on is variety and a good sense of mood.

I did my best to listen for Cassie's cues, her moans and whimpers and the speed of her breath. Did she need it faster or slower, and was the pressure just right? The answer was never consistent, and I fucking loved it. Every time I earned a reward through the curl of her toes or a squeeze of her knees, it made me work harder.

I licked and sucked, and she writhed her slick heat against my face. Her skin flushed the color of her nipples from her toes to her nose, and my dick jumped in response.

"God, yes. Lick it, Thatch," she commanded, and I hummed into her soft, bare skin. Never in my life had I had a woman order me around and take control like this, but I didn't mind—far from it.

When she came, it would be because I had gotten her there, and that was all the incentive I'd ever need. This wild woman was a fucking goddess, and anytime she wanted her pussy licked, I'd do it—no questions asked.

Come on, honey. Come on my face.

Just when I was ready, she robbed me of it, jumping from my face with a moan and scooting quickly back down my body and onto my dick.

"*Fuck me*," I breathed.

"No, baby," she corrected with a shake of her head. "Not this time. This time, I'm fucking *me*."

And by God, she did, up and down, she fucked herself on my dick, never even giving me an opportunity to show any of my moves. I was an instrument, and she didn't mind doing all the goddamn work. It wasn't an impossibility, but I had to admit it was rare I encountered a woman with this much sexual work ethic.

I reached for her tits as they swung in front of me, and I smiled internally when no hands slapped mine away. They were heavy and heaving, and when I rubbed the tips with my thumbs, she licked her lips and fell over the edge.

Her head shot back, her eyes closed, and the taut muscles in her thighs squeezed harder at my hips.

When she fell forward onto my chest with long, even breaths, I let my hands settle on her hips and rubbed gently to give her a minute to get her strength and energy back. She'd been tired when we came in here, and now she'd done enough work for both of us.

"You okay, honey?" I asked, touching my lips to the side of her face and breathing in the scent of her skin. God, she smelled delicious. Like oranges and us. I licked at the curve of her shoulder.

She didn't move or speak.

"Cassie?" I questioned.

Soft snores tickled my inner ear, and I knew in an instant.

She'd just fucked herself to sleep. She'd *fucked* herself to *sleep*. *Jesus.*

My overexcited dick wasn't getting his happy ending tonight. No, this fucker was doomed by the cliffhanger, and I was the messenger who had to break the news.

Sorry, buddy. No full eight-second ride this time.

Up and off my dick, I moved Sleeping Beauty as gently as possible. But when I shook her arm to get her attention without any kind of response, I knew I shouldn't have bothered.

"Goddammit," I grumbled, picking myself up off the bed and walking bowlegged into the bathroom. I may not have been happy, but my cock was spitting mad. Yanking off the condom, I found just a tiny bit of precome at the tip but absolutely no relief.

Don't be mad at me, asshole, I told my dick. *This is not my fault…I don't think.*

The whole thing was confusing. I didn't understand how it'd happened or why it'd stopped before it was over. None of it made one fucking lick of sense.

The taps to the shower squealed slightly as I turned them and stepped into the not yet warm spray.

My fist was a horrendously poor substitute for the grip of Cassie's pussy, but it would have to do. I worked myself while picturing the motion of her tits and the weight of each one in my palms. She'd looked me in the eye on more than one occasion, even studied my face with a closeness that made it damn near impossible to forget who she fucked.

And she wasn't the only one. After tonight, I'd be able to picture every part of her body for the rest of my life.

A mediocre climax brought practically the opposite of relief, but I took it for what it was, did a half-assed job of drying off, and climbed into the bed next to my new favorite woman.

She was deep in sleep, but that didn't stop me from watching the way her chest rose and fell with each breath or noticing the absence of intensity her face normally carried.

She was beautiful in the way all women were, but she was also different. All this individuality that she never apologized for. It consumed her, and if I was honest, it was starting to consume me.

The bleating reminder of work blared from the alarm on my phone the next morning. I reached to shut it off, but instead of finding it in its normal place on my nightstand, it was across the room in the pocket of my pants, long forgotten thanks to the naked woman in my bed.

Tossing the covers off, I crossed the room in a hurry and shut it off, looking back over my shoulder to the bed, but Cassie never even stirred.

She was obviously a sound sleeper.

Venturing into the bathroom again, I took a quick shower since I'd just had one last night, and I dressed for work quickly enough. Out into the main room, I walked with my suit jacket in hand and laid it over the back of the couch before setting a pot of coffee to brew.

I was used to going without sleep. Having a stake in so many companies and putting extra time into the tattoo shop whenever I could, I spent a lot of extra hours awake. But this was different. Because I was sleepy and sexually frustrated, and I may have been proficient in the first, but I wasn't a frequent victim of the last. Getting off often was the tension release I needed to keep me moving, and I knew all that frustration, combined with the memory of Cassie's body, was going to make this workday one of the longest in my history.

As the time to leave approached, I went back into the bedroom and rounded the bed to Cassie's side. I settled a hip into the crook of hers and wiped a clump of untamed hair from her face.

"Cassie," I whispered, shaking her hip. "Wake up, honey."

She didn't move until I shook harder, and when she did, it wasn't nice and easy.

A right hook came for my head that I just barely dodged, and then up and out of the bed she jumped until her wild eyes found mine.

"You don't do anything easy, huh?" I asked with a laugh.

Her eyes pinched together as she looked around, but it must have all come back to her quick enough. She strolled to my dresser, yanked out a T-shirt, and pulled it over her head without a word.

"Is there coffee?" she asked, pointing out the door in the direction of the kitchen.

"Yeah," I answered and followed her as she walked down the hall. "Sorry to wake you up, but I have to leave for work."

"No worries," she said with a wave as she poured the fresh brew into her cup.

I smiled and started to open my mouth, but as soon as she was finished pouring, she turned on her foot and headed back toward my room.

I followed again, expecting to find her gathering her clothes, but she climbed into the bed and pulled the down comforter and her cup up to her nose.

"I, uh..." I started. "I have to leave for work."

"I know," she confirmed with a nod. "Have a good day."

What the...?

"Oh—okay. I'll, uh, see you later?" I said with the lilt of a question.

"Yeah, sure thing," she agreed, gulping down a slurp of coffee and reaching to the nightstand for my remote.

"Do you get the Bravo network?"

"I..." I shook my head. "What?"

"I missed the latest episode of *Vanderpump Rules*, and Georgie's got me hooked on that shit."

"Yeah," I agreed without being able to understand why. "I'm pretty sure I get all the channels there are to get."

"Fucking excellent."

I tried my hardest to understand what was happening again. "So...I'm leaving for work now. You're gonna hang out for a little while?"

"Yep," she said with a smile and wave. "You have any food? I'm dying for some breakfast."

I tried my hardest to wrap my brain around what she was asking. I knew mornings were rough for her, so maybe she just needed a little extra time.

"Yeah, I think there are some eggs in there. Maybe some bacon."

"Ooh, bacon," she hummed. "Have any lettuce and tomato?"

I thought about it. "Yeah."

"Fantastic. I love BLTs for lunch."

"Lunch?"

She nodded and shushed me. The playback of her show was starting, and she snuggled even deeper into my covers.

"So. Bye?" I said with uncertainty.

She smiled impatiently. "See ya. Good luck."

"Thanks."

I turned and left my room, walked down the hall, grabbed my jacket, wallet, and keys, and stepped out the door.

Only when it shut behind me did I let all of my manic, unorganized thoughts channel themselves into one burning question. "What the ever-loving fuck is going on?"

My focus today had been almost nonexistent. The night. The morning. All of it together had my brain sprinting all out around one fucked-up loop. I'd barely been able to do any work, and if I remembered the highlights from any of my meetings, it'd be a miracle.

Normally, I worked efficiently from one task to the next. Today, I couldn't even find the surface of my desk.

Paralyzed by the unknown, I'd fired off an experimental text to Cassie in an attempt to push her until she broke. All it had done was perplex me more. She'd been overzealously responsive—to the tune of nearly a dozen texts—and so comfortable with her banter that I would have sworn we chatted all the time.

I grabbed my phone and stared down at the text conversation in question.

Me: Can you run the dishwasher?

Cassie: I can't right now. I'm trying to figure out your DVR. I don't want to miss this Lifetime movie that's on at 2.

Me: What are you doing at 2? And you realize it takes all of two seconds and a press of a button to run the dishwasher, right? I know you can multitask, honey. I've seen you play with your tits while riding my cock.

Cassie: But that was for an orgasm. Your dishes aren't that much fun. Anyway, I'm very

"Kline Brooks is on the phone for you," my assistant, Madeline, buzzed in.

I shook off the confused stupor, moved the rogue folder that had slightly muffled her voice, and answered the phone.

"Kline."

"Hey, T," he greeted casually. I bounced my knee, and the sole of my dress shoe tapped erratically on the tile underneath my desk. "I need to talk to you about—"

"You don't need to talk to me about shit," I broke in, knowing I wouldn't be able to sit through a hot minute of him going on about mergers and acquisitions and technical internet mumbo jumbo. "But I sure as fuck need to talk to you."

"Huh? What are you talking about?"

Too amped up, I did the exact opposite of burying the lede. I shot that shit straight into the stratosphere before a launch countdown even commenced. "I fucked Cassie last night."

"What?" he asked on a shout.

"Well, I guess," I corrected, "she actually fucked me. I don't even know how it happened or what happened or, shit, any of it, really. I'm confused as fuck."

Shock would never keep Kline stumbling for long. As expected, he composed himself quickly and started asking questions. "How are you confused? Weren't you there? Aren't you the reason it happened?"

"No!" I snapped, just as flabbergasted as he was. "That's the thing. I mean, I was there, but I didn't need to be. I didn't start anything. It just sort of happened, and then it was happening, and *fuck me*, it was really fucking good. But I still wasn't in control of anything."

"Maybe that's why it was good," he joked.

I scrunched up my face in mock laughter. "Not the fucking time, dude."

"No. Oh, no," he denied. "It's exactly the right time. This is what you would do to me, and I can't tell you how good it feels to be the one doing it to you."

"Fuck you." Both middle fingers saluted him rapid fire like rounds from a gun. It didn't matter that he couldn't see it. It made me feel better.

Kline just laughed.

"Ah, shit," I grumbled when I realized my only other option was to hang up the phone. A sounding board had never been more necessary in my day-to-day life, and I didn't have anyone else to talk to right now, so I was just going to have to take his shit and like it.

"Fine. Make your jokes."

"Thanks," he said. "I will."

My eyes narrowed at his glee, but I dove right into the basics anyway. "She fell asleep on my dick."

"O-kay," he ventured. "Maybe I shouldn't be hearing these details."

I ignored his delicate sensibilities. "*Right* after she orgasmed. Like creamed all over my dick—"

"Jesus!"

"And then, boom. Out like a light. There I was with my dick in the sweetest pussy it's ever entered, and I literally *couldn't* fuck it. I mean, I could have, but even I draw the line somewhere, and that would have been creepy as fuck."

"I don't know what to do with this," Kline admitted. If my savant of a friend didn't have the answers, I didn't know if anyone would.

"I don't either. She used me as a goddamn sleep aid!"

The roll of what I now considered his constant chuckle clucked in my ear.

One thought bled into the next with no transition, and as all of the worsening details came back to me in waves, I just kept on blurting. "She's still at my apartment!"

"What?"

"This morning, she wouldn't leave." I rubbed at the tense skin of my forehead. "I think maybe she's moving in with me."

"Good God. Slow down. She's not moving in with you, for fuck's sake. And if she is, this is completely out of my depth."

Fuck. I knew she probably wasn't moving in with me. I mean, that'd be fucked. But so was last night, so really, maybe that was right on point. I didn't know. It was a miracle I even knew my left hand from my right anymore.

"I'm going to have to consult with Georgie."

"Don't spread this shit around!"

"If you think I'm not telling my wife this as a way to earn points, you're cracked."

"I hate you right now."

"Yeah, well, I've hated you for years, and you're still around. I'd imagine it works the same way in the other direction."

No answers. No advice.

And no chance of getting over any of this until I got to the bottom of it.

CHAPTER 9

Cassie

Around noon, I decided to take a break from screwing with Thatch via text message and took a shower. As I brushed my wet locks with one hand, I ran the other across the granite counters of his bathroom and checked the pads of my fingers for evidence. *Nothing.* Not even a speck of dust. For a single dude, he did a relatively good job of keeping his place clean. Almost a little *too* clean.

Yeah, maybe I'd screw with Thatch just a *teensy* bit more. Because, let's be honest, I was finding an awful lot of enjoyment out of bugging the hell out of him.

I grabbed my phone off the counter and typed out a text as I headed into his closet.

Me: Do you have a maid?

Thatch: Rita is a very nice lady who comes to my apartment twice a week.

Me: I knew there was no way a single guy kept his shit this clean.

The shower clued me in.

Thatch: You're in my shower?

Me: Not anymore, Numbnuts. Right now, I'm in your closet.

Thatch: My closet?

Me: Um. Yeah. That's where the clothes are. I needed something to wear.

Thatch: Do NOT steal my favorite shirt.

I didn't even have to ask to know he was referring to his "Single and Ready to Mingle" shirt.

Me: You can calm the fuck down because I found an even better one.

Thatch: Which one?

I walked over to his freshly made bed—*see, I* was *a good houseguest*—and laid the shirt in question out, then snapped a quick picture and sent it to him.

Thatch: What in the fuck did you do to my shirt?

Me: It was too big.

Obviously, I'd had no other option but to put my amateur seamstress skills to good use. His T-shirt could've easily been a dress, and I was talking more muumuu than stylish maxi. Lucky for me, I only had to cut off a few inches, utilize some needle and thread, and *boom,*

Thatch's old shirt was now an adorable crop top.

Thatch: Wait...why isn't that shirt on you? Are you naked in my bedroom right now?

Me: No. As a matter of fact, I have on a pair of tighty whities. Which, I gotta say, that's real cute, Thatch. I love that you actually wear these.

Thatch: I have to when I play rugby, smartass.

Me: Better support for your Supercock?

Thatch: Yes, and speaking of my Supercock (perfect nickname), he wants to FaceTime your tits. Put them on the phone, please.

Me: Meh. You should have texted me sooner. I already rubbed one out.

Thatch: In my shower???

Me: No way. I prefer to masturbate in a bed, Thatcher.

Thatch: So what you're saying is you've just been lying around in my bed all day (during breaks from snooping through my place), rubbing your pussy all over my sheets?

Me: Is that a problem?

Thatch: Hell no, but my apartment has rules.

Me: Rules?

Thatch: If I'm not there to witness, then you have to record it for my viewing pleasure.

Me: Put your boner away, Thatcher.

Thatch: Pretty sure you started this, Crazy. I'm not the one hanging out at your apartment, swinging my dick around and jizzing all over your sheets.

Me: Okay. I'll give you that.

Thatch: I'll be done with this meeting at 1:30. Prep those gorgeous tits for FaceTime with my Supercock.

Me: Sorry to disappoint, but I've got lunch with Georgie.

Thatch: You owe me.

Me: I owe you nothing.

Thatch: Once the details of last night become clear in that pretty little head of yours, you'll realize you actually do. Enjoy your lunch, honey.

What was that supposed to mean?

We fucked, we came, we fell asleep. Pretty sure none of those things constituted an IOU on my part. I didn't bother trying to read between the lines, figuring it was just Thatch being Thatch more than anything else, and finished getting ready. Even though I had to borrow a pair of his underwear and alter one of his shirts, I was thankful to find a knee-length black, knit skirt inside my purse. And it was clean. *Jackpot.*

I walked into Georgia's office forty-five minutes later to find her sitting behind her desk, staring at her computer and shaking her head. "The answer is no," she said. I ruled out any possibility of a business-related FaceTime because she was grinning like a loon. The coast seemed clear to slide in for a closer investigation.

Moving around her desk, I found Kline on the screen, smiling back at his wife.

I met Kline's eyes over her shoulder. "Hey, Big Dick, how's it hanging? Am I interrupting a lunchtime jerk-off sesh?"

He chuckled in response and looked up and to the side. From the vast knowledge afforded to me by TV crime drama, I took that as a yes.

"Christ," Georgia muttered, the color of her perfect cheeks deepening to a rosy flush. "Can you stop calling my husband that?"

"When you stop being embarrassed about it, I'll stop doing it."

"And this isn't a 'jerk-off sesh,'" she corrected, air quotes accompanying her words. "This is Kline's daily video chat where he offers me a job and I politely decline."

"Come on, Benny. You'll have way more fun at my office," he chimed in, waggling his eyebrows. His blue eyes shone with innuendo.

This frequent conversation between the two of them wasn't a surprise. Kline had been trying to get her to come back to Brooks Media ever since she had resigned and had taken a job working for Wes at the New York Mavericks. But Georgia was her own woman, and even though he teased her about working for him again, he was ultimately proud of his wife and everything she had accomplished.

Kline was so good for Georgia it wasn't even funny. His presence in her life didn't hold her back from anything. *No,* he made her flourish into an awesome woman, who also happened to be getting some fan-fucking-tastic loving on the regular.

"Gotta go, baby. It's lunchtime, and I'm starving," she said, and despite Kline's best efforts to keep her on the phone with pouts and good-natured humor, she managed to end the call.

"Where to?" she asked as she got out of her chair and grabbed her purse.

Orange-yellow gooey goodness flashed before my eyes. "Shake Shack? I've been jonesin' for their cheese fries."

"Sounds good to me."

We headed out of her office, and after a three-block walk, we were sitting at an outside table, feasting on chocolate shakes and cheese fries, and enjoying the sweet summer air laced with the delicious aroma of burger grease. And human excrement. You never really escaped the lingering hint of every form of human foulness in New York.

I know it sounds awful, but upward of a million people put up with it daily. It's all about priorities.

"All right, spill it. What happened between you and Thatch last night?" she asked after taking a hearty sip from her straw. Her eyebrow hooked up with intrigue, and I couldn't help but notice she'd plucked a really nice shape for her brow bed this time around.

"How'd you know about last night?"

"Oh, come on," she said through a laugh. "Kline, Thatch, and Wes are worse than gossiping teenage girls. My husband was way too excited to share his conversation with Thatch this morning. Normally, his video chats start with, 'Come on, Benny. Come back to work for me,'" she imitated his deep voice. "But today, he went straight for the juicy gossip."

"What did Thatch tell him?"

"Nope. I want to hear your side first."

"Fine," I said around half-chewed meat and cheese sauce, wiping the grease off my fingers with a napkin. I was obviously a delicate lady. "It was typical Thatch and Cass. We talked about his boner. You know, same old shit, different day."

She rolled her powdery blue eyes. "You spent the whole day *and* night together, Cass. Tell me you talked about something else besides his boner."

"And my tits, too. He's a big fan."

"Your boobs are the size of my head. Of course, he's a big fan."

"They're not *that* big."

She snorted. "You have double Ds. And both Ds stand for *damn*."

I laughed at the inflection of her voice and the size-specific gesture she added to the front of her own chest. "True."

"So, did you make *any* progress on the topics of conversation?"

"Sorta. We fucked last night. That seems to have helped. It at least channeled part of his focus to my pussy."

"Jesus! You what? Talk about burying the goddamn lede."

"Why are you so shocked? I figured that was the first thing Thatch would've told Kline."

She shook her head.

"Yeah." I shrugged. "I sleep-fucked him."

"God, I hate when you call it that. Do you know how bad it sounds?"

"Okay, I didn't exactly *sleep-fuck* him, but he woke me up after I fell asleep on his couch, and then next thing I knew, I was horny and trying to bang him. You know how I get when I'm tired but can't fall asleep. I need a release or else I'll just be staring at the ceiling all night, watching the time pass at a snail's pace."

"Tell me you were awake while fucking him."

"Oh, yeah. I was fully aware of what was happening."

"Was he?"

I flashed an annoyed look. "Of course, he was. If a man falls asleep while a chick is grinding her pussy on him and shoving her tits in his face, then he is either narcoleptic, gay, or should seek medical attention."

What? If men can have double standards, so can we.

"True." Georgia grinned. "*So...*"

"So?"

"How was it?"

I tilted my head to the side. "How was what?"

"The sex!" she exclaimed, slamming her hands down on the table. Our cups shook from the vibrations, and a few people turned in our direction.

"Slow your roll, Susie. You're about ten seconds away from reenacting *When Harry Met Sally,* and I'm not so sure that couple feeding their dog ice cream is going to appreciate it."

She giggled, grabbing a fry from the basket. "Great movie."

Oh yeah, only murderers and puppy-mill directors didn't recognize that showing of cinematic genius. "Fan-fucking-tastic movie."

"All right," she said, leaning across the table. "Tell. Me. Everything."

"Wheorgie encouraging an overshare? Color me impressed."

She gestured with an impatient hand for me to continue.

"Well, it was good sex. *Great* sex, actually. His dick and mouth are talented, that's for damn sure. I would have come twice had my pussy not demanded to be penetrated."

"Da-yum, that's a good session of sleep-fucking, then."

I laughed, and I couldn't stop myself from replaying the night's events in my head. I really had enjoyed last night. Thatch had a body made for fucking. That was pretty much all there was to it.

"So I'm assuming Thatch enjoyed himself too?"

I rolled my eyes. "His cock was inside me, and my tits were in his hands... Of course, he enjoyed it."

"Are you sure about that?" she pushed, even though I'd spoken perfect fucking English.

I tilted my head, scrutinizing her secretive expression. "What do you know that I don't know?"

"Nothing," she said, but her shifty eyes said otherwise.

"Spill it."

"I don't know anything," she tried to convince me, but the grin she was fighting made it quite obvious she was full of shit. God, she was about the worst liar in the history of liars.

"Georgia." I stared at her, unleashing the crazy eyes. It was my biggest weapon when trying to get her to fess up to something. She called it the creepy stare, and it generally only took about ten seconds of half-assed effort to get her to spill her secrets.

Five.

Four.

Three.

Two.

One.

"Fine!" She gave in, raising both hands in the air. "Cool it on the creepy staring. You know it freaks me out."

Works like a charm. Every time.

"Okay, so maybe I already knew you guys had sex," she confessed.

"Wheorgie!" I admonished, equal parts shocked and impressed she was able to convince me otherwise for even the short window she had.

"Sorry." She shrugged, her button nose scrunching up in a text-book gesture of *sorry, not sorry*. "I just wanted to hear it from you first before I told you what I actually knew."

"That was way too persuasive." She had *almost* convinced me. "I think you've been practicing the fake tears on Kline too much."

She laughed. "I know, right?"

"All right, what did Thatcher tell Kline?"

"Well…he called my husband this morning all freaked out that you were actually moving in with him."

That had me smiling big. I loved that my plan to mess with him this morning actually worked. I didn't usually set a precedent of making myself at home at someone else's place. I just had a feeling Thatch wouldn't know what the fuck to do if I made myself comfortable in his bed while he was getting ready to leave for work.

She pointed at my face. "So, you *were* screwing with him this morning!"

"Oh, yeah," I said, nodding in confirmation. "I was most definitely screwing with him. You should have seen his face when I got back in his bed, turned on the TV, and started asking him what channels he got."

But really, I'd had a blast lounging all over his apartment this morning. If I didn't love Georgie so much, I'd probably still be there, drowning hours in bacon and DVR and anything else I could get my hands on.

Georgia laughed, loud and boisterous. "Holy shit, that's awesome! I love that you did that. He's the ultimate prankster. It's about time he got a taste of his own medicine."

I smirked. "I know. I wish I would've recorded it."

"The only other thing he told Kline was that…*well*…" She paused, eyeing me with an amused look. "The sleep-fucking worked. Like it *really* worked."

I thought over her words for a good thirty seconds until I finally caught what she was putting down. "Oh, *fuck*," I said through a laugh. "Definitely not *Sleepless in Seattle*."

"Nope. More like Comatose in New York," she agreed.

I replayed the sex in my head and realized I had actually passed out—*on his cock*—and I did this *before* he finished. "Man, talk about a bitch move."

"Yep. It was like something out of *How to Lose a Guy in Ten Days*," she agreed again.

I cringed before asking, "Are we speaking only in movie-isms now?"

She shrugged, but she didn't look like she thought it was the worst idea in the world.

My usual devil-may-care attitude had up and gone hiking. "In my defense, I was running on two hours of sleep from the night before. But still, I kind of feel like an asshole." Doing the ole dine and dash on someone's dick was almost never called for.

Georgia let out a quiet laugh. "Yeah, you probably should."

The ogre was right; I *did* owe him. Because, let's face it, if Thatch had done that to me, I would've been fucking pissed. I honestly had to give the guy props for handling it so well, seeing as I was still alive and everything.

I had always lived my life by one motto: I couldn't please everyone, I didn't care to please everyone, but I could motherfucking please myself. Which I did, *often*.

But for some odd reason, I found myself actually caring about what Thatch thought and trying to find a way to make it right. And the more I thought about it, the worse I felt. It was a foreign concept to me, but even I couldn't deny I had pulled a *big-time* bitch move last night.

Maybe there's some way I can make it right?

Georgia pointed at my face. "I know that look. What are you planning?"

Man, those cheese fries are really wreaking havoc on my stomach. It was in turmoil.

When I shrugged my uncertainty, she made a suggestion of her own. "Maybe he's finally getting a little glimpse into what he puts everyone else through."

"Little Wheorgie is encouraging my scheming ways?"

Georgia nodded, and a devilish smile consumed her lips.

"Is it safe to assume this has everything to do with Thatch including the gargoyle dick in his best man speech?"

"You bet that prankster's ass it does."

Thatcher had finally met his match in me.

His match.

At pranking, I told myself. But the seed was already planted, and there was no way I'd be able to keep it from growing.

I strode through Thatch's building and straight for his assistant's desk.

"Hi, I've got a last-minute meeting with Thatcher Kelly."

She looked up from her computer, and hesitance etched her face. "Uh...he's in the middle of a conference call right now."

"Oh, I know." I played it off. "That's why he asked me to come."

She squinted in confusion and took in my not-exactly-business attire. I was pretty sure the waistband of Thatch's underwear was sticking out of the top of my skirt like a rapper, for fuck's sake. But people were always hesitant to deny you if you acted self-assured enough. "And you're supposed to be on that conference call?"

"Yep," I said, tapping her desk and walking toward his office door. "He'll be happy I was able to make it in time."

"But...wait...let me..." She stuttered over her words as she stood up from her desk. "I should probably let him know you're here."

"No worries. I got it from here." I waved her off and proceeded to open his office door.

Thatch sat behind his big mahogany desk. His brown eyes rested behind a pair of sexy glasses and were lacking their playful edge. He was obviously concerned and very distracted with whatever was being said on the other end of the call. He didn't look up from his desk until he heard the door close and the lock being flipped with a quiet click.

His hair was rough and unkempt as though he'd been running his hands through it constantly, and it made me want his hands in my hair. Tugging, pulling, you name it.

Oh, yeah.

My arousal was plain to see, and those brown eyes switched from serious to intrigued in a matter of seconds.

"Hi," I mouthed, holding up a bag of "I'm sorry for falling asleep on your dick" fries. I moved around his desk until I was standing beside his chair.

He turned to face me and held up one finger, responding into the phone, "Unless you want your balls handed to you on a silver platter, I strongly suggest rethinking those investments."

I smirked at the way Thatcher Kelly did business. I doubted many other people threatened their clients' balls and got away with it.

I set the bag on his desk and went about my ogling. A sleek gray suit covered his huge, masculine body, and I wanted it uncovered. My pussy was pounding thanks to his all-motherfucking-business expression and its enhancement of his strong features.

He oozed power and authority, and I was getting all kinds of sexy-as-hell alpha vibes.

Oh yeah, Thatcher Kelly was a stud, and I was about to show him how sorry I was for falling asleep on his dick. The fries wouldn't be the only meal consumed in the name of forgiveness.

I grabbed a pen and notepad off his desk as I heard him rattle off a few investment figures into the phone. I scribbled out a quick note and held it up for him to see.

Will there be anyone coming by your office in the next ten minutes?

He read the note and then met my eyes, shaking his head.

I flashed a smirk and a wink as I got down on my knees and placed my hands on his thick thighs, pushing them apart to make room. His eyebrows rose to his forehead as I undid his belt and slid down his zipper.

The second I slipped his cock out of his pants, he placed his hand over the receiver, whispering, "Cass, honey, what are you doing?"

"Telling you I'm sorry," I responded as I stroked him in my hand. "Is that okay?" I asked, but I didn't wait for a response, grazing my lips around his crown. Slowly, inch by inch, I slid him into my mouth as his eyes stayed fixated on what I was doing.

"Fuck," he muttered and then cleared his throat. "No, I'm still here, Mike."

He tasted delicious, and I loved the feel of him against my tongue—velvety smooth and *hard,* really fucking hard. It was all I could do to pull it out of my mouth for a little more teasing. I used my hand to outline my lips with the tip of his thick cock, alternating that move with sucking the head into my mouth. Every time his cock jumped, I sucked harder.

"I already told you what I…I…th-thought about that," he stammered as I tortured the underside with the flat of my tongue.

My gaze locked with his as I pumped my mouth quickly up and down his shaft. He couldn't take his eyes off of me, and I watched his Adam's apple bob with a swallowed groan when I tapped the end of him to the very back of my throat.

Then he swallowed another.

And…*another.*

It was safe to say he was thoroughly enjoying the blow job, maybe even a little too much for a conference call. But turned-on Cassie had absolutely no consideration. Even less than the normal me.

Seconds later, he mumbled a near-incoherent "I'll call you back" to Mike and tossed his phone onto his desk with reckless abandon as he started to move his hips in rhythm with my mouth and hand.

"I have no idea why you're doing this, but please don't fucking stop." His hands were in my hair, just like I wanted, encouraging me to continue with gentle yet firm movements.

The soft hum of the fluorescent lights was the only noise that wasn't a distinct result of him and me and sex. I released him with a loud pop and continued to stroke his length as I gazed up at him. My chest heaved and my voice was nothing more than a sexy rasp. "Don't worry, Thatcher. I won't stop until you come in my mouth."

A deep, throaty groan left his lips. "Keep talking like that, and I won't last another thirty seconds."

I lapped up a few drops of precome and moaned. "You taste

good, Thatch," I said with a smirk before wrapping my lips around him again and sucking down his shaft.

"God, your mouth is heaven, honey."

As I continued to work him over, the ache of arousal became too much. I needed just a little relief. I slid my shirt and bra up and over my breasts, baring them to his greedy gaze. "Baby, play with my tits while I suck you off."

I didn't have to ask him twice. He grabbed my breasts with his large hands and rubbed his thumbs across both nipples. I throbbed between my legs from his expert touch and had to fight the urge to turn the situation into an outcome where we both found release.

But this wasn't about me. This was about him.

I lightly glided the surface of my teeth down his length, trailing it with my tongue.

"God, you're good. Too goddamn good."

"Oh, just wait, baby. I'm going to make you come...*hard*."

As I watched him slowly unravel, I felt empowered by having this much control over his pleasure. And every thrust of his hips, every deep, heady groan, only spurred me on more. Hell, I was getting all kinds of good blo-jo vibes from Thatch, damn near getting off on it as much as he was.

I sucked him deeper and stroked him harder as I flicked my tongue against him in rhythmic movements.

"Fuck. Yes," he hissed, and then groaned in a staccato rhythm. "Keep doing that."

That's it, baby. Come in my mouth.

When I knew he was close, I gently tugged on his balls and watched that little move push him right over the edge.

"*Oh, fuck,*" he shouted, his voice bouncing off the walls of his office. He gripped my hair as his head fell back, and then Thatch growled the sexiest fucking sound my ears had ever heard as he finished in my mouth.

I gave him a minute to catch his breath, and to talk myself out of spreading out on his desk and finger-fucking myself while he watched, and then gently tucked him back into his pants.

Carefully, I got to my feet and placed a soft kiss to his shocked lips. "Have a good rest of the day at work, honey," I said, grabbing my purse off the floor and tossing it over my shoulder and walking toward the door.

"Cass?" he asked, voice filled with surprise and awe and utter confusion.

My mind was a mess of unsatisfied arousal and surprising affection, and I knew I had to do something to get my head back in the game.

Before leaving his office, I glanced over my shoulder and left him with the only defense I had against the way my emotions were fucking with me—*fucking with him.*

"Oh, and enjoy the fries. They're from the Shake Shack." I waved with a little wiggle of my fingers. "See you at home, Thatch."

Boom. Suck on that, prankster, I thought to myself as I strode down the hall.

But the elation over screwing with him only lasted a few seconds, and as I got on the elevator, I found myself touching my lips and grinning over what I had just done.

And I wasn't completely sure it had anything to do with a declaration of a prank war.

CHAPTER 10

Thatch

Cassie winked and closed the door to my office with a soft click, but I still hadn't moved a muscle.

Behind the solid wood of my desk, my wood was fading in the still-open fly of my pants. Shock didn't really fucking cover what I was feeling at that moment—the surprise visit, the bag of takeout, the blow job, and the way she left things as soon as my dick left her mouth.

I'd done a lot of shit in my life, but I'd never been sucked off behind my desk. The whole showing up at work without warning thing was a boundary only crossed in serious, long-term relationships or between involved coworkers, and I'd never really had either.

I'd been in love with Margo, but the love had been young. Still a teenager, I'd been naïve and self-centered and completely focused on what she could do for me rather than the other way around. It'd probably have been a fleeting memory of adolescent hormones and mistakes had it not ended the way it had. But that was the kind of thing that never left you, was never forgotten. After all these years, all that was left of her in my day-to-day life were Frankie, Claire, and

Mila—and I wouldn't trade them for anything.

"Mr. Kelly?" Madeline's voice called, freaking me the fuck out and jump-starting the rush to zip up my pants.

I pushed the tails of my shirt in, zipped the fly, buttoned my pants, and then fastened my belt, all before taking a deep breath, running a hand through my hair, and pushing the button to respond to her call.

"Yeah, Mad?"

"Wes Lancaster is on the phone for you."

Jesus. I wasn't sure now was the best time to talk to him, but he was on a recruiting trip, so I'd expected him to call at some point wanting to run numbers. He didn't have me on staff, but as much as we teased each other, he trusted me more than anyone else when it came to money. Thus, he brought me in to consult from time to time.

A puff of air left me as I fought for quick composure.

"Hey, Wes. What's up?" I said as I answered, trying my best to sound casual.

That was my first mistake.

"No jokes?" he asked cautiously without even saying hello. "Something's wrong. What's wrong?"

I rolled my eyes. "I can be serious on occasion, you know."

"Not with me. Not ever. Not in the history of our friendship."

Pushing my back firmly into my chair, I rubbed at my facial hair. "God, you're fucking dramatic, Whitney."

"That's better. But, yeah, you're not getting off the hook. What's going on?"

"I just got my dick sucked, how's that?" I asked when no other explanation came to mind, trying to put him off by oversharing.

"Nope. I'd say that's pretty normal too. What's *abnormal*, T-Rex?"

"You're a pain in my goddamn ass."

"I've heard. I'm waiting."

"Jesus Christ—"

"Mr. Kelly?" Mad buzzed in on the intercom. "Kline Brooks is on line two."

"Hold on, Wes," I said into the phone and pushed the button to answer her. "You might as well conference him in, Mad."

She didn't answer, but in a matter of moments, Kline was in on our call.

"Thatch."

"Wes is on the line too, Kline."

"What's wrong with you?" Kline asked suspiciously.

Fucking hell. I didn't crack jokes *all* the time. I could answer a call normally, for fuck's sake.

"I've been wondering the same thing!" Wes exclaimed, fucking victorious.

"I hate you both."

"You love me," they both said at the same time.

I rubbed at the pinched center of my forehead.

"Does this have anything to do with Cassie?" Kline asked astutely. The clever fuck. I'd be murdering him later for bringing this up now.

"What? What about Cassie?" Wes asked like a teenage girl hungry for gossip.

"He fucked her last night," Kline supplied helpfully, and I sighed.

"Holy shit!" Wes exclaimed.

"Then she fell asleep on his dick before he came," fucking asshole Brooks went on. Wes guffawed.

"She just blew me in my office, thank you very much," I told him as though I had something to prove. I regretted it the minute the words left my lips.

Kline's voice vibrated with glee. "There it is!" That asshole had baited me, and I'd gulped that shit down without hesitation.

"So you were serious," Wes put in.

"And what did Crazy Cassie do after she blew you?" Kline asked way more sincerely than I'd ever heard anyone deliver those words before.

I dropped my head back, and I pulled at the choking tie at my neck. "She said to enjoy the bag of French fries she'd brought me and that she'd see me at fucking home."

"Fucking home?" Wes replied like a smartass. "What's that?"

"At home, jackhole. My home. I swear to God, Kline, she's moving in with me. I don't know what happened, but I think she's suffering from some kind of psychotic break. With Georgia in the middle, you and I probably won't be able to be friends anymore."

The sounds of two varying degrees of laughter filled my ear.

"This isn't funny! One sleepy bone, and this chick thinks she lives with me!"

Wes stopped trying to soften his laughter and dove into it full out. "This is fucking hilarious."

Kline finally took pity on me. He found compassion through his laughter, but he found it. He was definitely above Wes on my list of friendship today. "Relax, man. She's probably fucking with you."

My elbows went to the surface of my desk as I leaned forward quickly. "Why would she do that?"

"Would *you* fuck with you right now?"

Obviously, I would. He took my silence as an affirmative.

"Exactly."

"Shit." I hadn't even considered how similar we were.

"Plus," he went on, "I told Georgie about your freak-out this morning, and she *may* have been getting ready to leave for lunch with Cassie when I did."

"Fuck! Kline, I told you not to spread this shit around."

"And I told you I was going to tell Georgie. I'm not even sorry."

Wes continued to laugh.

"Yeah, yeah. Laugh it up."

"Listen," Wes said, just barely softening his chuckles enough so that he could speak. "If she's gonna fuck with you, why don't you fuck with her?"

My eyes narrowed at the empty spot on my office floor. "What do you mean?"

"She's obviously expecting you to squirm. Turn it around on her."

"That's the best idea I've heard all day," Kline agreed.

I pondered to myself and decided I could do that. I was way more comfortable as the messer than I was as the messee. "Fine. I'll text her something."

"Make sure you tell us what it is," Wes demanded.

"Didn't you guys call me for fucking reasons?"

"Mine can wait," Wes said just as Kline murmured, "This is suddenly more important."

"Fuck you guys."

"Bye, Princess Peach," Kline said in dismissal through his chuckles.

Wes's laugh trailed on after Kline hung up.

"You seriously don't have questions for me?" I asked.

"We'll talk about it all when I get back. But you better fucking tell me how this plays out."

"Don't worry, Samantha. I'll fill you in on all the happenings of *Sex and the City*."

Slamming the phone into the cradle before he could say more, I picked up my cell phone off the corner of the desk and pulled up her number to text.

Me: Thanks for "lunch." I need to stop by the drugstore on my way home. Need me to pick you up anything, honey? 😏

Sent. *Think you can mess with me? Think again, honey.*
Student, meet teacher.

CHAPTER 11

Cassie

I reread the text and triple-checked that the message was in fact from Thatch.

Did he just send me a goddamn kissy-face emoji?

I opened and closed my eyes a few times, just to be sure what I was seeing was real.

For the love of freaks, he really sent that.

I knew I was a talented cocksucker, but I had told him I would *see him at home* after putting him back into his pants. Home, meaning his home, meaning he should've thought I was off my rocker and actually trying to move in with him, meaning that text message should've been him freaking the hell out. Not all kissy-faced and asking me if I needed anything from the store.

Why wasn't he losing his shit over this?

I grabbed my phone off my coffee table and called Georgia.

"Hell—" she started to answer, but I immediately interrupted.

"I think he's fucking crazy."

"—o," she finished with too much amusement in her voice.

"I'm being serious, Wheorgie. I think Thatch might be crazier than me, and believe me, I know that's a fuckload of crazy."

She laughed. "Why do you think he's crazy?"

"He just texted me after I gave him an 'I'm sorry for falling asleep on your dick before you blew your load' blow job in his office and asked me if I needed anything from the store on his way home. Not to mention he sent me a goddamn kissy-face emoji. He's nuts, that's all there is to it. A total whack-job with a Supercock."

Yeah, no doubt about it, that kissy-face-emoji-sending-mother-fucker needed to spend some time in a padded room and reevaluate his life choices. At least, that's what I needed Georgie to *think* I was thinking.

"Hold up. Please repeat that because I'm not sure my brain was able to process what you just said."

"I know," I said as I stood up from the couch and started pacing my living room. "I had to check that text message fifteen times to believe he sent that. What grown-ass man even uses emojis?"

"That's not the part I'm having a hard time processing."

I sighed, shaking my head. "I hear you, G. The store part threw me for a loop too."

"*No*," she voiced. "I'm talking about the blow job, Casshead."

I rolled my eyes. "Don't worry, I didn't go narcoleptic on his dick this time. He got the full-service treatment, if you know what I'm saying. Came right in my—"

"That's not the part either! *Jesus*," she said through a laugh. "You went to his office after we had lunch and *sucked him off*? Are you fucking with me right now?"

I scrunched up my face in annoyance. "Please explain what you're trying to get at here. I'm not seeing where the confusion is coming from on your end."

"Cassie!" she exclaimed, bursting into full-belly laughs. "You told me you were going to *tell him* you were sorry. I thought that meant bringing him lunch, not using *his dick* as *your* second lunch."

I'd thought that too. But goddamn, he'd looked like a culinary delight when I got there. A woman can only be so strong.

"Actions speak louder than words, G."

It'd been a deviation from the flight plan, but there was no doubt in my mind Thatch appreciated a blow job way more than lunch and a Hallmark card. Hell, I'd much rather a guy show me he was sorry by tonguing my puss-ay than sending me flowers. Flowers died, but fantastic orgasms? Yeah, those fuckers lived on forever by fueling fantasies and becoming priceless spank-bank material.

"Please tell me this without giving too much detail. How does one start off the whole 'I'm going to apologize by putting your penis in my mouth' conversation?"

"What conversation? There wasn't one. I went in, locked the door, got on my knees, and unzipped his pants."

"Like a drive-by blow job?"

"Exactly like that."

"Wow. I still don't understand how you can manage to shock me after all these years."

"You've never blown Kline in his office?"

"Um. No, I have not."

"You need to do that," I recommended.

"Brilliant idea, Cass!" Kline's voice filled my ears. "I'm on board with this plan, Benny."

"Well, hey there, Big Dick. I see I'm on speaker phone."

"Sorry, Cass," Georgia chimed in. "We're heading home from taking the boys to the park. And you didn't exactly give me a chance to give you a heads-up."

And by "boys" she meant their asshole cat, Walter, and his boyfriend, Stan—who also happened to be a one-hundred-pound Great Dane that was still growing by the day. They were star-crossed lovers who had happened to meet in a vet's office when Thatch had lost Walter.

It only took one sniff of Stan's asshole, and Walter had found his soul mate. Well, *life* mate. I was pretty sure that cat didn't have a soul.

He was Satan in feline form.

"No worries," I responded. "So, Kline, how should we handle this?"

"Handle this?" he asked, voice equal parts amused and uncertain. "What are we handling?"

"Thatch. I mean, isn't it obvious? He's fucking lost it. He thinks I'm moving in with him, and he's actually okay with that. Not freaking out in the least."

Kline chuckled a few times and paused before offering, "Don't you think it's odd that loud—*obnoxious most of the time*—Thatch seems very reserved about all of this?"

"*Yeah,* that's why—" I started to respond, but I stopped when my brain started to process his words. "Wait...no way...*no way.* You think he's calling my bluff?"

"I'm not saying I think that, but I'm not saying I *don't* think that either."

"Oh, that devious bastard. He's good, but he's not *that* good." I headed straight into my bedroom and started pulling shit out of my closet.

"What are you doing?" Georgia asked.

"Obviously, moving on to Plan B."

"And what's Plan B, exactly? Isn't that the name of the morning-after pill? Tell me you're not pregnant."

"No, I'm not pregnant! There's been no completion in this tank, remember?"

Big-brained Brooks felt it was important to take me back to sex ed. "A guy doesn't have to finish to get you pregnant."

"So true," Georgia agreed.

"I'm not pregnant, fuckers. There was a condom. Plan B is me taking this prank to a new level."

"Uh...is anyone going to get hurt in this scenario?"

"Nope. But I'm about to take that trickster's ego down several notches."

Kline chuckled. "Man, I really wish I was privy to seeing this shit go down."

"Let's just hope I don't have to resort to Plan C."

"Wait…what happens in Plan C?" Georgia questioned.

"You and Kline will have to help me hide the body, obviously. That's generally what Plan C involves."

"*What!*" she shrieked.

I laughed. "Calm your tits, G. I'm kidding…*sort of.*"

"Cassie!"

"He'll be fine…as long as he cooperates," I lied. "Enjoy your night! Bye!" I ended the call with sounds of Kline chuckling and Georgia shouting for me not to hang up the phone.

Sometimes I was almost disappointed in how easy she was to tease.

Georgia: YOU'RE AN ASSHOLE. I know you're joking, but on the off chance your crazy ass isn't joking, I'M NOT HELPING WITH PLAN C. He's too fucking big. I couldn't even lift a leg.

Me: I'm glad we never had to resort to robbing banks for money. You'd be a terrible accomplice.

Georgia: Yes, remember that. Me = terrible accomplice.

Me: Tell me something I don't already know. If you were a hooker, you'd probably track your payments on an Excel spreadsheet and claim them on your taxes. (Add terrible hooker to the list.)

Georgia: Whatever. I'd be the most organized hooker. I'd get one of those credit card swipe-y things.

Me: When is the right time to complete the transaction in that scenario?

Georgia: I think they'd swipe before, and sign their PayPal receipt after.

Me: Prostitute Georgia is classy AF.

Georgia: I know, right?

Me: Strippers should use those swipe-y things. If I had a dollar for every time I've run out of money at a strip club, I'd never run out of money at a strip club.

Georgia: Those are some deep thoughts, Cass. I'm a little disturbed you frequent strip clubs that often.

Me: I generally go for the steak and stay for the lap dances.

Georgia: Strip clubs serve steak?

Me: Only the good ones.

Georgia: Please don't kill Thatch until after Kline's birthday. He's helping me plan the secret shindig.

Me: When is Big Dick's bday?

Georgia: June 28th.

Me: Okay. You have my word. Thatcher will live to see June 28th.

Georgia: You're the best.
Me: I'm ending this convo now, asshole. I've got some serious

packing to do.

Georgia:

I laughed and tossed my phone onto my bed. It landed with a soft bounce beside a few stacks of clothes I had already managed to get out of my closet while chatting with Georgia. I had a plan to execute, and it needed to be in place by the time Thatch got home from work.

My original plan was to use the key Georgia had kindly given me and be sitting on his couch when he got home from work, but now the stakes had been raised.

And since I was pretty much in love with screwing with him, the Jolly Green Giant was about to be on the receiving end of the best prank I had ever come up with.

Oh yeah, let the games begin.

CHAPTER 12

Thatch

Worn out from one of the weirdest days of my life, I shoved the key in the lock of my door and turned it, and then pushed the door open cautiously so I could poke my head in without having to fully commit to entering.

Everyone kept assuring me Cass was only crazy in the sense of wild—not in the put-her-in-a-muzzle-and-straitjacket kind of way. And for the most part, I believed them. But I'd experienced a few things in the last twenty-four hours at her hands that I didn't think anyone else in my circle of trust ever had, so a little skepticism was understandable.

All was quiet, and I could finally hear myself think as I stepped inside. I wasn't exactly *hating* everything she'd thrown my way. In fact, I mostly felt the opposite—giddy and elated and anxious inside every time she said something that should have made me cringe. But that kind of reaction made me question *my own* sanity, and well, that's a dangerous little loop of psychosis.

Moving into the space, I tossed my suit jacket on the back of my couch and my keys on the entry table and made my way into the kitchen. I yanked open the fridge and surveyed the contents. Not because I was actually hungry, but because I was antsy, anxious for something to fill the time and mute the downright excessive amount of thinking going on in my head.

In general, I was a pretty simple guy. Eat, sleep, laugh, fuck, repeat. If I was having a good time, I was at ease. I didn't analyze or question, I just did.

Shaking my head, I closed the refrigerator with a slam and tugged at my too-tight tie. I needed to change into comfier clothes and just relax.

I moved toward my bedroom at a prowl, frustrated at myself for being *disappointed* that Cassie wasn't here. Saddened that my evening would be like normal—relaxing and completely of my own making. Upset that I didn't have to be on my toes every second of the night, watch what I said, or constantly dodge flying objects and tiny but aggressive fists.

I must have been losing my mind.

The end of my tie came loose with a final tug, and it landed somewhere in the middle of my bed as I discarded it with a mindless throw. Two buttons undone at the top of my dress shirt, I reached behind and over my head with one hand, tugging at the fabric between my shoulder blades until it gave way and slid over my head.

Still blinded by fabric, I turned the corner into my closet and ran so hard into an unexpected wall it nearly knocked me over.

"Ow! What the fuck?" I snapped, pulling the shirt free from my head. My gaze met cardboard.

Several moving boxes cluttered the walk-in space, the set I'd just run into stacked four high.

I pinched my eyebrows together as I peeked around it. More boxes but nothing else.

I moved deeper into the space and then turned around slowly, suspiciously, as objects clinked softly together in my bathroom.

I reached into the open box in front of me, grabbing hold of the first object my hand came in contact with and holding it loosely at my side in case I needed a weapon.

Yes, the chances of my needing a weapon are slim, but I'm pretty sure most robbers don't ring the doorbell either, ladies. Yeah, I'm looking at you, crawling out of your living room so the person at the front door won't see you. I know your game.

Vigilantly, I rounded the doorjamb into the bathroom and—

"Boo!" the intruder shouted right in my face. I swung the object before I realized it was Cassie, but I pulled up short just before it would have smacked her in the face.

"Fucking hell," I snapped as my eyes focused on the *vibrator* in my hand and Cassie dissolved into an all-out *fit* of laughter.

"Oh. My. God," she wheezed. She dropped to the floor and went fetal, the power of her laughter too much to maintain while standing. "Holy shit, this is the best thing that's ever happened to me," she said around big gulps of air. "I'd say you don't know how to use that thing on me, but this is seriously the most pleasure I've ever gotten out of it," she went on as I towered over her.

I shook my head to clear the tingle of excitement in my spine and focused on my irritation. "What are you doing here?"

"Pretty sure I told you I'd see you at home, boss man."

My thoughts collided and fought for supremacy, but in the end, I couldn't focus on any of them. "Right," I mumbled, turning from her to the boxes and back again.

"What do you think, Thatcher?" she asked with a smirk and held out her hand. "Can I put *my* boner away?" I glanced down at my hand to find her toy still clutched tightly in my grasp.

I smiled then. "And by put it away, you mean…?"

The smart smirk dropped from her features, and her eyes narrowed.

Ah, and the tables turn.

"I mean put it away in my box."

"Your box?" I questioned further with the raise of an eyebrow.

"Shut up," she snapped at me.

"Later," I teased. "I won't say anything else."

I looked around at the general female apparel and accessories hanging next to mine in the closet and all the product filling the counter of my bathroom vanity and tried to keep my brain on task. She didn't like that I was calm, so I very much intended to stay that way.

"This sure is a lot of girl shit."

She waggled her eyebrows and prompted me excitedly. "Yeah?"

I brushed a piece of hair from her face and murmured, "You must be worn out."

She scrunched her eyebrows again. "Huh?"

"From all the packing and unpacking. How about I go get us some dinner?"

"Dinner?"

"Yeah. You know, the last meal of the day where we shouldn't overeat but obviously do."

"Dinner."

"Yep," I said with a pop of my p.

"I—" she started, but I cut her off.

For seemingly the first time during this interaction, she focused on my naked chest and torso. I unbuckled my belt and unbuttoned my dress pants as she watched.

"I'll just shower quick and then run out," I told her, stepping out of my shoes and socks and pushing my pants and boxer briefs to the floor. Her gaze followed every movement, but her mouth did absolutely zero talking.

"Did you want to join me, honey?" I asked.

"No," she answered yet nodded her head at the same time.

I bit my lip to contain my laugh. "Throw those clothes in the hamper, okay?" I prompted with a wink and then climbed under the spray. I hadn't even needed a shower, but fuck if the warm water didn't feel good on my buzzing nerves as I watched the most obstinate woman on the planet stoop down to scoop up my dirty clothes. Confusion was an extremely powerful thing.

Showered and dressed, I walked out into the living room to find Cassie stretched out on the couch with the TV remote in hand. The screen was still black.

When I made it to her and she didn't move, I reached toward her hand and pushed the power button without saying a word and then leaned down to touch my lips to her cheek. Her skin was warm and smelled like citrus. Immediately caught up in the memories of sex and us, I had to fight the urge to linger.

"I'll be back," I called as I walked out the door. When I settled on the other side, I was overwhelmed by déjà vu, but this time, the all-encompassing question had more to do with me than it did her. "What the ever-loving fuck is going on?"

The situation, my reaction, the way it made me feel. All of it felt completely foreign.

Pulling my phone from my pocket, I scrolled through recent calls and hit Kline before I moved an inch.

"Yeah?" he asked, laughter in his voice.

I closed my eyes and shook my head. I should have known. "You gave her a key, didn't you?"

"I didn't," he denied. "But Georgie did."

"What the fuck, man? Is there no bro code in that cold heart of yours?"

His chuckles were obnoxious. "I thought it was hilarious. And she's just messing with you. You should be in heaven. You're always messing with everyone."

"That's right," I corrected. "*I* mess with everyone. Not the other way around."

"Ah," he breathed. "I see how it is."

I narrowed my eyes at the realization he was making me out to be a pussy.

"I can handle it. I'm just not used to it."

"Poor Thatch," Kline fake pouted.

"Screw you. I don't know why I call you."

"Because you're looking for reason, and I'm normally the voice of it."

"Yeah, normally," I agreed.

He laughed again, and I sighed long and deep. "Just have fun with it. That's what you do with everything else."

He was right. And there was one thing I found enjoyable above all others.

"That's it," Kline said with excitement in his voice just before I hung up. "That's the sound of plotting."

Fuck right.

CHAPTER 13

Cassie

The door clicked shut behind Thatch, and I stayed on his couch, a bit taken aback by the events that had just gone down. My gaze roamed his apartment—*now, my apartment?*—taking in the neutral yet sleek décor. Unable to comprehend what had happened between Thatch and me, or any of the implications of it, I came to the only conclusion I could: he had definitely paid someone to decorate his bachelor pad.

No fucking way he was this forward thinking in the interior decoration department.

The minimalist approach was completely modern and highlighted with strategically placed black, white, and gray accents.

Whoever had designed this place had a very keen eye. They had known the huge window framing the living room would bring in natural light that would make the darker style appear warm and inviting versus drab and melancholy.

The photographer inside me wanted to add a few black-and-white photographs of places I had traveled to the walls beside that huge window, which only led to my confusion.

Was I really moving in now? Decorating his shit?

Needing information, I found the ability to move my body off his couch and into his bedroom, where I had last left my purse. I grabbed my phone, plopped down on his big-ass bed, and called the one and only person I could call in a moment like this.

"Well, hello, Cass," Georgia answered, and her voice hinted at amusement.

My eyebrows rose with suspicion. "It sounds like you were expecting my call."

"Why would you say that?" She feigned bewilderment. The day Georgia Brooks was able to lie with a straight face and a convincing voice, hell would freeze over and I'd be able to teleport myself onto David Gandy's cock whenever I wanted.

"Oh, I don't know," I answered, laughing a little at how truly terrible my best friend was at lying. "Maybe because you can barely hold back your giggles. And I know for a fact, when you're two seconds away from turning giggly, you're one hundred percent full of shit."

"I am not full of shit," she responded, but I could literally hear her swallow the urge to burst into laughter.

"Acting would've been a horrible career path for you, by the way," I teased. "But since I love you, I'm going to take the bait and act like I actually believe the words coming out of your mouth."

"I'm not lying!" she exclaimed.

"Uh-huh, sure you're not… Would you like me to tell you about what just happened?"

"Yes," she responded far too quickly. My spidey sense was tingling. She already knew something.

"Well, I'm at Thatch's apartment, and honestly, I'm not sure if I should start calling it *my* apartment." I sat up from the bed and stared out the floor-to-ceiling windows that gave a gracious view of the city. "My original plan was to *fake move in* and ruffle the prankster's feathers a bit, but things didn't exactly go as planned."

"What happened?"

"Well, he didn't freak out or try to get a restraining order. He got naked, took a shower, and then went out to get us dinner. Not gonna lie, I'm not quite sure what to do with this."

"Do you think he's...maybe...screwing with you back?"

"Do *you* think he's doing that?" I tossed her question back. "Why don't you just go ahead and tell me what you already know?"

Fabric rustled in the background like maybe she was covering the mouthpiece of her phone.

"I'm not saying I know anything, but I'm not saying I don't either," she answered vaguely when a slight hum of ambient noise returned to the line.

Georgia was a special brand of fiddle. You had to really tune her up right, and begging wasn't the way to do it. But, as her longtime best friend, I knew the one thing that *would* make her little informational bow fly—act like I was freaking the fuck out. Her immune system had absolute shit defense against hysteria.

"So...I shouldn't be concerned? I mean, what if when he says he's got his hands in all kinds of things, he's actually living a secret life? What if I just accidentally moved in with the next Ted Bundy?" I forced my voice to rise a few octaves toward panic.

"Cassie," she started to chime in, but I cut her off, going all out with the dramatics.

"What am I supposed to do now? I think I just moved myself in with a psychopath! What if he's a serial killer, Wheorgie?" I started rummaging through his nightstand for added effect, knowing full well she'd be able to hear the commotion. Condoms. Ticket stubs. An old cell phone. No Beretta 9mm or bowl of teeth.

"Cass, calm down." She tried to talk over me, but I kept up the charade.

"There's nothing in his nightstand, but serial killers are notorious for covering all of their tracks. They don't hide shit in their nightstands, do they! *Oh God,* they hide things under floorboards and behind secret doors where they have their stash of crazy and walls filled with pictures of their victims! *Oh. My. God.* I'm going to end up on one of those FBI Files shows, and it will be all your fault!"

I hopped off the bed and put the phone on speaker as I started stomping my feet along the hardwood floor. "The secret floorboards would sound hollow, right? And what are secret doors supposed to sound like when you find them?"

"Cassie!" Georgia's voice echoed inside the bedroom.

"What?" I asked as I continued stomping my feet along the floor.

"Stop going through his shit. Thatch is not a serial killer."

Once my feet got tired, I grabbed a nail file from my purse and sat down on the beige chaise in front of the window. "Then why is he going to get us dinner?" I yelled as I filed my nails. "Why isn't he freaking out that some stranger—*albeit a very attractive woman*—took it upon herself to just move in with him?"

Come on, Georgia. Spill the juicy gossip. You know you want to...

"I'm like ninety-nine percent sure he's messing with you back. He might be on to your prank," she finally admitted on a whisper.

"Ninety-nine percent sure is not reassuring, Wheorgie! That one percent could be the one percent that has me ending up on a missing persons' website!" I shouted as I held my right hand out in front of me. *Man, oh man, I really need a manicure.*

"I think he might be mentally disturbed, G! I wonder if I should try to get out of here before he comes back with dinner. *Holy. Fuck.* What if dinner is code for something else?" I asked on a dramatic gasp.

"Oh. My. God. Seriously, calm down and stop yelling in my ear," she responded in irritation. "Thatch isn't a serial killer. He's not a psychopath or mentally disturbed. He called Kline the second he left his apartment to grab dinner. He knows you're pranking him."

Bingo.

"Oh, okay. Thanks for the info," I answered in a normal tone.

The phone went silent for a few seconds.

"You are such an asshole," she eventually responded with an incredulous laugh. "Why do I always fall for your bullshit?"

I shrugged. "I have no idea, sweetheart, but I can't believe that big motherfucker is trying to one-up me. He's in for a rude awakening if he thinks I'm going to be the one to raise the white flag," I announced, determined.

"Uh oh... This sounds like it could end badly," Georgia said in concern. Although, her concern didn't really sound all that concerned. It sounded more excited than anything else.

"Yeah, you're right. This could end badly, but I will not be the one to say uncle. Even if I have to continue this little prank war until I'm on my deathbed, you can bet your sweet ass I will come out victorious."

"Oh, Jesus," she responded with a laugh. "What exactly are you plotting? You promised you wouldn't kill Thatch until after Kline's birthday."

"The only thing that will die at the end of this is a big part of the Jolly Green Giant's ego."

She laughed. "There's a small part of me that feels bad for wanting to encourage this."

"If anything, Thatch deserves this."

He has to pay for making my steel-barricaded heart feel like maybe it isn't impenetrable after all.

"I think that's pretty debatable, Casshead. And mostly depends on what you have planned. Thatch is actually a really good guy. Kline says he's—"

I didn't want to hear it. I already liked the guy enough all on my own.

"Yeah, speaking of plans, I gotta scoot. My roommate will be coming home with dinner soon, and I need to make myself nice and comfortable in my new humble abode."

"Okay..." she said and then paused. "You should probably avoid a few things, though. You know, just a few things that might *make him mad*."

Well, I'll be damned, Georgia could be a little devious when she wanted to.

"And what exactly would those things be?"

"Well, for starters, he only keeps one item of junk food in his pantry, and he gets pretty pissed when someone eats it. So, *don't* eat his Trix cereal. Whatever you do, I *wouldn't* do that."

"Jesus, he's like a giant toddler. I'll be sure to stay away from his favorite sugar fix."

Or I'll eat the whole fucking box in one sitting.

"And don't mess with his DVR. He records all of his favorite teams and a few shows. One of which is *America's Next Top Model*, which I gotta say, I kind of find endearing."

"Got it. Don't mess with the sports." Or I'd delete the games and, obviously, keep *Top Model*. "Any other no-gos?"

"And he's a bit of stickler for keeping your shoes off in his apartment. So I would always make sure you take your shoes off at the door. Do *not* wear them around his place."

"Shoes off, always. Got it."

Or I'd never take my shoes off. Ever. Hell, I'd probably start showering in them.

"All right, G. I better go and make sure I'm not doing any of those things."

"Good plan."

After I hung up the phone, I slid on my oldest pair of Chucks and headed into the kitchen. I found a serving bowl, filled it to the brim with Trix and milk, and made my way into the living room where I proceeded to sprawl out on his couch and scroll through his DVR recordings.

ESPN *SportsCenter… Goddammit, I can't delete that.*

America's Next Top Model… Of course, keep.

The Late Late Show with James Corden… Keep.

Family Guy… Keep.

It's Always Sunny… Keep.

The Voice… Fuck. Keep.

Well, this wasn't going as planned. *At. All.* He had the same taste in television as I did.

"Honey, I'm home!" Thatch called as he came through the door. I heard his footfalls stop in the entryway while he was predictably taking his shoes off. "Where are you, Cass?"

"I'm on the couch. Bring the food in here, baby!" I yelled over my shoulder, adding my own endearment as a counterpart to his. If he wanted to crawl up my ass, I could do the same to him. I was Cassie fucking Phillips. I could handle whatever he threw my way.

Well, maybe not literal anal fisting. I don't think I could handle that. His hands were big.

He strode into the living room with two bags of Chinese takeout in hand and stopped dead in his tracks when he found me on his sofa.

"Hi," I greeted with a sugary smile as I took an equally sugary bite of his favorite cereal. "Sorry," I continued over a mouthful, "I got too hungry waiting for you to get back."

His brown eyes looked me over, and once they saw the shoe-covered foot resting on his pristine leather couch, I swore I saw his jaw tick a few times in response, but somehow, he managed to force his face into an annoyingly neutral expression.

I swallowed the bite and asked, "What'd ya get?"

"I hope you like Chinese. I would've gotten your favorite food, but I don't know it." He flashed a smirk in my direction as he set the bags on the coffee table and sat down beside me. "But I guess that's how all serious, live-in relationships start out, right? Not knowing anything about each other. Seems normal to me," he said with a shrug as he pulled cartons from the bag.

God, he was such a smartass, and I couldn't deny that I enjoyed that aspect of his personality endlessly.

"Well, mystery is what makes a good relationship." I set my serving bowl onto the table and started opening up the cartons. "At least I've heard that somewhere…like *Cosmo* or *Georgie*? I mean, look at them. They were catfishing each other, and it worked out pretty damn good."

He chuckled at that. "Yeah, I'd say it worked out well for both of them."

"Can I have the orange chicken, sweetie pie?" I asked, holding up the carton in his direction.

"Anything for you, *honeybunch*," he said, flashing a wink. He grabbed the remote from my lap and turned on *SportsCenter*. As the sportscaster rolled through the Top Ten Highlights, Thatch leaned back on the couch and started to dig into a container of Kung Pao Chicken.

I made myself even more comfortable, stretching my legs out and placing my shoe-clad feet in his lap, but to my disappointment, he briefly glanced down and then his eyes went back to the TV as he continued eating his food. And even though I had eaten the equivalent of half a box of cereal, I couldn't resist gorging on Chinese while we sat in silence for a while, just eating and watching *SportsCenter*. It was oddly comforting.

I didn't realize he had finished his food until he was busy untying my laces and gently removing my shoes and socks. Next thing I knew, his big hands were massaging the soles of my feet while his gaze stayed fixated on the television.

The whole scene felt way too instinctive on his part. I honestly didn't know if he even realized he was doing it, and that was probably why I found myself asking, "Have you ever had a roommate before?"

"Kline and I were roommates in college," he answered without looking in my direction.

I removed my foot from his grip and tapped his thigh, urging his attention.

He looked at me, tilting his head in slight confusion.

"I meant roommate of the female persuasion."

"No." He shook his head. "I've never lived with a woman."

Interesting. Maybe he had just had a lot of girlfriends? Because, yeah, his hands were real fucking good at giving massages.

"When was your last girlfriend?"

"It's been a while," he answered cryptically.

"A while? Like a few years?"

"I haven't had a girlfriend since high school."

"High school?" I questioned in shock.

He nodded. "Like I said, it's been a while."

"Wow. That's a really long time."

He turned his body toward mine while he kept my feet firmly in his lap and his hands kept massaging all of the most perfect spots. I had to fight the urge to moan when he started using his thumbs on my heels.

"What about you? Have you ever lived with a guy before?" he asked, turning the tables on me.

"No."

"When was your last relationship?"

"Um...*a while ago.*" Or never.

He raised an eyebrow and smirked. "A while? Like a few months or a few years?"

"What constitutes a relationship, exactly?"

Thatch laughed. "I'd say it would be the last time you considered someone your boyfriend."

"Then I guess I'd have to say a while, meaning never."

His brow scrunched into a firm line. "You've never had a boyfriend?"

"Nope." I shook my head. "I've dated, but never long enough to hit the boyfriend-girlfriend milestone."

"Any particular reason?"

"Not really." I shrugged. "I've just never found anyone who kept my interest longer than three or four dates. I'm aware that makes me sound like I'm scared of commitment, but in reality, I just don't like wasting time. And not just my time—*anyone's* time. If I'm not feeling it or shit feels forced, then it's better to end it than let something continue when I know it's not going to work out in the end."

Thatch nodded in agreement. "I respect that."

"Really?" I asked and squinted a little in surprise. Not that I had ever made a point to care what other people thought about my life choices, but Thatch's neutral reaction was the opposite of pretty much *everyone*. Hell, even my mother—who for most of her life had encouraged me to do what made me happy—had recently started bombarding me with questions about whether or not I'd ever settle down. Although, I had a feeling that concern was more focused on the second female biological clock, the one people forgot to mention, than anything else: *Grandchildren*.

"Yes, Cass." He tapped my foot and offered a small smile. "I definitely respect the fact that you're open and honest and don't beat around the fucking bush when it comes to relationships. I wish more women had that mind-set. Most would probably find that waiting on the right man is better than settling with some dipshit who doesn't deserve them. And it's more respectful to the other party than pretending to be all in when you're not."

For some reason, the softness in his coffee-colored eyes had me giving him more insight into my life and lack of relationship history. "In college, I never had a boyfriend because I didn't want a boyfriend. I was one of those rare girls who enjoyed being single and just doing my own thing. And once I graduated and started my career, I was traveling all the time in the beginning. Four months would go by, and I'd maybe be in New York for a week or two, tops. That lifestyle never really made a relationship possible."

"Do you still travel that much?"

"*Fuck* no. But that's only because all of that traveling paid off. I paved my own path and created a good reputation for myself."

"A reputation that generally revolves around taking pics of half-naked men?" he asked in a teasing tone.

"What can I say? I have an eye for good-looking men, muscles, and sometimes, a nice, *thick* bulge in a pair of Calvin Klein's," I declared with a wink.

I expected him to retort with something about *his* thick bulge, but he merely laughed and continued to massage my feet, working those big hands up to my calves.

Hmmm…maybe Thatcher Kelly could be serious every once in a while?

I glanced at the clock on the cable box and saw it was nearly ten o'clock. "Well, roomie, I better hit the hay. I have to be out the door before dawn for a shoot in the Hamptons."

He removed my feet from his lap and stood, holding out a hand to help pull me off the couch.

"What are you doing?" I asked as I got to my feet in front of him. My eyes scrutinized his, waiting for him to raise the white flag and tell me to go home—which would mean the ultimate prankster would officially be dethroned from his royal throne of pranking and I would walk away victorious.

Say it! Say it! Say it! I chanted in my head.

"I'm going to bed too."

Huh?

"We're both going to bed? Right now? In *your* bed?"

"I think you can start calling it *our* bed now, baby," he said with a wink as he walked toward the hall.

I followed his lead into his bedroom, until we were both standing in front of the his and hers sinks in his master bathroom. Thatch seemed to be completely at ease, brushing his teeth, peeing—*in front of me*—and then, washing his hands. A few minutes later, he was cozied up in bed while I remained in the bathroom, just staring at my toothbrush, which he had kindly set in my hand.

"If you forgot toothpaste, feel free to borrow mine," he called from the bed.

"Uh…thanks," I muttered.

As I brushed my teeth and stared at my reflection in the mirror, I started to wonder what tricks Thatch had up his sleeve. I had a feeling he had a plan in place, and no way in hell was I going to let him one-up me without already having some plans of my own.

I crawled into bed beside him, fluffing the pillows and patting the plush white comforter around my body. "Good night," I said into the dark room.

"Night, Cass," he responded, and I swore I could hear a smirk in his voice.

And because I truly loved fucking with him, I finished the "good nights" off by reaching under the covers, grabbing his package, and whispering, "Good night, Supercock."

He chuckled softly a few times, and to my surprise, Thatch's big hands didn't even try to cop a feel of my tits.

That's not disappointment you're feeling, I told myself as a weird hollowness took shape in my belly. *Really.*

Within a few minutes, I could hear his breaths easing in and out at a slow and steady pace.

As I lay awake beside the sleeping giant, his soft breaths lulling me toward sleep of my own, I tried to make sense of his act of utter contentment.

The only explanation I could find was that the prankster had already planned his next move.

Game on, motherfucker.

CHAPTER 14

Thatch

"A week," I said into the webcam, rubbing at the tight skin of my forehead.

"What?" Kline asked. I wanted to poke out his overly amused blue eyes.

"She's been living with me for a fucking week, dude."

Boisterous laughter filled my ears, and I flipped him the bird since I knew he could see it. Well, he'd be able to see it when his head came forward again after his all-out humor-seizure, anyway.

"So she's there a week. What's the big deal?" he asked as he shuffled some stupid papers from one side of his desk to the other. His voice had finally evened, but a smile still swallowed his face from ear to ear.

"The big deal is that I made her an omelet this morning because she told me to, and we haven't had any more sex. That office blow job is the last activity my dick saw. Taking orders and not being rewarded? I don't even know who I am anymore."

"Have you tried to have sex with her?"

Well, I mean… Not really. I'd expected it would just happen. I chose not to tell Kline that, and he pretty obviously took it to mean the opposite.

"Right. I forgot who I was talking to."

Yeah, yeah. I had the friend vote for *Most Likely to Become a Prostitute* wrapped up.

"So ask her to leave," he said seriously, looking straight into the camera and raising an eyebrow in challenge.

This was a test, and I was definitely going to fail. Or pass, depending on what he wanted from me. *Fuck.*

I didn't *want* her to leave. She was entertaining and funny and so goddamn hot my retinas burned just thinking about her. But the whole "look but don't touch" thing was really starting to wear out my stamina, and not in the good way. Plus, I still couldn't figure out what the fuck was going on. I knew she was pranking me. *I knew it.* But it didn't even remotely feel like it.

I also didn't really want to give Kline the inch he was so desperately stretching for.

I fought the natural change in my features to keep my expression neutral. "And give in first? No fucking way."

I never give in first.

He smiled at that and shook his head, tilting it down to look at his phone at some kind of naked picture of Georgie, no doubt. His eyes came back to me, a full Tyra Banks *smize* engaged.

What? So I like America's Next Top Model. *Sue me.*

"Why aren't you driving this little game?" he asked, clicking the lock button on the side of his phone and setting it on his desk. "You seem to be sitting back and letting her call the shots, and that's not normally your style."

"You're right," I agreed, doodling some flames on a nearby Post-it note. "That's *not* my style."

I didn't wait and see, I *did.* I didn't let things happen; I made them. And no woman was going to outlast me. First rule of life: the woman always goes first. Through doors, into orgasm, and in this case, crumbling to the pressure in a battle of wills.

"Fuck right," I went on, truly fired up now. I probably should have paid more attention to the smirk on Kline's face, but apparently, I wasn't quite done being young and impressionable no matter how old I got.

"Oh, honey!" I called as I stepped through the door to my apartment, a new sense of purpose in my step. I'd been inside Cassie's mouth, and pussy, and by the end of this night, I was going to repeat both.

I was fucking determined.

"Cassie?" I called when she didn't answer, surveying the apartment with a keen eye. Nothing looked amiss. No new boxes of tampons littered the kitchen counter, and there was no Hello Kitty throw blanket on the couch.

I smiled to myself and shook my head, curious to see what else she'd come up with. She thought outside the normal box. I take that back—my favorite brand of woman wasn't constrained inside a box. She was sitting dead center inside her endless loop of crazy.

"Yo, Cass!" I called down the hall to no answer.

Anxiety tightened my chest as I moved in that direction toward my bedroom. Maybe she had given in, moved out—gone on some shoot with exotic men in an exotic location—and my apartment would be all mine again.

God, I hope not.

I stopped dead in my tracks at my line of thinking. I hoped not? That was ridiculous.

Still, it drove me forward again, the quiet in my bedroom and lack of activity in my closet sinking a pit into my stomach.

Before I could look around, hunt for her belongings that I'd battled so heartily to hide throughout the week, the doorbell rang.

I changed direction and headed back out of my room, down the hall, and straight to the door. When I opened it, a flower version of a centaur filled the doorway.

He wasn't actually half man, half flowers, but the enormous bouquet blocking the entirety of his body from his waist to his face sure made him look like it.

"Delivery for Cassie Phillips?" he asked. My heart swelled and sank at once as soon as he said the words, an extreme war of wills between the two versions of me playing out in my head. She was getting deliveries to my apartment, which was insane *and* insanely comforting. But she was getting flowers, *fucking blood-red roses*, and those fucks usually came from pricks with dicks.

Six feet, five inches worth of blood started to boil.

"Yeah, thanks," I said, nearly yanking the huge vase from his arms. He shrugged and took off as I shut the door behind him.

Two angry steps ate the distance between me and the kitchen counter. The glass of the vase clanged against the stone as I slammed it down and rifled through the blooms to find a card without shame.

"Aha!" I shouted as my forefinger and thumb closed around the soft paper of the envelope and yanked it out.

It was too fucking tiny for my big fingers to open delicately, and it ended up looking like I'd chewed it open, but I could throw that evidence away.

The first side was blank, but the second was filled with the scrawl of whatever employee had taken the order.

Dearest Cassie,
You're so bangable.
Love, Thatcher's Boner

"Did you send these?" I looked from the card to my dick in question, but after several seconds of irrational thought, I knew he couldn't have done it. He'd been with me all day.

The only other explanation, however, was that she'd sent them to herself, as *me*. Or as part of me.

Jesus.

"Is she actually crazy?" I asked myself aloud. I shook my head and laughed, talking to myself again. "Maybe. But you definitely are, asshole."

CHAPTER 15

Cassie

"I wrote the best fan fiction scene during my break," I gushed to Georgia as I hopped on the A train after finishing up a late shoot in Hell's Kitchen.

"Fan fiction?"

"Uh, yeah," I scoffed and adjusted my camera bag over my shoulder. "You know I *love* to write *Fifty Shades of Grey* fanfic. Don't you ever check my Wattpad page?"

"You still write on there?" she questioned in surprise.

"Hell yes, I do. I'm still waiting for E.L. James to read my work and fall madly in love with me." I'd been writing *Fifty Shades of Grey* fanfic since I devoured the entire series a few years back. I had always loved to write, but it was *that* series that had actually motivated me to put my fingers to the keys for my own enjoyment. It was probably one of the best things I had ever decided to do. There was just something about writing your own little world of whatever the hell you wanted. It was downright liberating.

"Pretty sure she's a little busy to be reading fanfic on Wattpad."

"You're ruining my BDSM buzz."

"Sorry," she said through a laugh. "I honestly had no idea you still did that. I thought that was a 2013 thing."

"And here I thought, every time I published something new, my Wheorgie was actually reading it. Some best friend you are," I teased even though I couldn't blame her. I didn't normally stick with things this long.

"So, explain how this works to me. Do you just rewrite Ana and Christian's story or what?"

"No. I apply their story to my life and create my own little fantasy world of BDSM, hot sex, a sweet-ass apartment that isn't located anywhere near my shitty place in Chelsea, and a perfect cock that can get it up on demand."

When the word cock left my lips, a woman across from me, dressed in plaid loafers and a Mickey Mouse T-shirt, threw the stink-eye in my direction. "Disgusting," she muttered loud enough for my ears.

Oh, for fuck's sake, lady. Don't eavesdrop if you're going to get pissed about what you're hearing.

"Hold on, G." I stared at Loafers until her gaze met mine again. "Would you prefer I say *penis*?" I questioned brashly. "Please, let me know how *you* would like for me to continue *my* phone conversation."

She scoffed and stood up from her seat, moving down the aisle to the opposite end of the train.

"For the love of God, don't get arrested on the subway," Georgia said into my ear on a laugh. "Chelsea is not shitty. Especially not our building. There's a fucking elevator and a doorman. And, *technically*, you're not even living in Chelsea anymore."

Thank fuck. I told myself it was just the apartment making me feel that way and not the giant ogre whose bed I shared.

"God, I can't wait to get out of there. Between the construction, the constant dust, and the overall depressing vibe I get every time I walk through the neighborhood, I'm ready to move out."

I couldn't see her, but I knew my little Wheorgie was shaking her head in silent defense of Chelsea. But I was my own woman, goddammit, and if I said Chelsea was shitty, it *was*.

Especially compared to Thatch's floorplan.

"Are you going to find a new place once you're done playing house with Thatch?"

I laughed. "Actually, I am. While Thatch is busy trying to one-up me, I've been busy getting our old apartment back up to snuff. I'm meeting with a contractor tomorrow to get the floors and kitchen redone."

"Well, shit. That's convenient," she responded. "But I'll reiterate... Chelsea isn't that bad."

"Oh, *puh-lease*." I laughed, loud and boisterous. "You are so far out of the Chelsea loop it isn't even funny, sweetcheeks. Your opinion means jack shit when you're living in a goddamn suburban oasis with your mogul husband where all you have to worry about is which room to bone him in."

A guy had replaced Mickey's number one fan across the aisle, and he grinned at me. I held his eyes until he started to blush.

Georgia giggled. "Speaking of my husband, he just walked into the bedroom. Are you almost home? I'd sleep better if I knew you were back."

Right. Like Big Dick was going to let her go right to sleep.

"Wait...*which* home are you going to?"

"Yes," I answered as I walked off the train and headed for the steps that would get me to street level. "And my swank new pad in Midtown, of course."

"Okay, well, call me tomorrow if you're free for lunch."

"Sounds good." I ended the call and slid my phone into the pocket of my jean shorts.

The walk to Thatch's apartment was about five blocks, and since I was getting home so late, the sidewalk traffic was a breeze. Six minutes later, I was getting off the elevator and unlocking the front door of my home away from home.

"Thatcher, I'm home, and I'm hungry as a motherfucker!" I shouted as I kicked the door shut with my Converse-clad heel. My mind was already one-tracking straight for the special delivery of roses I had sent around two this afternoon, and I didn't give two fucks if I woke him up.

I probably should have cared, but I wanted at least one interaction with him. Now *that*, wanting it so bad I didn't really have control of my actions anymore, I cared more about.

Perfect, I thought to myself once I saw the outrageously large bouquet sitting on the kitchen table. They looked ridiculous in his neutral apartment, their blood-red petals damn near blinding compared to the black-and-white décor. I plucked the note from the center of the vase and couldn't stop myself from grinning as I read the brilliant words.

God, I'm a fucking genius.

Well, a *horny* genius.

I had come up with the flower delivery plan on my break, while I was three spanks deep into my fanfic scene. My brain had been so goddamn fixated on Thatch while I was writing that I could *not* stop thinking about having sex with him again. Hell, my pussy might as well have written that chapter. *If only she could hold a pen.*

But I wanted Thatch to ask for it. And if I couldn't have that, I wanted some outside reason, like a floral offering from his dick.

"Well, look who's home," Thatch greeted as he walked into the kitchen, wide awake and completely fucking fuckable. He was freshly showered and dressed comfortably. It should've been illegal for a man to look as good as he did in a simple pair of black jersey shorts and a white cotton tee. His eyes caught sight of the note in my hand. "You're getting in a little late. *Busy* day?" he asked with a knowing smirk.

"Very busy day," I answered and held the note up for his amused gaze. "It looks like someone else was busy too. And thoughtful, I might add."

He shrugged and crossed his arms over his chest. The muscles bulged, and I swallowed a groan. "What can I say? My cock is generous. And considering I'm having a hard time recalling when he found the time to send those to you, I'd say he's pretty fucking smart too."

I grinned. "Well, he definitely has great taste in flowers." I leaned forward, sniffing the sweet aroma of roses. "You know, I almost feel compelled to thank him."

Thatch leaned forward against the counter, stretching his arms wide and making the veins of his forearms stand out, and I could practically feel my breasts swell. "Almost?"

"Yeah. *Almost.*" I set the note down beside the vase and turned to give him my full attention.

He smirked. "Honey, my dick sent you two dozen roses. I think you can go ahead and take out the almost and just leave it as you feeling compelled."

I moved toward him, into his space until he leaned back and made room for me to stand between his legs. "Today was a really good day."

He smiled.

"Do you want to hear about my day, Thatcher?" I asked as I ran an index finger down one of his arms.

He stared down at me with an intrigued smirk. "Tell me all about it."

"I'm surprised I got anything done. I was very distracted by thoughts of you." I stood on my tiptoes and softly pressed my lips to his. "Did you know I like to write?"

"No, honey, I didn't know that." He gripped my hips with both hands. "What do you write?"

I skimmed my mouth across his lips and then his jaw, and I savored the sound of his soft intake of breath. "Have you ever heard of *Fifty Shades of Grey*?" I asked as I pressed soft yet biting kisses down his neck.

"The BDSM books with all of the spanking and hot sex? Yeah, I've heard of them."

"I like to write stories based on those books. And today, I wrote a little scene with you in mind. You want me to tell you about it?" I asked coyly, gazing up into his warm eyes.

His hands slid up my T-shirt until his fingers were resting beneath the swell of my breasts. "If by telling, you mean showing…" He leaned down and took my mouth in a soft, seductive kiss. "Tell me all fucking about it," he whispered, his breath warm against my lips.

I kissed him once more and then bit his bottom lip, tugging gently before finally pulling away. "Meet me in the bedroom." I turned around and headed for the hallway.

"Do I need to bring anything?"

"Just your cock," I called over my shoulder.

He didn't waste any time. Thatch was hot on my heels and removing my clothes before I could say otherwise. Within seconds, we were both gloriously naked, standing beside his bed, and kissing the hell out of each other.

He grabbed my ass and lifted me up with ease until my legs were wrapped around his waist. "Show me what you were fantasizing about today, honey," he groaned against my mouth as he laid us on the bed. His cock was hard and ready between my thighs and pressing against the oh-so-perfect place. "Fuck, I can't wait to bury myself inside you."

I gripped his hair and tugged his lips away from mine. "Beg me for it," I demanded. "Say, 'let me feel your perfect pussy.'"

He smirked down at me as he thrust forward, sliding teasingly across where I was already wet and throbbing for him. "Is that what you want, baby? My dirty mouth?"

I nodded. *God, yes. Dirty talk me, you sexy giant.* His body spanned the space of two regular men. He didn't have two dicks, but he sure knew how to use the one.

"Please, let me feel this perfect fucking pussy wrapped around my cock."

"Mistress Cassie Grey," I added.

One of his brows quirked up, confused.

"Say it, Thatchastasia."

"Thatch-astasia?" He sat back on his heels and stared down at me. "What the fuck are you talking about?"

I grinned. "I'm *showing* you, remember?"

"Let me get this straight." He ran a hand through his hair. "You wrote yourself as the male dominant, and *I'm* the female submissive?"

"It's the only way it would work, Thatchastasia."

"Excuse me?"

"You're way more submissive than I am, baby," I explained.

He started to shake his head, but I kept talking. "And speaking of the whole submissive thing, you're not very good at it right now. You should be saying Mistress Cassie Grey every time you address me." I patted his knee. "But don't worry, we'll work up to it."

He stared at me for a minute before an amused smirk raised the corner of his mouth. "You planning on spanking me, *Mistress Cassie Grey?*"

"Only if you're bad."

He waggled his brows and grabbed my ankle with one of his large hands. "Oh, believe me, I'm going to be all kinds of bad, honey." His lips started a slow and heated path from my ankle to my inner thigh. "I'm going to blow your mind."

"You're a terrible submissive," I said through a soft moan. "I should spank the shit out of you for topping from the bottom and not addressing me properly."

"Spank me later. Right now, I have to put my mouth on you." His hands gripped my thighs, spreading me wide for his heated gaze. "You gonna come right on my tongue?"

Well, shit, I didn't have to think twice about that. *"Fuck, yes,"* I moaned as my head fell back on the pillows.

His mouth was on me before I could take my next breath. With tiny, insistent strokes, his tongue thrummed against my clit as his lips applied the perfect amount of suction. I clenched the sheets in my fists, and my thighs shook in anticipation.

"You taste so fucking good," he whispered against my aching skin sloppily, still eating me as he spoke.

I gripped his hair as my hips started to move against his mouth of their own accord.

"You're so close. Your pussy's already trying to trap my tongue." He slid his hands up my body, past my hips, until they reached my panting chest. "These fucking tits are going to be the death of me someday," he groaned as he gripped my breasts and brushed his thumbs across my nipples.

God, the man had some serious skills. I was convinced his tongue had graduated with an Ivy League doctorate in oral. Within seconds, thanks to a perfect swirl and two quick flicks of my clit, I was screaming his name through a mind-blowing orgasm. I expected the fog to last, but I wanted him too badly. Each roll of pleasure only drove me to want more.

"Now, Thatch," I panted as he rolled a condom down his length. "Please, fuck me now," I begged.

"I don't think either of us are born submissives, baby. But your sweet voice begging me to fuck you sure makes me think you could be." He smirked down at me as he kneeled between my thighs.

Before I could offer a snappy retort, he gripped my thighs and pushed inside me, hard and so deliciously deep. "Holy. Shit."

He groaned. "I'm never leaving this pussy." He increased his rhythm, driving into me with wild and uninhibited movements. "I'm just going to eat, fuck, and sleep inside this perfect cunt for the rest of my life."

"Yes. Let's do that," I agreed on a whimper. "Just fuck me all the time."

He wrapped his arms around me and flipped us around so he was lying on his back and I was straddling his thighs. "Ride me, Cassie," he demanded as he sat up to grab my breasts and suck a hard nipple into his mouth. "Let me see those gorgeous tits bounce."

God. Following his command, I noticed each jolt from the weight of my breasts as though they were connected by a live wire to my pussy. I knew he was watching them, and the unbelievably sexy feeling I got from it was overwhelming.

I didn't stop riding the Jolly Green Giant's cock until I was shouting through another perfect orgasm. The climax was so strong I felt like it had wrung me out from the inside and left my body limp and sated as I laid my head against his chest.

Holy hell. I just need a minute to catch my breath.

Yeah, just a minute.

Just one...

CHAPTER 16

Thatch

How did that saying go?

Fall asleep in the middle of sex once, shame on you. Fall asleep in the middle of sex twice, shame on me. What would happen on the third time? Cassie needed to see a doctor?

Fuck. I was positive if I had to experience her falling asleep on my dick for a third time, I'd end up permanently bowlegged and my balls would shrivel up inside my body.

I'd at least partially understood the first bout of coitus interruptus since I'd been shocked to the point of off my game, but this go 'round, I'd been highly engaged in some of my best moves. And still, her orgasmic bliss was the end of my own. Out like a light, she'd started to snore into my already damp skin, slick with her drool.

I probably needed to skip to the third scenario and find a doctor who made sleep-sex house calls. *Maybe Dr. Savannah Cummings is available.* Yeah, no. Definitely not a good idea.

Is this what real life looked like?

Unceasingly unsatisfied sexually while being covered in other people's bodily fluids?

The drool I could handle, but the blue balls were another thing entirely. I'd never liked it, not in the seventeen some odd years since I'd first lost my virginity, so I didn't imagine I'd start now.

But for the first time in nearly the same length of time, I wasn't longing for the physical companionship of some nameless, faceless woman with a body of my choosing. Instead, I fantasized exclusively about the flawless face of the very known woman currently mouth-breathing into my nipple.

"Cass?" I whispered, trying to rouse her from her coma. "Cass!" But I wasn't surprised when she didn't respond, truly entranced in the deep recesses of REM sleep.

"Goddamn fucking sound sleeper," I grumbled as I shifted her off and slid away from the heat of her body. I was upset with her, but I was a hundred times more distressed by the fact I didn't want to put distance between us, didn't want to move to my side of the bed or leave it out of spite.

I wanted to lie there and listen to her breathe, something she so rarely gave anyone the opportunity to do. Bold and the complete antithesis of bashful, Cassie Phillips seldom shut up, and when she did, the violence of her overactive eyes spoke for her. But like this, she was completely at rest and her so often aggressive features melted into softness.

It made me wonder if there was a vulnerable woman inside of her anywhere, or if the fight she so naturally manifested was the way of her mind. I wasn't sure what I wanted the answer to be, but I knew I wanted to search for it.

She was naked, and her skin still held the glow of a healthy arousal-induced blush. Loose strands of chocolate hair fell around her mouth, one of them sticking to the moisture between her lips, so I reached out and pulled it free, my fingertips ghosting along the edge of her jaw as I pushed it to rest behind her ear.

Looking from her serene face to the glow of the clock behind her, I transitioned from inquisitive to agitated once again. I had to be up for work in three hours, and the steel rod in my dick made it nearly impossible to even consider sleep. I could work out the frustration on my own again, but I knew it'd leave me nothing but angry and no more satisfied.

I punched at the pillow beside my head and rolled over, closing my eyes to keep myself from staring at Cassie all night like I wanted to.

There was something about her that stirred something in me. She'd joked about mystery being a good foundation for a relationship, but she was at least partially right.

In the beginning, not understanding everything about someone was what made me want to know more. I'd been in this place before, but never for this long. Two dates, maybe three, and women always seemed to fall short of what I'd hoped. I wasn't looking for someone who was perfect, just someone who perfectly affected me. Cassie had held my interest for far longer than any woman in the last fifteen years, and she wasn't even trying for it.

If anything, she'd been trying to drive me away.

Staring out the window, I blinked into the lights of the building across the street and let my mind wander. To the things I'd done wrong, the ones I'd done right, and the majority that I wouldn't change either way.

Three full hours without sleep and a cold shower later, and my irritation was starting to grow into impatience.

"Cass," I called at normal volume, shaking her awake. "Wake up, fucking Narcoleptic Nancy."

Her eyes fluttered delicately as her long lashes fought to unstick themselves from one another. She cleared her throat and touched my chest in confusion, the first moments of waking up some of her most interesting. It took a lot of work to transform from the peace of sleeping to the chaos of awake, and I enjoyed the opportunity to watch. Violent or soft, it was never the same.

"Thatcher?"

"Yep," I answered shortly, frustrated by my feelings of the *exact opposite of frustration*. With a repeat of this kind of stunt, I should be fucking over it. Instead, all I could concentrate on was how undeniably attracted I was to her. *Goddamn, why do I have to make everything so difficult for myself?*

"It feels fucking early. Why are you waking me up early?" she asked and accused at once, her eyes still fully closed and her small hand resting on my shoulder. I could feel the heat of it all the way through my shirt.

"I have to go to work," I said. I wanted to whisper, but I forced myself to speak loudly. After last night, she deserved this. And it didn't hurt that it meant getting to see her, talk to her, *take her in*, before I headed out for the day.

"Ah, fuck. We've got to talk about this you going to work thing," she replied as she cracked open one eye. "It's really not working well for me."

I raised my eyebrows in response but said nothing else.

"Is there coffee?" she asked, pouting her lip in a way that normally made me crumble. She'd only been around for a week, but women learned fast. They preyed on your weakness and then used it against you shamelessly. I kind of admired it.

"No," I told her. "There's no coffee."

"No coffee?" she shrieked.

"No fucking coffee."

"What's wrong? Why is there no coffee?"

"Stop saying 'no coffee.'"

"Then get me coffee!" she snapped, eyes open and alert.

"No. You're a terrible fucking roommate. Only good roommates get coffee in bed in the morning."

"What the hell did I do?"

I got right into her space, all the way in her face, my eyes staring directly into hers. She moved back until her back hit the headboard, and I followed her in. My voice was a rough whisper. "What face do I make when I come?"

"What?"

"What *face* do *I* make when I *come* during sex?" I asked again.

She searched for the answer, her eyes lifting up and to the right as she did, but it didn't take long for her to figure out why she didn't know the answer.

"Shit."

I nodded. "Yeah."

I pushed up and off the bed and stalked down the hall, grabbing my suit jacket from the back of the couch and throwing it on. Glancing at the clock on the wall, I picked up my wallet, keys, and phone and headed for the door.

Feet pounded behind me, but I didn't bother to turn at the sound. She was everything no serious man should want—selfish, fucking crazy, and miles away from wanting a commitment. But when I thought about the past week with her, I couldn't seem to convince myself I didn't want it. And that was fucking dangerous.

"Thatch!" she yelled from the mouth of the hallway when I reached for the doorknob.

I looked over my shoulder in question, but I kept my body to the door.

"I just…I'm sorry."

Her words hit me right in the chest. I hadn't been expecting an unashamed, unmasked apology. My body turned toward her on its own.

"What are you sorry for?" I pushed, and my eyes took in the fact that she'd managed to throw on a pair of tiny shorts and a tank-top before leaving my bedroom.

She avoided the question. "I've never done that to anyone twice."

I forced a dry chuckle, before turning back toward the door.

"Great. I guess I'm just special."

"Thatch."

I turned once more and leaned my back into the door on an exhale. "What, Cass? You're forgiven, okay? Neither of us owes the other anything in this scenario, and you know it just as well as I do."

I didn't want to be the one to give in, but this was turning into something I had never expected. I didn't know how much one-sided interest I could take.

Her face shifted in a way I didn't like, so I looked to the floor.

I'd never seen her coming.

At a dead run, she jumped up to wrap her arms around my neck and sealed her lips to mine. They tasted like regret and Cassie, and her smell enveloped me on a delay.

Hands at her ass, I lifted her higher and opened my mouth to her, and she didn't squander the opportunity. Light licks tickled the tip of my tongue, and she yanked at my hair. I tried to find my bearings, figure out what was happening, but the feel of her body pressed to mine made it pretty much impossible.

She pushed herself closer, and I pulled at her hips. I needed more, and after a long night thinking about nothing but her, my body refused to accept any other answer.

I stroked her face with my thumbs as I forced our tongues to her mouth. Control was mine this time around, and I'd be damned if it ended in anything other than satisfaction.

Her legs tightened around my waist as I slid my hands down her sides, pausing at her perfect tits to slide my thumbs under their weight.

She moaned in my mouth, and that was all the incentive my feet needed to move.

Heading straight for the bedroom, I navigated to my hallway blindly, shoving my hands into the bottoms of her pajamas and kneading at the naked skin of her ass. She wore no underwear underneath.

"Fuck," I breathed as one hand traced the crack of her ass all the way to her pussy. She was wet and wild and bucked at the intrusion of one of my thick fingers.

My tie came over my head with a few solid yanks from her, and she worked at the buttons of my shirt, nibbling at the skin as she exposed it.

Each pinch of her teeth made my already hard dick harder. Forcing her up when my shins hit the comforter, I unwrapped her legs and stood her up on the edge of the bed in front of me. She was breathing hard as I pulled her shorts down roughly and shoved up her shirt to put my mouth to her tit. Her legs shook as I released her nipple with a pop, and I cut her legs right out from under her with a yank.

"Holy shit!" she yelled as her back hit the bed with a bounce.

Up and over, I flipped her on a roll, yanked her hips to mine and forced her knees into the bed. When her pussy glistened at me from between the cheeks of her ass, I reddened the skin with one sharp slap.

She yelped and shoved her ass back at me harder. My blood pounded.

"Go ahead, baby. Fall asleep on me now," I taunted. "I dare you."

CHAPTER 17

Cassie

Thatch kneeled on the bed while I straddled his thighs. He had one arm wrapped around my waist, while the other skimmed up my back and into the messy locks at the nape of my neck. Soft moans fell from my lips with each upward thrust of his hips.

"Come with me," he demanded as his heady gaze stayed locked with mine.

Two bouts of giving him the Come Coma, and he wasn't taking no for an answer this time. We'd been at it for a while, but I had no fucking concept of time. Thatch ensured I couldn't focus on anything but him, holding my eyes with an intensity I'd never experienced.

My hands slid across this skin of his chest, his arms, until they found their way into his hair. I gripped the strands and pulled his mouth closer to mine as the initial sensations of my orgasm started to course through my veins. "Thatch, I'm there. I'm there," I chanted. My lips brushed against his as panting breaths started to fall from my lungs.

He growled. "God, you're gripping my cock so tight, honey." His rhythm turned wild and reckless as he followed my lead, but he wasn't taking any chances. As my release pulsed inside of me and my eyes wanted to roll closed, he slapped my ass hard. The sting faded straight to pleasure and rolled into another orgasm. I had to admit it was a smart move. Even I couldn't fall asleep while his big hand was reddening my ass.

"Yes. *Fuck,*" he groaned as his long-awaited orgasm finally came to fruition. He wrapped both arms around my body, holding me tightly to his chest, as he rode out his climax inside me.

The sound of ragged air overwhelmed the space for several long moments.

Once we caught our breath, Thatch lay back on the bed, stretching out and maneuvering my body so that I was sprawled across his chest.

Holy hell. I was convinced this man had the stamina of a fucking superhero. Every past sexual experience paled in comparison to the workout he had given me. I had been fucked in every position possible. I glanced at the clock, and my eyes nearly bugged out. *For three hours straight,* my body had been flipped, turned, and sexed on just about every surface of his apartment.

He had taken me slow and deep in his bed. Rough and quick against the tile wall of his shower. Spread out across his kitchen table, where he literally ate me for breakfast.

He'd even fucked me against the terrace doors, with the sounds of the city below us.

But he'd brought it home in his bed, and goddamn, I had to admire the confidence it took to bring me there, to the scene of the crime, after putting me through the paces for hours on end. But then, maybe proving he could do it was the whole point.

His fingers ran through my damp hair. "You still awake, honey?" he asked with a hint of amusement.

I rested my chin on his chest and gazed into his big, brown eyes. "As a matter of fact, I am." The corners of his mouth nearly touched his ears. "You're looking awfully pleased with yourself right now."

"Oh, believe me, I am. You were offering up some pretty sweet declarations of love for my cock."

I shook my head in denial. "I can't be held accountable for anything I say during sex."

But he was right. I had pretty much waxed poetic for his penis. At one point, I'd told him I was going to buy a bigger purse so I could carry it around with me all day, *every* day. Even announced that I would find a new TSA-approved carry-on for air travel.

Honestly, I don't normally have the urge to carry dudes' dicks around in my bag.
But in my defense, Thatch is a fucking fantasy in the sack.
His good points?
1. Insatiable endurance.
2. Sexy as fuck body.
3. Huge and thick schlong.
4. Delicious dirty-talker.
5. His PhD in oral.
See what I mean?
You'd be trolling Amazon for a dick carry-on too.

"It was definitely the first time someone has offered to carry my dick in a bouquet as they walked down the aisle. Honestly, I'm flattered," he teased.

I shrugged. "Well, he does send me flowers. I'd say it's a normal progression for him to *become* the flowers."

And motivate you to marry him, my pussy screamed.

Whoa. Slow down there, Pussy Promiser.

He chuckled in response, causing his chest to vibrate against mine.

I couldn't stop myself from smiling and laughing along with him. Hands down, Thatch had *the best* laugh. It was husky and deep and downright infectious.

To his core, he was a happy, carefree guy. He went with the flow, and most importantly, he enjoyed his life. He wasn't the type of man who would spend his weekends holed up in his apartment. *No.* Thatch *lived.* He *experienced.* He was more alive than anyone I had ever met.

He was a bright light I wanted to reach out and catch in my hands.

And I found myself craving more of him—his laughter, his smiles, his stupid winks, and witty retorts. I couldn't deny that I genuinely wanted to get lost in all of it.

He tapped my nose with his index finger. "You know, when you're not going narcoleptic after getting off, you're a bit wild, honey."

I quirked a brow. "A *bit* wild?"

"Real fucking wild." He smirked and pressed a flirty kiss to my mouth. "I'm a fan of *your* brand of wild," his whispered against my lips.

"I'm a fan of your stamina."

"And my cock," he added, and one of his signature winks followed suit.

I laughed. "Yeah, that too."

"Rule number ten," he announced. "Don't hold back your girlish giggles."

At some point, we'd started a list of ridiculous roommate rules. Most of them were so outlandish, I had to keep a list in the notes on my phone to remember what they were.

I know I'd be fucking curious if I were you.
Here's the rundown of The Rules of Thatch & Cass thus far.
#1. If someone forgets to run the dishwasher, they have to walk around the apartment shirtless for one hour.
#2. Thatch is always the big spoon in bed.
#3. Cassie isn't allowed to go to strip clubs without Thatch. Ever.
#4. Never delete an episode of America's Next Top Model before Thatch sees it. (See Rule #1's punishment, but add stilettos and Cass reenacting the episode in her underwear.)

#5. Thatch has to watch a Lifetime movie with Cass once a week.
#6. Cass isn't allowed to drink diet soda. Only regular.
#7. Thatch isn't allowed to mention ice cream unless it's in the freezer.
Otherwise, consider himself dick slapped.
#8. Cass has to hit a minimum daily word count of fifteen fucks in
front of Thatch.
#9. Pinkie promises aren't for pussies. If you hook that finger, it's as
good as a blood oath, but less messy.
And now, Rule #10. Cass can't hide her girlish giggle.

I rolled my eyes. "I do *not* giggle."

"Yeah, honey, you do." He nodded slowly. "Not often, but you do."

I groaned and buried my face in his chest.

"Don't be embarrassed. I love seeing tough as nails Cassie all girly and soft."

My eyes met his again. "I'm not embarrassed. I'm annoyed. There's a difference."

"Oh, so you blush when you get annoyed? My bad," he teased.

"I'm not blushing!" I smacked his chest.

"Ow. Fuck," he responded through a laugh as he flipped me onto my back before I could stop him. His hands held my arms above my head as his mouth brushed across my lips. "Spend the day with me today," he demanded, his eyes gazing into mine.

"Pretty sure I've been spending the day letting you fuck me senseless."

He smirked. "Yeah, but I want you to actually spend the *whole* day with me. No last-minute shoots for you. No work meetings for me. Just me and you, fucking and laughing and occasionally taking breaks for food."

"I'm not going to be able to walk tomorrow."

He waggled his eyebrows. "That's what I'm hoping for."

I smiled. "Okay. Count me in."

"Fantastic." He pressed a soft kiss to my lips. "Now, *Mistress Cas-*

sie, I need to order us some lunch." He hopped off the bed and tossed on a pair of boxer briefs. "Anything in particular sound good?" he asked as he moved toward the doorway.

"Rule number eleven," I called from my comfortable position on the bed. "Don't lose your stamina."

He stopped and turned toward me. His eyes glinted with amusement. "My stamina?"

I nodded slowly. "Yeah. Don't lose that. *Ever.*"

Thatch's answering smile was as wide as Texas. "Oh, honey, as long as you're around, I don't think there's any danger of that."

CHAPTER 18

Thatch

"What's wrong with all these people? Don't they have lives?" Cassie asked as we weaved through a predictably crowded Times Square.

I chuckled and pulled her closer to my side as the space on the sidewalk around us closed up. "Yes, they do. Believe it or not, this is *actually* the sight of them living them."

We'd stayed holed up in the apartment for most of the day and evening. I knew more about her body than I'd ever known about anyone's other than my own. One-night stands weren't exactly about the details, and I'd been too young and horny to ever pay attention to anything specific about Margo. My brilliant thoughts had pretty much ended at *I like it*.

Now we were out, and I was on a mission to fulfill my urge to let her *know* me. I'd never felt this motivated.

"Fucking fuckers! I reject that idea! Anyone who thinks this is living is—" Cassie started on a curse only to be interrupted by the jarring bump of a group coming to a stop for a picture. "Goddammit, watch where you're going, assholes!"

I smiled at the irony that they weren't "going" at all and tightened my hold on her hand, pulling her away from the confrontation with an Asian tourist and into motion through the crowd. We were only a block away at this point, the distinct neon of Fu-Get-About-Ink catching the attention of my trained eyes despite its proximity to all the other flash and flare of Times Square, but with the lead weight of my companion on my arm, it was liable to take us years to get there.

Even that thought didn't make me feel the need to rush. I had what I really needed beside me.

"Sweet fucking cocksuckers, I thought I got annoyed in Chelsea, but I'd mate with that place over Times Square."

"It's not that bad," I replied, smiling the whole time and tugging gently on her hand when she slowed to shoot a glare at some innocent children.

"Not that bad?" she shrieked. "It's like the seventh circle of hell."

"Well, then, just be glad it's not the eighth," I teased.

"What the hell were you guys thinking, putting your business this close to Times Square?"

I laughed. "Uh, that we wanted to make money?"

"From the bottom of my gold-digging soul, I never thought I'd feel this way, but don't you have enough money?"

"It's mostly Frankie's money," I lied. Technically, I had fifty-one percent ownership.

"I don't know if I can deal with this," she went on. Her face was set into the opposite of relaxed.

I pulled her to an abrupt stop, knowing I couldn't wait another minute.

Twisted like the front section of her hair, I found myself fucking *attracted* to all the things by which I should only be put off.

She started to grumble at first, but the ability to speak quickly left her as I pushed her back against the nearest building and skimmed my lips against the warm, pink skin of hers. "If you don't want my tongue in your mouth, you better say so fast."

Her eyes had only the time to widen before my tongue traced the seam of her lips and forced their blue ferocity closed. All the air in her lungs left in a rush, traveling from her mouth to mine and straight down the line of my throat and into my chest. I knew it didn't work like that, the actual air that she breathed out sustaining me—the science of oxygen and carbon dioxide wouldn't allow it—but, *God*, in that moment, as her tongue circled the tip of mine, it couldn't have felt more like it did.

Hands eager, I dove into her hair, tangling the tresses among my fingers until she couldn't easily pull free. Each flick of her tongue pushed me further, begged me to come closer, and I obliged, overjoyed to make any one of her wishes and desires come true. Her nails dug into the skin of my biceps, scratching noticeably deeper when I pushed her tongue back into her mouth with my own and ate at the corners of her lips with sucking nibbles and slight pinches of my teeth.

At her moan, my dick swelled, and the feeling of getting jostled closer was the only thing that stopped me from running my lips from throat to nipple.

Sweet *fuck*, her skin tasted like a dream. If I hadn't spent the entire day in her company, I would have thought she'd showered in the juice of the sweetest fruit. But she'd only taken one shower, and it had been with me.

I pulled away slightly, but she followed, sealing her lips to mine until I was too tall to reach.

"Come on, honey," I urged gently, running a hand through her tangled hair courtesy of the rough bricks of the building behind her and finishing with a wink. "I'll give you more of that later."

Her eyes narrowed, but the tightening of her lids did nothing to lessen the sparkle of arousal in her eyes.

With a tug at her hips, I pulled her off the wall and pushed her in front of me with a hand at her back to guide her.

She glanced back at it in disgust, ever independent, but I didn't move it an inch. I'd always been a fan of affection, but I *liked* touching her every opportunity I got in a way that it would take more than a few dirty looks to make me stop.

When we came to a stop in front of the building, I watched as she looked up at the two-story-tall neon sign and stared.

"This is it."

She nodded. Not in disinterest, and not in a you're-an-idiot kind of way. No, the fire in her eyes was more proud than passive, and I had the strangest feeling of growth in my chest.

I'd obviously done my fair share in the world of business, but most of it had been born of natural talent rather than interest. This, however, was something that came straight from my heart.

It was Frankie's livelihood, but it was my home. I felt comfortable here in a way I didn't really even understand.

But she looked like she did. I wanted desperately to see through a window into her mind.

Maybe then I'd be able to understand if she was feeling all of the things I was feeling.

What started out as a game of pranks and a constant battle of wills had turned into something that didn't feel superficial at all.

Somewhere along the line, the playbook had changed for me. I didn't understand the details of how I'd gotten here, and I had no idea if anything had changed for her, but I knew to my soul that I wanted more.

Of her laughter, her attitude, her ability to keep me on my fucking toes—the way she lived her life. I was nearly insatiable for all of it. *All of her.*

"Come on," I called, bringing her eyes from their exploration to me. "Let's go inside."

The bell over the door rang as we stepped in, and Frankie's eyes came up from the portrait tattoo he was working on in the open station in the back. We had private rooms too, but when Frankie was working by himself, he stayed up front to keep an eye on things.

He gave an interested nod, seeing as bringing a woman here was pretty much the exact opposite of my normal routine, but then went back to it.

Come to think of it, I'd never brought a woman here. Something about everything it meant to me had stopped me.

I'd never even considered *not* bringing Cass here tonight.

My eyebrows pinched together involuntarily. I wasn't quite sure why that was.

"Wow, this place is fantastic!" she spouted, her eyes bouncing from one piece of artwork on the walls to the next. Some of them were mine, but I wasn't quite ready to tell her that yet.

"Yeah?"

She nodded enthusiastically and hiked herself to sitting up on the counter. I smiled at her no-cares attitude. No one else I'd ever met would blatantly jump up on the counter of a business without permission.

Her gaze moved around, but when it came back to me, her face was reminiscent. "I actually thought about opening my own photography studio when I was younger, but Georgia talked me out of it."

I stepped forward and pulled her legs apart to stand between them. "Why's that? A studio sounds cool."

She laughed and shrugged before rolling her eyes. "It probably had something to do with the fact that I wanted to call it Let Me Shoot Your Kids."

Frankie and I laughed. Cass and I both turned to look at him now that we knew he was listening. His green eyes sparkled, but he feigned concentration on his work.

"What about you? A tattoo parlor and a... Jesus, what do you do?"

I shook my head and smiled. "A financial consultant."

"That means next to nothing to me. I'm assuming there are numbers and money involved?"

"Am I like the Chandler Bing of the group? No one knows what I do?"

She shrugged shamelessly. "At least you're taller."

"Oh yeah, thank God I'm taller," I joked.

"So how'd your business portfolio become so diversified?" She bounced her brows as if to say, *See, I can speak work jargon.*

"Well, I went to college with the idea that I needed to do something respectable."

"An interesting concept for you," she teased.

I pushed forward as though she hadn't spoken, but I smiled and squeezed at her bare thighs.

Fuck, her skin was like quicksand. I could get lost in it for hours. I shook my head slightly to bring back my concentration.

"And, well, it turned out I was really good at it. Kind of a savant with numbers."

"An idiot savant," she said with a smile.

"Right," I agreed.

"It's starting to make more sense now," she said and smiled, but I didn't take the bait.

"Once I started to make a lot of money, I got bored."

She shook her head and swung her legs at my sides. "Oh, man, that sounds familiar."

"You too?" I asked to which she answered earnestly, "Always."

"Well, I had the cash to invest in things I was interested in. A lot of property and small businesses trying to get off the ground, that kind of thing."

"So you opened this."

"Nope," I corrected with a smile. "Frankie opened this place. I just stepped in as an investor about four years ago."

"You're obviously more than a silent partner, though."

I shrugged. "I liked it. And Frankie liked having the help."

"Sure did!" Frankie yelled from the back, again confirming shamelessly that he was listening to every word we said.

Cassie smiled, lips and eyes and the apples of her cheeks all falling victim to her amusement as her hair flipped effortlessly over her shoulder. She pushed me back slightly so she could tuck her foot under her ass and leaned onto her hand, and I couldn't help but notice that she looked comfortable here.

"Get us some fucking food, T!" Frankie called from his station.

Cassie joined in enthusiastically. "Seriously! And make it a pizza, pineapple and ham."

"I don't get a say in this?"

The two of them glanced briefly to one another before turning back to me and speaking in unison. "No."

I grumbled, but what I didn't do was tell them to fuck off. It was just us, no clients to speak of, and I was liking being with both of them.

Knowing it'd take nearly a year for a pizza to be delivered to this location at this time of night, I considered going out to get it myself. But all it took was one glance at Cassie's face, relaxed with genuine interest and wonder as she hunched over Frankie showing her the inner workings of his tattoo machine, to know I wasn't going fucking anywhere.

Kline and Wes knew nearly everything about me—my wild teenage antics and Margo's death. But neither of them knew I'd been apprenticing to actually become a tattoo artist.

I wanted to tell Cassie, though. So much so I had to fight the urge to just blurt it out.

Grabbing my phone off the counter, I reached for my wallet from my back pocket, but when my fingers met the seam, I knew immediately something was wrong. I patted at the fabric in shock, but that didn't change the outcome.

"Fuck!"

"What?" Cassie asked, jumping up from her spot next to Frankie and coming toward me.

Over a goddamn decade in this city, and I'd finally been pick-pocketed. All because my brain had been more concerned about the bump in the front of my pants than keeping the one in the rear.

"What happened?" Frankie called with a crease in his brow as the corners of my mouth started to turn up.

It was completely possible I was actually losing my mental stability. I'd just been taken for the first time in my life. I'd have to get on the phone immediately to cancel all of my shit, go to the DMV for a new license, alert the doorman of my apartment, and never, ever get back the cash I'd had in there, and *still*, I was smiling. Because when I thought about how distracted I'd been, how irresponsible it was to let my guard down like that, it made me think about why I'd done it— and the way her lips had followed mine like they couldn't get enough.

I shook my head with a laugh. "Somebody stole my wallet."

"What?" Cassie shrieked, and Frankie's brows pushed even closer together.

"How'd that happen?" Frankie asked.

I looked to Cassie's face and didn't even try to stop the smile on my own. "I guess I was distracted."

She blushed, something I didn't even think was possible when it came to her. She was not the kind of woman who dissolved into a puddle of embarrassment or should-haves, and she never apologized for anything. But she'd felt the same thing I had, that much was more apparent than ever, and the only thing that could make her flush like that was the unexpected.

I knew that was true because the same was true for me.

"I guess rule number twelve should be no kissing in public," she said with a quick glance at Frankie as she hopped onto the counter in front of me.

I just shook my head. "No way."

"Come on, Thatcher. The rules need a good, solid foundation, and it seems like this one is warranted."

"I'll burn the whole house of rules down. No rule number twelve."

"Not ever?" she asked with faux seriousness.

I couldn't find it in me to care that she was mocking me.

"Nope. It'll be like the thirteenth floor of buildings. It just doesn't exist."

"Is it because you're afraid of it?" she teased.

I shook my head. "It's because if that rule exists, it'll only be as a literal example of *made to be broken*."

"Why waste the paperwork, then, huh?"

"Exactly."

CHAPTER 19

Cassie

Me: Rule #25: Don't use my body wash.

Thatch: But what if I'm using it on you?

Me: Are you asking for shower sex, Thatcher?

Thatch: I'm not asking, honey.

Me: Ohhhhh, T's going all alpha male. Will Sir spank me later too?

Thatch: Only if Mistress Cassie begs.

Me: On my knees?

Thatch: You're making me hard.

Me: Considering a fucking breeze could get you hard, this is not surprising.

Thatch: YOU make me hard. All the fucking time.

Me: Charming me with your snake?

Thatch: What can I say? I have my sweet moments.

Thatch: What are your plans today? Can you do me a favor?

Me: Nothing major. Just editing some photos. You want another office blow job?

Thatch: Yes, but let's put that on the books for tomorrow. Today, I've got something else going on.

Me: And what's that?

Thatch called my phone thirty seconds later.

"Well, hello, *Master*," I teased.

His deep chuckle filled my ear. "Can you be flexible with your schedule today?"

"I can probably work something out. What'd you have in mind?"

"Well, I'm supposed to pick Mila up at one for a Central Park date, but I've got a last-minute investors meeting at noon that I can't skip out on. By the time I get out of this, it will only give me ten minutes to get to Claire and Frankie's."

"You want me to pick her up and bring her to your office?" I offered. I generally wasn't one to rearrange my schedule for a man, but Mila was an exception. I looked around Thatch's apartment. It wasn't like I had to travel from Guatemala to do it either.

Next time you have the opportunity to spend time with Mila you probably will *be doing a shoot in Guatemala,* the little voice inside my head told me. *Don't pass this up.*

"Do you mind? Mila is always waiting for me on the front porch, and I'd feel like a bastard for showing up forty minutes late."

"I'll do it under one condition," I negotiated.

I could tell he was smiling when he said, "And what would that be?"

"I'm driving your Audi."

He laughed again. "You can drive the Audi, but only if you promise to stick around and hang out with us today."

Yeah, I would have done that anyway. No way was I driving all the way up there to get her and not get to spend the day with her.

"Awwww…Thatcher can't get enough of me?"

"Something like that."

"Okay. I'm in. Text me their address, and I'll get ready to head out now."

"Thanks, honey."

I hung up the phone and saved the open files on my laptop before shutting it off. Even though I was on a deadline, and would probably need to put in a sixteen-hour day tomorrow to finish up the pictorial I owed *Men's Health*, I decided Mila was more important. And, well, hanging out with Thatch for the day wasn't exactly a chore.

Actually, I was finding it was the opposite; I really enjoyed spending time with him. He teased and flirted with me relentlessly, and he always found a way to make me laugh.

Last night, I had come home to Thatch sitting in a bubble bath with my favorite exfoliating treatment smeared across his face. The fact that he had finished off a fifty-dollar bottle of face cream—*that bastard's big head had some serious square footage*—should have earned him a dick slap, but even I couldn't deny he had looked fucking adorable.

So adorable, I'd stripped right out of my clothes and joined him.

God, he was a creative motherfucker. And so goddamn much fun. I couldn't remember the last time I'd enjoyed being with someone so much that the tank never topped up—I always wanted more. His ridiculous smirk or stupid fucking winks or the feel of his big body spooned around mine. No matter how much he did it, it never felt like enough.

When in the hell had he become so vital to my daily life?

It had to be the Supercock. Or his big hands. Or maybe it was his talented mouth.

Yeah, it's none of those things, moron. This isn't a game anymore, my brain whispered. *You're falling straight into the real deal with the charming ogre.*

I quickly shook off those thoughts and set my focus on less confusing things, like getting ready to pick up Mila.

An hour later, I was pulling up in front of Frankie and Claire's sweet house in Thatch's sweet-ass ride. The Audi in question was red, a convertible, and drove like a fucking dream. Since owning a car in New York was generally more hassle than it was worth, it was nice to be able to drive on occasion. And the car made it that much nicer. I made a note to myself to find more reasons to borrow this car. Or one of the others. The proud owner of several, he was no Kline Brooks in that department.

Mila jumped up from the porch swing and came barreling down their front steps, sprinting toward the car before I had a chance to get out of the driver's seat.

"Aunt Cass!" she shouted.

"Slow down, Mila," Claire called behind her, following her daughter's lead while shaking her head in amusement.

Mila didn't waste any time, opening the passenger door and hopping into the back seat. "Where's Uncle Thatch?" she asked, meeting my eyes in the rearview mirror.

I turned in my seat to face her, taking in her current attire with tickled eyes. From the *Harry Styles is my boyfriend* T-shirt to her rain boots covered in cut-out magazine pictures of the band, she was decked out, head to toe, in One Direction gear.

"We're meeting him at his office. Is it okay that I'm coming along today?"

She pumped her little fist in the air. "Yes! I'm so excited!"

"Hey, Cass," Claire said once she reached the vehicle. "I'm surprised to see you today."

"I thought I'd tag along, but only because I wanted to hang out with Mila," I said, winking at the adorable little girl in the back seat.

"Please excuse her outfit," Claire whispered, leaning over the passenger door and into my space so I could hear her. "But I couldn't convince her to change."

"I'm glad you didn't," I whispered back and then said loud enough for Mila to hear, "One Direction is the coolest."

"I love One Direction!" Mila agreed excitedly.

Claire laughed. "She literally made those boots this morning. I have a feeling you'll be losing pictures of Harry and the gang all over Central Park this afternoon."

"Let's go!" Mila encouraged. "Bye, Mom!"

Claire laughed. "You think she's a little eager to leave?"

"Maybe just a little bit," I agreed, grinning.

After Claire got Mila settled in her booster seat in the back and kissed her daughter good-bye, we were on our way, sunglasses on and ready to rumble.

"You wanna listen to some music?" I asked at a stoplight.

"One Direction!"

Of course, I thought to myself and smiled. "You got it, girlfriend." I grabbed my phone and pulled up Spotify. Once the perfect playlist— *every single One Direction album*—was set up, I hit play and headed for Manhattan.

"Wooohoooo!" Mila yelled from the back seat. She alternated between singing the lyrics to every song at the top of her little lungs and throwing her hands in the air as we cruised back into the city.

Traffic was bustling as we drove up 5th Avenue, but that was the New York norm. The streets were cluttered with yellow cabs honking their horns and pedestrians hurriedly crossing the busy intersections. Tourists stared up at the enormous skyscrapers from the sidewalks and natives abruptly moved around them, annoyed and desperate to get to their next destination.

"We need to make a quick stop, okay?" I told Mila as I pulled up in front of Brooks Media.

She clapped her hands. "I hope it's somewhere fun!"

Paul—one of the security guards for Kline's building—strode over toward our car, irritation etched across his face. "Ma'am, you can't park—wait...*Cassie Phillips*?" Paul's irritation turned to intrigue, a soft smirk covering his lips.

"Hey, handsome." I winked. "How are you?"

"It's been a while, sweetheart. Ever since Georgia left, we never see your gorgeous face around here."

"I guess I should change that, huh?"

He nodded. "Definitely."

"Listen, I need to leave the car here for about fifteen minutes. I just need to run inside and grab something from Dean."

"Cass...I don't know..."

"Oh, c'mon, Paulie." I batted my eyelashes. "I promise we'll be quick."

He shrugged. "Okay. But make it quick."

"You're the best," I said, getting out of the driver's seat and helping Mila out of her booster. "I owe you one."

"Dinner with me, and we'll call it even."

I grinned in his direction as I grabbed Mila's hand. "I'm not sure my boyfriend would be too thrilled with me going out with other men."

"Boyfriend?" His eyebrows rose. "Cassie Phillips has a boyfriend?"

"Her boyfriend is my Uncle Thatch!" Mila chimed in.

Surprise consumed Paul's face. "Thatch? As in Thatch Kelly?"

"That's him!" The little chatterbox continued to speak for me.

I laughed. "This is his niece and fan club, Mila."

Paul kneeled in front of her, holding out his hand. "Well, pretty Mila, it's a pleasure to meet you," he said as he took her hand and kissed the top.

She giggled, batting her eyelashes flirtatiously, and I couldn't help but laugh. This little girl already had men eating out of the palm of her hand. Her teenage years would give Frankie, Claire, and probably Thatch, a run for their money.

"Thanks again, Paul," I called over my shoulder as we strode inside Brooks Media.

"Where are we?" Mila asked, looking around the lobby of the Winthrop Building in wonder.

"We're heading to my friend's office. I need to borrow something from him," I explained as I led her onto the elevator.

"I think I've been here before," she said as we stepped off the elevator and walked through the hallway outlined by various offices. "Does Uncle Thatch's friend work here?"

"Who? Kline?"

"Yep," she said with a nod, and her ponytail bounced up and down in response. "Last time I was here, Kline let me play games on his computer."

"He does work here." Owned the place. Same thing. Knowing Kline, he'd probably told her he was his own secretary. I grabbed her hand and led her to the end of the hall, where Dean's office was located. Mila looked on as I turned the knob and opened the door just slightly. "Is this where the One Direction fan club meetings are held?" I asked, peeking my head in to find him typing away on his laptop.

He looked up and grinned. "Only if you brought a ready and willing Harry Styles with you."

I laughed, opening the door wider and ushering Mila inside. "Well, I brought their biggest fan. Does that count?"

Dean stood up and walked around his desk. His grin widened as he took in Mila's attire. "Little Miss, you are my new favorite person. I want Harry to be my boyfriend, too."

Mila's hand went straight to her hip, and a determined look crossed her tiny face. "He can't be your boyfriend cuz he's gonna be *my* boyfriend. When I'm thirteen, Harry is gonna marry me. I'm gonna wear a pink dress and he's gonna kiss me." And she punctuated that statement with a snap in the air.

Dean laughed, visibly amused by her pint-sized sass. "Will you at least invite me to your wedding?"

She eyed him skeptically and pointed her little index finger in his direction. "Only if you promise to not eat all the pizza and donuts."

I raised an eyebrow. "Donuts?"

She nodded. "Um, yeah. Harry and me is gonna have pizza and a donut cake at our wedding."

Man, I loved her little mind. My perfect wedding would be pizza and a donut cake, too. And hell, to be honest, I had never really been completely sold on kids. But Mila was the kind of little girl who could maybe get me to consider purchasing some little monsters of my own.

"Deal, little diva," Dean agreed, smiling down at her.

I tugged on her ponytail. "I hope you're going to invite me."

"Duh." She rolled her eyes. "You and Uncle Thatch have to bring my baby cousin to the wedding, Aunt Cassie!"

Dean's eyes bugged out of his head. *"Baby?"*

I laughed and sliced a hand through the air for emphasis. "No baby."

"Not yet," Mila insisted. "But soon. You just gotta marry Uncle Thatch first."

His head tilted to the side. "Uncle Thatch? Something you need to tell me?"

"Nope."

"Lies-a-Minnelli," he retorted, and I laughed again.

"Later," I agreed. "When little ears aren't around."

"I'm holding you to that because you know I have got to know *everything.*" He pointed at me and winked. "Okay, so not that I don't love that you're here, but seriously, why are you here?"

"Well, as you can see, Mila is dressed to impress, but I'm kind of lacking," I hinted. "I'm a sad excuse for a *Directioner*."

He raised a sharp brow. "Who told you?"

"I have no idea what you're talking about," I lied. "I just felt like maybe you had some gear I could borrow."

Dean definitely had the goods. A few years back, One Direction had had a tour stop in the city, and there was a pop-up store for fans inside Madison Square Garden. Georgia might have told me homeboy had cleaned out on anything and everything Brit boy-band themed.

"Don't ask questions and follow me," he said, striding out of his office. Mila looked up at me excitedly and pretended to zip her lips.

A few turns through back hallways I'd never been privy to venturing later, he ushered us inside a storeroom on the other side of the floor. Once he switched on the light, the entire room looked like a teenage girl had vomited up her fandom. The walls were lined with posters. There was not one, not two, but *three* racks cluttered with clothing. And cardboard cutouts of the band stood in the corner.

"Omigod! This is so cool!" Mila jumped up and down.

"I know," Dean agreed. "This is my favorite place in the building."

"I'm shocked Kline lets you use this for your undying One Direction love." I glanced around the room, while Mila helped herself to the racks of clothes.

"We have an understanding."

I raised an eyebrow, and it pulled one corner of my mouth up with it involuntarily. "You have an understanding?"

He flashed a secret smile. "Yeah, he understands that whatever he doesn't know won't hurt him."

I smiled full out. "Kline Brooks would lose his shit if he saw this."

A hand went to his hip. "Well, good thing he'll never know, *right?*"

"Cool it, diva," I teased. "I won't spill the deets on your shrine to One D."

He feigned offense. "Oh, no, honey. You did *not* just call me a diva."

"Oh, but I did," I said, walking over by Mila.

"You're lucky I refuse to corrupt the young and innocent. Otherwise, you'd be dealing with a full-on catfight, *Cassandra*."

"Knock, knock," I announced as Mila and I opened the door to Thatch's office.

He glanced up from his computer, and a giant smile consumed his face.

My chest grew tight at the sight of his radiating affection, and I inhaled a cleansing breath to ease the discomfort.

Man, I probably needed to see a doctor. No one under thirty should be experiencing chest pain. Well, unless they dabbled in cocaine and attended drug-fueled raves on the weekends. Which, obviously, I didn't.

Although, I could probably make good use of glow sticks with a naked Thatch. I'd rave all over his Supercock, minus the drugs of course. That man didn't need any performance enhancers. Any increase to his stamina and my pussy would need a cane to hobble herself onto his dick.

Mila let go of my hand, ran around his desk, and hopped up into his lap. "Hi, Uncle Thatch!" she greeted and placed her hands on each side of his face before kissing his nose. "Ready to go?"

He nodded and kissed her forehead. "What's on the agenda today, sweetheart?"

She jumped off his lap and handed him a T-shirt and hat out of her backpack. "You have to change your clothes first so everybody matches."

He tilted his head to the side and glanced up at me. His eyes made the circuit down my body and then back up again—paying particular attention to my T-shirt that read, *Liam is my spirit animal.* They were fully amused by the time they met my gaze again.

"I'm supposed to wear these?" he asked Mila.

She nodded. "Yep. You're gonna look so awesome!"

Five minutes later, Thatch was walking out of the en suite bathroom in his office and lifting Mila up to carry her piggyback style. He looked outrageous with a *Niall is my boyfriend* T-shirt stretched tight across his huge chest and a One Direction baseball cap worn backward on his head.

"How do I look, Mila?" he asked.

"So cool!" Mila said, resting her chin on his shoulder.

His eyes met mine and he grinned. "Next time, Aunt Cassie and I are going to switch. I like Liam more than Niall."

"No way," I disagreed, running a hand across the words on the front of my shirt. "You'll have to fight me for this dreamboat."

"I have no issues with wrestling you, Crazy." He winked.

"Can we go?" Mila asked impatiently. "I'm hungry."

Thatch grabbed his new wallet, keys, and phone and slid them into his pockets and managed it all with Mila still hanging from his back. "Let's hit it," he said and grabbed my hand, leading us out of his office and toward the elevator.

As we rode the cart down to ground level, I couldn't stop myself from smiling as I looked at Thatch, decked out in One Direction fan gear, with Mila on his back. No man in his right mind would subject himself to this willingly.

But Thatch wasn't a normal kind of guy.

He was different.

And I really liked his kind of different.

CHAPTER 20

Thatch

"Call on line one from Mr. Sanchez," Madeline buzzed in as I closed the first-quarter financial statement for Hughes International. They were a relatively new client, so I'd been scouring the details of their money management and hiring expenses and comparing it to their investment portfolio in an attempt to map out a new system of checks and balances. They'd had a plan in place, but they obviously hadn't been making optimal financial decisions for a while. In fact, the best one they'd made was paying me to get them back on track.

"Thanks, Mad," I responded after saving my spreadsheet. I kept backups for backups, but I wasn't particularly keen on having even a chance of losing weeks' worth of work.

"Hey, Carl," I greeted one of my longtime clients as I clicked on to the line. "What can I do for you?"

"In a hurry to get me off the phone, Thatch?" he greeted, his voice amused.

"No way. Just a man with many tasks and know you're the same. I also have a feeling you're calling to invite me on an all-expenses-paid vacation, and the sooner I get off the phone with you, the sooner I can get a tan in the Southern California sun."

He laughed and I smiled and rubbed at the edge of my desk. He started talking about a new plant in Encino and all of the questions they had about what that kind of long-term investment would do to their long-term financial goals, so I picked up a pen and doodled on the edge of my calendar as he ran through the particulars.

Squiggles turned into a sun, and before I knew it, a stick woman with a fantastic rack appeared with a bouquet of roses next to her. I scribbled it out and dropped the pen before I ended up dropping Carl's financially motivated ball.

"I know it's short notice, but I've got the projections team creating a mock plan, and this is the only date our contractor can walk the property for the next six months."

"When did you say you needed me there again?" I asked, knowing I hadn't been paying enough attention to hear it the first time.

"Tomorrow. I went ahead and put a hold on a ticket for you out of JFK at noon, but I can have Ashley change it if that doesn't work for you. We walk the plant on Thursday morning."

I glanced back at my scratched out doodle and the clock on the wall. Just about twenty-four hours away. The trip actually sounded like a nice reprieve from my uncharacteristically empty apartment.

I'd lived there alone for nearly seven years, and now, two days without Cassie while she was on a shoot in Las Vegas, and the place seemed hollow. We'd transitioned into a different place in our relationship sometime during the last week, coexisting in the same apartment so naturally, it was almost scary.

Our mornings always started with a cup of coffee together, after an initial superficial battle over having woken her up, and our nights ended with Cass cuddled inside my arms whether we were watching TV or catching our breath after orgasms—or both. We filled the time in between with frequent texts and phone calls and making plans for dinner or something to do for the evening.

Cass had even taken it upon herself to pick up my dry cleaning on Monday afternoons, and I'd found myself in the checkout line at the grocery store with a cart full of random, girly bullshit that she'd added to *our* list more than once.

Sure, we still pushed at each other with pranks and surprises, but I was really fucking enjoying it. It made things interesting, and I couldn't seem to get enough.

We'd even started a little joint prank of our own, texting Kline from her number with the same kind of bullshit subscription messages she'd sent me what seemed like a lifetime ago. She was seriously gifted at coming up with different shit to say, and when I found out over dinner one night that Kline didn't know her new number yet, the opportunity to mess with him was too good to pass up.

"I'll be there. I'll expect donuts and coffee on Thursday morning, though. No industrial tour is acceptable without them."

He laughed openly. "You drive a hard bargain, but it's done. I'll make sure there are donuts and coffee waiting."

"Fantastic."

If anything could pull me out of my funk, it'd be sweet treats and a run under the California sun to burn them off.

As soon as my desk phone landed in the cradle, I picked up my cell and unlocked the screen.

Me: How's Las Vegas?

Cassie: Hotter than a ball sac.

Me: Is that your chosen analogy because the actual temperature of a ball sac is fresh in your mind?

Cassie: Huh?

Me: Have you been fondling anyone's balls?

Cassie: Fuck no. Do you have any idea how quickly I'd have to make contact after showering to avoid ball sweat? It's pretty much impossible, and I'm not really into that kind of thing like Georgie.

Me: Wait…what about Georgia being into ball sweat?

Cassie: Nevermind. It was a whole thing during the Kleorgie breakup debacle. I think you had to be there.

My thumb hovered over the little phone icon when a banner for another message crossed the top of my screen. I tapped the icon to open my messages again instead.

Cassie: I gotta go. My entourage is calling. Say hi to your boner for me.

Me: He says hi back. And he misses your tits.

I miss you. I sighed and took a deep breath as I stared at my phone for an embarrassingly long amount of time before accepting there wouldn't be any more messages. She was busy working, the very thing I should have been doing, but my concentration was pretty much shot.

There wasn't a snowball's chance in hell I'd be able to get my head back into third-quarter analytics and projections based off my suggested budget cuts and advertisement allocation for Hughes International.

I considered calling Kline, but I knew he'd actually be working.

I dialed Wes instead. He answered on the third ring.

"What's up?"

I spun in my chair to face the window. "Just seeing what you're up to, Whitney."

"On the West Coast again."

"Ah. Back for another round. Where are you this time? I'm head-ed toward that end of the country tomorrow."

"Seahawk territory. I've got a couple of meetings with guys com-ing to the end of their contract."

"A Tuesday afternoon and everyone is actually working? I don't understand."

"It's that whole being an adult thing. I can see why you wouldn't be familiar with it."

"Ha-ha," I mocked.

"Why aren't you working?"

"My eyes were starting to cross," I lied.

"Ah. Well, sorry I can't spend hours on the phone giving you a cuddle."

"I'm flipping you off right now, in case you were wondering."

"We don't have time for that either. Go get something to eat. Pref-erably at my restaurant."

"Discount?" I asked even though I knew his answer.

"Fuck no."

"You know, it's okay to admit you're in love with me. It won't make you less of a man."

"Bye, Thatch."

I laughed as I pulled the phone away from my ear. That had actu-ally made me feel better. *Fuck, I have weird comforts.*

I looked down at my phone once more before deciding to be done for the day. I had work, but I didn't have meetings, so I could pretend I had nothing.

Shutting down both of my monitors, I grabbed my suit jacket from the coat hook and filled my pockets with my keys, wallet, and phone.

Madeline looked up as I walked out. "I'm gonna take off for the day. I just got a last-minute meeting with Carl Sanchez, so I'm headed out there tomorrow on a noon flight out of JFK."

"I'll book you a car," she replied, making a note on a convenient stack of Post-it notes.

"Thanks. Feel free to work from home while I'm gone, okay?"

She smiled, and I knew it'd been the right move to offer. She worked really fucking hard for me no matter where I was or what time I called. I had other people who worked for me in a sense, but she was the only other one I kept in the office, and she did a pretty bang-up job of managing my entire life.

I spent a large portion of my time out of the office, meeting with clients and doing a lot of it after hours. The time clock never really stopped, but no matter how much I took on, it never turned into a group activity. When these people came to me, they paid a very large premium to get financial advice or planning from *me*—not someone working for me.

She smirked. "I would have done it with or without your permission."

I laughed outright. "See, Mad, that's why we work well together. You don't take any of my shit."

"I'm also an organizational genius."

"That too."

"Have fun in L.A.," she said in dismissal, and I laughed.

"Okay, I get it. I'm going now."

She just raised her brows.

I jumped toward the exit and laughed while raising my hands in the air. "Okay, okay. Geez. And in my own office."

L.A. looked pretty much the same as the last time I'd seen it. Bright and bustling and filled with traffic.

Big palms lined the streets, and the sun beat down on the exposed skin of my forearms. The intensity of the rays seemed stronger here, but at least it didn't feel like you were being choked by the humidity.

The overwhelming odor of piss also wasn't as strong as in New York. It existed, kind of lingering in the background, but it wasn't nearly as pungent.

Pulling my arm back through the window and into the cab, I grabbed my phone from my pocket and opened up the text messages. I hadn't heard from Cassie since yesterday.

Me: Rule #40: Take at least one recreational trip to L.A. a year.

Cassie: Recreational? Are you talking about drugs, Thatcher?

Me: I'm here on business. I'd rather be here for fun.

With you.

Cassie: How did I not know you were going to L.A.?

Me: I just found out I was coming yesterday. After we talked.

Technically, I'd found out before we talked. I wasn't sure why I hadn't said anything, but it was probably more because she'd cut the conversation short than anything nefarious.

Cassie: Oh.

My eyebrows pulled together at her uncharacteristically nor-mal—simple—response.

Me: Everything okay?

Cassie: Yeah. It's nothing.

Me: What's nothing?

Cassie: Just my assistant. It's not really worth going into it. We had a little disagreement earlier today, but I think it's resolved. Honestly, it's nothing.

It seemed like she was trying awfully hard to convince someone. I didn't know if it was her or me.

Me: Call me. We can talk about it.

Cassie: Thanks, but I can't right now. About to start shooting.

Desperate to make her laugh, I typed out a message.

Me: With your camera, right? I know how much you're dying to shoot some kids.

Cassie: Ha fucking ha. The FBI is probably monitoring both of our phones now.

Me: You better send a tit shot, then. That'll save us.

Cassie: Put your boner away, Thatcher.

I smiled then and started to type a message when her text bubbles stopped me.

Cassie: Would I ever be able to manage your ego if I told you I missed you?

I smiled and typed the least funny thing I'd ever been excited to say.

Me: I miss you too, honey.

CHAPTER 21

Cassie

I needed a new assistant. That much was clear to me.

Over the past two days, Olivia had started to show her true colors. Her motives for turning the tables were unclear, but whatever the reason, her professional attitude was sorely lacking and she seemed to enjoy doing the exact opposite of everything I asked. When I'd needed the lights dimmed, she had blinded everyone on set by making them fluorescent. When I'd asked her to let two of the male models know we'd changed their shoot time, she had made sure their arrival was two hours later than I needed.

If she could break it, she would, and she did.

And I was beyond tired of her shit.

Normally, I wouldn't sweat something like this; I'd just fire her and be done with it.

But this was a girl I had generously taken under my wing and shown the ropes. She'd been with me for more than a blip in time, and I had given her an all-access pass into my career in hopes that it would help her once she started to establish herself.

Obviously, that had been a big fat fucking mistake.

Olivia was a user. Rather than utilizing what I'd offered respectfully, she had chosen to try to screw me over. I'd found out from one of my close friends at *Men's Health* that she had already started reaching out to *my* contacts and worming her way into their good graces. The girl appeared hell-bent on destroying me and then taking my career.

I hated that this was bothering me as much as it was. I hated that I was letting this cunt get the best of me. And I hated that I'd even tried to make nice with her yesterday. I should've kicked her lying ass to the curb and been done with it.

I plodded through my hotel suite at the Wynn and grabbed my phone off the nightstand. As I stood in front of the floor-to-ceiling windows with a view of the Vegas Strip, I wasn't real sure what to do with myself.

I felt pathetic. I mean, fuck, I was in Vegas, and I was holed up inside my suite. I should have been out on the Strip, grabbing a drink, playing a little blackjack. Basically, anything but moping around like a sad sack.

The desert sun shone down across the concrete utopia, glittering rays bouncing from one ornate building to the next, and instead of thinking of something fun to do, all I could think was, *I wish Thatch were here.*

Maybe that line of thinking should have surprised me, but it didn't. He had barged his way into my life—*or maybe I'd barged my way into his?*—and I wasn't sure if I ever wanted him to leave.

Thatch just made everything better.

Which was crazy. He should have made things worse. He was loud and obnoxious and couldn't stay serious for more than a minute. He made a career out of bugging the hell out of me and spent most of his day sending me texts requesting tit pics.

But damn, that man.

That crazy fucking lunatic.

I *liked* him.

I tapped the last number in my call log, and it rang two times before his husky voice filled my ear.

"What are you doing, Crazy?" Thatch was smiling. I could hear it in his voice.

"Just finished having lunch with a few strippers from Spearmint Rhino, and now I'm about to head into a brothel. You know, the usual Vegas shit."

"Just fitting in a little sightseeing, then?"

"Yeah, you know that saying, 'What happens in Vegas, stays in Vegas.'"

"Unless you get chlamydia," he pointed out. "That won't stay in Vegas. That comes home with you."

"I'll make sure my hooker wears a dental dam, then."

He chuckled. "You're a smart woman. Putting your sexual health above all things."

I wanted to laugh, but my mood just wasn't feeling it. "You know me, safe sex and all that jazz," I muttered halfheartedly.

"You okay, honey?" His tone had changed from teasing to concerned in the span of a heartbeat.

"No," I answered as I rested my head against the window. "It's been a shit trip."

"What happened?"

"My assistant, who also happens to be the cunt I was kind enough to mentor, is doing her best to ruin everything. She can choke on a big fat dick while sitting on a parking cone."

"Did you fire her?"

"No," I mumbled. "Which is ridiculous. I mean, I found out that she had commandeered half of my professional contacts list and reached out to them for work. For *herself*. Which, obviously, makes me look really bad. Talk about an asshole move, right?" I sighed, long and deep. "I've done nothing but bend over backward for that chick. I've taught her everything I know. Normally, I wouldn't tolerate one second of the bullshit she's been pulling. Normally, I would have given her the boot."

"Why isn't this 'normally'?"

"I'm not sure," I answered honestly. "It's all so unlike me. What's wrong with me, T?"

"It sounds like she hurt your feelings, honey. You two were obviously close."

"That's what these are? *Feelings?*" I questioned in feigned shock. "I don't like these fuckers. They're killing my Vegas buzz."

He chuckled softly into the phone. "You want some advice?"

"Please," I responded and sat down on the chaise beside the window.

"Even though I think this chick deserves the whole fat-dick-and-parking-cone scenario, I think you need to approach this professionally."

God, could he have suggested anything more unnatural? "And how do I go about that?"

"Find out who she reached out to, and contact them. Let them know the situation, *without the use of f-bombs or cunt sentiments.* I'd also probably leave out the parking cone and dick sucking, too. Then, tell her to pack her tube tops and glittery eye shadow and take a fucking hike."

A small laugh escaped my lips. "Glittery eye shadow and tube tops?"

"Only one type of woman would pull a dick move like that, and she ain't doing it while wearing Louboutins."

"What about a guy who would pull that kind of shit? What's he wearing?"

"Tommy Hilfiger."

"Thatchastasia is a bit of a fashionista. I had no idea."

He chuckled. "I'll let you spank me later."

Normally, I'd toss back another snappy retort, but I was finding my humor to still be miles away. "Awesome," I replied, lacking any sort of enthusiasm.

"I don't like when you're sad, honey."

"I'm not sad," I lied.

"Hey, I hate to cut this short, but I've got to run," he said.

"Okay, bye," I answered and couldn't hide my irrational irritation.

"Now, wait a minute, sassy pants. Before I go, I'm adding a new rule. Number forty-five. No moping while in Vegas."

A sharp laugh escaped my lungs. "Yeah, I'll do my best to get right on that rule, even though I'd rather curl up in the fetal position and watch reruns of *The Office* from my hotel bed."

"I mean it, honey. No moping."

"You're not the boss of me, T."

"We'll see about that, Crazy."

"Number forty-six. Take a hot bath and a nap."

"Stop adding rules," I demanded. "And that's a weird rule."

"Everything feels better after a hot bath."

"I forgot bubble baths are one of your and Oprah's favorite things."

He laughed. "When you're in them, they are. But I can't speak for Oprah. I'm not sure what she digs."

"All right. Consider me naked and in the bath, then," I teased.

"Consider me hard and annoyed that I'm not there."

Six hours later, I had taken a hot bath—twice—and charged eighty bucks' worth of room service and movies to my room. Nothing was making me feel better. Not even the phone call I'd made to Olivia to tell her she was no longer my assistant.

That should have been an awesome call. I should have savored every second of telling her she'd been blacklisted from everyone she'd attempted to contact behind my back and she no longer had a job. But it didn't make me feel better.

I felt worse.

I hated that someone I had considered a close friend had screwed me over and forced my hand like that. If I was being honest, I had enjoyed mentoring her. I'd wanted to see her succeed, and if she had handled things the right way, I would have done everything in my power to get her foot in the right doors.

But greed and power and success made people do stupid things. The world was filled with good people who had genuine intentions, but it was also filled with manipulative users like Olivia.

Good riddance, asshole.

The sun was starting to set, and my mood was no better than it had been prior to calling Thatch.

I grabbed my phone off the nightstand and sent him a quick text.

Me: Rules #45 & #46 suck. I want to remove them from the list.

Thatch: Rule #47. See Britney in concert whenever you're in Vegas.

Me: Stop adding rules!

Thatch: Rule #48. Answer the door.

Me: Huh?

Three soft knocks sounded from the door, but instead of getting out of bed to answer it, I sent him another text.

Me: Did your cock send me more roses?

Thatch: Rule #49. Always, ALWAYS follow rule #48 when I tell you to.

Two hard knocks on the door spurred me into action. I hopped off the bed and padded toward the entry. "Who is it?" I asked.

"Housekeeping," a male voice mimicking a tiny female's voice replied back.

I grinned. "I don't need housekeeping."

"Do you need towels?"

"Nope."

"Toilet paper?"

"Nope."

"Pillow mints?" He continued the charade.

I fought my laugh as I peeked through the peephole and found Thatch standing on the other side of the black metal barrier. "Nope."

He smirked. "What about a massage? Do you like happy endings?"

"Sure. Okay," I finally agreed as I swung open the door.

And there he was, standing in front of me in all of his handsome glory. His brown eyes gazed into mine as a giant grin consumed his face. I had the overwhelming compulsion to burst into tears and maniacal laughter at the same time.

"You flew all the way from L.A. to give me a massage?"

He shook his head. "I drove, actually. There weren't any last-minute Vegas flights available."

"You *drove?*"

"Yeah," he confirmed, his voice dropping to an even sexier level. "I drove all the way here to cheer you up. So, are you going to invite me in?"

I launched myself at him and wrapped my arms and legs around his body like a little monkey. I buried my face in the crook of his neck and savored the smell of his cologne and the inherent scent that was only Thatch.

God, I hadn't known how much I wanted him to be here until he was actually here.

"What about your meetings?" I mumbled into his skin, unwilling to let go of the hold I had on him.

He squeezed his arms tighter. "I only really needed to be there for the walk-through I did this morning. I can work on the rest from home."

"You're fucking insane," I whispered into his ear. "Thank you for this."

"You're welcome, honey." He held me tight and carried us inside my hotel suite. "Did you take a hot bath and get a nap?" he asked as his long legs crossed the room. He sat down on the bed and adjusted me so that I was straddling his lap, making my hotel robe fall open slightly.

I nodded. "Two baths, actually."

He smirked and ran a finger along the swells of my breasts. "Did you fire your assistant?"

I nodded and breathed a little faster.

"Are you ready to have some fun with me in Vegas?"

I shrugged as my fingers found the nape of his neck and played with the edges of his hair. "Depends on what you have in mind."

My eyes followed his as he glanced down at his T-shirt.

It's Britney, bitch.

He winked. "Rule number forty-seven."

Fuck, I haven't had time to enter all of these into my phone. I struggled to remember for two seconds before it clicked.

"You're taking me to see Britney?" I shouted and hopped off his lap. "Don't fuck with me, Thatcher. Don't you dare fuck with me right now." I pointed an accusing finger in his direction.

He laughed and slid his hand into his back pocket to pull out two tickets. He held them up for my excited eyes.

I snatched them out of his hand and made sure they were real. "Holy shit! These are like front-row seats!" I exclaimed as I danced around the suite. "How in the hell did you manage these?"

"I've got friends in high places," he said with a boyish grin. "Good surprise?"

"Fantastic surprise!" I threw myself at him, forcing us to fall back onto the bed in a tumble. "You're so getting laid tonight!"

His playful eyes met mine as his hands slid into my hair and pulled my mouth in for a soft kiss. The kiss turned heated, and it was Thatch who pulled away with a groan.

"I hate what I'm about to say, but we'll have to take a rain check on the sex," he said as he lifted me to a standing position. "You've got thirty minutes to get dressed." He turned my body toward the bathroom and spanked my ass into motion. "So get that sexy ass moving, Crazy. We can't miss Britney."

Planet Hollywood was unreal. So many shops filled the glitter-floor-lined hallways that led to the actual theater within the hotel. After buying me a matching *It's Britney, bitch* T-shirt, Thatch carried me into the venue on his giant shoulders, shouting random things like, "I hope she plays *Hit Me Baby One More Time*," until we reached our seats.

Women stared. I laughed. And the giant ogre never faltered in his ability to not give a single fuck what anyone thought of us.

We were a pair. A loud, outrageous-as-fuck pair.

It was awesome.

Fans screamed around me, and I joined in relentlessly. I was in my element with all the other diehards, watching Britney Spears shake her little ass and hypnotize the audience on stage with her sexy dance moves and catchy lyrics. As she finished up a hot rendition of "I Wanna Go," I glanced up at Thatch, who appeared to be enjoying himself as much as I was.

He looked outrageous, sticking out like a sore thumb. His large frame—*still clad in a Britney tee*—towered over everyone in the audience. He was one of the few male attendants for the night, but in true Thatch fashion, he didn't care. He sang when he knew the lyrics, and he danced like a lunatic during each song, often grabbing my hips and grinding against me playfully.

God, he made things fun. *So much fun.*

The neon lights glittered and gleamed across the stage as Britney seductively sang the opening lyrics to "I'm a Slave 4 U." She moved down the stage, rotating her hips in hypnotic motions, and I watched on in amazement.

Thatch wrapped his arms around my shoulders and tugged me back against his chest. And as Brit sang, he sang directly into my ear, swaying us back and forth to the addictive beat.

"I'm having fun with you," he whispered in my ear between lyrics.

I leaned my head against his chest and looked up at him. His eyes met mine, smirking down at me as he continued to serenade me with the help of Britney herself.

I smiled. "I'm having fun with you too."

"Good." My heart jumped as he leaned down and pressed his mouth to mine for a sweet kiss. "It doesn't sit well with me when you're sad."

I turned in his arms and stood on tiptoes to kiss the corner of his mouth. "Thanks for cheering me up, Thatcher." It felt completely natural to admit how much he meant to me. "You're starting to become one of my favorite people."

He smirked. "Likewise, honey."

"Vegas! Let me hear you!" Britney's voice filled the venue, and I turned back toward the stage and hooted and hollered with the rest of the crowd. "I need a volunteer. Who's willing to help me get a little freaky?" She smiled at the audience and started to search through the numerous hands waving frantically.

Thatch watched on with amusement until I abruptly grabbed his hand and threw it roughly into the air. "This guy!" I called toward the pop goddess at an ear-splitting decibel. "He loves to get freaky!"

He chuckled in response, but then his eyes went wide as Britney pointed directly at him and started to walk across the stage until she was standing in front of us.

"Oh, *fuck*," he muttered.

"Don't be shy." She giggled into the mic. "Come up here, big guy.

I need your help," Britney instructed him.

Thatch started to shake his head, but it was too late; two security guys were already beside him. "You owe me, Crazy," he growled into my ear before he let them lead him stage right and up the steps.

And there he was, standing tall and proud in his *It's Britney, bitch* T-shirt, in front of an entire audience of Britney Army. Women catcalled and screamed for him to look in their direction. I couldn't blame them. Hell, I even joined in, wolf-whistling and shouting, "Take off your pants!" as loud as my voice could manage.

"Whoa, you're big," Britney said once he was standing beside her and her entourage of talented dancers. "What's your name?"

"Thatch, and I hear that a lot," he responded without missing a beat.

She laughed. "Well, Thatch, who are you here with tonight, baby?"

"That crazy woman right there." He pointed directly at me and smirked like the devil as he added, "My girlfriend, Cassie."

Girlfriend? If I hadn't been so fucking mesmerized that Britney Spears was within touching distance, I probably would have had the foresight to flip him off.

Sure, that's exactly why your not contesting that sentiment. Keep telling yourself that.

But seriously, was that him trying to one-up me?

Or was it him trying to tell me something?

I didn't know what I was to him. Fuck, I didn't even know what he was to me. But I was certain of two things: the lines of our relationship were starting to become more blurred and confusing by the second, and I didn't want anything to change. I wanted him all up in my space.

I wanted his jokes and surprises and uncanny ability to raise the stakes.

Britney's gaze met mine and she grinned. "Damn, girl, you're gorgeous too! What's with all of the beautiful people in Vegas tonight?"

The crowd shouted their approval.

"So, Thatch," she said as her dancers moved around him and started sliding something over his neck. "Would Cassie say you're a naughty boy?"

Where most guys would have been dying from embarrassment, standing up on stage while wearing a shirt with Britney's face, Thatch did the complete opposite. He just chuckled and answered, "She sure as hell wouldn't say I'm nice."

I bit my lip as the crowd lost their fucking minds, shouting proposals and innuendos so loud I had to cover my ears to dull the roar.

Britney laughed as Thatch met my eyes and shrugged at the attention.

"Let's get freaky, Vegas!" Britney shouted as the beat of "Freakshow" pounded from the speakers.

My gaze followed the dancers as they crowded around the sexy ogre in the center of the stage. They rocked it out, dancing in sync with one another with gyrations and short flicks of their arms and hair to the sexy beat.

I slid my phone out of my back pocket and started to record every second of this perfect, blackmail-worthy moment.

A giant grin consumed my face as Thatcher Kelly became a prop at a Britney Spears concert. I wolf-whistled as the dancers led him by a harness-leash across the stage and he followed on his motherfucking *hands and knees,* crawling across the stage until his leash was handed off to the pop diva herself. Britney led him down the center platform, and he followed without an ounce of shame or embarrassment on his face.

He was urged to his feet by the dancers and moved toward the center of their freestyle circle.

And that's when Thatch got freaky as fuck. My cheeks threatened to cover my eyes as I watched him grind and move with seriously impressive moves.

Goddamn. Channing who?

For a guy his size, he could get down, and I decided I'd need to test his reaction to "Pony" at some point in the future. His body moved in sync with the seductive beat, and every woman in attendance was screaming her excitement. He even obliged the woman stage left who screamed for him to "Take it off, hot stuff!"

With a cocky grin, Thatch slid off his T-shirt and tucked it into the back pocket of his jeans. His muscular chest and ripped arms shone beneath the spotlight, and the venue was filled with high-pitched screams. He danced. Britney sang. And by the end of the song, I was pretty sure the charming, sexy idiot had won over every female in attendance, including the pop princess.

"Rule number fifty. Never volunteer me to go on stage unless you want some serious paybacks," was the first thing he said to me when he made it back to our seats.

I laughed. "Oh, get over yourself. You took your fucking shirt off. We both know you were enjoying every minute of that."

He winked. "Don't be jealous, honey. I'll take my shirt *and* pants off for you tonight."

"Cool the fucking ego," I teased and playfully smacked his arm.

He grinned and wrapped his arms around my shoulders, tugging my back to his chest. "If you're a good girl, Cass," he whispered in my ear, "I'll lick your cunt just the way you like."

Crude? Yes.

But did it turn me on? *Of course.*

I looked up at him underneath my lashes and smiled. "Deal."

We stayed in that position until Britney finished the show. As the venue started to clear out, Thatch grabbed my hand to lead me out of our aisle, but I couldn't find the will to move my feet. I just stood there, looking around the half-filled room, while I tried like hell to wrap my mind around the night's events.

I was overwhelmed, and it had nothing to do with Britney Spears or front-row seats or getting a video of Thatch crawling across a stage on a leash.

It was *him*. He was overwhelming me.

But not in a bad way.

It was in an all-consuming kind of way.

I just couldn't believe he had done this. He'd changed his plans in L.A. to drive five hours to Vegas to cheer me up. And he hadn't just shown up and taken me to dinner. No. He'd pulled some serious strings for tickets to a concert I had been dying to go to. A concert I had maybe mentioned to him once that I had been wanting to see.

But he'd remembered.

And he hadn't hesitated to drop everything for me.

He tugged on my hand again, but he stopped and glanced back when he realized I wasn't moving.

"You okay, honey?" he asked.

I shook my head.

He stepped toward me. "What's wrong?"

"Nothing is wrong," I answered truthfully. "I'm just overwhelmed by how right everything feels."

Placing his fingers under my chin, he lifted my eyes to his. His eyes turned soft as his gaze locked with mine.

"Thank you for tonight. This was the sweetest thing anyone has ever done for me."

He caressed the skin of my cheek with the stroke of his thumb. "When it comes to you, I have an endless supply of sweet, Cassie."

"You're sweet for me and only me?" I asked, without saying the words I really wanted to say.

Be mine. Only mine. No other women. Just me and you.

"Yes," he answered without a second thought before tossing back, "You're good for me and only me?"

I smiled and nodded, adding, "And your cock too."

"When it comes to my cock, you can feel free to be bad."

And then, right there, in the still-crowded venue at Planet Hollywood, Thatch lifted me into his arms and brushed his mouth against mine, taking my lips in a kiss that made me feel like we were the only two people in the room.

CHAPTER 22

Thatch

Clothes littered the space between the door and the bed as I pushed Cassie backward at a near run. Her hair, her smile, the smell of her skin—I hadn't been able to get enough of any of it tonight.

Steps stuttered and stumbled as she tried to keep up with the unfair advantage of my long legs. A moan filled the air as I palmed the cheeks of her ass and lifted her feet right off the ground.

"Thatch," she whispered, her voice nothing more than an aroused hum.

"Right here, honeys," I answered, dropping her to the bed, whipping off her shirt, and speaking directly to her tits.

Cassie smiled and swatted at my face, and I did my best to dodge it as I laughed.

"Jesus Christ, can't you be serious? Ever?" she huffed. I nuzzled at the sweet skin of her neck.

"You want me to be?" I whispered.

Her pause was brief and not at all nerve-racking because the more I was around her, the more I found I didn't care what the answer was. Contentment for me was becoming synonymous with contentment for her. I didn't understand it, but right then, with her tits in my face, I didn't even try.

"No. I don't want you to be serious." Her eyes said, *I just want you to be you.*

Like an animal, I forced her weight into the bed by covering her with my own and licked a line from her jaw straight down the middle of her chest. I circled the perfect edge of her belly button, lapping at the jewelry there, and then tugged at the fabric of her jeans with my teeth.

Her hips jumped, and heat from the flames in her eyes singed my skin.

When I pulled at her pants again but didn't unbutton them, she snapped. "Stop teasing me!"

I smiled into her skin, rubbing my lips back and forth as my gaze met hers. "Why, baby? Did something turn you on tonight?"

She nodded and licked her lips. "There was one thing I can't get out of my head."

"Tell me," I demanded as a surge of new blood filled my already stiff cock.

"You on the ground."

"Yeah."

"On your knees."

"*Yeah.*"

"With a collar around your neck—"

"Cass," I warned, pulling her down the bed by the hips and slamming her to my cock. Her head shot back, and a gasp broke through the heavy, arousal-filled air.

"Fine. Just take off my pants, for fuck's sake. No freak show necessary."

Cognizant of her impatience, I ripped her pants and thong down her legs, shoved them open, and licked a path straight from her ass to her clit.

Her pussy convulsed right in front of my eyes.

"Fuck, honey. Wait to do that until some part of me is in there," I chastised with a smirk. Tongue, finger, cock, I didn't care what she squeezed.

I pushed back from her and the bed and grabbed her phone from the back pocket of the pants I'd just stripped off her.

"Password?" I asked as I swiped to unlock it.

"Fuck off," she told me with a smile, so I stepped forward, dropped to my knees in front of the bed and licked a circle around her clit. I filled her pussy with two thick fingers at the same time.

Her head shot back, and she moaned.

"Password," I repeated again.

Her eyes were far less obstinate when they found mine, but I could tell it was a fight she didn't want to give up.

It meant next to nothing, but goddamn, I wanted it. In and out I pumped, working the bud up top with my tongue until she couldn't stop herself from bunching the white comforter in her hands.

"Password, Cassie." This time, I said it as a command, and she broke, her pussy convulsing on my fingers as she did.

"It's fucking CASS, you prick." I smiled at her ability to be on the very brink of orgasm and insult me at the same time.

There wasn't anyone else like her.

As for the password, I should have known.

Finally inside, I did my best to show her that sometimes it pays to do what someone else says. As the distinct beat of Britney Spears' "Freakshow" filled the room, surprise made a bid to do the same in her eyes.

"Come on, honey," I called, pulling her to the edge of the bed and settling her legs wide and to the sides so her glistening pussy shone in the dim lights.

"What are you doing?" she asked, and I winked.

"There may be no leash, but I can dance for you, honey."

She smiled, and I literally lost myself in it. In her, in the ridiculous moment, in everything we could be.

Oh yeah, baby. Tonight, you and I are going to dance.

"I can't believe you're coming to my parents' house with me," Cassie grumbled as we got into the cab waiting at the curb outside Portland International Airport. To be fair, I hadn't told her I was coming until we were at the airport, through security, and I was following her to *our* gate. She'd thought I was flying home to New York.

A smile had become pretty much permanently affixed to my face after the weekend we'd had, and like always, her complaining only made me more cheerful. I was in a strange place, getting all of my jollies from a recipe book that suggested two cups of Cassie with a teaspoon of messing with her stirred in.

It was the weirdest fucking catalyst for happiness, but I embraced it. It meant more of her. More laughs. More sex. More everything I was finding I didn't want to go a day without.

"Believe it because I am," I advised. "If you didn't want me to come, you should have told me before I got on the big metal bird and flew over nine hundred miles in a direction other than home."

She scoffed indelicately, and I bit my lip so as not to laugh. "How the fuck do you know how many miles are between here and Las Vegas?"

I shrugged. "Miles are a number. I know numbers."

"Okay, Chandler."

"What's the big deal, anyway?" I asked seriously, trying to get to the root of the issue.

"Meeting the parents? Hello? That's a big deal."

"I asked you to meet my parents," I pointed out.

"Yeah, while I was wearing a T-shirt about my pussy. You knew I wasn't going to go inside. You're coming with me to stay over!"

"And?"

"And I've never brought a guy home before."

I laughed and apparently angered her more by pointing out the obvious. "No kidding."

"Excuse me?" Her stare was lethal. I glanced to the cab driver to see the whites of his eyes in the mirror, but they shot back to the road when I widened mine. No doubt this would be showing up in some *New York Times* bestselling book at some point. Cab driver turned romance novelist.

Actually, that sounded kind of interesting. *I should pitch that idea to someone.*

"You've never been in an actual relationship, honey. You told me that yourself. So I just assumed you'd never brought anyone home before."

"Oh."

"Oh," I mocked with a rise of my brows.

She slapped my dick.

"Fuck, Cass!" I said, pressing a hand to my crotch to stave off the burn.

Satisfaction turned her eyes downright mischievous. "Serves you right."

Thankfully, since it'd been a fairly superficial blow, it only took me a few seconds to catch my breath. "So what do I need to know about…" I started to ask.

"About?"

"Insert your parents' names here," I explained.

"Oh. Diane and Greg."

"Ah, Diane and Greg. And what do I need to know about them?"

"My mom is on the local news."

"She commits that many crimes, huh?" I teased.

Her gaze turned out the window, and the corners of her lips turned up just slightly. *She was close with her mom.*

"She's been with KTLJ for nineteen years. She has pretty middle-of-the-road political views, but she's a lot more traditional than I am. Really into mission work. My dad is a doctor, but he's retired now. He mostly just does volunteer work at the local shelters and kids' group homes and stuff."

"Wow, your parents sound very—"

"Philanthropic?" she offered, turning back to look right at me.

"Exactly. And like really fucking great people."

"They are. They've always supported me, and I haven't exactly been the easiest person to support." Her face was warm with genuine familial affection.

"I know exactly how that feels," I admitted honestly. I'd put my own parents through some serious bullshit in my lifetime.

Moments before I could ask what else I needed to know, Cassie's smiling eyes turned from me to the window. "We're here!" she declared, and for the first time since I'd decided to come along, I got a little nervous.

She shoved open the door and then turned back to me to put a hand on my arm. "Oh, one more thing."

"Yeah?"

"Don't curse in front of my parents at all. They fucking hate that." She turned and scooted out the door and left me sputtering in the back seat.

My immobility didn't last long, though, and I scrambled after her. "What?"

She booked it toward the door, but I chased her down in two long strides and turned her toward me. "What do you mean don't curse?"

"I mean don't curse," she repeated, scrunching up her face in a fantastic display of *you're an idiot.*

"Do you even know me at all?" I asked, and she laughed before patting me on the ass.

"I know you well, *honey.* Pull up your panties and be an adult."

The door opened, and a well-dressed woman with perfectly placed chocolate hair, creamy skin, and familiar fiery blue eyes stepped out onto the stoop. Cassie dropped her bag and rushed forward into her arms.

I turned back to the waiting cab and paid the fare before scooping her bag up off the ground and walking in their direction.

Cassie's mom took Cass's face into her hands and looked her over the way only a mother could. Studying the changes since she'd last seen her daughter and logging every single one into the memory on her heart.

It was a biological impossibility, but it existed nonetheless. Every woman I'd ever known had two sets of memories: the ones they wanted to remember and the ones their heart wouldn't let them forget. The first kind were chosen, mostly positive and personality building, but the second would live on forever, despite age and fatigue and life-stealing diseases like Dementia and Alzheimer's. Coded on the heart like a hard drive, the feelings never vanished.

"Greg, Sean!" Diane called back into the house. "Cassie's here!"

I arrived at Cassie's back just as Diane turned back around. Her next words were mumbled. "And she brought a giant of a friend." She glanced at Cassie. "No heads-up?"

"There was no heads-up to give. This strange man just followed me home." Cassie shrugged. "He seemed pretty nice, though, and I doubt he could've gotten an ax through TSA, so I'm pretty sure we should all be safe this weekend."

Diane scrutinized her daughter's neutral expression for a beat until her mouth turned up at the corners. "You're ridiculous."

Cassie grinned. "Okay, so maybe I *do* know him, but I didn't know he was going to make the trek to Portlandia until the last minute."

I smiled and gently pulled Cassie out of the way so I could wrap her mom in a friendly hug. "Nice to meet you, Mrs. Phillips," I said into the top of her head before stepping back. "I'm Thatch."

"Thatch?"

"Short for Thatcher, Mom," Cassie explained.

"Well, it's nice to meet you too, Thatcher."

Like mother, like daughter, I thought.

"Come in, come in," she buzzed after breaking out of her stupor.

All the feelings of home surrounded me as we stepped inside. The house was exactly like my parents'. Homey and comfortable for everyone except me. The doorways were a little too small, the ceilings a little too low, and every single aspect of it made me smile.

I'd gladly hunch for a house and people who felt this genuine right off the bat.

"Cassie!" Greg greeted as we stepped into the kitchen at the end of the hall.

"Hey, Dad," she said with a smile as she jogged around the island to give him a hug.

"What's all the noise?" I heard just as the last person I ever expected rounded the corner.

"Sean, Greg, honey," Cassie's mom called, "this is Thatcher. Cassie's…"

"Boyfriend," I supplied when Cassie stayed silent.

Sean was the first to speak. "Huh. Look at that. You're dating an actual giant."

"Sean!" Diane chastised. I laughed.

"It's okay," I interjected with a shrug before speaking directly to Sean. "I saw a picture of you on her phone and thought you were an ex." Whereas Cass was silk and curves etched in creamy white, her brother was the opposite—muscular, hard lines defined by dark, black skin.

She had only recently revealed to me that Sean was her *adopted* brother.

"You couldn't see the family resemblance?" he deadpanned. Cassie was the first to laugh, and the sight of her at-ease face made a smile spread across mine.

As soon as the awkwardness broke, the conversation continued as though I wasn't there. I just soaked it all in. Cassie chatted about her job, and her mom and dad talked about the mission trip they were planning on attending soon. Cassie tried to talk to Sean about football, but he directed her pretty sternly to move on.

It was the reunion of a family who loved each other deeply but didn't get together nearly enough. It made me feel like I needed to visit my parents more often. The Phillips still had Sean at home, at least for now, but the only thing my parents had was me. I needed to do a better job.

"We still going out tonight, little S?" Cassie asked her brother with a pat to his face.

"Sure. Are you going to be embarrassing?"

"Most definitely," I answered for her with a smile, earning me a punch to the bicep from her and a laugh from Sean.

"I figured. We'll go to a place where I won't know anyone."

"Whoop it up," Cassie shouted over both of us as we laughed. "I'm going to get ready." I pushed off the counter, and she turned to me with a stern finger. "Don't even think about following me, Thatcher."

Her eyes weren't angry at all, so I knew she was just pushing my buttons the way I loved to push hers.

"I'll be up in just a second, honey. I'll help you with your zipper."

"I don't have a zipper," she remarked just as Sean said, "Ew. Sister."

Cassie turned toward the stairs with a smirk, and Sean just shook his head. "Make sure you're both ready in an hour. Not an hour for screwing and an hour for getting ready. An hour total."

"I—"

"I don't need to know details," he interrupted me.

I laughed and slapped a friendly hand on his shoulder. "See you in an hour."

I walked calmly until I got to the stairs, and then took them two at a time and jogged down the hall until I found the room her mom had led me to to drop our stuff halfway through the family hellos.

I opened the door and scooted through before leaning against it when I caught sight of Cassie's completely bare back. A bare back usually meant a bare front, and I couldn't wait for the moment when she turned around.

"I know you're back there, Thatcher," she called without turning around as she lifted a foot up onto the bed and started smoothing lotion onto her thigh.

"I wasn't trying to hide it, Cassie."

I shoved off the door and moved forward when she didn't say anything else, pressing my hips to her ass and squeezing the bare skin at the bottom of her stomach.

"You have the sexiest fucking body," I breathed into the crook of her neck. She shivered.

"We don't have time for sex right now," she told me, pulling away from my lips and leaning forward. She pressed her ass into my dick, and her tits swung out in front of her just enough that I caught a peek of her nipples from above. I groaned.

"There's always time for sex."

"Nope." She slapped my hand away as it sought the weight of her breast.

"Does that mean we'll have time for sex later? I really like the sex time."

"We'll see." She awarded me with a smile as she turned in my arms and pushed her tits to my stomach. "Maybe if you're a real good *boyfriend.*"

I was wondering how long it would take for her to start exchanging that sentiment now that I had. I had a feeling she was tossing that out there to test me, *challenge* me, but it didn't matter. I liked the sound of it no matter how it came, and I found myself wanting to set her up to use it even more.

"I can be good. Can you?"

She shook her head, pushed up on her toes, and nipped at the vein in my throat. "Not tonight, baby. I'm too good at being bad."

"How many drinks has she had?" Sean shouted over the crowd noise and music.

I watched as Cassie climbed on the stage and pulled a man in his seventies up with her. Disco lights strobed, and the beat of the music made the floor shake under our feet.

"Five," I answered with a smile before taking a sip of my water. I'd been watching out for her and soaking in all the entertainment she offered. I, myself, hadn't had a drop, content to get to know Sean and be the designated driver.

A lot of men would be upset watching, but I didn't get the point. She was enjoying herself, and I was here to make sure she did it safely. I certainly never thought she'd be grinding on some old guy, but I never wanted a woman I could predict.

I was also very rationally aware of the plethora of attention she'd been getting from young guys, guys she'd actually entertain the idea of dating, and she hadn't paid a single one any attention. Even in the throes of her drunken good time, she respected me. That's all I needed. A wild woman I could trust.

The rare combination had seemed damn near impossible to find until now.

Her phone buzzed in her purse on my shoulder, so I pulled it out and read the drunken text message thread she had going with an unsuspecting Kline.

And yes, I said on my shoulder. You should know by now I have very little shame.

Cassie: Get 25% off onesies this Sunday at Carter's by subscribing now. Text NO to opt out of messages.

Kline: NO

Cassie: No baby? No problem! Text YES to subscribe to deals from our sister company, Trojan. Text NO to opt out of messages.

Kline: NO. Take my number off your list!

My eyes went back to my genius girlfriend. I knew Kline was too smart to let this go on forever without paying someone to hack Verizon, but I was enjoying it while it lasted.

Sean pulled my attention away from the sway of Cassie's hips as she bumped and grinded into the older guy and back to him. "I like you for her."

"Huh?" I asked as though I couldn't hear him over the noise even though I'd heard him just fine. I wanted him to elaborate.

He knew I'd heard, but he smirked and humored me anyway.

"Cassie is a certain kind of girl. She gets bored easily, needs the thrill of a dance with some fucking grandpa and the freedom to drink however much she wants. But I usually worry about her while she's doing it, wondering who's got her back. I like that I won't have to wonder anymore."

I liked it too.

"You won't," I promised, and he nodded.

Somehow I'd passed Cassie's twenty-one-year-old brother's test. It wasn't exactly the entrance exam to NASA, but right then, to me, it felt even better.

CHAPTER 23

Cassie

My eyes fluttered open as the Oregon sun filtered in through the windowpanes of my childhood bedroom. The warmth of a large body enveloping mine had me peeking out of one eye to survey my surroundings. Thatch was curled around me—one hand holding my boob, while his head used my chest as a pillow.

His handsome face looked so young, blissfully unaware and deep in sleep. His dark lashes rested softly against his cheeks as soft breaths puffed out from his lips. I ran my fingers through the messy strands of his jet-black hair as I tried to recount last night's events.

One thing was certain; I had definitely danced and drunk my ass off. It had been an all-in kind of night, and I had forced Sean and Thatch to close the bar down with me, even demanding Taco Bell on the drive home. *Good thinking, Cassie.* That fast food had probably saved me from a morning of praying to the porcelain gods.

Thatch stirred in his sleep. His foggy, dark eyes met mine.

"Good morning," I said with a soft smile.

"Morning, honey," he said in a raspy voice, but he didn't move his head from my chest. Both of his hands were now holding on to my boobs and squeezing them playfully. "Mmm," he moaned. "I need to add a new rule. Number fifty-one. These tits are *my* pillows."

I laughed and flicked his forehead with my index finger.

"Ow, fuck," he responded through a laugh. "What was that for?"

"I'm about to revoke your rule-making rights. You've made over twelve rules in the past forty-eight hours."

He peeked up at me through sleepy eyes. "Rule number fifty-two. You can never revoke my rule-making rights."

I grinned and decided to add a rule of my own. "Rule number fifty-three. If one of us has to be the designated driver, it will always be you."

He chuckled. "I'll actually agree to that one."

I quirked a brow in surprise. "Really?"

"I think I have more fun watching you get drunk and wild than I actually do getting blitzed myself."

"That's crazy talk," I refuted. "No one likes being the sober person dealing with a drunken idiot."

"Yeah, but you're an exception. You're my favorite drunken idiot."

A few giggles slipped past my lips, and his smile turned wide and blinding in response. He rested his chin on my chest and gazed up at me. His eyes were so endearing—full of zero pretense or judgment—and their dark depths revealed that every word coming out of his mouth was the truth.

"You took care of me last night, didn't you?"

He shrugged. "I kept an eye on things, but I mostly just sat back, chatted with Sean, and let you do your thing. Did you have fun last night?"

I was with you. Of course, I had fun.

"I did," I answered with a nod. "What about you?"

"Besides worrying about that old guy having a heart attack, I had a fantastic night."

I tilted my head to the side. "What old guy?"

"Your dance partner for most of the night."

"I danced with an old guy?"

He nodded as a slow, amused grin consumed his face.

The wheels started to turn, and my brain caught up with the hazy memories. "*Oh...*the old guy in the blue blazer? The one who kept pelvic thrusting his geriatric crotch into my ass?"

Thatch's face turned up with hilarity. "In his defense, you were encouraging his senior citizen dance moves."

I cracked up at that. "Oh, man. I bet Sean was thrilled. How bad did I embarrass him last night?"

"Like on a scale of zero to ten?"

I nodded.

One of his hands left my boobs and slid a lock of hair behind my ear. "I'd say a twelve, maybe? Twelve and a half, tops?"

"Fantastic." I fist-pumped the air. "The night was a success, then."

He chuckled.

"What about you? How bad did I embarrass you?"

He tilted his head in amusement. "You didn't embarrass me."

"Oh, come on." I raised a knowing brow. "Be honest, Thatcher."

"Honey, you didn't embarrass me," he responded in an even tone. "I thoroughly enjoyed watching you have a good time."

"Even when I was grinding on the old dude?"

He grinned. "Especially when you were grinding on the old dude."

My sleepy brain buzzed at the abnormality overload. That was *never* a guy's reaction.

This man. What was I going to do with him?

He never failed to amaze me with his abnormal yet refreshing responses to my behavior. Thatch had become someone in my life that I could always rely on. Someone I could trust to have my back no matter what. Those kinds of people were so rare in a world filled with selfish motives and one-track minds. I felt lucky I had found someone like that in him.

Yeah, but how long will it last?

Anxiety clawed at my chest at that train of thought. We had started our relationship on a joke, constantly trying to one-up and out-prank each other, but somewhere along the way, things had changed. Sure, I was highly skilled at avoiding anything related to commitment or giving someone else any form of control over me, but I also wasn't blind to what was happening with us. Somewhere along the way we had hopped on this path of something that resembled an actual relationship.

And if I was honest with myself, I didn't want this, *whatever it was*, to end.

I didn't know where I wanted it to go, but I knew to the root of my soul, I didn't want it to be over. I was never one who looked toward the future, but with Thatch, I was having a hard time *not* looking toward the future.

I couldn't imagine my day-to-day life without him in it.

"What are you thinking about, honey?" he asked, voice soft. His hand caressed my cheek as his eyes stared into mine.

I don't want to fuck this up. I don't want to lose you.

I leaned into his touch. "No matter what happens between us, we'll always be close, right?"

His brows raised in confusion. "Close?"

"Yeah," I answered. "Me and you, we'll always be…" I stopped midsentence when I couldn't find the strength to say all of the things I really wanted to say. My heart and brain were at war, one wanting to profess something far stronger than *like*, while the other froze up in fear of the unknown.

I had never been the type of woman who stayed with one thing for more than a short amount of time. So how could I ask him for any kind of long-term commitment or declaration of his feelings for me if I wasn't certain my current feelings for him would never change?

But they won't change. He's your person, you fucking commitment-phobic moron.

Thatch didn't pry or press for an explanation. For several quiet moments, his gaze didn't leave mine. His eyes searched for my unsaid words, and when he found whatever he was looking for, he changed positions—his body hovering over mine and his hands resting beside my head.

"Don't worry, honey," he said, his lips mere inches from mine. "We're on the same page."

"But how do you know?" I asked. "What if we're not even reading the same fucking book?"

"Because I know." His mouth quirked up at the corners as a confident smile took over his lips. "We're on the same word, in the same paragraph, on the same page, in the same fantastic fucking book."

"But *how* do you know?"

"Because it's our book, Cassie. Yours and mine. This is our story, and I'll be damned if I let it end badly."

I know what you're thinking.
Avoiding party of two?
Our table is ready.
But should you expect anything less confusing from us? This is Thatch
and me we're talking about here. We could have a reality show called
Defying Normal.
But at least we are on the same show.

He chuckled softly as his eyes softened to caramel. Nose to nose, all I could see was Thatch's face highlighted by the soft morning sun. His eyes were gleaming and dark as they studied me. His gaze moved to my lips and stayed there for a beat as he just took me in. His mouth was close. So close that our breaths mingled. And God, I loved his mouth. His full, soft lips. I loved the taste and lush feel of those perfect lips.

Heat pooled in my belly until it consumed my entire body. I was desperate for him, for everything he could give me. I reached up and traced his jaw with my fingers.

"*Same fucking page*," he repeated, but he didn't wait for my response.

He crushed his lips to mine and kissed me like a man starved for my taste, my breaths, my heart. Around and straight down the center, his tongue worked mine until I couldn't tell where his ended and mine began. The fabric of my pajama shorts bunched easily in the grip of his hands as he pulled them away from my hips and down until his palms met the bare skin of my ass.

"You feel so goddamn good," he breathed into the tiny sliver of space between my lips. I sucked it in and let it overwhelm me, my head falling back until his lips had nowhere to go but my throat.

His tongue traced the line of my pulsing vein, and my chest heaved. *Fuck. This would make some fantastic vampire porn.*

Easing his weight off of me, he forced my shorts down the rest of the way and licked his top lip before biting the bottom with a groan. "No panties, baby?" One thick finger filled me in a stroke, but it didn't stay long. He pulled it back and sucked it clean. "You have the sweetest pussy. All that attitude must turn right to sugar."

I rolled my eyes until he stood up and shoved his boxer briefs straight to the ground.

A lot of fucking inches, hard, purple, and angry, brought my gaze right back.

"Tits out," he ordered with a wink. "They just put in a direct request."

Smiling, I pulled my shirt up and over my head and spread my legs wide.

Both of his big hands went straight to my calves and up, smoothing the line of each leg with a touch so gentle I didn't know it was possible.

His sweet eyes said so much as they held mine. They didn't look at my tits or my spread pussy. They looked right into mine and stayed there. My skin tingled from head to toe.

"You are *the most* beautiful woman I have ever seen."

"Thatch," I whispered. A rarity, I didn't have anything else to say.

He covered me with his body, his forearms in the bed, pressed every accessible inch of his skin to mine, and slid into me all the way.

I moaned at the feel of him, bare and pressed deep. His hips moved slowly, with measured motion as he positioned his cock at just the right spot to put friction on my clit.

"*Shit*," he muttered and stopped midthrust. "I forgot a condom."

He started to pull out, but I wrapped my legs around his waist and urged him to go deeper with my heels. "Don't stop, Thatch. Please, don't stop," I begged. "I'm clean. I'm on the pill. Just don't stop. I *need* to feel you."

"Fuck," he groaned. "Believe me, I don't want to stop. But are you sure, honey?" He moved both of his hands to my face and cupped my cheeks gently in his palms. "You know I would never put you at risk, right? I'm clean. I get tested often."

But what is often? How many women has he been with since his last test? I hated to think it, and honestly hadn't until his gentle insistence, but Thatch's pussy persuasion was strong. But what I did know managed to drown out those thoughts. I knew Thatch, or at least I was starting to, and he wouldn't put me in a precarious position. Not like this, not for some cheap thrill.

"I trust you." I tilted my hips and encouraged him deeper. "I. Trust. You," I repeated the words, and I wasn't sure if was for me or for him. But I knew I needed him. Needed this. Needed to reinforce the difference between this and every other sexual encounter I'd ever had. This was personal, planned, and most definitely devoid of regret.

His eyes glazed over at my words, a guttural groan filling the room so distinctly it felt like it'd been mined from his chest. He crushed his mouth to mine again and pushed his cock to the hilt. Everywhere he could reach—and with his size, he could reach a lot of things—he touched me, his hands and fingers moving over my heated skin and setting every nerve ending on fire.

Once his tongue found mine again, it didn't leave, delving deeper and harder, just to slow down and linger on every stroke. I wasn't sure if either of us was actually capable of stopping, both starved for one other, but it never entered my mind to find out.

His hips picked up the pace, the sound of skin slapping skin filling the otherwise quiet room, as his hands slid up my sides and caressed the pliant flesh of my breasts. I trembled in response, and my breaths turned to erratic pants mixed with pleading words falling from my lips. "More. More. More," I chanted, mindless of my volume despite our proximity to my family.

"You feel so good. God, Cassie, what are you doing to me?" He pumped his hips slowly then, moving in and out of me and completely changing the angle, while low, husky groans escaped from his lungs.

Each slide of his cock felt like it skimmed a live wire inside me. "Oh, fuck." I gasped into his mouth as a shiver tore down my spine from the building intensity of my climax. The rising intensity so great I feared I'd literally fall to pieces if I let it go completely.

"Don't hold back, honey," he demanded, speeding up again to move his hips in raw and greedy drives.

"Thatch. I…" All of the oxygen had been removed from the room, and I couldn't breathe. "I need…Fuck…I need…" *You. I need you so much.*

His large palm cupped my cheek as his gaze stayed locked with mine. "I know," he rasped as if he had heard my silent plea. "I know, honey. *Same fucking page.* Always."

I grabbed hold of his hair, trying like hell to anchor myself, but the climax took over and consumed me. He watched with rapt attention, eyes burning. My back arched and my hips lifted toward his, ravenous and frantic for each wave that washed over me. Heat pooled in my core until it spread like wildfire through every nerve, every cell, every fucking molecule of my body.

Each thrust of his hips came faster, harder, deeper, until he lost himself inside me. "Cassie. *My Cassie,*" he whispered, the sound of my name guttural and penetrating and completely unfiltered. I felt it all the way to my toes.

I sat at the kitchen table, watching Thatch's toned ass stand in front of my mother's sink while he helped her wash the dishes from break-fast. He washed. She dried. And they kept up a steady gab session in between.

"Someone's got it bad," my father whispered before he took his last sip of coffee and stood up from his seat.

I rolled my eyes but didn't give him the satisfaction of a response.

He walked over to my chair and urged me to my feet before envel-oping me in a warm hug. The smell of my dad and home and love and my childhood wrapped me up in nostalgia. I returned his embrace and buried my face in his chest. "I missed you, guys," I whispered.

"I missed you too, baby. Don't wait so long to come home, okay?"

I nodded into his shoulder.

He leaned back and took me in with an affectionate grin. "It's hard to believe my little Cassie is all grown up, living her life in New York, and excelling in her career. You make me so proud, sweetheart."

"Thanks, Daddy." I returned his smile.

"You know, you look different from the last time I saw you."

"I do?"

He nodded. "You look happy."

My brow scrunched in confusion. "I'm always happy, Dad. I have nothing to be sad about in my life."

He shook his head. "Not like this, baby. This is a different kind of happy," he said and glanced toward Thatch standing at the kitchen sink. "But I'm sure I don't have to tell you the reason for those bright eyes or glowing smile."

I started to respond, but my dad stopped me by pulling me in for another quick hug.

"Risking my heart was the hardest thing I ever did with your mom," he whispered into my ear. "But it's the single best decision of my life." He squeezed my shoulders and then headed for his study.

I stood frozen in my spot until Sean bounded down the hallway and nearly barreled into me.

"Yo, Thatch! You fucking coming or what?" he practically shouted as he sat down on a chair and slipped on his trainers.

"Jesus," I muttered and slapped him upside the head. "You scared the shit out of me."

Sean ignored me and tied his laces.

"Are you going now?" Thatch asked as he turned toward us. His eyes bounced like ping-pong balls between me, Sean, and my mom as he wiped his hands off with a dry dish towel.

"Yeah," my brother answered and stood. "You ready?"

"Wait. Where are you going?" I crossed my arms over my chest.

"Your boyfriend is coming to the gym with me."

"Is that okay?" Thatch walked toward me and placed his hands on my hips. "What time is our flight?"

"If you make it back by three, we'll have plenty of time to get to the airport."

"How about I'll get back by one, and I'll take you to lunch before we leave?" he offered.

My eyes lit up. "Italian?"

He smirked. "Anything you want, honey."

"Okay. Deal. But go easy on my brother. He's still recovering from an injury."

Sean scoffed. "I'm one hundred percent healthy, Cass. Stop being such a fucking mother hen."

I shot a glare in his direction. "I'm your big sister. I'm supposed to fucking worry about you."

"That's e-fucking-nough," my mother called over her shoulder as she put dishes away. "No bickering on Sundays. Those are the rules."

Thatch narrowed his eyes. He'd been on to us before, but we'd pretty much dumped the bucket of truth on him now. He glanced between Sean and me and then my mother until his eyes met mine again with a knowing raise of his brow. "The whole no-cursing bit? You were screwing with me, weren't you?"

I grinned. "Oh, yeah. I was totally fucking with you. My mom sounds like a sailor compared to me."

He smirked and pointed an accusing finger in my direction. "I'm getting you back for that one, Crazy."

"I don't give a—" I said and finished the sentence by scratching the side of my nose with my middle finger.

He laughed and shook his head, before turning toward Sean. "You had an injury?" he asked him.

My brother sighed. "Yeah. ACL. College football. But it's been a year, and I've been training my ass off."

"He's going to go pro," I added.

Thatch's brows shot up, intrigued.

"Hoping to go pro. Nothing set in stone yet," Sean chimed in.

"He'll go pro," I announced. "He's *that* good."

"He'll go fucking pro!" my mother added.

Thatch grinned.

Sean rolled his eyes but didn't say anything else. He knew better. When Momma Diane says you're going to fucking do something, you'll do it.

My brother would have been drafted into the NFL had he not gotten injured at the end of his junior year. But he had been training his ass off for the past year, and I was more than confident he'd get there. His talent wasn't something you could teach. It was ingrained in him. And one day soon, he'd achieve his dream of playing professional football.

"All right, let's get a move on it," my brother said as he grabbed his keys, wallet, and cell phone from the kitchen counter. "It's leg day, and I've gotta get at least two hours of weights in before cardio."

Thatch pressed a soft kiss to my lips. "Be fucking good while I'm gone, Crazy," he whispered into my ear before heading upstairs to my bedroom to change his clothes.

My mother's gaze met mine—after I'd thoroughly exhausted the watch on Thatch's retreat—and she held up her watering can and gestured for me to follow her out onto the back deck.

While she watered her potted plants, I stared at the breathtaking view of clear skies and mountains. I would never get tired of this view or the fresh Oregon air. It all felt worlds away from the cluttered, noisy streets of New York.

"I really like Thatch," my mother announced as she moved from her roses to her lilies. "I think he's good for you."

"But what if I'm not good for him?"

She turned toward me and searched my eyes. "What do you mean *not good for him?*"

"I don't know." I plopped down onto one of the deck chairs and let out a long sigh. "It's just that I've never been very good at committing to things. Have I always been this way?"

"You've always been pretty spontaneous," she answered. "But I wouldn't say you're bad at commitment."

"Oh, for fuck's sake, Mom," I scoffed. "Don't blow smoke up my ass. Remember fifth grade when I wanted to try the piano?"

She smiled and nodded. "Yes. You only lasted one month."

"And then gymnastics? How long did I last with that?"

"Three weeks," she answered.

"There's at least ten more hobbies we could add to that list, and we haven't even started on my lack of relationship history. I'm starting to think there's something wrong with me. Like maybe I'm lacking some kind of gene."

"Sweetheart, there is nothing wrong with you," she disagreed.

"Yes, there is. I'm flighty and flaky."

"Yeah, maybe you're a little flighty when it comes to things you're not really into, but I think you're selling yourself short, Cassie. I've seen you when you really want something, *really love something,* and there's no stopping you. You commit yourself one hundred and ten percent."

"Like when?"

"Photography," she responded without a second thought. "You wanted it, and look at you now," she pointed out. "You have a highly successful photography career that most people would kill for."

"Yeah, but I think photography is different, Mom. That's my career, not my love life."

"I don't think it's different, baby. I think when you meet the man you're supposed to spend the rest of your life with, it'll be like photography all over again, but more intense, more all-consuming. You'll want to spend more time with him. You won't be able to stop yourself from picturing a future with him."

"Is that how it was with Dad?"

She set her watering can down and leaned her hip against the deck railing. "I just knew with him. To my fucking soul, I knew I didn't want to live a life without him in it," she said with a wistful smile. "So don't be so hard on yourself. Thatch will be one lucky bastard if he ends up being that person for you. You're beautiful, kind, funny, and have one of the biggest hearts I've ever seen. Don't ever forget that."

I want to be good for Thatch, and I want him to be that person for me.

In that moment, I was really hoping Momma Diane was right.

CHAPTER 24

Thatch

Sirens rang out loud and shrill as fire trucks forced their way through jam-packed Midtown traffic.

On the way to Wes's office to go over some of the players he was hoping to draft and the kind of money he'd have to put into their contracts, I looked down a 7th Avenue that seemed to have no end.

Cars and people and streetlights as far as the eye could see cluttered the space between the two rows of buildings. My height afforded me better vision than most, though, and as a shorter woman swam her way upstream through the crowd in front of me, I found myself picturing how different the city might look from Cassie's perspective. She wasn't short, so to speak, but she still came in nearly a foot below me and certainly wouldn't be taller than most New York men.

I really couldn't imagine it. I'd been tall since the end of high school, all of my childhood fluff disappearing in one distinct vertical burst. I'd never walked these streets as anything other than huge, and as I passed one of the many people of "questionable sanity" peppering the way through the city, my reverie took on an entirely different angle.

Did Cass ever feel unsafe here, or with her rough and tough exterior did she feel some kind of false sense of exemption? And more
importantly, was she always responsible with her personal safety, or
did she take it lightly?

As I approached the front of Wes's office building just up the
block from his restaurant, BAD, I nearly came out of my skin over the
fact that I didn't know the answer.

*Me: Rule #55: You start carrying Mace with you every-fucking-
where you go.*

*Cassie: Is this some kind of new fetish where I spray you in the
face and lick your balls at the same time? I've heard of spicing
things up, but most couples don't need it this early.*

Me: Don't be cute.

*Cassie: Fuck, Thatcher. That's like telling me not to breathe or
eat nachos. I just can't stop doing any of it.*

I shook my head and smiled. I'd have to remember to pick up
nachos on the way home tonight.

*Me: Just...I was just thinking about how vulnerable a woman
can be in the city.*

Cassie: I carry a switchblade between my tits.

Me: Now, I know that's not true. It'd never stay put.

Cassie: Actually, my tits are pretty hospitable.

Me: I fucking bet they are. Are they going to offer me a drink later? ;)

Cassie: Gross. And don't ever use a wink emoji again. Text messages are the only place I know I can escape your fucking wink.

Me: Is that an official rule?

Cassie: YES. Consider it #56.

Me: So you accept #55?

Cassie: Sure. I've always wanted to pepper spray somebody anyway.

Me: Jesus. Don't just go spraying random people.

Cassie: They won't be completely random. Just people that piss me off.

Me: Fuck. The Mace is just gonna get you in even more trouble, isn't it?

Cassie: Only time will tell, Thatcher.

Only when someone bumped me from behind did I remember I wasn't alone with her. All the sounds of the city came back immediately, finally penetrating the barrier her witty comebacks had formed around me. After getting back from Vegas and her parents' house a couple of days ago, it was starting to happen all the time.

I shook my head and dropped my phone back into the front pocket of my slacks before stepping up to the door of Wes's building and holding it open for a woman on her way out. Hair slicked back in a sleek ponytail and wearing skintight head to knee black, she smiled up at me from under her lashes and did a spin as she stepped past me so she could keep eye contact.

On more than one occasion that kind of move had led to dinner and horizontal dancing, but today, all I cared to exchange was a friendly smile. She raised a brow as if to ask me if I was sure, but it didn't slow her down. All in one move, she kept up her momentum, circling right back to her path and catwalking directly away from me.

I didn't even wait to watch her go.

"Hey, Mr. Kelly," one of the security guards greeted me. I wasn't at Mavericks headquarters a ton, but I'd definitely been there before, and Sam and I had a running commentary on Yankees baseball.

"Hey, Sam. You see the game two nights ago?"

"Nah, man. I had to work the night shift at my other job. I heard Rodriguez nailed that shit in the bottom of the ninth with the bases loaded, though. Saved our asses."

I just nodded as I strolled past him, past the elevators, and straight to the stairwell door.

The Mavericks were only on the fourth floor, so I didn't mind making the climb in my suit. And with the amount that I'd been sitting around my apartment with Cassie and eating, I needed to get in a little exercise.

The receptionist's head jerked up as I pushed open the stairwell door into the entry in front of the Mavericks offices, but the surprise on her face melted into a smile when she saw it was me.

She looked at me like she knew the dimensions of my cock, but I'd always been careful to keep that shit separate. I never slept with anyone my circle of friends worked with. I flirted with them, which was probably what had Susie's toothy smile making a bid to eat up her entire face, but I never actually messed around.

"Susie," I greeted as I approached her desk with a smile.

Her porcelain cheeks flushed pink. "Hi, Mr. Kelly."

"I've got a meeting with Wes."

She nodded as though she already knew, but she signaled me to wait one minute with her forefinger. Punching a couple of numbers into the phone that I assumed connected her to Wes's assistant, she checked to see if I could go back.

We exchanged a few words while I waited, and I moved my eyes around the office rather than keeping them on her. The old candid player photos were more interesting than Susie anyway. Don't get me wrong; she was pretty in the conventional way, soft features and golden-blond hair, but she didn't even register on my dick's radar.

Apparently, he only gave feedback to supercell women now, the kind that fucking lit up your world with lightning-like surprises and thunderous opinions—the ones whose looks were ominous and their bite was just as bad as their bark. The kind of women who weren't a kind of women at all, but instead, a woman all their own. The kind of woman who wasn't *just* a woman because she was fucking *Cassie*.

She was a dozen things at once, and I couldn't fucking get a single one out of my head.

"Mr. Kelly," Susie called, and I turned at the sound of her voice. Her eyes moved upward dramatically, and I had the feeling they'd been studying my ass. "He's just finishing up on a phone call, but you can go on back."

"Thanks," I said with a wink and smile. She flushed again, and only when she tried to surreptitiously hike her breasts higher in her bra did I realize that maybe I shouldn't have done it.

It was just second nature. Like a facial tic. I wasn't even sure I was in control of it.

Pulling my face to neutral, I moved past her space and down the hall, looking at the nameplates on the doors as I did. Wes didn't have a huge staff here at the offices since the stadium was actually in New Jersey, but he kept the people he needed to interact with on a regular basis close. And for him, and his multifaceted entrepreneurship, that meant being in Manhattan.

Since he was still busy on a phone call, I had time for a little visit with one of my favorite women.

I knocked on her closed door before turning the knob and peeking my head in. Her lips curved into a smile when she saw me—a completely different reaction from the first time she'd laid eyes on me in the Raines Law Room.

"Hey, Georgia girl," I whispered when I saw she had her phone up and in front of her like she was FaceTiming with someone.

"Hey, *Thatch*," she said dramatically, and my eyebrows pulled together.

"Thatcher?" I heard from her phone and immediately understood. "What's that motherfucker doing there?"

I moved around the desk and into Georgia's space until my big head came into the shot beside hers. "Hi, honey. Nice to see you too."

She rolled her eyes and smiled at the same time. "I just didn't know you were gonna be there."

"Yeah, baby, I have a meeting with Wes," I replied, and then noticed Georgia's eyes go comically wide out of the corner of my own at the unexpected genuineness of my endearment.

"Oh, okay."

"Hey, I meant to ask if you're going to be home early tonight?"

Georgia's head moved back and forth between us, but I tried not to notice. Instead, I watched Cassie look over her left shoulder and talk to someone out of frame and back again, her dark hair pulling across the top of her low-cut shirt as she did.

"Yeah, I should be done with this shoot in the next couple of hours. What about you?"

"Yep. I've got to run back to the office after this and work on a couple of third-quarter plans that I'm almost done with, stop by and open up for Frankie, and then I'll be home."

"Okay, I'll see you there. Need me to pick up your dry cleaning on my way?"

"That'd be great, honey. I'll get dinner."

"Perfect." Someone called for her attention in the background again, and she whipped her head back and forth once more. "I have to go," she said directly to me, and she *almost* looked disappointed. "I'll talk to you soon, Wheorgie. Let me know if you need me to do any last-minute stuff for Big Dick's party."

"I need you to cook," Georgie teased, and Cass just flipped her off.

"Let me know if you need me to do something I'm actually capable of."

"Like give blow jobs?"

Cassie smiled as she made a slicing motion across her throat.

I took the opportunity to interject. "I could actually use your help with one of those."

"Just how many of those are on your to-do list?" she asked, pretending to be annoyed. "Every time I check one off, another one gets added to the bottom."

"Yeah, it's more of a perpetual to-do."

I heard someone speed-talk about something from off to the side of her, and her eyes snapped back to us. "I really have to go now. Later."

And then she was gone. I missed her immediately.

"Picking up your dry cleaning?" Georgie questioned, and I waved her off.

"Georgie."

"No, Thatch, that was as domestic as I've ever seen my friend in the history of, well, ever, and she didn't even seem pissed about it."

"She's just determined not to let me win in a war of wills," I downplayed in an effort not to talk about it. I was pretty sure Cassie was on my wavelength, feeling all the things I was feeling, and I hoped my instincts were right.

"True enough, but this is not that."

I took a deep breath and changed the subject. "Where are we with Kline's party? All set?"

"Nice subtle avoidance," she mocked. I shook my head and stared directly into her gentle blue eyes.

"I wasn't trying to be subtle."

"O-kay," she agreed, the motion of her mouth exaggerated.

She turned to her computer and opened a document that had a checklist of party details two pages long.

"Jesus," I remarked. It was supposed to be to myself, but judging by the aggressive eyes she turned my way, I hadn't been successful.

"It's mostly just the details of what I've been telling Kline. You know he's too smart for anybody's good, and I've been trying to avoid getting caught in a lie."

"Especially because you're a shit liar."

"How do you know I'm a shit liar?" She pouted.

"Honey." I tilted my head. "Everybody knows."

"Goddammit. I'm gonna be good at it one day."

I shook my head with a smile and tucked a stray hair behind the ear of Kline's perfect match. "No. You won't. And that's a good thing. We are who we are for a reason. You're the perfect fit for my friend because you are the way you are. I'm pretty sure he'd be pissed if you changed."

She smiled, and the sincerity of it lit up the room. Yeah, Kline had picked well.

"Why are *you* the way you are?"

"How exactly am I?"

"Knock, knock," Wes said from the door, looking from Georgia to me curiously. "I've been waiting for you for at least five minutes, dude. I had a suspicion I might find you here, though."

"Just saying hello," I dismissed, leaning down to place a friendly kiss on Georgie's cheek.

"Does Kline know you like to kiss his wife?" Wes teased.

"As a matter of fact, he does, Whitney." He didn't fucking like it, but he *knew*. And it wasn't like I was giving her open-mouth tongue with a side of tit grab.

Georgia just shook her head and threw up a jaunty wave. "Bye, boys." Her eyes moved to me, a piercing promise of this-conversation-isn't-anywhere-near-over rolling tumultuously in their depths.

Wes and I both waved before moving down the hall toward his office.

"What did I interrupt?" Wes asked as we stepped inside and he closed the door behind me.

"Nothing." I pulled off my suit coat and took a seat in the chair in front of his desk. "We were just talking about Kline's birthday."

"It didn't sound like that."

"Jesus." I rubbed at my head. "What are you, the conversation police? It was nothing."

"So it doesn't have anything to do with your roommate?" he pushed with a smirk.

Narrowing my eyes, I told him the truth. Well, at least half the truth. "No. It doesn't."

He pulled out the chair from behind his desk and moved to sit down.

"And how do you know she's my roommate? I'm pretty sure you were still out of town when that happened."

"I was. Kline wasn't."

I twisted and lifted my leg so that my right ankle rested comfortably on my left knee and tried to tamp down the nervous swell in my stomach. Talking about everything with Cassie with other people made it real. And being real made me feel like I had everything to lose. My mind had rerouted the end goal, and winning a prank war wasn't my focus. I wanted to win *her*.

"He sure has made a flawless transition from Perfect Paul to Gossip Gabe."

Wes smirked. "He's just happy he isn't the center of attention anymore. It was never his thing. But you should feel at home here."

Both my hands raised to shoulder level in a gesture of *what can you do*. "I can't help it if I'm endlessly interesting."

His body shook with laughter as he reached for the files on the corner of his desk. "So I have a few guys I really want. And I need to find the number that's going to make that happen comfortably. A couple of them are coming to the end of their contracts with the Seahawks, but one kid is just finishing college."

"No draft?"

"He tore his ACL pretty early in this last season. And he'd been sitting second-string to that Pulchek kid for most of the first three years of his college career. No one else has even thought about touching him. At least not since his All-American years in high school."

"So why are *you* thinking about touching him?"

He raised a brow suggestively, so I flipped him off.

"Because he's fucking good."

A shocked laugh burst from my lips. "Well, fuck. I'd say that's a good reason." I held out a hand. "Here, let me see his file."

Wes pulled it from the bottom of the stack and passed it to me, leaning back in his chair and running a rough hand through his hair.

"You know it's not your job to help me pick people, right? I just need you to make sure I'm paying them the right amount of money."

"Oh, I know it's not my job. I do it as a favor out of the goodness of my heart."

"I don't really need—"

"To thank me?" I interrupted and pointed at him. He narrowed his eyes. "You're right. It doesn't need to be spoken between friends."

He just shook his head as I opened the folder, and I didn't bother to hide my smile. He was too easy to play with, and with the way I wasn't in control of anything else in my life right now, it felt good to be in control of this. It felt normal.

Recognition had me jumping to my feet when I saw the picture on top of the papers inside.

"Holy shit! Sean Phillips?" I'd had a flicker of a memory from Portland when Wes had said ACL, but it was a really fucking common injury and I wasn't expecting to be this lucky. I figured I'd have to drop hints about Sean to make Wes think it was his idea at some point, but this really saved me the trouble.

Wes's face scrunched in amused confusion. "Yeah. You know him?"

"Ha!" I shouted, a goofy smile making me feel nearly drugged. "Yeah. I know him."

He's gonna go fucking pro!

I tapped the folder almost aggressively. "This is Cassie's brother."

"Get the fuck out of here," Wes said through a laugh. "That kid is black."

I shook my head and chuckled. "I said the same thing when I saw his picture on her phone a couple months ago. I figured she was bullshitting me, but she wasn't. I was just at her parents' house, and this is her brother, Sean."

"Well, I didn't see that coming."

Fuck, I didn't see anything coming anymore. The thought made me smile.

CHAPTER 25

Cassie

"Listen, Phil. I need you to be cool," I said, fluffing up the dog bed I'd picked up on the way home. Following the mini-pig breeder's instructions, I placed the bed in the corner of the master bedroom with lots of blankets for him to root through. Since it had been nearly two decades since I had Dad, my childhood pig, I was a bit rusty on my pig-owning skills.

"Shit will probably go down once Thatch gets home, but if I'm cool, and you're cool, we should all be cool as a motherfucking cucumber."

The little guy snorted in response and proceeded to nudge my leg with his tiny pink nose while his little tail wiggled back and forth.

After straightening his bow tie, I stood up and pointed down at Phil's new bed. "This is where you'll sleep."

He grunted in response, his tail abruptly stopping its excited movement while he proceeded to just stare at the pile of blankets on top of the bed.

I sighed. "You haven't even tried it yet."

Another grunt.

"C'mon," I instructed, kneeling down and picking him up. "Once your little ass hits this cotton cloud of heaven, it will be love at first touch." I gently placed him on the bed, and he just sat there, looking at me.

"Philmore, you need to try better than that, dude."

He snorted but proceeded to root through the blankets with his nose. I watched avidly for a few minutes until he appeared to be enjoying his humble new abode.

I sat down beside the bed and softly ran my fingers over his back. "I think you'll be really happy here, buddy. New York is a pretty cool place to live. The rent is exorbitant, but yeah, that shouldn't concern you since you'll be mooching off us. Well, Thatch. Technically, I'm kind of mooching off him right now too. That makes you and me tight. An unbreakable bond, okay? Even though I bought you for him. Between me and you, it's solely because I'm focused on out-pranking the prankster, but I can't deny you're one cute little bastard."

Yeah, but your main focus isn't on pranks and one-upping Thatch anymore...

Okay, so maybe my focus had changed. Maybe my focus was just *him*, plain and simple. Well, confusing and complicated was probably more like it, but it didn't change the fact that I truly loved screwing with him. I fucking *loved* keeping Thatch on his toes.

Phil lay down on the bed, resting his chin on my thigh, and looked up at me.

I took in his little piggy face and grinned before continuing to give him the ins and outs of the city. "The food is phenomenal, but skip the sushi at Duane Reade. I made that mistake once and nearly shit my brains out for a week."

In hindsight, I really should have known. But I'm the kind of person who actually needs to touch the hot stove to confirm it's hot, even though you already fucking told me.

"I should probably warn you that pigs are illegal in the Big Apple, but don't worry, I found a way to get around that rule," I said as I rubbed the prickly hairs of his back.

"You're going to have to get used to walking places."

He grunted and nudged my arm with his nose.

"Sorry, but them's the breaks in New York. Cabs are too expensive when you live here full time. You should probably consider getting a MetroCard. And I know you'll *love* Central Park. It will be your happy place, for sure. Since I'm not really the type of chick that enjoys participating in movement outside of getting from one place to the next, I'll make sure Thatch takes you there. That big asshole is always running and working out and shit."

Eventually, his little eyes started to drift closed until he rolled to his side and fell fast asleep.

I headed into the kitchen and cleaned up the mess I had left during Phil's arrival. Empty bags, torn tags from his new toys and collar, and a half-empty bowl of food and water littered the stainless steel space. Once I had all of the trash thrown away and Phil's belongings set up the way I wanted, I made myself comfortable on the couch and flipped on the television.

By the time Thatch walked through the door, I was forty minutes into a Lifetime movie I couldn't stop watching. "Jesus, Deb, get your shit together," I yelled at the screen. "Oh, my God. Are you blind? Julianna is an asshole. She's going to kill everyone!"

"Honey, I'm home and I've got takeout," Thatch called from the kitchen. "Think maybe you can take a break from Lifetime and come enjoy it with me?" he asked in a teasing tone.

"Bring it out here," I whined. "I need to see the end of this movie even though I already know what's going to happen."

He walked into the living room and set the bag of food on the coffee table. "Already seen it?"

"Nope. But there are *always* two certainties with Lifetime movies. One," I said, holding up one finger in his direction, "is that the acting is always terrible. And two—" I held up another finger "—they're predictable as fuck."

He chuckled as he sat down beside me. "Then why watch them?"

"Are you kidding me? Because Lifetime movies are addictive. They're so awful they're good."

"That makes zero sense."

I shrugged. "Yeah, well, consider it another mystery of the female population. Who knows why women love these movies? But they do, and I'm a testament to that very fact."

"That's unfortunate for you," he teased.

"You know what's unfortunate?" I pointed the remote toward the screen. "That Deb can't figure out her twin sister Julianna is a fucking psychopath."

"Which one is which?" he asked, opening the bag and pulling out a large white foam container. After setting it on the table, he reached up to loosen his tie. Climbing to my knees, I pushed his hands out of the way and did it for him. His eyes looked like melted chocolate.

The leather felt cool on my shins, so I rolled back over to sit beside him.

"Deb is the one that looks like she just rose from the dead. She obviously needs a tutorial on good Goth makeup. And Julianna is the cunt with the long blond hair," I answered, watching him lift the lid of the container. Once the aroma of refried beans and cheese and salsa and chicken hit my nose, I damn near dove face first into the food. "Did you get nachos?" I asked excitedly.

He winked. "Sure did, honey."

"I'm going to let that fucking wink slide because you just made my night." I grabbed one of the chips from the container and took a crunchy bite. "Mmmmmmm," I moaned over a mouthful.

"Good?"

"Javelina has the best nachos in the city." I nodded. "I'd do a lot of things for these nachos."

"How about you give me a kiss as thanks?" he suggested, pointing to his cheek.

I got up on my knees once more and pressed my lips to his cheek.

"Thanks, honey. How'd you know I was in the mood for nachos?"

He grabbed my hips and lifted me into his lap with ease, and his strong hands rearranged my legs so that I straddled his thighs. "You mentioned them," he answered, tucking a piece of hair behind my ear.

I tilted my head, combing the flecks of subtle gold speckled throughout his irises. "I'm not much for spouting sentimental bullshit, but I should say that I really enjoy when you're sweet like this. Especially when you feed me my favorite nachos."

"I'll make a mental note that nachos are the true way to your heart." He smirked and pressed a soft kiss to the corner of my mouth.

I pointed to the other corner of my mouth.

He kissed that too.

I gestured to my nose.

His lips followed that demand as well.

When I pointed to my lips, he slid his fingers into my hair and held my gaze for a few poignant seconds, his eyes searching deep into mine. For what, I'm not sure, but I couldn't deny the flutter in my belly and the quickening of my breath as his mouth moved toward mine. I watched his lashes sweep down, and the second I felt his lips, my eyes fell closed.

The kiss was demanding from the onset, his tongue slipping past my lips and dancing with mine in the hopes of producing a moan. His fingers stayed in my hair, caressing the strands and encouraging me to deepen the kiss together. Which I did willingly, because fuck, this man could kiss. His soft, full lips held all sorts of power. They could've convinced me to do just about anything in that moment.

"Fuck, Cassie," he groaned as his hands slid down my back and grabbed my ass. He pulled my hips closer to his, and I finally gave him the moan he was hoping for, right against his mouth. The Supercock was hard and ready, pressed against me.

Delicious nachos and the Lifetime movie were long forgotten.

I wanted him. Hell, I *needed* him to the point that I was stunned by my desperation. The moment was fueled by lust yet laced with an undertone of something more, something different, something my brain couldn't fully process.

Far off in the distance—as in the same room—I heard a rustling behind us.

But I ignored it, too consumed with this sexy-as-fuck man. My hands moved down his broad shoulders and slid over the muscles of his biceps. He was cut. His body was one I could spend hours and hours examining with my mouth and probably never have my fill.

The rustling grew louder, and a few snorts accompanied the noise.

Shit.

Thatch paused and pulled away from the kiss. His head tilted to the side as his gaze stared deep into mine. "Did you just snort?"

I had two options in this scenario. Either fess up and risk popping the soon-to-be bubble of hot and sweaty sex *or...* "Yes," I lied.

Obviously, option two was the best choice. I wanted him naked and between my thighs, and I had a feeling if I revealed my teacup surprise, Thatch wouldn't be feeling all that horny.

Angry? Yes. Horny? Probably not.

His face grew skeptical, the line of his mouth turning down minutely, and he attempted to glance around me, but I grabbed both of his cheeks and forced our noses together.

A few more snorts came from behind us, and I joined in the barnyard orchestra, snorting louder and more obnoxiously than Phil—*who had obviously managed to wake up and make his way into the living room*—and doing it directly into Thatch's face.

He tried to gently disentangle my hands from his face, but I stayed resolute in our literal nose-to-nose position.

"*Cass,*" he said, and his brow furrowed. "What's going on?"

"It's that fucking time of year when everything is blooming. I'm all stuffy and snorty."

"Stuffy and *snorty?*"

"Yeah, you know, allergy season. It kicks my ass."

"This is the first time I've ever heard you complain about aller-gies."

"Well, they usually don't bother me, but…" I paused, searching for a reason. "But, I went for a run today in Central Park, and they were cutting the grass, and I think it just triggered the snorts."

He raised a curious brow. "*You* went for a run today?"

"Um, yeah. I love to run."

His eyes squinted in disbelief. "You love to run?"

Fuck, this hole felt deep. "All the time."

"Considering the last time I tried to wake you up for a run, you told me you'd bite my dick off, I'd say that seems a little farfetched, honey."

Before I could offer a retort, the soundtrack of snorts and rus-tling started to play again, which meant I had to snort along and, ob-viously, come up with a quick plan. Because, yeah, this was not going to work for any substantial amount of time. Christ, I had brought Phil home to help me mess with Thatch, not cockblock me from fucking the prankster. I'd just wanted to live through the high of another one of Thatch's unexpected reactions. They made me feel good.

My gaze found the tie loosened around Thatch's neck, and I quickly unfastened the Windsor knot the rest of the way. "Let's play, baby," I purred and held the tie in front of him.

His expression remained skeptical, but his cock showed a bio-logical reaction a little suspicion couldn't deny, hardening instantly between my thighs.

"We're going to play," I instructed as I secured the makeshift blindfold over his eyes, "What part of Cassie's body are you touching."

"I'll only play if by touching you actually mean your lips, pussy, or tits touching my mouth."

"Deal," I agreed, removing myself from his lap and turning around to find Phil face-deep in a bag of plain tortilla chips that had come inside the takeout bag.

"Shit," I muttered and silently prayed to the heavens above that the little piggy hadn't managed to reach the nachos. I wasn't an animal expert, but my general knowledge of Mexican food and digestive tracts told me that would have been the opposite of good.

"Wait, where'd you go?" Thatch asked behind me.

"Uh…I just wanted to freshen up my pussy and tits for you," I said, and even though I realized how gross that sounded, I was too determined to care.

I had to hide the porcine chastity belt so I could resume the sex bubble.

"Stay right there, baby. Don't move that big cock from the couch. I'll be right back."

It should be noted here that I do not have a tuna twat or hairy nipples.
I'm groomed and fresh as a motherfucking daisy in those goddamn
Irish Spring commercials.
Seriously, my pussy smells like a meadow full of flowers.
Well, the meadow with a hint of pussy.
Because let's face it, pussies smell like pussies.
And there's no avoiding that fact unless you want a yeast infection.

I picked up Phil and carried him down the hallway, muttering, "I gave you one fucking responsibility. *Be. Cool.* That was all you had to do, and you pretty much fucked it up."

Phil snorted, and his tail wiggled back and forth when I set him down on the bed.

"You're being a bit of a cock-block, dude," I chastised, but he didn't mind, seemingly more concerned with rooting through the comforter.

"Who's a cock-block?" Thatch's voice filled the room.

I turned to find his large frame—still clad in a sexy charcoal-gray suit—standing in the doorway, sans blindfold.

His jaw dropped the second his eyes met the tiny, teacup pig snorting and nudging his nose against the bed.

"What in the ever-loving fuck?"

Well, shit. So much for waiting until after *we boned.*

And since the cat—*well, pig*—was out of the bag, I did the only thing I could...

"Surprise!" I exclaimed and did jazz hands to punctuate the statement. "I bought you a pig!"

"You..." His gaze moved back and forth between Phil and me. *"What?"*

I picked Phil up from the bed, cuddled him close to my chest, and walked over toward Thatch, who appeared to be frozen in the doorway to his bedroom.

"I bought you this little guy," I explained. "I wanted to do something thoughtful for you."

"I brought home nachos for you, and you bought me a pig?"

I tried not to smile. God, this was *almost* as good as sex.

"Aw, babe, we aren't keeping score. Anyway, I'm sure you'll repay me with something even more thoughtful."

He just stared back at me. "I never said I wanted a pig, Cassie. I live in the city, for fuck's sake. What in the hell am I going to do with a pig? *Fuck.* I'm pretty sure they're illegal in New York."

"Don't worry," I said, handing Phil to Thatch. "I've got that covered," I assured, grabbing the ID off the nightstand. "He's a registered service pet."

"Service pet? For who?"

I held up the ID. "For you, silly."

His eyes scanned the ID. "Mr. Philmore F. Bacon?"

"Isn't that the best name ever?"

"What does the F stand for?"

"Mr. Philmore *Fucking* Bacon. He's classy, but he's also a badass. I think it suits him."

"How in the fuck is he a service pet?"

"He helps your anxiety and depression."

"I don't have anxiety and depression." Thatch adjusted Phil in his arms so he was holding him like a football.

"I know that, but the city doesn't know that."

"Cassie," he started to say, but I interrupted before he could continue.

"Thatch," I said quietly, fluttering my eyelashes as I prepared to unleash the big guns. "I really feel like this is the next big step in our relationship. You know, before marriage and kids. I want to make sure we're responsible together before we move forward. I figured a pet was the best way to do it. And, well," I whispered, feigning emotion. "He just reminded me so much of Dad. And you remember how much I loved Dad."

"Jesus," he muttered to himself.

"Do you want to move our relationship forward?" I asked, pretending to get choked up.

He stared at me for a few seconds before glancing down at Phil.

When his eyes met mine again, he finally answered, "Yeah, honey. I think this was a great idea."

I waited for my chest to fill with the usual disappointment and annoyance of not being able to get Thatch to fold, but it never came.

Thank fuck.

I never wanted him to fold.

"Wake up, honey," Thatch whispered in my ear.

"Go away." I groaned and swatted at his face.

"C'mon, Cassie. It's time to rise and shine."

I rolled onto my side and pulled the comforter over my head, and his chuckles practically followed me under the blankets. "It's too early for this shit."

We'd spent the rest of last night eating and watching trashy Lifetime movies while Phil fell asleep in Thatch's lap. And when I had fallen asleep, I'd relished the idea of spending today sleeping my ass off. This wake-up call was *not* on my agenda.

"You don't even know what time it is."

"I know it's *too* fucking early."

He wrapped his arm around my waist and turned me onto my back with ease, even managing to pull the comforter away from my face in the process. "But I've got a surprise for you."

"I don't want a boner, Thatcher." Though, my pussy hadn't gotten any kind of party last night, so maybe I did. *If only the pull of sleep wasn't so strong.*

He laughed. "It's not my dick."

I peeked out of one skeptical eye and turned my head to face him. "Then what is it?"

"Belgian waffles. What breakfast dreams are made of."

"As in *Wafles and Dinges*?" They were my favorite waffles. Think whipped cream and hot fudge and caramel and pretty much any topping you wanted, and that was *Wafles and Dinges.*

He nodded. "I figured we'd get Phil some fresh air in Central Park before the Saturday morning crowd hits and grab waffles on our way back."

"But what if you and Phil went together? You know, since you haven't really had a chance to get to know each other…" I trailed off and turned over on my side again. "I think that's the best idea. You take Phil to the park and bring me back a waffle on your way home." I made kissy noises as I pulled the comforter back over my face. "Kisses. You're the best, baby."

He chuckled, and I felt the mattress move as he stood up from the bed.

I sighed a breath of relief, but before I could snuggle myself back to sleep, Thatch yanked off the comforter and flipped me over his shoulder. *"Motherfucker!"* I shouted.

"Time to wake up!" He spanked my ass. "This is for the good of our relationship, honey. We need to be doing things with Phil together. We don't want to bring him into this world only to immediately make him feel like he's a part of a broken home. Which means, you get to accompany us to Central Park today."

"What time is it?"

"It's a little after six," he answered, setting me on my feet.

"A little after six?" I shouted and poked him directly in the chest. "Are you kidding me? It's too early! Way too goddamn early."

He smirked. "I would agree, but Phil would not agree. He's been whining—well, more like squealing—since about five thirty this morning." And right on cue, Phil came tip-tapping in on his tiny hoofed feet and grunted when he plopped his little ass down by Thatch's feet.

"See what I mean?" Thatch questioned, and Phil looked up at me.

"Fine," I groaned. "But I'm not even brushing my hair," I announced as I tossed my long locks into a messy bun.

"Just wear a bra and some gym shoes."

"Huh?" I questioned in the middle of brushing my teeth, but Thatch ignored me. He picked Phil up and walked into the bedroom, setting the pig on the bed and fastening the harness leash around his body.

Fifteen minutes later, we were headed toward Central Park, one of Thatch's hands holding mine and the other wrapped around the leash. Phil's head stood tall as he trotted down the sidewalk, his little ass swaying side to side with each step.

This pig knew how to bring all the girls to the yard. We had stopped four times for random people to kneel down and give him attention. Two of which were giggly women insisting on taking a picture with the pint-sized Casanova.

It didn't help that the man holding his leash proudly was bigger than a giant and soaked up the attention just as much as the snorting pig. Winks and smirks and hearty chuckles were being passed out like fucking candy. If I wasn't so pissed off for being woken up at six in the morning, I might have found it all amusing.

Liar. You're totally loving every second of the Jolly Green Giant and

Philmore show.

Thatch led us toward a table sitting just outside the entrance of Central Park and smiled down at the gray-haired lady holding a clipboard. "Thatch Kelly and Cassie Phillips."

She scrolled her paper with the tip of her pen until she tapped it twice and grinned. "Looks like you've already filled out the forms and paid the entry fee." She handed Thatch two square pieces of paper with safety pins attached. "Just pin on your numbers and head on over to the starting line. The race will start in ten minutes."

My eyes went wide. "The race? What race?"

"Thanks, honey," he told her and grabbed my hand, tugging me through the entrance of the park. He led us toward a bench, ignoring my persistent questions about what the hell was going on and urged my ass to sit down by giving my shoulders a gentle shove.

When he tried to pin the paper on my shirt, I slapped his hands away. "Thatcher," I snapped. "What the fuck is going on?"

"We're running this 5K together," he said like it was the most normal thing in the world.

"Oh, hell to the no," I disagreed. "I am not running in a fucking race. Do you even know me?" I questioned his sanity. Cassie Phillips did not run in races. The closest she came to running was when Macy's was having their end-of-year clearance sale on shoes. And even then, my pace was more speed-walk than run.

"But you love to run," he stated. "Isn't that what you said last night?" His gaze met mine, and I didn't like the devious glint of amusement that rested behind his eyes. "I'm really trying here. Trying to do nice things for the good of our relationship. I wanted to be thoughtful and do something with you that you said you loved to do."

His smile said sweet, but his eyes, well, they said *checkmate.*

"Do you not want to spend time with me today, honey?"

Oh man, he was evil.

The fucking king of one-upping had just laid down the gauntlet.

I plastered a sugary sweet smile on my face. "Of course, I want to spend time with you, baby. I'm so happy you did this," I lied, snatching the paper from his hands violently and pinning it to my shirt.

As we lined up at the starting line, I had the urge to kick Thatch in the nuts. The cute pig standing at his feet was the only thing that had stopped me.

The gun fired and everyone around us was off, their gym shoes slapping against the pavement in the direction of the finish line. I started off slow and silently prayed that Thatch would speed ahead so that I could sneak off the path and find a park bench to plop my already tired ass down on. But of course, he didn't do that. No way, that would have been too damn easy. Thatch jogged leisurely at my side, letting my pace lead us.

A minute into the run, I was silently cursing everyone and everything.

Fuck you. Fuck running. Fuck the beautiful sun. Fuck those chirping birds. Fuck that lady pushing her kid in the stroller. It should be me in that fucking stroller.

I looked up from the ground and found Thatch smiling down at me, his long legs running at a slow and easy rhythm and not an ounce of discomfort on his face. He paused briefly to pick up a squealing Phil and adjust him in his arms like a baby, and I took that moment to scratch the side of my face with my middle finger pointed directly in his direction.

He caught it and his smile grew wider. "You okay, honey?"

"I'm fine," I bit out between panting breaths. "Never been better."

I refused to let him know my body was practically screaming for me to stop.

But ten minutes after that I could no longer keep quiet.

"For fuck's sake!" I shouted, and the runners in front of me shot glares over their shoulders. "I can't go any longer, Thatch," I gasped and jogged off to the side of the path. My feet stayed firmly planted by a bench as I leaned forward and rested my hands on my knees. "I'm done. I'm fucking done. Why do people do this? This is so fucking stupid. Why would anyone want to run unless they were actually being chased or Prada was having a going-out-of-business sale?" I rambled through shallow breaths.

Thatch sat Phil down on the bench, and before I could stop him, he gripped my hips, lifted me over his head, and set me on his shoulders.

"Whoa! What the hell?" I cried. My head spun from the abrupt change in altitude.

"I'm really proud of you, Crazy," he said and picked Phil up from the bench. "For someone who's never run before, you kicked ass for the first mile and a half." He glanced up at me and winked. "So now, just sit back, relax, and hold on tight to Phil. I'll take it from here."

He lifted our little piggy above his head and put him into my arms.

Phil squealed in protest, but I slipped him inside the front of my shirt and held on tight to comfort him. "It's okay," I soothed. "I've got ya, little buddy."

Eventually, his squeals stopped, and he peeked his little head out above my neckline. He sniffed the air a few times and snorted his content, inside the warmth and safety of my shirt.

"That's the cutest fucking thing I've ever seen," Thatch said as he held his phone in front of us, catching all three of our faces in the shot. His gaze met mine in the screen and those chocolate eyes of his glimmered with affection. "Smile, honey," he said as his lips curled into a handsome smile.

I smiled.

Phil snorted.

Snap. And just like that, our happy little moment had been recorded.

Forever unchanged. *Just like your growing feelings for this beautiful, charming, perfect-for-you man...well, five minutes ago you would have thought perfect-for-you asshole.*

"All right," Thatch announced as he moved back toward the path and held my thighs tightly to his shoulders. "Let's hit it."

With pep in his step and occasional grinning glances in mine and Phil's direction, Thatch finished the last two miles of the race just like that—me on his shoulders and our teacup pig in my T-shirt. And beyond that, he did it with ease. The second he crossed the finish line, he pulled me off his shoulders and put his lips to mine. His breathing wasn't even labored.

Fuck, that man had some serious stamina.

An hour later, we were stuffed full of waffles and settled on a park bench—Phil asleep on my chest, while my legs were stretched out and rested in Thatch's lap. I watched him watch the people meandering by, his eyes following their Saturday paths with nothing but mild curiosity.

He untied my laces and slipped off my shoes and socks, leaving my feet bare beneath the late morning sun. His fingers kneaded into my soles and started their talented course of finding all of the sensitive spots that ached from the run.

A soft moan fell from my lips, and his gaze met mine.

"Feel good?"

"So good."

He grinned.

"You know, you're a really good boyfriend," I admitted. Even though our relationship had an undertone of pranks and jokes and relentless teasing, Thatch *was* a good boyfriend. I knew I wasn't an expert by any means when it came to relationships, but beneath that wicked sense of humor, he was thoughtful and caring and sweet. So fucking sweet sometimes I wondered if I'd get a stomachache from sugar overload.

His brow rose in question.

"I mean, look at you," I said, nodding toward his hands on my feet. "You're rubbing my gross feet after I just ran like fifty miles."

"You're feet aren't gross." He plucked one of my hot-pink painted toes with his index finger and thumb. "They're cute."

I wiggled my toes. He chuckled.

"And you only ran a mile. Mile and a half, tops," he added with an amused grin. "I ran more than half of the race with you and Phil on my shoulders."

"But I ran the hardest part of the trail. There were more hills on the first end."

Yeah, that was a lie. They weren't any hills.

He winked. "Of course, you did, honey."

I wiggled my toes again. "So who taught you how to be a good boyfriend? Your last girlfriend was in high school, right? What was her name?"

"Yes." He paused briefly and then started kneading at the balls of my feet. "Her name was Margo."

"How long did you guys date?"

"A little over a year."

"Why did you break up?"

"We didn't." He turned on the bench to face me. "She died at the end of our senior year."

Whoa. That had been unexpected. In the past, before Thatch, I would've shied away from going further with this conversation and tried to lighten the tone, but I didn't want to do that.

"Wow, Thatch…I'm so sorry…I don't really know what else to say."

"It was a long time ago," he reassured. "When it happened, of course, I was devastated. But as time passed, and wounds healed, I knew that my relationship with Margo was a huge part of my life because of the way it ended, not because of the actual relationship we had. We were both young, wild, and selfish. If she had lived, and every day I wish she had, I know Margo and I wouldn't have been sitting here together on this park bench. I just wish she could have had the opportunity to spread her wings and really fly, really find herself."

My heart grew two sizes bigger inside my chest. There were so many facets to Thatch's personality, so many tiny particulars and huge guarantees, but underneath all of that charming swagger and good-natured sense of humor was a good man. *The best man.*

I reached out my hand and grabbed his, squeezing it gently.

He smiled softly in response. My lips mimicked his, and I didn't try to stop the permeating affection from showing beneath my eyes. I wanted him to know I cared. I wanted him to know he was easily becoming my whole world.

Phil snorted in my lap. His little eyes peeked open and glanced around the outside oasis.

Thatch grinned down at him and then his eyes met mine again, "Ready to go home?"

Home. I couldn't deny my first thought was, *Home is wherever you are now.*

"Yeah, baby, let's go home."

CHAPTER 26

Thatch

"So you're good to get him to Monarch tonight, right?" Georgia asked as I stepped into the crosswalk with the phone to my ear.

Kline's birthday party was finally upon us, and we were all just living in Georgia's world until it was over.

I shook my head and smiled at the near panic in her sweet voice. "I won't let you down. I'll get him there no matter what it takes."

A bike messenger weaved up and around me to cut in front of the pedestrians. Cabs and cars filled the streets, the height of the commuting hour packing a half a dozen extra sardines into the can.

"But, like, you're not gonna drug him, right?"

A startled bark of laughter had the people in front of me looking over their shoulders. I ignored them and focused on the woman at my ear. "No. I won't be taking advantage of your husband in any way. But I will carry him there if I have to."

"Good."

"Not good," I corrected. "If I have to physically carry your husband to his party tonight, you better start planning my funeral."

She giggled. "Okay. At least I've gotten a little practice at event planning, so I'll make sure it's nice."

"That's not really comforting at all."

"I'll also make sure Cassie puts a picture of her boobs in the casket with you."

I smiled at the visual. "Okay, I'm feeling slightly comforted now."

"Fantastic!"

I heard some guy hoot in the background, and my eyebrows pulled together as I made my way across 5th Avenue. There was never any shortage of people talking to you when you didn't want them to, men hooting at the attractive women, as though yelling at them gave them a chance, or crazy people forgetting the meaning of personal space. But as hard as I focused my ears, I couldn't figure out which of those scenarios Georgia was currently encountering.

"Where are you? Do you need me to do anything else? I've got about an hour before rugby practice. I'm just running by the tattoo shop to make sure Frankie's good, but I can skip it if you need something."

"Thanks, but I think I've got everything covered. I'm meeting Cass in just a few minutes, and then we're going over to the bar to finish setting up."

Three beats in the space of what should have been one, my heart sped up at the mention of my roommate and lover. It was unexpected but not completely unwelcome. Still, the feeling was overpowering, so I tried to distract myself with meaningless questions.

"What did you tell Kline? I can't imagine he likes the idea of not being with you on his birthday."

I could practically hear her smile. "I told him it wasn't that he wouldn't be with me, just that he'd be with me *later*. And that I'd make sure *being with me* was verbiage for some very dirty activity."

"Ah," I breathed. "The real way to a man's heart. Your puss—"

"Yeah, I get it, thanks."

"Hey, I'm just saying, my stomach isn't really the answer unless it's got a pussy sitting on—"

"I said I get it!" she yelled, and I laughed at the mental visual of curious eyes turning her way on whatever busy street she was walking.

"What's that? Did you say you didn't get it? I said—"

"I will hang up on you!" she threatened in a way that was supposed to be scary but had all the danger of a chipmunk behind it. She was too cute to be lethal, and if she wasn't, I guess that was how I'd die.

"Okay, okay," I conceded with a laugh. "Just pass the message along to Cassie, okay?"

"I will not dirty-talk my best friend for you."

My face felt swollen as my cheeks climbed up around my nose, but I made sure to do my best impression of an audible pout for her benefit. "Ah, come on. The visual is *so* good."

"Kline would kill you if he could hear you right now," she said in my ear, just as I spotted what I knew was his back disappearing down the steps of the subway ahead. It didn't happen often, especially now that he was living outside the city, but on occasion, the world did its best to remind me how truly small it was. Quickening my steps, I strode after him.

"Good thing he can't, then, huh?" I teased.

"I'm not even sure why I talk to you."

"Because you love me. Everyone loves me," I deadpanned. The woman walking next to me glanced up with surreptitiously curious eyes. She didn't want me to know she was listening, but she also didn't want to miss a word.

Raising a hand, I gave her a wave and wink. Disgusted eyes met mine for a second before she sped up her stride to put distance between us. Given the natural length of my stride, her little legs looked like she was running a hamster wheel.

"Right," Georgia scoffed in my ear.

"I'll see you in a couple of hours, Georgia girl, and I'll have your dreamboat of a man at my side."

"You're ridiculous."

"—ly handsome? I know. Don't worry. I won't tell Kline you think so if you don't."

"Bye, Thatch."

I shook my head as I heard the sound of her hanging up on me before I could respond.

Everyone made it so easy.

Except Cassie.

That wild, beautiful woman brought her own game to the table, and as time went on, the truth was becoming more and more apparent—I fucking loved it. The challenge, the change, the way she didn't take any kind of shit without giving it right back. And somehow, she managed to maintain a certain amount of softness while she did it.

Whether it was a glance or a smile or a step closer to me in proximity, there was always some sign that she had vulnerability in there somewhere. That she cared about others and wanted them to care for her.

That she wanted all the things out of life that people often misunderstood about a woman like her—family, friendship...love.

I sped up, taking the steps down to the 57th and 6th station two at a time. The train sat on the tracks waiting, and with five huge strides, I slid on just before the doors closed. Kline glanced up from his paper at my Cosmo-Kramer-like entrance.

His lips formed the word "Great" with fantastic faux sarcasm but finished with a smile.

"Are you stalking me?" he asked as I took a seat close to him but left one in between us. Spatially, that was the only way if I wanted to maintain any use of my arms.

"Yes. I've actually been watching you from the little window to your office all day. Didn't you notice me?"

He shook his head and laughed, tucking the newspaper into the handles of his duffle bag between his feet. "I wouldn't be surprised. It's not like you're busy or anything."

"Exactly," I agreed, knowing he knew I was busy in the most literal sense of the word. Kline knew pretty much everything about me, so much so that I could barely even surprise him anymore. He actually pointed out tons of investment opportunities to me before I ever mentioned them. Granted, I was usually already looking into them, but he was just a millisecond behind me. And when it came to money moves, that was saying something.

"Ready for practice?" I asked as the train started to move.

"Honestly?"

I shrugged and nodded.

"I'd rather slice my eyeballs open. I just want to go home and be with my wife and our fucking wildlife refuge."

I smirked. "You have two animals. Hardly zoo material."

"It doesn't feel like two. Stan weighs a million pounds and shits bombs, but he's actually the easier of the two."

"Well, that much I believe," I conceded easily. "Walter is a little prick."

"But I still enjoy it because Georgie does. What's that say about me?"

"That you misplaced your balls?" I joked.

"Fuck you."

I leaned my elbows into my knees. "It means you're a lucky bastard. Above us right now, thousands of unhappy assholes are leaving their miserable jobs and going to the bar instead of home."

Kline raised his eyebrows.

"*By choice.* They'd much rather be there than go home, but you, my friend, are one of the wise ones."

"What about you?"

"What about me?"

"You're fine with going to the bar instead of home?"

"I rarely go to the bar anymore."

"Not my point at all, and you know it."

I shrugged with nonchalance and tried not to let my thoughts run away. "I want what you have."

He smiled. I pushed.

"You think Georgie would be into me?"

His smile turned into a scowl.

"Kidding," I said through a laugh. I almost told him I'd just gotten off the phone with his wife, but that would have raised at least one flag.

It wasn't like I didn't talk to her, but I didn't tell him about it every time I did.

"How's it feel to be a year older, Grandpa?"

He laughed. "You're older than I am."

"Yes, but I've aged better. Don't take it personally. I credit most of my looks to a rigid diet of Oreos, Nutella, and Trix. Plus, you know…"

"I know?" he questioned.

"Don't be embarrassed. You can't help it."

He lifted his brows and waited. The man had legendary patience, so of course, I caved.

"It's not your fault your growth was stunted."

"Jesus," Kline breathed out before a laugh. "The only thing embarrassing is you."

I lifted my shoulders to my ears. "I can live with that."

"Come on, Thumbelina, shower faster!" I yelled through the closed door of my guest room.

Since Kline didn't live in the city anymore, he had to use my pad as his locker room post-practice. Now that I was clean and had dropped off Phil with the sitter, I figured he'd had plenty of time.

The door swung open immediately, and I bobbed and weaved as Kline's fist punched the air an inch in front of my stomach.

"Oh, good," I stated calmly. "I thought you were going to take forever, and we don't have time. Places to be and all that."

He tried to hide his cringe. I did an equally poor job of hiding my laugh.

Since I'd run into Kline, I'd decided to forgo the tattoo shop and just head straight to practice with him. Frankie didn't mind, but really, it didn't matter if he did. My shares of ownership outweighed his. But it also did matter because I wasn't an asshole. Not most of the time, anyway.

"Sorry, buddy. The faster we go out, the faster I'll have you home to your brood. But for now, you're stuck with me."

"Which is obviously the worst-case scenario," he muttered in jest. "I'll have to suffer through it. Where are we headed?"

"Monarch Bar," I answered succinctly. "Thelma and Louise are already there."

His eyes narrowed in suspicion. "Thelma and Louise?"

"Oh," I said with pretense and a waggle of my eyebrows. "Twins. I can't remember their actual names."

He looked ready to interrupt, so I bowled right over him. "And they're both for me."

"What about Cassie?" he asked as we walked down the hall to the living room.

"What about her?" I replied with a hidden smirk.

"Her stuff is here, in your apartment, and you're meeting women?"

One of whom was her. "Yeah, she won't mind," I lied.

I wasn't quite sure how serious she was about our relationship—if she was as serious as I was—but I knew she was serious about being the only woman. I liked my balls, thank you very much. They weren't exactly the best-looking guys in the place, but they made sure I had a good time when it counted.

My phone vibrated in my pocket as I shoved Kline out the door and locked it behind me. His face was in full mope mode.

"Come on," I encouraged. "Once we're on the subway, you can text your little wife until we get there. Where is she again?"

"Working," he said with a sigh.

"Boy, Wes knows how to crack the whip."

"It's not him. I already confronted him about it. She's just fucking determined to do a good job."

"Well, I'd say that's a pretty good quality, right?" I asked as we stepped out onto the sidewalk in front of my building. My fingers itched to dig in my pocket for my phone knowing I had an unread text, but it was only a quick walk to the corner and we'd be on the train where I'd have a better chance of keeping it hidden from Kline's astute eyes.

"Of course, it's a good thing. There's a reason I'm always trying to hire her back."

"I thought it was horniness."

"Okay, so there are two reasons."

I laughed and kept walking, leading the way down the stairs and into the dim lighting of the subway station. We didn't have to wait long as the train pulled up and the doors opened. It was just a quick ride on the R down to the party, so neither of us bothered to go for a seat. Instead, we found a spot in the center around one of the stripper poles.

Okay, it wasn't actually a stripper pole, and guaranteed, you'd pick up some kind of disease if you rubbed yourself too thoroughly on one, but it sure looked like that's what it should be. I'd have to talk to the MTA.

My phone buzzed in my pocket again. Pulling it out carefully, I tilted the screen slightly away from Kline so I knew he wouldn't be able to read it.

Cassie: Has the Eagle landed?

Cassie: I will castrate you if you don't answer me.

Fuck. I typed out a quick reply.

Me: *The Eagle is in flight.*

Cassie: *What? What the fuck does that mean?*

I shook my head and smiled.

Me: *It means we're en route. If the Eagle had landed, you'd be able to see him yourself because he'd be there.*

I glanced up to see Kline staring at me in question.

"It's Cassie," I explained. "Just harassing me about using the last of the toothpaste."

He narrowed his eyes. Fuck him for being so smart.

"Oh, look," I said, jumping to turn toward the door. "Our stop."

"What's going on with Cassie?" he asked as we weaved our way through the moderate crowd and off the train car.

"What do you mean? She's still holding out, and so am I. You know how it is."

"Come on. Enough with the innocent bullshit. I don't care how strong-willed you are; there's no fucking way that chick would still be living with you if you didn't like it."

I shrugged but let my lips curve into a smile as we jogged up the concrete steps and out into the busy intersection at 34th Street.

"She always surprises me. I think I know what she's gonna do, but I never actually do."

"And that's it? The thrill?" he asked skeptically.

Not wanting to get into the details, but knowing he was one of my very best friends, I gave him the bare minimum. "It's not just the thrill."

A smile transformed his face.

And then, my friend Kline, a man who complained relentlessly about my one-eyed blinks, winked at *me*.

Georgia's angry eyes scoured me through the glass wall between us and the patio as Kline took his time ordering a drink at the bar.

He'd actually cheered up after I shared the little glimpse into my soft heart, and I wasn't about to ruin it just so everyone could yell the word "surprise" five minutes sooner.

Plus, I had been missing my friend.

But as Cassie started to gesture with a knife in her hand, I knew I didn't have much time to stall anymore.

"Thanks," Kline thanked the bartender before taking a slow sip of his scotch—no lime. I smiled.

The bar was filled with people seeking post-work solace, and quite a few men and women looked like they were on the hunt for their next one-night victim. I'd been one of those people not too long ago, small-talking my way into the panties of whatever woman caught my eye.

It was actually funny how different they all looked to me in such a short time. Sexy smirks were now desperate fake smiles, and what I once considered banging bodies held none of my interest.

"Do you ever wish you could drink it the way you used to?" I asked, even though I already knew the answer. The answer was in all the little things I'd never been able to see before.

"Not even a little," he replied without hesitation. It wasn't about the drink, but the life. We were both really happy guys. We were both content in our habits, hobbies, and careers, but some holes go unnoticed until something comes along that fills them.

"Come on," I gestured overzealously as he put the glass to his lips again. "Let's go out on the patio." I saw Georgia and Cassie turn their backs to the window out of the corner of my eye.

"I guess time's up, huh?" Kline smirked, and I narrowed my eyes.

"What are you talking about?" I asked in an empty attempt to continue our ruse.

"My wife. She's ready for me. You've killed enough time."

"How'd you know?"

He scoffed, and I smiled. Clever fucking bastard.

"If I hadn't known two weeks ago, I would have known as soon as I saw my wife's ass through the windows."

I laughed because, yeah, Georgia had a pretty memorable ass. I'd imagine the man who spent hours of his time paying it personal attention was highly attuned to it.

Well, whatever. If he hadn't known, I probably never would have convinced him to come. He played the part of being dragged along well, but Kline Brooks didn't do fuck-all he didn't want to. "Just don't tell her you knew."

"Unlike you, I don't have a death wish or a need to be right out of principle."

"Hey, I happen to think those are both admirable qualities."

"Having a death wish is admirable?" he asked skeptically as we walked through a crowd of women toward the patio doors. Several sets of eyes followed us as we did. I did my best not to make direct contact.

"Okay, maybe not. But there's a certain amount of bravery—"

"No," he denied, cutting me off. "You can't save this one."

Fair enough.

I chuckled and tipped my head in defeat.

"Surprise!" the crowd shouted as we walked out the doors, and I didn't waste the opportunity.

"Oh, my God," I squealed with a hand to my chest. "You guys shouldn't have!"

Plus, I knew Kline didn't really like the attention anyway.

"Thatcher Kelly!" Cassie chastised, waving her arm in a reprimand. Her tits bounced with her gesture. I waggled my eyebrows and made my advance while Kline rushed his wife and scooped her into his arms. He didn't make any other effort to address the crowd, and I wasn't surprised. It just wasn't his thing—especially not when Georgia was in the room; he only had eyes for her.

"Hey there, honey," I sweet-talked as I pulled Cass into my arms and tightened my hold. Her chest pushed deliciously against the bottom of mine, and her hands shot up to grab me by my belt. The tips of her fingers snuck under my shirt and grazed skin. I held back a shiver.

"Why do I spend most of my time plotting ways to kill you when we're apart, and then hug you when I see you?"

Hopefully because you're falling in love with me.

"My good looks and charm?" I joked.

She didn't answer, though, her eyes holding mine contemplatively until someone knocked into her from behind. We both swayed from the force, but I at least kept her from hitting the ground. She stepped away from me and our bubble after she gathered herself. I kept a hand at her elbow until I knew she was safely balanced back on her sickeningly hot heels.

Goddamn, her legs go on forever.

"Whoops, sorry," the clumsy woman apologized, putting a flirty hand to my arm and smiling.

I excused her politely but kept my face neutral. Cassie's eyes, however, became significantly smaller.

"I'm Jennifer," the intruder offered.

I stuck out my hand in an effort not to be rude. "Thatch."

"Oh, wow. That's a fantastic name."

I bit my lip to keep from laughing when Cassie's face took on the lethal edge of an assassin.

"It really is a great name, *honey*," Cassie emphasized before reaching around and brazenly giving my cock a squeeze. "He's got a monster—"

"Cass!" I shouted, startled.

"What?" she asked, raising an eyebrow in challenge.

Tucking her back snug to my chest, I put my hand over her mouth.

"It's nice to meet you, Jennifer. My *girlfriend* and I both think so."

"Where's Phil?" Cassie asked with a smirk as Jennifer mouthed a horrified "O-kay" and walked away.

"At home with the sitter."

"You left him with someone I've never met? Who is this person?"

I walked toward one of the beer coolers Georgia had arranged for the bar staff to set up. Longnecks stood out of a bath of sloppy, semi-melted ice, so I plucked one out with two fingers and gave it a gentle shake to shed some of the water. The cap gave way to my twist easily, landing right in the center of the garbage can as I tipped the bottle to my lips and took a swig before answering.

"Yep. I'm *paying someone* to watch my *pig*, thanks to you. And it's a sweet lady in the building next door."

She raised her hands palms out in front of her. "Phil is so much more than a pig."

"You're right. He's a manifestation of you trying to win our little game."

"I don't know what you're talking about," she denied, getting up in my space once again.

I opened my arms to accommodate her, leaned back against the wall, and pulled her between my legs. "Bullshit."

"Hey, guys," Wes said as he approached us, easy smile lighting up his green-hazel eyes. He was always running fifteen minutes behind schedule. Luckily, he'd somehow managed to make himself important enough that people waited for him.

I half expected Cassie to move away, go talk to Georgia or one of her other friends, but instead, she turned her back to my chest, pushed her ass to my crotch, and settled into me the way I was on the wall.

She pulled out her phone and glanced at it as she waved at Wes, but his eyes never left mine. And they were mighty fucking amused.

"Hey, Cass, did Thatch tell you—" Wes started, and I waved a wild arm frantically to head him off. I shook my head to emphasize the point just as her eyes left her phone and met Wes's.

A Wes who had paused midsentence because I'd activated the bat signal.

"Did Thatch tell me what?"

It wasn't that she wouldn't know about Sean eventually, but I knew she'd both flip her shit and be angry with me that I hadn't said anything sooner, and I wasn't ready for the negative side of that coin. My plans for tonight were going to be flirting the line with pissing her off enough.

"Um," Wes stalled and widened his eyes at me uncertainly. "Did he tell you how much he sucked at rugby practice earlier?"

I closed my eyes and waited for the fallout. I was surrounded by absolute shit liars. How could I be so gifted in something all of my friends struggled with? Wouldn't I start to rub off eventually?

But Cass didn't call him on it, instead dissolving into a gentle laugh. "Yeah, right. Have you seen this guy? He tosses people around for breakfast. Trust me, I know."

Wes's smile came back at that, and it'd taken on an air of insinuation. "Oh, yeah? How do you know that?"

"Fuck. Forget I said that shit, or I'll kill both of you." She shoved off of me so hard it made me grunt in the middle of my laugh.

Cassie's hand fell easily into mine as she talked to the people around her. She didn't notice the way people's eyes went there, the way they watched and smiled—or sneered in the case of a few women *and pricks with dicks*—but I did. Their eyes widened just slightly, and the corners of their lips turned up or down just enough. The tiny tics of a person's thoughts out there for anyone to see if they took the time.

I knew I hardly ever did, and I honestly don't think Cassie ever concentrated on anyone else's opinion. But tonight, as I publicly claimed her as mine over and over again, I found myself fascinated.

I gently tugged her hand before releasing it and sliding a posses-
sive hand around the curve of her waist to settle on her opposite hip.
She sank into me effortlessly, and I wasn't sure if she'd even noticed
what I'd done.

"Excuse me, ladies, but I'm going to steal my girlfriend for a little
while."

Once again, mouths turned up and down in equal supply, but the
corners of mine went distinctly north. Cassie hadn't even questioned
the sentiment. I'd obviously done a stellar job of desensitizing her to
it. And tonight, I had practically followed her everywhere she went,
touching her without permission and interjecting about our relationship anytime the opportunity presented itself. Pushing the boundar-
ies as always, I'd even told a couple of guys I was planning to propose
soon. She'd smiled. Of course, she'd felt secure in the fact that I was
joking.

I wasn't so sure.

It was the most fun I'd had in a long time.

Once we were several feet away, Cassie's commentary returned.
"You didn't even wink at any of those women, Thatcher. Is your game
failing?"

I bit my lip to stop a smile, but I didn't fight the urge to lean down
and press a subtle kiss to her lips. "It wasn't really necessary." When I
pulled back, I didn't deny her the pleasure, though.

"Ah, there it is," she breathed. "Just delayed a little, I guess."

"Something like that."

I held the door as we walked inside and then pushed through the
crowd until we came to another door on the other side. It read Emergency Exit in big official letters, but I knew there was no alarm on it.
At practice, one of the guys had been telling a story about drunkenly
stumbling through it while trying to woo a woman. Not exactly A
game material, but I wasn't going to be the one to tell him. That was a
lesson he really needed to learn for himself.

And tonight, I was going to make sure it paid off to pay attention.

"Where are we going?" Cass asked as we stepped out onto the deserted rooftop patio on the other side.

"Just doing a little experiment, honey."

"Experiment?" she questioned suspiciously.

She had good reason. I wasn't really sure how my plan was going to go over, but I had to try. This was the kind of opportunity smart men didn't pass up.

"Just a little pleasure versus fear tug of war."

"Fear?" she snapped. "What the fuck are you up to?"

"Come here, baby," I coaxed with a tug on her hand when she turned for the door. "I promise to make this whole ordeal worth your while."

"Ordeal? That's not a fucking promising word. Ordeal suggests pain and suffering."

I laughed.

"I don't like to suffer, and if you make me, I'll be sure to return the favor."

"Duly noted," I agreed.

All the way across the patio now, I pulled her toward the fire escape ladder and urged her to go up in front of me. She didn't exactly do cartwheels.

"You want me to go higher? Are you crazy? You know I fucking *hate* heights. I already threatened to murder Georgie in her sleep for choosing this as the venue, and she's my best friend. I like her better than you."

"Really?"

"Yes."

I laughed. "I do love your honesty."

"Oh, yeah," she grumbled as I pushed her to the ladder and put her foot on the first rung for her. "Well, I honestly hate you right now."

Tucking my chin into her neck, I breathed her in before whispering my words out. "No, you don't." My lips smoothed over the skin as I twisted my head back and forth. I nipped the soft flesh with my teeth and then sucked it into my mouth, sliding the tip of my tongue over it gently to soothe the sting. My beard rubbed at the surrounding skin, and she shivered.

"Thatch," she whispered but didn't say more.

"Go up the ladder, Cassie," I ordered softly, giving her one last squeeze with my arms before stepping back to spot her.

She paused for a moment but didn't look back, scurrying up the ladder and moving quickly away from the edge.

As soon as I reached the top and traversed a safe number of paces away from certain death, she charged me. Her nerves were driving the conversation, and it felt unnatural to see her anything but confident and in control. I actually felt bad for a minute, that her discomfort was making me feel special, but when she fisted her hand in the material of my shirt at my chest, any regret retreated immediately.

"What's this about, Thatcher?"

I smiled. She glared.

"Do you trust me?"

"No." Her answer was emphatic and immediate and completely devoid of thought.

"*Cass*," I stressed.

"Fuck!" she shouted, frustrated, and squeezed her eyes shut. "Yes. For some completely insane reason, I do. And I have not one clue why since you're a psychopath."

"Takes one to know one."

"Thatcher—" she snapped, and I lunged.

My lips slammed to hers aggressively, and she didn't delay or hold back.

A gasp moved from her mouth to mine as I pulled her body flush with a hand at her ass. Her skirt was short, and the tips of my fingers just barely grazed the skin of her thigh.

My hand flexed at the feeling, doing its best to leave my mark on the perfect canvas of her skin whether either of us gave it permission or not.

I nibbled at the plush padding at the center of her lower lip, and she tugged at the short strands of hair where my beard met my hairline.

"You want me to take your mind off the heights, baby?" I asked, pulling my lips off of hers just enough to speak clearly.

"You already were, you idiot. Now I'm thinking about it again."

When I put my mouth on her, I had a feeling she'd forget again.

I smiled with my lips against hers. "Not for long."

Starting slow, I wrapped my arms around her body until they met in the middle of her ass. I gripped her soft flesh until she moaned.

"You have on panties, baby?" I whispered against her mouth.

When she bit her lip and shook her head, I couldn't hold back my groan or desperate need to know if she was telling the truth.

Roughly, I bunched the fabric of her skirt in my hands and slid it up until there wasn't anything between my palms and skin. I dropped to my knees in one smooth motion, and her head fell back as her hands found my hair and tugged.

Leaning forward, I put my tongue right to her bare clit.

"Goddamn. I will never be the same," I told her pussy honestly. Now that I knew she really would go out without anything under a little skirt like this, I'd be constantly out of my mind wondering when she'd do it again.

Settling one leg over my shoulder, I licked and sucked her pussy until her knees started to shake. With two hands at her hips, I lifted her other foot off the ground and urged her to settle the other leg over my shoulder too.

"Holy shit," she breathed. "I am literally sitting on your face right now."

Right where I want you. I nodded and flicked the tip of my tongue against her clit.

Pulling back just enough to speak, I rubbed at the juncture of her thighs. "Close your eyes, baby."

She took a minute, staring down at me between her legs, but

eventually, something she saw made her comply.

A scream left her lips as I climbed to my feet with her sitting reverse cowgirl on my shoulders.

"Oh, holy fuck!"

"Keep your eyes closed," I soothed.

Five careful strides brought me to the alcove on the edge, a little cutout of the main exterior wall of the building that had a platform three feet down.

I set her down carefully, kissing each eyelid when she gasped at the feel of cool concrete on her bare ass.

"Trust me, honey. I'm gonna make this so good."

"Less talk and more action, then!" she chastised. I laughed and climbed over the edge, behind her, and onto the small platform.

"Thatch," she said nervously as my lips touched her shoulder from behind.

"It's okay, baby."

With an arm around her back and another under her legs, I lifted her off the concrete to protect her skin and spun her to face the city.

I hit my knees again and spread her legs one at a time, a foot on each of the surrounding ledges, until she was wide open and ready for me.

Her eyes squeezed shut tighter. I kissed the inside of both of her thighs. "I'll take care of you," I promised. "You just keep your eyes closed until right before you come. I'll do the rest."

Breathing her in, I put my mouth back to her pussy and worked. Around the rim, I teased her with the tip of my tongue before moving up to suck on her clit and filling her with two fingers. She gasped at the intrusion and reached for the concrete at her hips.

I groaned as her excitement coated my lips and spilled to the back of my tongue.

Goddamn, she tastes good.

"Oh...My...God," she breathed as I pushed her higher and higher, chasing her orgasm hard and fast, and nearly coming in my pants from the fucking excitement of her pussy's eagerness to please.

"I'm gonna...I'm gonna," she called, and I pulled my mouth away just long enough to remind her to open her eyes.

She gasped loudly, the sight of the city before her mingling her fear and pleasure together into one heady mix of perfection, and her nipples pebbled through the thin fabric of her tank top.

Definitely no bra. She did it on purpose now just to drive me crazy; I knew she did.

I stayed there and drank all of her in, careful not to waste a drop or miss one moment of her face. When it all became too much, her eyes shut again and her head fell back in the most perfect display of everything I'd ever wanted.

She shook as I pulled her into my arms and tucked her face into my neck.

"How'd I do, honey?"

Her arms tightened around me reflexively.

"You did a good job," she told me. "Of showing my pussy to the top fifty floors of the Empire State Building."

I laughed and pressed my lips to hers.

"Trust me, baby. They enjoyed the view."

CHAPTER 27

Cassie

I cradled my cell phone between the crook of my neck and shoulder in order to grab a mint out of my bag. These Wintergreen Lifesavers were like crack.

"Will you have time to stop by the apartment and feed Phil before your meeting this afternoon?" I asked as I walked down 28th Street, weaving in and out of lunchtime pedestrian traffic. "I'd do it, but I'm supposed to meet Georgie and Will for lunch, and then I have to stop by ESPN's offices to drop off some files."

"Yeah, that's not a problem," Thatch responded in my ear, and the sound of papers shuffling filled the receiver.

"Boy, you're awfully accommodating today," I teased. "Does it have anything to do with this morning?"

"I'll do pretty much anything you ask if you wake me up like that every morning."

I grinned. "Sometimes I forget how happy blow jobs make you."

"First of all, *rule number sixty*, don't *ever* forget that. And secondly, *your* blow jobs make me happy," he clarified.

"You don't want blow jobs from anyone else?" I tested. I knew the answer he better fucking say.

"No," he responded quickly. "Once you've experienced a Dyson, no other brands come close to cleaning the carpets anymore."

I grinned. "What about my tits?"

"Those too."

"My pussy?"

"You're just fishing for compliments now, but I'll play along," he said with an amused tone. "Yes, luscious Cassie, your pussy gets my dick hard."

"What about my ass?"

"Are you extending an offer? Because I'll drop everything I'm doing right now to sign on the dotted line that leads to claiming your ass."

Good try, Thatcher, but it's not going to happen. A lady has to keep one get out of jail free card in the tank.

I laughed and remembered the other reason for the phone call. "Stop distracting me. I actually called you for a reason."

"What else can I do for you, honey?"

"Well, I have a bit of surprise," I announced as I crossed 5th Avenue. "Are you getting excited?"

"No," he responded in a flat tone. Two long drags of a cab horn punctuated the sentiment.

"Well, that's really fucking ungrateful of you."

He showed no signs of remorse. "The last time you got me a surprise, I ended up with a pig and the city of New York thinking I have chronic anxiety."

I laughed. "But you love Phil!"

"Yeah, *now,* I do," he answered. "He's grown on me. But initially, *no.* I wasn't thrilled with the idea of a barnyard animal sleeping in the corner of my bedroom."

"Well, this is even *more* exciting than Phil," I announced. My voice was ecstatic over the idea of getting a rise out of him again. It was literally one of my favorite things. And after his little "fear of

heights" test last week, I was really itching to one-up him again. Although, it should be noted, that test had gifted me with the *most powerful* orgasm of my *entire life.*

But those were just minor details, right?

"Get ready, Thatcher, because guess what? You're going to be a
Big Brother!"

"Huh?"

"A Big Brother!" I repeated.

"What are you talking about?"

"I signed you up to be a Big Brother for the Boys and Girls Club
of Manhattan."

The line went silent before he finally asked, "Why on earth would
you do that?"

"Because I felt like it was the next big step in our relationship," I
explained as a devilish grin kissed my lips. "It will prepare us both for
kids someday."

"How does *me* being a Big Brother prepare *you* for kids?"

This fucker. He kept my bullshit game on its toes.

And I kind of loved it.

And him.

"You can teach me everything you know. One of us has to be
the expert on children, and I just felt like this was more your realm
than mine," I explained. "There are just a few confidentiality papers
and other legal mumbo jumbo that you have to sign, but otherwise,
you're all set. You'll get to meet your little brother next week!" I exclaimed, but stopped abruptly in the middle of the sidewalk when I
came across a booth with the word *GuyFi* displayed on the side.

My eyes scanned the fine print below the logo. *Masturbation
Booth for men that comes equipped with a chair, a privacy curtain, and
a laptop.*

"What in the ever-loving fuck is this shit?"

A twenty-something woman dressed in Doc Martens and a ba-
by-doll dress stopped beside me and stared at the booth with a dis-

gusted look on her face. "Gross, huh?"

"What shit?" Thatch questioned, but his call wasn't my number-one priority anymore. I needed my own answers, and I needed them now.

"How long has this been here?" I asked her.

"I think about a month." She shook her head. "I swear, girlfriend, New York just keeps getting weirder, and men are pigs," she added before resuming her stroll down the sidewalk.

I agreed with her one hundred percent. My blood started to boil, and my anger rose by the second as I continued to glare at the vile display.

"*Cassie,*" Thatch voiced louder in my ear. "What shit?"

"This shit!" I shouted and pointed to the booth in an erratic gesture, even though he couldn't see me. "This fucking jerk-off booth in the middle of the sidewalk!" I stomped my boot-clad heel against the concrete.

"And it figures it's just for men! What if I'm a horny broad who needs to rub one out?"

For fuck's sake, I *was* a horny broad.

"Can I not go into this stupid little booth and work things out?"

"Cass—" he tried to interrupt me, but it was too late. I was already on a tirade.

I pointed at a man walking past me. "How about you, baldy? You need alone time to tug on your wang?" He averted his eyes and picked up his pace to an almost sprint and crossed the street in a blur of uncomfortable avoidance.

"*Cass—*"

"Hey, guy in the red hat! What about you?" I gestured toward the booth. "You need a little afternoon jerk sesh before you head back to work?" I threw my hands in the air in disgust. "Fucking perverts! Goddammit, Manhattan! Get your shit together!"

Why couldn't they choke the chicken at home into their socks or in the bathroom at work like every other goddamn guy in the country?

"Hey, Crazy." Thatch's loud voice caught my attention.

"What?" I snapped.

"Stop verbally assaulting every man who walks past you."

"I can't help it, Thatcher. I'm appalled."

Quite frankly, it was probably more about the blatant gender discrimination than anything else.

"Wait, where are you?" he asked. "Are you on the corner of 28th and 5th?"

"Yeah, why?"

"Do you have the Big Brother paperwork with you?"

"Um, yeah."

"Fantastic. I'm in the booth, enjoying my lunch break. Just bring them in here."

My face scrunched up in confusion. *"What?"*

"Bring the papers in here," he instructed again, speaking slowly as if that'd help me understand.

"Shut up, you liar. You're not in that booth."

"Just come inside the *GuyFi* booth, honey. I could use your tits for the motivation. All of the commotion outside the curtain has kind of ruined the mood."

"How'd you know it's called a *GuyFi* booth?"

"How do you think? Because I'm in here."

My jaw dropped, and before I could think through the situation with a rational head, I was stomping toward the booth like a madwoman. I fisted the black curtain and yanked it back hard enough to shake the walls of the metal cubicle.

The second my eyes met the shocked expression of a guy I'd never met before, holding a penis I didn't recognize, I shrieked. "Oh my God, I don't know that dick!"

"Close the curtain!" the man shouted. "Close the fucking curtain!"

"Sorry," I apologized and yanked the curtain shut. Then, on a whim, pulled it open to add, "Happy jerking!" before closing him back in.

Thatch's loud, boisterous laughter filled my ear as I damn near sprinted away from the booth.

"You're such an asshole!" My words had the undertone of a wheeze thanks to the adrenaline and abnormal exercise.

Thatch never stopped cracking up. "I can't believe that actually worked on you."

"You just forced me, your girlfriend, to look at some other dude's dick, Thatcher. That is totally fucked."

"Aw, honey, do you need to cleanse the palate and come stare at my cock for a few minutes? Would that make you feel better?"

"Fuck you, T. Fuck you hard," I said and hung up the phone before more of his laughter could fill my ear.

Me: Rule #61. Don't trick me into looking at other dudes' dicks.

Thatch: HAHAHAHAHAHAHAHAHAHAHAHAHA

I snapped a picture of my middle finger between my tits and sent it his way, adding the words, Say good-bye to blow jobs for the next three weeks.

Thatch: Hey, now. Let's not get too hasty here.

Me: Too late for negotiations. Three weeks. Suck on that.

Thatch: You can serve me your pussy for breakfast, every morning, for the next month, if you change your mind.

Well, shit. That was a hard offer to decline.

Me: Fine.

Thatch: In the words of Richard Gere, I would have paid four.

Suddenly, I was Julia Roberts in a bath of bubbles on the set of *Pretty Woman*. We really were visual entertainment spirit animals. Sure, I was the hooker in this scenario, but if Julia Roberts could play the part of one, I could too.

Me: I would have stayed for two.

Fifteen minutes later, I walked through the doors of the Starline Diner, glancing around the joint for Georgia and Will. Old-time chrome diamond plates and records lined the walls, and the red pleather on the seats of each booth looked like it was made of glitter.

"Over here, Cass!" My best friend waved to me from a table in the back corner when my eyes didn't immediately find them.

I walked the aisle lined with booths in their direction, careful to keep my eyes away from any patrons I didn't know personally. The tempo of my heart suggested I might still be in danger of attacking an innocent bystander.

When it was safe to look up at the only table I cared about, I found a woman I had never met before sitting beside Georgia's brother, Will.

"Hey, *William*," I greeted with a knowing smirk before glancing back toward his extremely attractive female companion. Generally, I tried to avoid associating my opinions in any way with conventional society, but in this instance, I could really see what the fuss was about—blond hair, blue eyes, and from what I could tell, one hell of a body underneath her silky blouse and form-fitting pencil skirt. This woman was the epitome of stunning.

"She's not my girlfriend," Will responded without even waiting for me to ask, and I smirked.

Will stood up and gestured between us as if we couldn't follow who he was talking about. "Cassie, this is Winnie, my friend *and* boss. Winnie, this is Cassie."

Since I was making a first impression and all, I chose to forgo ribbing him too hard about it.

We exchanged friendly greetings, and Winnie added, "I hope you don't mind that I'm crashing your lunch," as I sat down across from her.

I waved her off. "Don't be crazy. A friend of Will's is a friend of mine."

"Honestly," Georgia chimed in, "anyone who can put up with my brother wins my friendship right off the bat."

Winnie grinned, and Will just laughed it off with ease.

"So, what's it like to be Will's boss?" I asked, more than curious to know all the dirty ER hospital gossip. I knew Will had said she wasn't his girlfriend, but he hadn't said he wasn't fucking her. Trust me, I knew from plenty of fun experience they were not mutually exclusive.

"Is it as terrible as I think it would be?" Georgia asked as a follow-up.

Winnie laughed. "Will's actually one of my favorite residents."

Georgia's expression fell. "Well, that's disappointing. I was hoping you'd have some awful things to say about him."

Not to worry, Wheorgie. I'll get to the bottom of this rabbit hole.

"Okay, I've got questions." I leaned forward and rested my elbows on the table.

"Here we go," Will muttered.

"Tell me the truth. Do doctors and nurses really fuck around with each other like on *Grey's Anatomy*?"

"Oh, yeah!" Georgia's eyes lit up. "Tell us everything the hospital doesn't advertise… Well, unless it involves you two hooking up. Don't tell me any of that."

My pout was instinctual, and Georgia laughed. "He's my brother!"

"Cover your ears, then," I retorted.

Will sighed. "We've never hooked up, Gigi. We're just friends."

"Yeah, Will and I are about as platonic as two people can get," Winnie agreed. "Unless McDreamy walks in, I probably won't ever fuck one of my coworkers."

Will half smirked, half grimaced like he couldn't say the same.

Winnie noticed. "Oh, my God. Who are you fucking at work? How do I miss all the good stuff?"

"I'm gonna guess it's because you're too busy working or taking care of your daughter. And it's fucked, past tense. No office romance currently."

"You have a daughter?" I asked, more intrigued by kids lately than I had ever been in my life. It was a little disturbing, but instead of panicking, I went with it.

"I have a six-year-old." Her eyes brightened and lips crested into a loving smile. "Her name is Lexi, and she's my whole entire world."

"Winnie here is like the superwoman of single moms," Will interjected. "She runs the ED, works eighty-hour weeks, and somehow manages to raise an awesome kid."

"You're totally kissing my ass right now. And no, I will not take you off call next weekend."

Will shrugged. "It was worth a shot."

She laughed. "But he's right. I'm pretty much awesome at everything besides having a life outside of my daughter and work."

Winnie girl was spunky. I liked her already. "I'm demanding that you hang out with us more often."

"Yes," Georgia agreed. "Like actual nights out. Minus Will, of course."

Winnie smiled. "Let me work on getting a new job where my schedule isn't so demanding, and I will definitely take you up on that. I can't tell you the last time I actually went out for a drink."

"You know," Georgia continued, "the Mavericks are looking for a new team physician."

Her eyes perked up. "Really?"

"I don't know all the details of the position, but I know it would be less demanding than your current eighty-hour workweeks. Especially in the off-season. I could email you more info if you'd like."

"Less work and football players? Color me interested." She reached into her purse, pulled out a business card, and slid it across the table.

I glanced over Georgia's shoulder and caught sight of the name printed in black. "Winnie Winslow," I read it aloud. "Hell, that's one badass name."

She shrugged nonchalantly. "Well, I'm a bit of a badass bitch."

Yeah, I was definitely going to be friends with this chick.

Feeling that any gossip about her brother and the blonde had been settled, Georgia's prying eyes came to me.

"And what about you?"

"What about me?" I challenged.

"You are just like your boyfriend!" she accused with a laugh, and as much as I tried to stop it, I started to blush.

"Boyfriend?" Will asked. "What boyfriend?"

My skin started to tingle, and my voice locked up.

"Look at you," Georgia prodded. "You'd think you'd be able to talk about it. You should be able to talk about a relationship where you're living with the guy, for fuck's sake."

"Wait a second? Living with the guy? When did this happen?" Will asked rapid fire, while Winnie looked on with interest.

"It's Thatch," Georgia announced.

"Holy fuck. Why didn't he say anything either?"

My eyebrows pulled together. "It's relatively new."

"You're living together," Will insisted with a laugh.

"I'm aware, thank you very much. I moved in as a prank."

"Nuh-uh-uh," Georgia said. "Don't give me that. When you move in as a prank, you move out. You don't fuck like rabbits and make moony eyes at one another and talk about picking up stuff for each other from the store."

I wonder how hard it would be to wring Georgia's neck.

"I like him, okay?" I admitted in a rush. "He's funny and fun, and goddamn, he's got a cock that won't quit."

"Oh, Jesus," Will cried.

"I like him already," Winnie put in with an encouraging smile.

"Right?" I blubbered in a rush. "The stupid asshole makes it nearly impossible to *not* like him. It's not my fault."

Georgia's smile was practically nuclear. "So...what's that mean? What's going on with you two?"

I shrugged.

"Have you tried talking to him about what's actually going on?" she pushed, and Will groaned. She turned cold eyes in his direction and snapped. "You, shut it. This is girl time, and you'll deal with it."

He shut up and Winnie laughed. "I'm gonna start talking to you like that at work. You obeyed more quickly than usual."

He groaned again and sank his head into his hands.

Georgia turned back to me, but I was happy to use the distraction to my advantage. "Just drop it for now, okay? Let me worry about Thatcher's boner, and you just concentrate on Big Dick." I smiled to take some of the sting out and hoped she'd understand.

I knew I needed to talk to Thatch about where we were. But I couldn't help but worry about the chance that, for once, for the first time in all the years I'd been dating, I was the one who was sure we *were*—an item, an us, all the things I wanted in my life for a long time and maybe forever—and he was the one thinking we *weren't*.

CHAPTER 28

Thatch

"**W**ake up, honey," I cooed in Cassie's ear.

Phil snorted awake and started rooting at my hand.

"Look out, Phil. I'm trying to wake up your mom, and you know that's not gonna be easy."

"I can hear you, asshole," Cassie grumbled into the pillow.

"Oh, so you only sleep like the dead when I'm trying to fuck you?"

"Hey! I haven't fallen asleep on your dick in a while."

I smiled and touched my lips to her bare shoulder. "Let's keep it that way."

"Ugh. God. Where's the coffee? Is there coffee?" she asked, her eyes still closed tight.

I picked up the mug from the nightstand and held it carefully under her nose. "There's coffee."

One eye peeked open to make sure. "Thank God," she said as she grabbed the mug and pushed up to sitting.

She took three sips before bothering to speak again. "What time is it? I feel like ass."

"Don't worry about what time it is."

Her eyes narrowed and jumped to the nightstand to look for what I'd been careful to move earlier. "Where's the clock?"

"Hmm," I said, playing innocent. "Look at that. Phil must have done something with it."

"Don't you dare blame Phil!" she shouted. "What godforsaken time is it? You tell me right now, Thatcher!"

"It's not important. Just drink your coffee and wake up," I tried to say soothingly. She wasn't buying it.

Out of the bed, she jumped and ran, coffee in hand and Phil hot on her heels. He snorted and she cursed and I pushed up and off the bed to follow at a slow walk.

This had to be what men felt like when they were walking to their execution.

"Three a.m.?" she shrieked from the kitchen. I winced. "Three o'clock was made as a time for going to bed, not waking up," she yelled just as I cleared the mouth of the hall into the living room.

"Occasionally, it's a time to get up. Radio DJs do it. As do people with flights first thing in the morning."

"Do I look like any of those people to you?" she asked, and my eyes bugged out with the effort it took not to laugh.

Her hair was a fucking rat's nest of epic proportions, and her tits were hanging there perfectly out in the open like they did so often. Mascara smudged the creamy skin under her fierce blue eyes, and her nipples stood at full attention.

She was the best thing I'd ever seen in my life.

"I'm sorry about the early wake-up call," I apologized. "But I've got a surprise."

Her eyes softened a little. "I like surprises."

"I know, honey."

"All right. I'll get dressed. But Phil and I are putting you on our blacklist. Right, Phil?"

Phil didn't even look up from where he was rooting around at the bottom of the island.

"Fuck, Phil. Would it kill you to give me a little support?" Cassie asked.

"Phil's more of a guy's guy, honey. Bro code and all that. Don't feel bad."

"Well, he better get his act together and remember who brought him here." Her voice dropped to the one women generally used with kids, but the words she used made it creepy. "Or else someone is gonna be on a sandwich, right little Phil boo-boo? Mommy won't hesitate to make a little PLT." She poured more coffee into her cup and headed my direction.

"Wear comfortable clothes," I instructed as she passed me on her way back to the bedroom.

With a little more thought, I added specifics. "And a bra."

She screeched to a stop, leaned into the wall, and turned to face me. "A bra? This better not be another fucking run, Thatcher."

"No running," I assured her. When she still looked skeptical, I broke out the big guns. "Pinkie promise."

She took the two steps back and hooked her tiniest finger with mine. I smiled at the sight of them intertwined.

I swatted her ass when she didn't move immediately. "Go on. Get a move on."

She disappeared down the hall, but she did it walking backward and gesturing one-handed threats to me the entire way.

If you think she wants to kill me now, just wait.

"Where are we?" she asked as we pulled into the airfield. Luckily for me, it was hard to tell what it was in the pitch dark if you didn't already have knowledge going in.

"You'll find out."

"You know, maybe I don't like surprises," she grumbled.

I chuckled. "Yes, you do. Just have a little patience. You'll find out soon enough."

You also wouldn't be this eager if you knew what it is.

"I wish Phil could have come with us," she pouted, and I barked out a laugh.

"You were just threatening to make him bacon, and now you wish he was here?"

"It's called tough love. All the good parents use it every once in a while."

God, she was cute. Ridiculous. But cute.

The gravel of the empty parking lot crunched under our tires as we came to a stop and I put the car in park. "We're here."

She rolled her eyes. "I can tell we're here. But *where* is here?"

I asked her for the one and only thing I needed from her. "You trust me?"

She leaned her head back into the seat and covered her face with her hands. A groan filled the otherwise silent air. "Ah, *shit.* You only ask me that before you make me do things I don't like."

"But they normally turn out well for you, right?"

"I fucking guess," she grumbled. I took her hand between mine and turned it over so I could trace the lines of her palm.

"I'll look out for you, okay? And I don't just mean right now. I'll always look out for you."

"Jesus Christ." She forced open the door, climbed out, and slammed it. I sat stunned for a second before following her on my side. "Now I know how Georgie feels," she went on as she rounded the hood and pushed right into my arms. "Always dealing with that big-dicked bastard saying all sorts of swoony shit."

I shook my head and squeezed her to me tightly. This was how Cassie Phillips reacted when you said something she liked. *Unexpected.*

Bending at the neck, I kissed the top of her head and breathed in the scent of her shampoo. Normally, I'd have been searching to place the scent of a woman, but not her. I knew she used the pink kind of

Herbal Essences, could picture the fucking bottle in my shower, and the thought of it made me smile. It didn't feel like the mystery was gone or some other clichéd nonsense men told themselves they wanted to avoid. It felt *good*. Like we were starting to become familiar in the best kind of way.

Like I knew things about her that other men only wished they did.

"Ready?" I asked into her hair.

"I'm guessing I don't have a choice," she muttered, pulling her head from beneath my chin and looking up at me through her freakishly long lashes.

I didn't answer with words. Instead, I touched my mouth to hers and pulled away, clasping her hand in mine. A smile tipped the ends of her lips up.

We walked across the parking lot in silence, the echo of crunching gravel the only sound in the early dawn light. When we stepped inside the hangar, she had to shield her eyes because of the sudden intrusion of light.

Our companions were waiting across the space, already suited up. Cassie noticed them at the same time I did.

"Claire? Frankie?" She turned briefly to me and then back to them. "What are you guys doing here?"

She didn't realize she was the truly unexpected guest.

Claire stepped forward first, returning Cassie's enthusiastic hug, and Frankie followed not far behind.

Cassie turned back to me when she noticed their attire, and her eyebrows pulled together, but she didn't put it together yet. "Do you guys know what we're doing?"

Claire's face was a mask of trying to figure me the fuck out, but Frankie's slightly annoyed gaze just came straight to me. "She doesn't know what we're doing?"

"It's a surprise," Cassie said in my defense.

"Oh," Frankie mouthed. "Well, then, yes. We know what we're

doing." He hesitated, glancing to me for direction. "It's a yearly activity. We always do this on this day."

I appreciated his attempt to cover for me, but I hadn't gone into this with any plans to keep secrets. I'd brought her here because I wanted her to know. I wanted her to know everything about me, and more than that, I wanted her to be part of it. Every day I spent with her made me want her to be part of everything I did.

"Margo was Frankie's little sister and Claire's best friend. And today was her birthday," I told her freely. "Me, Frankie, Claire—and now you—do this every year to celebrate her life."

Her face softened, and goddamn, I fell right into her trap. So hard, so brash for the rest of the world. But in that moment, she didn't think about herself and how awkward it might have been. She thought about me.

"That's amazing. Are you guys sure you're okay with me being here?" she asked, stepping back to include all three of us in her line of sight and questioning.

"Yes," I answered conclusively with absolutely no hesitation.

Cassie nodded. "Okay."

She smiled at me and then glanced back at Frankie and Claire. Her eyes moved from their faces to their bodies, taking in the protective suit and the harness. "Wait…why are they wearing that?"

I took her hand, pulled her toward the office to grab our gear, and ruined her happy place all in one moment. "Because we're going skydiving."

"If I make it to the ground alive," Cassie yelled over the roar of the twin-engine jump plane, "I'm going to straight up murder you."

My arms wrapped tight around her chest even though I knew she couldn't get away from me if she tried. She was strapped to me because I was her jump buddy, and we were forty seconds away from our jump point.

"I look forward to it, honey," I yelled over the noise, sneaking in a kiss to her cheek and earning a world-class glare and two middle fingers.

Frankie and Claire looked on with smiles on their faces from across the plane.

"I can't believe you're a part of this madness, Claire!" Cassie screamed as loud as she could. Frankie laughed, and Claire gave two thumbs up.

"You ready?" I asked, maneuvering the two of us toward the door as the pilot gave the fifteen-second signal.

"No, I'm not ready, you motherfucker. I can't believe you got me up here!"

With a reach around her perfect body, I pulled open the door and scooted us toward the edge.

"Oh, sweet baby unicorns," Cassie breathed.

"It's okay, honey," I soothed. "Just close your eyes and enjoy the ride."

"Close my eyes? What's with you and always making me close my goddamn eyes?" she shrieked.

"Only until you feel like you can open them," I clarified with a laugh. "I promise I'll take care of you."

One hand on each side of the opening, I moved us to the very edge and watched for the pilot's signal. As soon as the thumbs-up flashed in my peripheral vision, I started my countdown.

"Three, two—"

"Oh, fuck. Oh, fuck, fuck, *fuck*!" Cassie screamed.

"One!"

I shoved us out and cleared the plane. The wind immediately hit me hard enough to knock the scream right out of my lungs. Surrounded by no sound but the roar of our descent to earth, I knew the same had happened to Cassie. I would have wondered if she was conscious had she not assumed the position we'd spent time instructing her on.

Her outstretched hands found my forearms and locked on, and I smiled against the force of the wind so hard that my lips started to curl back.

The fall was exhilarating and the scenery unparalleled. But as many times as I'd made this jump before, and it was a whole hell of a lot, the company had never been better. The whole thing had never been better.

I reached for the parachute as we hit our mark on altitude and gave it a solid yank. Slowing down so quickly that it felt like we went back up, Cassie's screams could definitely be heard this time. But they mingled in with manic laughter.

"You okay, honey?" I asked now that she could hear me, and all I got back was a squeal.

"Give me something other than Phil's language, baby," I said with a laugh.

"That. Was. Incredible. Holy fucking shit, I might throw up."

I chuckled and wrapped one of my long legs around hers. "Do me a favor and wait until we're on the ground, okay?"

"I'm not in control," she told me honestly.

"Just look around and breathe, baby. We'll be down soon."

I looked up to see Claire and Frankie floating not too far above us. Claire gave another thumbs-up when she caught my gaze.

"Wave hi to Claire and Frankie," I told Cassie. She looked up and let out a scream so loud I wished I'd been able to cover my ears. But it was happy.

And so was I.

The landing zone was coming up fast, so I started reminding Cassie of the important points. "Remember what I told you to do? Legs up in front of you like you're gonna sit down, okay?"

"Got it!" she yelled in answer.

Down we went, me maneuvering the chute so that we moved slow enough and in the right direction. She did terrific on impact, executing my instructions exactly until we came completely to a stop.

"Wooo!" she screamed in excitement once more. I laughed as I unhooked her from my chest and tapped her on the shoulder to let her know I was done. Before I could move to get up, she turned and tackled me, taking me back to the ground, wrapping her arms around my neck, and pushing her lips to mine.

I had *never* experienced anything better than that moment.

She let me go and jumped up, hopping around from foot to foot in excitement. I watched her smile, and as the sun glinted off her hair, I just *knew*.

I never wanted to do this without her.

I didn't want to do *any of it* without her anymore.

I was in love with her.

"Cassie," I called, and her eyes came to me. Claire and Frankie were landing thirty feet away and her attention was split, so I called her name again. "Cassie."

"What, Thatcher?" she asked. As soon as her eyes locked with mine, I dropped to one knee. We were still nearly the same height.

"What are you doing?" she asked through nervous laughter. I just shook my head and took her hips in my hands.

"Marry me."

"What?" she yelled.

"I said…*marry me.*"

"Thatch," she breathed, just slightly shaking her head in disbelief.

With a clench of my hands, I dug my fingertips into the cushion of her ass and laid down a challenge I knew she wouldn't be able to resist. Because when it came to this, this truly selfish request to have her as mine for the rest of my life, I didn't care why she said yes as long as she did.

"What's the matter, honey? You scared?"

Her brows scrunched, and her eyes searched mine, deep and unrelenting.

And then, after what felt like an eternity, she said the one word that nearly knocked me on my ass and had my heart pounding so hard I thought it might jump out of my chest and into hers.

"Yes."

CHAPTER 29

Cassie

"How much farther until we get to my soon-to-be in-laws' house?"

I glanced over toward the driver's seat, taking in the relaxed posture of the motherfucking one-upper sitting beside me.

Thatch drove down the highway with one hand on the wheel and the other holding mine, the crowded edges of the street filled with trees rather than people. It was like a different world up here outside of the city, the only bonding characteristic the name of the state.

But my concentration on nature was next to none thanks to Thatch.

I knew what he was doing. The occasional tap or soft caress of his fingers to my left ring finger. Yeah, I knew. He was trying to egg me on, to make sure I couldn't forget what I'd agreed to or what this trip meant. Maybe he should have been soothing my nerves or whispering encouraging mantras into my ear, but I sure as hell wouldn't have been if the roles were reversed.

All I knew was, despite our attitudes toward nearly everything, the proposal had felt serious. Serious in nature and serious in meaning. Of course, I hadn't asked him about it like a fucking coward. It was so unlike me, but…everything was so good. And I didn't want to ruin it with details.

This just meant I had to figure out where to go with this little prank war next. I wasn't sure about the particulars, but the possibilities lay somewhere between an unplanned pregnancy, hiring Dean as my wedding planner, or me wearing a strap-on, and this time, the war would be waged outward—against our friends—as a unit.

I was positive I'd find a perfect middle ground—or a nice balance of all three.

Although, I wasn't sure if a pregnant woman wearing a strap-on was a violation of some unspoken rules of morality. I'd have to Google it when we got home.

Thatch grinned beside me. "About twenty minutes or so, honey. You getting nervous?"

"Me? Nervous?" I scoffed. "I haven't been this excited since *Magic Mike XXL* came out, and even that feels a little lame in comparison. And that's saying something, Thatcher. I almost caught a glimpse of Channing's cock in that one."

"You're excited to meet my parents?"

I tapped the handle of the passenger door. "*Oh, yeah*, baby. I get to meet my future in-laws. Check out teenage Thatch's masturbation suite. Talk your mom into showing me pictures of baby Thatch. I feel like you're taking me to a sex shop," I said with a waggle of my brows. "I won't even know where to start." I was excited and surprisingly comfortable, given the situation. But Thatch was at ease, so I was too.

"I should've strip-searched you before you got in the car. If you pull a black light and white gloves out of that suitcase you call a purse, I'm carrying your ass straight back to the car."

"Shut up. You're making me horny," I said, and he winked. The music faded with a quick flick of my wrist, and I grabbed my phone from the console. "Did you tell Kline about our engagement yet?"

He shook his head.

Hmm. The gossip train had slowed. Though, I guess it had been only a couple of days since he'd demanded I enter the ultimate lifelong prank war. Because that's what a marriage between Thatch and me would mean—a lifetime of one-upmanship and laughs. My chest felt warm and heavy at the possibility.

"Perfect." I hit Georgia's number in my contacts and prepared myself for one of the best conversations I would probably ever have with her.

"Put her on speaker. I need to hear this."

My body buzzed with the thrill of having a ready and willing accomplice while I tortured people. I tapped the speaker icon, and Thatch and I waited, practically bouncing in our seats, until Georgia picked up on the third ring. "Hey, Cass!" she greeted in her normal bubbly voice. Thatch smiled out of the corner of my eye. "What are you up to?"

"Oh, not too much. Just heading to meet the parents." Thatch smiled again, and I decided right then maybe solo gigs were better. This fucker's attractiveness was distracting.

Everything in my head slowed as I tried to force my concentration back to the conversation with Georgie.

"You're on a plane right now?" Confusion swirled up and out of the phone like tear gas.

"Not my parents."

"Then whose parents?"

"Thatcher's parents. Who else's parents would I be meeting?"

She laughed. "Honestly, I'm not sure. But I didn't think you'd be on your way to meet his either. I need to get my calendar and mark this date down. This is a momentous occasion that should be documented."

Thatch flashed me a smirk as he got off the exit for Frogsneck.

"Go ahead and keep that calendar out, because there's a few other dates I need you to mark down."

She groaned. "I'm not watching Phil. I'm busy. Every day until I die."

I grinned, and Thatch squeezed my knee. "How does October 28th sound for a wedding? Will that give you enough time to plan my bachelorette party?"

Part of me fluttered at the thought of walking down a multicolored leaf-covered aisle toward Thatch at sunset. I focused on Georgia instead of putting the cart before the horse. Pranking our friends was one thing, but we hadn't even discussed this in any real terms yet. Planning it in my head might jinx it.

"Huh?"

"Will you be my matron of honor?" A few fake tears pooled at the corners of my eyes. *Fuck, they must be missing me in Hollywood.*

"Matron of honor?" She sounded baffled, and it made me smile more.

"Are you going to answer every one of my questions with another question? If that's the case, it's going to be really fucking hard to accomplish anything in this conversation."

"Are you having a stroke?"

"Are *you* having a stroke?" I repeated.

"What are the signs? I think I might be," she muttered.

"Kline really needs to stop banging you into the headboard, G. I think you're losing brain cells," I teased.

"I agree, sweetheart," Thatch chimed in. "You're not as quick as you used to be."

"What in the hell is going on right now? *Kline!*" Georgia called away from the phone. "Kline! Get your ass in here!"

A few seconds later, Kline's voice was muffled in the background. "Jesus Christ, Benny. What's wrong?"

"I think something is wrong with Cassie and Thatch!" she continued to shout.

Thatch and I grinned at one another.

"What?" It was Kline's turn to sound confused.

"Something is wrong with Cassie and Thatch! I think they've been abducted by aliens. Or possessed. Call a priest! I know zilch about exorcisms, but I know we need a priest. Get Maureen on the phone. I bet she knows a Catholic priest who can help them," she rambled.

"Give me the phone, baby," Kline coaxed in a calm voice.

A rustling noise echoed from the receiver, and then he was on the line. "Why is my wife looking through the yellow pages for priests right now?"

"Why does your wife have a phone book is what I wanna know?" Thatch chimed in. "I haven't seen one of those since 2005."

I ignored him and started a conversation of my own. "Hey, Big Dick, how's it hanging? Thatch has a big question to ask you."

"Fuck, honey, I haven't decided yet," he played along. "Can I have two best men?"

GEORGIA would like FaceTime popped up on my phone. I showed it to Thatch, and he nodded with an amused glint in his eyes.

Two seconds later, Kline's face filled my screen. "What is happening?"

"Get excited, Brooks," I said with a smile. "Because Thatch and I are getting married!"

Kline's eyes narrowed, but before he could say anything, Georgia's face replaced his. Her blue eyes were practically bugging out of her head. "Are you fucking with me right now?"

"Of course not, Wheorgie. I thought you'd be more excited about this. Aren't you happy for us?" I feigned concern.

"No. No. No." She kept shaking her head. "There's just no way. I know you're screwing with me."

Thatch tilted the screen toward his face. "We're not screwing with you, Georgia girl. Your beautiful best friend is going to be my wife."

I turned the phone back to me, and I had to fight the urge to laugh when I saw Georgia's face scrunched up in absolute shock. "How many months do you need to plan my bachelorette party? I know you're busy at work, and I don't want to overwhelm—"

Her jaw headed straight for the floor. "You're serious?"

I nodded.

She looked away from the screen and took a deep breath. Eventually, her eyes met mine again. "He asked you to marry him?"

I nodded again. "Yes."

"And you said yes?"

"Yes."

"And you want me to be your matron of honor? Because you're really getting married?"

"Yes."

"How are you being so calm about this right now? This is, like, a big step, Cass. Like, the biggest step you can possibly take into a pool of lava that will swallow your soul for life."

"Hey!" Kline said through a laugh in the background. She turned to him with a soft smirk and wild eyes. "Except us. Our marriage isn't like that."

Kline shook his head. "Yeah, right."

I shrugged and bit back my smile as I went in for the kill. "You know, the marriage part isn't scary to me. The unplanned pregnancy? Yeah, not gonna lie, that scares me a little bit. But it has nothing to do with Thatch being my baby daddy and more so with the fact that my boobs are already big. I mean, can you imagine what they're—"

She looked like she sucked on a lemon. "You're pregnant?"

"I can't be one hundred percent sure yet. But—"

"You're pregnant?"

"The wedding makes sense now," Kline muttered in the background.

I ignored him and focused on Georgia, giving in a little and changing the storyline just slightly. "Well, no, not yet. But I think I'm ovulating, and Thatch is like real virile, if you know what I'm sayin'."

She put a distressed hand to her face. "I think I need to lie down."

"Will you and Kline be the godparents?"

The screen flashed across their kitchen in a blur until it hit the ground with a loud thud. Footsteps echoed across the hardwood until

Kline's face came into view again. "I'm convinced you're trying to kill my wife."

I couldn't hold back the laughter. "Okay, so the pregnancy thing was a joke, but I couldn't help myself."

His face turned skeptical. "You two are really getting married?"

Thatch tilted the phone toward himself again. "I want Vegas for my bachelor party, K. But I think Wes should plan it. No offense, but his pockets are deep and won't have us cruising the Strip in a mini-van."

"You've got to be shitting me right now."

"Just hang up the phone, Kline!" Georgia shouted in the background. "Just hang it up and call 911. I think they've pranked each other into having nervous breakdowns."

Thatch chuckled and I smirked.

"I want to hear you say it," Kline said, his blue eyes scrutinizing Thatch's face. "Tell me you're getting married."

Thatch stopped at a red light and gave Kline his full attention. "I'm getting married."

"Tell me you asked Cassie to marry you."

"I asked Cassie to marry me."

"Tell me you want to spend the rest of your life with her."

Thatch paused for a few seconds, and then his face lit up with a soft grin. "I want to spend the rest of my life with her."

My breath caught in my lungs when I heard those words pass his lips. His response felt way too genuine to just be playing along. Half of me had begged the gods to make him serious, while the other half lobbied for the exact opposite. Because I needed both to be a reality. Him joking was the only thing keeping me from freaking out.

He's not joking, the little voice in my head told me, and then answered itself with, *thank God.*

What in the fuck was happening to me?

My brain screamed one word: *love.*

My stomach clenched in response.

I fought the urge to slap Thatch in the dick. Or in the face. Or maybe I needed to slap myself. Someone in this car needed to have some sense knocked into them.

But my heart? Yeah, it motherfucking smiled.

Kline stayed quiet for a minute, and then his face morphed into a huge smile. "Holy. Shit." His smile got even bigger. *"Dude?"*

Thatch returned the smile. "Dude."

"Well, I'll be damned. Congrats, buddy. I'm happy for you."

"Thanks, man," Thatch answered. "We're almost to my parents' house. Give Georgia girl a kiss for me, okay?"

Kline flipped him off. "Tell Cass I'll have my wife call her when she's wrapped her head around this *and* forgiven you guys."

I ended the call as Thatch took a right onto a dirt road.

And before I could slip my phone back into my purse, it pinged with a text notification.

Georgia: We're not friends anymore.

Me: Yes, we are.

Georgia: You should've worn a bra to meet his parents.

Me: I know your game, G.

Georgia: His mom is going to think you're a floozy.

Yeah, she was definitely trying to freak me out as payback.

Me: I'm not taking the bait on this one.

Georgia: You really want me to be your matron of honor?

Me: And my future child's godmother.

Georgia: Even though I hate you right now, I love you. I'll be anything you need me to be. Even if I think you've lost your mind. You better call me tomorrow. You've got some serious explaining to do.

Me: I love you too, Wheorgie. We'll chat tomorrow.

A few minutes later, we pulled up in front of his parents' house, and he shut off the engine. He turned in his seat and took me in with amused eyes. "That was actually more fun than I thought it would be."

"I know, right?" I laughed. "I should probably feel a little bad about it, but man, I can't help myself. Georgia is easily one of my favorite people to mess with."

He glanced toward his parents' house and back at me. "You ready?"

Shutters and window boxes framed the summery floral wreath on the front door. Before I could think of what that might mean about Thatch's mom, I took a little breath and dove in with both feet.

"Let's do the damn thing. Let's show Ken and Sally I'm actually a really nice girl who just so happens to have a fabulous rack."

"Let's not get *too* far ahead of ourselves," he teased, and I flipped him off.

He laughed in response, but he hopped out of the car and walked around the front to open my door and help me out. "Come on, honey," he said as he led me up the porch steps. My feet felt a little heavier than normal, so I leaned on him a little extra. "I've got a surprise for you."

I tilted my head to the side, confused, but I didn't get a chance to question him. The door swung open, and both of his parents greeted us with wide smiles.

"Mom, Dad, this is my fiancée, Cassie," Thatch introduced us.

Wow. Introducing me as his fiancée right from the get-go. *Definitely not joking*, my brain taunted.

I held my breath for his mother's reaction to turn from welcoming to murderous—because, yeah, I generally made a great first impression, but my tits weren't usually mom-friendly, if you know what I mean. But she did the complete opposite of what I had expected. She ignored Thatch completely and made a beeline for me, pulling me straight into her arms.

"Cassie, it is so great to finally meet you!" she exclaimed and hugged me tightly. She leaned back and took me in with soft eyes and an easy smile. "I can't tell you how excited I am to finally meet the woman who can keep my Thatcher in line."

"Finally?" I blurted without thinking. We hadn't been together long enough to use words like finally.

"He's been talking about you since Kline got married."

I whipped my head to the side.

Thatch's deep chuckles filled my ears, and a barely-there blush rosied the cheeks under his scruff.

"It's so nice to meet you, Mrs. Kelly," I answered as I pulled myself together. My smile was confused but genuine. The idea of being on his mind that long made my chest ache.

"Please, call me Sally."

Thatch pouted. "No hug for me, Mom?"

She waved him off and wrapped her arm around my shoulder. "Isn't she gorgeous, Ken?" she asked her husband.

"Too pretty for Thatch, that's for damn sure," Ken remarked with a smirk. "Seriously, Cassie? Is he blackmailing you? Do we need to alert the authorities? Blink twice if he kidnapped you. Three times if you fear for your life."

The teasing personality was a family trait. I loved his parents already.

I blinked three times, and his dad cracked up.

"Turncoats," Thatch responded. "You've known her for all of two minutes, and immediately, you're on her side."

Both of his parents grinned, and his mom finally wrapped him up in a loving hug. "I'm glad you're home, sweetie. But I have a feeling she's less trouble than you are."

"Thanks, Mom," he replied with a grimace before smiling down at her with affectionate eyes. Right off the bat, it was apparent he was very close with his folks. The idea warmed my heart. "But she's definitely not less trouble."

My warm heart felt ragey all of a sudden.

"Well, let's go inside," Sally insisted, unfazed. "Dinner is almost ready."

"Dinner was delicious." I dried off the last dish and set it in the cabinet carefully. Sally had served us dinner on the good china, and a constant film reel played in my mind of somehow shattering all of them. But I wanted to make a good first impression, and if I knew anything from Rom Coms and my first encounter with Claire, helping a woman clean up when no one else did usually racked up serious points.

Sally grinned and wiped her hands off with a dish towel. "I'm glad you enjoyed it."

"I did. Thank you so much for having me."

"You're welcome here anytime, sweetheart." She lovingly tucked a strand of hair behind my ear. It seemed intimate in a way I wasn't expecting, like she really did intend to consider me a daughter. My thought-crazed brain wasn't exactly sure what to make of it right then, but I knew I'd figure it out eventually. "I hope you'll force Thatcher to stop by and see us more often."

The longing in her voice made me nod without hesitation. "Consider it a done deal."

"I have a feeling you know all the right things to say and do to keep my son on a tight leash. And I can't tell you how happy that makes me. He's a good boy, but someone needs to keep his ass in line."

I laughed. Little did she know, I never had walked very straight myself. I'd do my best not to burst her bubble, though. "Speaking of him being a good boy, I'd love to see some baby photos." I thought it over. "Or blackmail-worthy stories and photos of teenage Thatch."

"Oh, sweetheart. All you have to do is say the word."

"Yeah, I think it's time I steal Cassie before you bust out the scrapbooks, Mom." Thatch walked into the kitchen and wrapped his arms around my waist. "I know your game, and this is me effectively blocking it before you get started."

Sally held up her middle finger in response, and I died laughing.

Thatch feigned offense. "I swear, the two most important women in my life are the ones who flip me the bird more than anyone else. I'm feeling seriously short on the love right now."

His mom grinned at me and retorted, "Your head is already big enough, Thatcher. If we showered you in love all the time, you wouldn't be able to walk upright."

"Sally! Come sit on the couch and give me some sugar, honey!" Ken called from his cozy spot on the sofa in the living room.

"I'm too busy cleaning up after you to toss out affection!" she shouted back, but she still managed to meander his way.

"Are you ready for your surprise?" Thatch whispered into my ear once we were alone in the kitchen.

I looked up at him with curious eyes. "What surprise?"

He kissed the tip of my nose and took my hand, leading me out the terrace doors and through the backyard. He urged me to sit down on a bench that rested beneath the shade of a big oak tree before taking a deep breath, reaching into his pocket, and pulling out a small black box.

Flies, small birds…waterfowl—any or all of them could have flown right into my mouth for as wide as it opened. "What are you doing?"

He smiled and got down on one knee in front of me. The tiny hinges squeaked lightly as he popped open the box, and my eyes met the sparkly, gorgeous, overwhelmingly beautiful sight of a pink diamond nestled in the center of a platinum band.

It was the one and only ring I had ever pictured as my perfect engagement ring.

Definitely, definitely not joking, my brain whispered in awe.

Was he fucking serious right now?

I slapped him clear across the face.

"Ow, fuck, Cass," he said, but he kept grinning like a lunatic.

I pointed an accusing finger in his direction. "How did you know about this ring?"

"Because I know you." I narrowed my eyes. He wasn't *that* good. "And maybe you mentioned this ring to me several months ago when we were searching for a missing cat."

I shoved his shoulder hard enough that he nearly fell back on his ass, but somehow, he stood his ground and just kept smiling like this crazy proposal made any sense. Like I wasn't completely losing my shit. Like it was normal to propose to someone. *Twice.*

"That was forever ago. How did you even remember that? Are you on drugs?"

"There are certain things I'll never forget. In my lifetime, so far, most of those memories include you."

I stared down at him in shock, and my heart continued to pound inside my chest. I felt like it was trying to escape my body.

His eyes softened to caramel. "Be my wife, Cassie Phillips."

I stood up and paced in front of him. "Jesus H Christ," I muttered to myself.

He grabbed my hips and stopped my momentum. "Marry me, honey. Spend the rest of your life making outrageous, wild, insane kinds of trouble with me."

I smacked him in the dick so hard that he fell onto his side and held his balls.

"Ow! Holy fucking shit!"

I snatched the box out of his hand and stared down at the ring while he lay fetal and struggled to catch his breath. "This isn't really going as planned," he wheezed.

I took in the gorgeous ring, and my heart grew three sizes.

This was my ring. *The* ring.

God, he was such an idiot. A perfect idiot. My idiot. But a fucking idiot for sure.

And for some reason, I didn't ask any of the questions a sane human being would ask in that moment. What this meant for us or if he was sure or if he thought it was fucking crazy that it had all started as a prank.

Love had taken over. And I was finding, when it came to that stupid four-letter word, all rational thought fled the building. Love made you senseless—*me, more so*—and it made you follow your heart even if your brain was shouting, *What in the fuck is happening right now?*

We had never once exchanged the sentiment, but as I stared into the eyes of this man, who looked like he might want to strangle me or possibly needed to ice his balls, I knew it didn't matter. My heart had taken control and was driving this crazy train of spontaneity.

Eventually, Thatch got himself to standing and made his way over to the bench and sat down.

I stomped my way over to him and held the box in front of his face. He covered his crotch and stared up at me with confusion.

"Yes." I shook the box in his face.

His brows rose to his forehead. "Yes?"

"*Yes, you crazy asshole,*" I said and held out my left hand. "Put that gorgeous fucking ring on my finger before I slap you in the dick again."

Thatch sat there for a few moments just gazing back me, his eyes searching mine.

And then, the motherfucker grinned.

He took the box from my persistent hand and slid the ring down my finger. His lips kissed it softly once it was in place. "Come here," he said as he stood and lifted me into his arms. "Kiss the hell out of me with that perfect, crazy mouth of yours."

He didn't have to ask twice.

I wrapped my legs around his waist and crushed my lips to his.

I'd come to his parents' as his fiancée, but I'd be leaving as a woman planning to get married. There wasn't normally a difference, but the change for me was staggering.

CHAPTER 30

Thatch

Cassie was wrapped around me like second skin as we sat together beneath the old tree in my parents' backyard. Crickets chirped and fireflies glowed in the distance.

I didn't want to be anywhere but here, with my soon-to-be wife, breathing her air, smelling her sweet skin, and just holding on to her, savoring this quiet sliver of time where nothing else mattered but us.

I wasn't sure if I'd be able to have kids in the future after the number of times she'd slapped me in the dick, but no doubt, I didn't want to be anywhere else but here, with her—my fucking lunatic of a woman.

Twice, she'd said yes. And the second time she wasn't high off of an adrenaline rush and taunted by a challenge. When she had said yes—well, *yes, you crazy asshole*—I'd seen her wild, untamed heart inside the depths of her blue eyes, and I'd known instantly she wasn't saying yes because she didn't want to fold. She'd said yes because she wanted this as much as I did.

Same fucking page.

Yeah, I know. Same unspoken page.
No offense, but fuck you guys.
We'll talk about it when we're good and ready.

"Come on, Thatcher. Take me somewhere good," Cassie whispered in my ear. My lips curved into a grin at the feel of her mouth skimming lightly across the skin.

"Somewhere good, huh? What'd you have in mind?"

"Nope. No way. That's not the way this works. You just have to surprise me."

I spanned the whole of her knee with my hand and gave it a squeeze.

"Okay, honey. I think I can manage that."

Up and off the bench, I did the same for her, lifting her to standing with ease.

Her breath caught, and my cock jerked awake. "I swear, I never get used to your size."

I waggled my eyebrows. "I've heard it's the kind of thing that takes a while to acclimate to."

Mischief sparkled in her eyes, right next to the moonlight. "Put your boner away, Thatcher."

I smiled and pulled her farther into my arms. My mouth met the skin of her neck, and I inhaled as I spoke. "Not a goddamn chance."

"At least wait until we're not in your parents' backyard," she said through a laugh.

"We better move fast, then, huh?" I teased, pulling away from the allure of her skin and leading her down and toward the garage at a jog.

"Slow down, you giant!"

I just laughed and pulled her harder, making her legs move at twice the speed.

"What is it with you? Always making me run and shit," she grumbled, and I shot her a cocky wink.

"Uh oh," she huffed with a smile. "Not the wink too. I'm gonna be in fucking trouble tonight, aren't I?"

"God, I hope so." Grabbing her hips, I lifted her up, and over my shoulder she went. I ran across the lawn, and she squealed the whole way. I'd had dreams about this—this girl, my Nova, this kind of evening—even if I'd never known it.

The door to the garage slammed behind me, and I put her on her feet so I could get the car ready to go.

She flipped on the light switch for me as I pulled the cover off the Nova and pulled the chain to manually raise the larger garage door.

I folded the cover and tossed it on the tool bench, dumping the keys out of the jar that hung on the cork wall before rounding the car and pulling open the driver's side door.

"What do you say? You ready to go for a ride?"

Cassie's eyes flared at the innuendo, and I didn't think I'd ever get used to a woman who didn't shy away from being challenged. She loved it, fed off it. Every reactive muscle in her body begged me for more.

"I am." She raised an eyebrow, and my smile deepened as though the two were physically connected. "Are you?"

"Always, honey." I winked and she shook her head. Half the time I did it anymore, it was just to see her reaction. I couldn't get enough of it. "Jump in," I offered as I folded into the seat.

"Where are we going?" she asked as she climbed in beside me.

I shook my head and laughed as I reached out to tuck a hair behind her tiny ear. "Nope. No way," I spouted back. "I have to surprise you."

Her eyes turned heated, but I knew her well enough by now.

"What if I…" she started, leaning over and rubbing a hand slowly up the inside of my thigh.

"Good try," I replied, and she scoffed. "Save it for later."

I put the key in the ignition and gave it a turn until the big block under the hood roared to life. The car shook violently, and lucky for me, it wasn't the only thing.

"Goddamn," I told Cassie's tits. "I'm never driving you in anything other than this car ever again."

Her head flew back in an arc of hilarity, and the line of her throat opened up like she was taking a shot. I wanted to drink from her in that moment, the sweet glow of her skin the only thing brightening the dim cab of my car.

Her laughs echoed and the engine rumbled, and with my ring on her finger, I had an honest moment of wondering if there'd ever been a better instant in my thirty-five years of life.

"Eyes to the windshield and drive," she demanded with a wave of her hand. But the fact that she thrust it straight out from her chest at tit level didn't go unnoticed. She secretly wanted me to have what I was after, even if she wouldn't admit it.

I shoved in the clutch, pushed the shifter into first gear, and revved up the idle as we coasted out of the garage.

Cassie settled into her seat with ease, reaching forward to toggle the radio just as a streak of moonlight forced its way through the large front window.

Soft rock filled the silence, Bob Seger's "Night Moves" deepening the already curved line of my lips.

Cassie looked from the road to me several times before sliding her way across the bench style seat and settling her entire body into the crook of my arm.

I didn't waste time pulling her closer and keeping her there as I drove down the gravel line of my parents' driveway and out onto the mostly deserted road.

I'd made this drive before. In this car, with a girl in exactly this position, but I'd never felt this at ease. Like no matter where the night led, it would be somewhere good.

Cassie hummed along to the music as I drove and listened, and before I knew it, it'd been a full ten minutes and we were pulling down the dark, muddy tracks that led to the lake deep in the woods.

"Is this what I think it is?" she asked, perking up and forcing my arm to fall from her shoulders.

"I don't know. What do you think it is?"

"It's either the place of teenage dreams, premature ejaculation, and first-time fondles, or the site of my death."

I laughed. "Door number one, honey."

"Holy shit. This place must be legendary for you. Do you store all the bras in your trunk? There's a shrine, isn't there?" she asked, rapid fire.

"I'll have you know I've only been here with five women." She raised an eyebrow, and I pretended to think it over. "Okay, six." She rolled her eyes. I threw my hands in the air. "Fifteen, max."

"Quit now while you're not even remotely ahead."

"Good idea," I agreed as I pulled to a stop and dumped us into immediate silence with one turn of the key.

"Come on," I called when she didn't move or say anything. I pulled myself up and out of the car and watched as she did the same, gesturing for her to follow me to the trunk with the crook of a finger.

Mentally, she didn't come willingly, but her body wouldn't let her say no.

God, I loved the idea that I affected her that strongly.

"Is this where I have to volunteer my bra as tribute? Because I've got bad news."

"I know. You're not wearing one." We both smiled. "And that's not even remotely bad news."

"Does this mean I have to donate something creepy to your collection? Like teeth?"

I barked a startled burst of laughter. "There's no collection," I told her. "Pinkie swear."

"Oh, man," she muttered as she linked her smallest finger with mine. Mine was double the size of hers. "Now I know you're serious. Breaking out rule number nine."

Rule number nine: No pinkie swears unless you mean it. Of course,

I'm paraphrasing here.

She huffed adorably at the sight of my wink. I ignored the mock frost and popped open the trunk to find all the good stuff still there.

"A blanket?" she asked as I pulled it out and reached deeper into the dark opening. "And a CD player? Wow. Welcome back to the 90s."

The corners of my eyes crinkled as I slammed the heavy metal trunk shut. "Come on."

"Oh, I'm coming. Tell me you've got some 90s CDs in the car to play on that sucker."

"Sorry to disappoint, but it's the radio or silence."

"Or you could serenade me?" she offered.

"I get it. How you'd think I'd have the voice of an angel, what with my obvious good looks and all-around above-average talent, but trust me, my voice isn't performance worthy."

"Are you actually *admitting* to being bad at something? Do you feel okay?" she teased.

"It took fifteen years and several video recordings for Kline, Frankie, and Wes to convince me that I was anything less than superior. I mean, it's so unlike me."

"You're also not top-notch at being modest. Just saying."

"Pshh," I said as I spread the blanket on the ground close to the edge of the water. "Who needs modesty?"

"Um, most people. Public figures. Polite society."

"Girls in cotillion?" I added with a skeptical eye. "Those rules are archaic. The only people who need to be modest are those who feel genetically inclined."

"So, not me or you, I guess."

"Exactly."

"And what *am* I supposed to be?" she asked as I sat down on the blanket and leaned back onto my elbows. It was a completely different perspective to see her from below rather than towering above. I took advantage by surveying the line of her jaw and the curve of her creamy cheek to see which angle I liked better.

"That's easy." She put her hands on her hips and waited for my revolutionary answer. "*You.* All you're supposed to be is you."

"Am I supposed to be sexy?" she asked with a smirk as she leaned down to turn the radio on. The simple beats of Chris Stapleton's "Tennessee Whiskey" were just starting to build on the very first station, and she left it to play softly into the night.

Subtle but sure, she started a sway of her hips, back and forth like a form of hypnosis.

"Oh, yeah," I agreed as I watched them move. "Sexy is *definitely* you."

Her eyes lit, a reflection of moonlight making them shine bright across the distance to mine. Like a tree in the breeze, she moved with ease, just barely mimicking the beat of the music but leaving no doubt that she'd fully embraced it.

She started to move in my direction, up from the outstretched location of my feet to the side of my hip and back again. Her eyes followed mine the whole time, and my heartbeat seemed to build in intensity.

Her back became my focus as she turned away with a flick of her hair and a wave of her arm, before bending at the hip like a hinge. Excited eyes sought mine from the gap between her legs, but the sight of her ass in the air made compliance a struggle.

"You okay, Thatcher?" she asked, her voice a tease.

My answer came out in a hearty rasp. "Yeah, baby. I'm real fucking good."

Back up to standing, she moved quickly, spinning her way to my head and dropping to her knees directly behind it. I dropped flat to my back, pushing my elbows down into the blanket roughly.

She leaned over my face, her tits swinging the front of her dress with every sweet movement. I was fucking spellbound.

Her dance was more sensual than overtly sexual, but my dick obviously didn't know the difference.

Sweet Jesus.

I reached behind my head with the cock of an arm until the palm of my hand met the warm skin of her thigh. It was soft and luscious, and I could feel the muscle move underneath it as she continued her torture.

And then my hand wasn't on her anymore as that leg kicked up behind her into a full extension. Her whole body turned on a pivot with a flourish until she fell to my chest—executing a split directly on top of me as though I was an apparatus.

"Holy fuck," I muttered to myself, and she smiled.

"Strip aerobics, baby. You wanna be my pole?" she asked with a wink of her own.

Goddamn.

"Count me in seven nights a week."

CHAPTER 31

Cassie

As we sat at the bar, drinking beers, eating peanuts, and enjoying the ambiance that was a small-town bar, I could still feel the pulse of Thatch between my thighs.

There'd been no stopping him after showing him some of my best naked dance moves under the stars. One orgasm, two, he'd worked me over like we weren't outside on the edge of some random lake, but instead, like we were putting on a porny performance for millions. Just the thought of it made me smile.

But the sex had done the opposite of its usual, waking me up to a level that I knew I'd need something else to soothe the pounding pulse of my energy enough that I could fall asleep. So I had convinced him to take me to the infamous Sticky Pickle for a nightcap.

The satisfied look in his eyes told me I could have swayed him into pretty much anything.

He kept up a steady stream of affection in my direction—kissing my forehead, sliding a lock of hair behind my ear, flashing flirty winks and charming smiles. And every time he grabbed my left hand and kissed my ring, I'd threatened to slap him in the dick again.

Honestly, I couldn't remember the last time I'd had so much fun.

"Shit," Thatch muttered as his eyes glanced toward the front of the bar.

"What?" I asked and swiveled on my stool to watch three guys stroll in through the door. They were loud and boisterous, and my initial thought was that they looked like small-town douchebags looking for trouble.

I turned back toward Thatch. "You know those guys?"

He nodded. "Yeah, I grew up with them."

"They look like assholes."

He smirked. "Hit the nail on the head, honey."

One of the guys made his way to the bar and stood as close to Thatch as was humanly possible without sitting in his lap. "I'll take three Buds, Charlie," he told the bartender before turning his attention to us. "Oh, hey, Thatch," he greeted, and it was anything but friendly. "You brought a friend. How fucking precious."

Thatch ignored him, stood, and turned to me. "Wanna shoot some pool?"

His blatant avoidance had me tilting my head in confusion.

"Uh, sure, okay," I agreed and took his outstretched hand. I let him lead me over to the back corner where three pool tables stood in a row before I started asking questions.

"What was that about?"

He handed me a pool stick and grabbed the rack. "That was me avoiding trouble."

"Was this the same kind of trouble that I had to bail you out of?"

"Exactly that kind of trouble," he muttered.

His body language was all off—stiff neck, clenched jaw, and his normally playful brown eyes were practically black with irritation. I hated seeing him like that, strung so tight that I feared he might snap in half. Thatch needed a distraction, and he needed it quick.

I set my pool stick down and slid my body under and between the long arms that were currently racking the balls. My back was pressed against the green felt, and our faces were mere inches from one another.

His brows rose in curiosity. "What are you doing?"

I wrapped my arms around his neck and grinned. "Just flirting with my fiancé."

"Is that right?" His mouth turned soft, quirking up at the corners.

"That's right, baby," I whispered against his lips before taking his mouth in a slow kiss. My tongue teased his in a slow circuit.

He grabbed my hips and responded with a dirty, sexy, wet fuck of my mouth as he pressed himself against me. My body was practically clinging to his by the time he found the willpower to pull away.

"Thank you." He pressed one final kiss to the corner of my lips. He knew my game, but he didn't make a big thing of it, so I didn't either.

I grinned while he stood and straightened the bulge in his jeans with amused eyes pointed in my direction.

"Can I break?" I asked as my fingers slid the chalk over the tip of my pool stick.

"Be my guest." He gestured toward the table.

Things had managed to stay pretty smooth after that. We played two rounds of pool without any trouble from the three dickheads milling about the bar. Thatch had won both times and was adamant each win equaled three blow jobs.

"Your math is all wrong," I retorted with a hand on my hip. "One round. One blow job."

"I'm a numbers guy, honey. My math is never wrong."

I laughed and flipped him off.

"Just rack the balls while I go play some songs," I ordered and walked over toward the jukebox, sliding a few dollars out of my back pocket.

As I scrolled through the depressing list of song choices, I wondered if I'd find anything worth playing.

Conway Twitty? *No.*

"The Thong Song"? *Nope.*

"She Thinks My Tractor's Sexy"? *Jesus, take the wheel before someone in this small town dies from shitty music.*

R. Kelly, "Stuck in the Closet"? *Fuck no.*

Shania Twain, "Any Man of Mine"? *Okay, now this I can handle.*

As I waited for the machine to process my credits, the dickhead from earlier decided to make his appearance. He leaned one greasy elbow against the wall and crowded my personal space.

"I'm Johnny. And you must be one of Thatch's fuck buddies." His skeevy gaze honed in on my chest before it finally met my eyes.

I glanced around the room to find none of Johnny's friends in sight and Thatch chatting with an older guy by the pool tables, his back to me.

Looks like I'm handling this asshole by myself. Game on.

"I'm his *only* fuck buddy," I corrected. "I'm his fiancée."

"Oh, that's fucking fresh."

I feigned confusion and battened down the hatches. This fuck-face was going to do his best to surprise me, but he didn't have one goddamn clue who he was dealing with. "What was that, Joanie?"

"It's *Johnny,* and I said *that's fucking fresh.*" He flashed an evil smile. "How much are New York hookers these days, dollface? I'm sure I've got enough cash on me tonight to take your pussy for a ride."

Dollface? Man, oh man, this guy *really* had no idea who he was trying to fuck with.

"*Joanie,* you wouldn't know what to do with a pussy if it smacked you in the face and said *lick my clit.*"

His face turned hard as stone.

Obviously, I'd hit a nerve. Which wasn't that hard to figure out. Guys like Johnny didn't get pussy. Guys like Johnny got their right hand, a bottle of lube, and fuzzy porn in their parents' basement. And if they did somehow manage to get some, they juggled and jostled it until it couldn't take one more fucking second.

"Aw, Joanie. It's okay." I schooled my face into a sympathetic smile. "One day you'll find your perfect hooker who's willing to take one for the team and let you pay her to fuck you. Keep your chin up, Joanie. It'll happen."

He got all up in my personal space, his harsh breath smacking me in the face. "You must be a special kind of *bitch*. You'd have to be to marry a *murderer*."

Murderer? Yeah. I knew without a doubt whatever bullshit Joanie was peddling was purely fiction. And now I understood why Thatch had ended up in jail the last time he was home.

The asshole just stood there, staring down at me, and his mouth morphed into a devious grin. *That's it, motherfucker. Keep smiling,* I thought to myself as I stared up at him, a spineless man picking fights with women who were half his size.

He had some balls; that was for fucking sure.

But so did I. And mine were bigger.

"*Cass*—" Thatch called from behind me, but he was too late. No way was I walking away from this fight. And it's not like I couldn't defend myself. You didn't walk around with a mouth like mine without knowing how to throw punches.

I reared back with my right arm and upper-cut Johnny hard enough to knock the grin straight off his face. His body crumpled to the ground within seconds.

I ignored the sting in my hand as I stood over his prone form and looked down at the pathetic display. "Who's the *bitch* now, mother-fucker?"

"*Cassie.*" Thatch's concerned voice grabbed my attention. He lifted me up and away from the scene of the crime, and his hands moved over my face, my arms, my shoulders, searching for any sign of injury. "Shit, honey. Are you okay?"

"Oh, I'm fine, T."

His gaze was wild with concern. "What the fuck happened?"

Thatch's desire to kill the asswipe showed plainly on his face, so I chose my words carefully.

I pointed to Johnny, who was now being tapped in the stomach by the foot of the bartender.

"That guy, Joanie," I responded. "He doesn't have any manners."

Thatch blinked three times like he couldn't process what I was saying.

"*Wait*...did you just call him Joanie?"

"Oh, is that not his name?" I feigned confusion.

He barked out a laugh. "His name is Johnny. But I have a feeling you already knew that."

I flashed a knowing smirk.

Thatch's eyes turned from murderously concerned to filled with hilarity in the span of a heartbeat. "So, you took it upon yourself to teach Joanie some manners?"

I shrugged. "Obviously, someone had to."

"This shit can't keep happening every time you stop by, Thatch," Charlie grumbled behind us as he tried to rouse a snoozing Johnny. "I'm calling the sheriff."

"C'mon, Charlie," Thatch begged as he stared down at me with a tickled grin. "Just let it go. He assaulted my fiancée."

I grinned back.

God, we were both fucking insane. It made my belly flutter and my smile consume my face until I felt like my cheeks might burst.

Charlie laughed incredulously. "He didn't lay a finger on your fiancée. I watched it all from behind the bar. And you know this cock-sucker is gonna try to press charges the second he comes to. Hell if I'm going to be the one who has to deal with Miller tomorrow morning."

Thatch put both of his hands on my shoulders. "Honey," he said with amusement in his voice, "I have a feeling I'm going to be the one bailing you out of jail this time."

"Well..." I shrugged. "It was worth it."

"Hey, Sheriff Miller, do you mind if I use the ladies' room and grab a snack from the vending machine?"

"Call me Bill, darling," he responded from his comfortable position behind his desk—chair leaned back, boots kicked up on the metal table. "And help yourself to the snacks in the break room."

"Thanks, honey."

After I knocked Johnny out in one shot, I got arrested by the Frogstown Police. Sheriff Miller had placed me in cuffs and put me in the back of his patrol car while Thatch had tried to convince him otherwise.

But it hadn't worked. Obviously, my fiancé had been a troublemaker back in the day and had zero pull in his hometown. The sheriff had actually made it pretty clear that if Thatch tried to come with me right away, he'd put him in cuffs right next to me. The sweet fucking giant had looked like he was considering it.

But thirty minutes of flirty banter and fluttering eyelashes had gotten me on the sheriff's good side, and he had taken the cuffs off and given me free rein of the station.

He had even apologized for having to keep me for the required six hours.

Yeah, Bill and I were good buddies now.

Once I took a quick pee break and grabbed a bag of chips from the station's break room, I plopped down behind one of the deputies' desks and mimicked the same position as the sheriff. "Mind if I use my phone for a minute?"

"Go ahead, darling." Bill flashed a grin in my direction before returning his attention to the small TV across from his desk. He was three episodes deep into a *Bonanza* marathon.

Thatch answered on the first ring. "You okay, honey?"

"Oh, yeah, I'm fine. You can pick me up in about thirty minutes."

"I'll be there."

"Fantastic. See you in a few." I ended the call and relocated to a chair beside Bill. "Mind if I join you?"

He glanced over his shoulder and shook his head.

"I love these old shows," I said as I opened my bag of chips. "I used to watch them all the time with my dad when I was a kid."

"They don't make 'em like they used to, that's for damn sure," he answered with a wistful smile.

Bill and I got through another episode of *Bonanza* before Thatch powered into the station to pick me up exactly thirty minutes later. He'd obviously timed it so I didn't have to be here even a minute longer than necessary. He stopped dead in his tracks when he saw me sitting behind the sheriff's desk, teaching him how to use Facebook.

"Honestly, Bill, it's not as hard as you think it is," I told him as I scrolled through my newsfeed. "Plus, it's pretty awesome how you can keep in touch with pretty much everyone in your life without having to pick up the phone."

He chuckled. "I think I could get used to that."

"Well, my ride is here," I said as I logged out of my account. "But don't be a stranger, okay?"

Bill grinned. "Same goes for you."

"Did you get me all bailed out?" I asked Thatch as I stood up from my chair and threw my snack wrappers away in the trash.

"Pretty ladies don't pay, darling." The sheriff didn't give him a chance to answer. "Now, you've had a late night, so be sure to go home and get a good night's rest, okay?"

"Thanks, Bill." I leaned down and kissed his cheek. "Don't work too hard."

I grabbed my purse and walked over to Thatch. "Ready?"

He glanced around the room in confusion. "Did they change jail?"

"What?"

His chocolate eyes were equal parts amused and surprised. "This is not the kind of jail experience I got the last time I was here."

I grinned up at him.

"I should've fucking known," he said as he wrapped his arm

around my shoulder and led me toward the doors.

"Should've known what?"

"That you'd be the one person to get Sheriff Miller wrapped around your finger."

Once we got in his car, I turned in his direction.

"Can I ask you a question?"

His eyes met mine. "Of course, honey."

"And you'll be honest with me?"

He nodded. "Always."

"Why did Johnny call you a murderer?"

Thatch's face grew tight. His jaw ticked several times in response. "Is that what pushed you to hit him?"

"Yeah," I answered honestly. "Obviously, I *knew* his words were complete shit. But it was the fact he had the balls to say something like that. It didn't sit well with me, Thatch. Someone saying something like that about you."

He watched me for a few quiet moments, and I gave him his space.

"When Margo died, she was with me," he explained. "She was spontaneous and stubborn, and when she was set on doing something, there was no stopping her. She made a reckless decision that took her life, and I couldn't stop her. I tried to stop her, but I couldn't."

I grabbed his hand and squeezed it gently. There was more to tell, but he'd tell me in his own time if he wanted too. Knowing that much was enough. "Thanks for telling me, Thatch."

He stared out the window while his thumb rubbed soothing circles over my hand. "Thanks for being you, Cassie."

Eventually, he glanced over at me and smirked. "And thanks for defending my honor."

I grinned. "Thanks for letting me go all *Fight Club* on someone *and* for stopping by McDonald's on the way home."

He chuckled. "You're hungry?"

"So hungry," I groaned. "The Frogstown Police have shit snacks in their break room."

"You've got to be fucking kidding me. You were in their break room?"

"I'm not kidding about that or the fact that I'm hungry." I snapped at the windshield and held my stomach. "Get moving, baby. I've got a Big Mac with my name on it."

CHAPTER 32

Thatch

"You've got to be kidding me," Kline said as he and Georgia walked up to us arm in arm. "You brought the pig? To this?"

"Hey! Watch it, Big Dick. Not everyone's animal is an asshole," Cassie retorted.

"Um, excuse me?" Georgia cut in, and I tuned the women out.

"We couldn't get our usual sitter," I told Kline ridiculously. He looked like he was constipated with amusement—fucking dying to get it out, but it was all backed up in there.

We'd just gotten back from my parents' house last night, but we'd both promised Maureen we'd be here, at her charity Black Light Slide event, months ago. Of course, we'd responded separately, to two very separate invitations. Now, we were a real "we." Living together. Engaged. Fuck, I'd been the one to do it, to demand that it happen, and part of me still couldn't wrap my mind around it.

Two serial daters with nearly blank relationship histories were engaged. *To each other.* I'd have been tempted to call an exorcist if I weren't fucking thrilled to be chained to this devil.

"Georgie!" Georgia's dad, Dick, called from the opposite side of the slide. People filled the closed-down street, and only the bright lights of several light trees on the perimeter made it so you could see anything. The whole thing about a black-light event is that it needs to happen at night.

"Hey, Dad!" Georgia yelled back. We all waved like little puppets in time with one another.

Dick looked to us and back again, trying to find an easy way to get around the slide. It ran nearly an entire block in length, and people clogged the only available space along its sides. When seconds turned into a minute of trying to navigate the people and stuff around him, Dick gave up and just climbed right fucking through it, sloshing the glowing water with his feet and ignoring anyone who called after him.

I didn't even try to stop my laugh as Georgia grumbled, "Oh, for fuck's sake."

Kline wrapped his arm around her shoulder as her mom, Savannah, followed in Dick's footsteps, clad in nothing but a string bikini. Cassie tucked her face into my chest to hide her laughter. She might have even snorted, but when I looked at her, she pointed down at Phil.

"It was the pig."

"Hey there, Kline!" Dick greeted with excitement, slapping him on the shoulder first, then his back, and then finally pulling him into a tight man-hug. Their little father-son-in-law bromance never got old.

"Thatch, Cassie," he acknowledged when he finally released Kline, and then wrapped Georgia in a hug. "This is some shindig, huh? Not Maur's usual charity scene."

I glanced around the neon spectacle. "Yeah, I don't think the crusty upper-class crowd is happy about it, but it seems to be a big hit."

There were more people here than I'd ever seen at one of these things, and the atmosphere was really fucking cool. Glowing shirts and neon-looking water all the way down a giant Slip'N Slide that had to be five hundred feet long. There was nothing adults—especially ones like me—liked more than acting like a big fucking kid. Doing it for the good of someone else was even better.

"Thank fuck," Dick snapped. "Only so many times I can sit through one of those fucking hoity-toity dinners."

"Dad!" Georgia scolded.

"Hey, I'm with Dick," I said, and Cassie agreed, "Me too."

I raised an innuendo-filled eyebrow. Savannah noticed. "Wow. There's some really great sexual energy between you two."

I smiled, but Cassie didn't stop there. She never did. "That's because we're banging like bunnies." When other people got embarrassed, Cassie became emboldened. It was so fucking sexy.

"Fantastic!" Savannah shouted. Dick held out his knuckles for me to give him a pound, and Georgia dropped her head into her hands. "Why me, God?"

"Baby," Kline said through a laugh, tucking her into his chest.

"Where's your mom, Kline?" Savannah asked. "I want to say hi."

"She's here somewhere," he muttered. All our eyes scanned the surrounding crowd to see if we could find her, but really, it was like looking for a little piece of conservative fluff in a giant lint ball.

"Oh!" Cassie pointed out, completely defying the odds. "There she is."

"Maureen!" Dick yelled loudly. I shook my head and looked to the ground. "Here! Here! Over here, Maur!" Kline's mom struggled to lock on to the face in the crowd calling her name.

"Goddamn these crowds," Dick grumbled.

Cassie let go an ear-piercing whistle that silenced the entire crowd and made them turn to us. Maureen's eyes found the group along with everyone else's.

"I knew there was a reason I liked you, other than your rack," Dick told Cassie.

Georgia sighed. "Oh, Dad."

Cassie didn't mind at all. "Thanks, Dick."

I pulled her a little closer, and she laughed. Phil tugged on his leash occasionally but mostly just rooted around at everyone's ankles.

Normally, Kline would have reacted, but I guess a horse-sized dog and his asshole feline lover had really desensitized him to animal distractions.

Bob caught up to Maureen just as she shuffled over to the group.

"Good job on the one-dollar beers, Maur," Bob said, lifting his cup in salute.

"Are you already drinking?" Maureen asked, aghast. "I still have things for you to do."

"Relax. I'll do them. But you can't get a one-dollar beer anywhere anymore!"

"I know a place," I put in, and Kline shook his head. Probably at the image of Bob and me out on the town together.

Bob wasn't deterred, pointing to me with pizazz. "You're on."

"Bob, please," Maureen said. "Can you keep your eyes on the prize?"

"Uncle Thatch!" I heard the scream just as a little body ran into the backs of my legs. Handing the leash to Cass, I turned and picked up my favorite *girl*. I had a favorite woman now too.

"Hey, hey, Princess Mila. Where are your mom and dad?" I asked just as Frankie and Claire came into view. She pointed anyway. The crowd was thick, and they didn't have the same ability to run through people's legs.

"She took off as soon as she saw you," Claire huffed, out of breath, as they made it to us.

I smiled and looked at Mila. "You ready to do your slide thing, girlfriend?"

"I'm not your girlfriend," she laughed. "Aunt Cassie is!"

"Who's this?" Bob interjected.

"I'm Mila," she said in answer. "I'm six years old, and those are my parents." She pointed at Claire and Frankie. "I used to think I was gonna be a school crossemguard, but now I want to take pictures like my Aunt Cassie."

"She better wait a few years to take pictures like you," I whispered into Cassie's ear, picturing the half-naked men, and she smirked.

"Welp," Dick muttered. People had started to go down the slide in the background. "Just saw a nipple."

I bugged out my eyes as Mila asked, "What's a mipple?"

"A—" Savannah only got out one word before Georgia shrieked in panic. "Mom! No!"

"I got this," Claire said as she stepped in and pulled Mila from my arms. Thank fuck.

Meanwhile, satisfied that her mom wasn't going to corrupt any more youth, Georgia had gotten a good look at the nipple offender. "Is that fucking Leslie?"

"Good thing Mila's gone," Cassie muttered in an aside. I looked back to see Claire and Frankie taking her for a closeup view of the slide. She dipped her little fingers into the water and pulled them out to see them glow.

"What's Leslie doing here?" Georgia went on.

"I had to invite her," Kline defended cautiously. "I invited the whole office."

His wife scoffed. "*Ugh*. Why does it have to be Leslie? How is it even possible you haven't fired her yet?"

Kline shrugged.

Her eyes narrowed, and she started quizzing him. "Where's Meryl?"

Kline kept his calm like he always did, assuring her in a very diplomatic tone that he was in no way paying favoritism to Leslie of all people. "Meryl said very explicitly that I'd see her here, and I quote, over her dead body."

All of our heads swung back and forth with their verbal volley.

Dean popped up out of nowhere. "Did you guys just see that? The witch is officially wet. I'm hoping her skanky tits will melt."

"Maybe you shouldn't go down the slide," I told Cass. She laughed and fluffed her tits higher with a squeeze of her arms for me. I groaned, bit my lip, and when my dick jerked in my shorts, I forced my eyes to safer locations.

"Dean," I greeted.

"Hey, Mr. Man. Goodness, you are a tall drink of water. You wanna be my slide buddy?"

"Back off, Dean," Cassie threatened teasingly.

"Shoot." He turned to Kline. "How about you, BDB? You need somebody to grease your Slip'N Slide?"

"Dean!" Georgia yelled through a laugh. "He's still your boss."

Maureen had already flitted off to deal with something, but that was the last straw for Bob and Dick.

"I think we better go do that thing, Dick."

"Good idea, Bob. You coming, Vanna?"

"Sure thing," she muttered as she winked at Dean and spoke to him directly. "We'll chat more later, sweetcheeks."

"Kisses," Dean agreed in dismissal.

I smiled and looked around us aimlessly, only to spot someone I knew. "Hey, it's Clinton."

"Clinton?" Dean asked.

"Thatch's little brother," Kline explained with a laugh.

"There's a little mini-me version of you?" Dean asked with interest.

I turned to get Clint's attention, but I heard Georgia explaining in the background. "Down, boy. It's the Big Brothers Big Sisters program with the city. Cassie set it up for him."

"Clint!" I called loudly to get his attention. He turned on a dime, eyes scanning the crowd. I was easier to find since I towered above almost everyone.

He waved as if to say, "*Oh, hey, Thatch.*" I wasn't really sure if it was out of obligation or excitement. I wasn't exactly used to being forced on someone by an organization. Forced on people by myself, sure.

"I'm glad you came out," I told him as I got to him. "Looks like you've already made a trip down." His skin and big white T-shirt glowed with the fluorescent water, neon green, yellow, and orange tingeing every exposed surface.

He looked down at himself and laughed. "Yeah."

Cassie had set this up as one of her many jokes, but I had to admit I was having a blast. Helping Clint and mentoring him was one of the best things I'd ever done. I didn't know if I was the best fucking example, but I was trying.

"How'd that math test go?"

"All right, I guess."

"Just all right?"

He shrugged.

"Let me know when you want to get together, and we'll go over everything again."

"You don't gotta do that," he said. "You already taught it to me once."

"I know I don't have to," I replied. "But I want to."

His face seemed blank, but I knew he was actively thinking it over.

"You here with your friends?" I asked.

"Yep."

They stood behind him, watching us with interest. I stuck out my fist for a pound. "Okay, man. I'll let you get back to it."

He nodded and turned to leave, but after a brief pause, turned back. "Thanks, Thatch."

I smiled wide enough that I knew my teeth had to be glowing like Ross's in that "The One with Ross's Teeth" episode of *Friends*. "Yeah, man. No problem. See you soon."

This time, I turned to go so he wouldn't have to. Cassie stood watching me while Phil tangled the leash around her legs. She shook her head and winked when I blew her a kiss.

"Where's Will? I need more man meat," Dean pouted as I returned to the group and wrapped an arm around Cass's shoulder.

"He's working," Georgia said with a frown.

"Oh!" Cassie said as though she'd just remembered. "What about Winnie? Did anyone invite her?"

Georgia nodded. "I did. She couldn't get a sitter."

From what Cassie had told me, Winnie seemed like another ball-buster of a woman. I was really looking forward to meeting her.

Always late to the party, Wes walked up right then. "Who couldn't get a sitter?"

"Winnie," Cassie told him. "You'd really like her, actually. She works with Will."

Wes waved it off. "Last thing I need is a woman with a kid."

Kline and I cringed in sympathy.

"That's fucking awful," Cassie snapped.

"Oh no, he didn't," Dean whispered dramatically.

"Seriously. Forget that, then. She deserves better than you," Cassie scoffed, and Wes just shook his head, looking to the men, but not a single one of us was willing to go down with his ship.

Sorry, dude.

I had a woman to think about now.

One I very much hoped would reward me for my loyalty tonight.

Her eyes said she would.

Wild for wild, prank for prank.

As soon as I found someone to watch my goddamn pig, I was going to take that woman for a *ride*.

We looked radioactive as we tumbled through the door to *our* apartment that night. Cassie was wrapped around me like a glove, and I didn't have any desire to come up for air.

I didn't care if the apartment looked like a goddamn pride parade under a black light.

Phil barely made it through the opening before I shoved it shut with the weight of Cassie's perfect body.

"God," she moaned as I ate my way down the line of her throat with my teeth.

"No, baby. *Thatch.*"

Her fingers shot out and pinched my nipple ring with a rough tug. Thankfully, the state of my dick was too important to her right now.

Redistribution of blood flow made the move even more painful. When she licked the seam of my lips, it transitioned straight to pleasure.

I hiked her higher on the door and put my face directly between her tits. Her hands worked to loosen the waistband of my jersey shorts, pulling them and my boxer briefs free of my fully erect dick in one motion. I shoved it against her as soon as it was free, trapping her hand between us.

"You wet for me, baby?"

"I could be wetter," she challenged, and I growled. Phil snorted relentlessly at my feet until finally climbing into my shorts and underwear at my ankles. Cassie looked down and cackled.

"This gives a whole new meaning to having an animal in your pants."

I laughed as she pushed my shirt up and over my head, leaving me completely naked, save the pig and pants around my ankles.

She shoved off the door with her palms to get us moving, and I stumbled, nearly going down in a tangle of epic proportions. Squeals pierced my ears from her and Phil.

I laughed and righted myself before shuffling down the hall with her ass in my hands. She giggled and threw her hands in the air as I licked at her neck.

When we finally made it to the bed, I dumped her down with a flourish and stood back with my hands on my hips. Her eyes gleamed as they locked on my dick.

"You've got on way more clothes than I do," I told her. "Way too many clothes."

She smirked, sat up, and grabbed the hem of her tank top, pulling it up and over her head. I watched as her tits held until the last second and then bounced down, bare and pebbled and perfect.

My dick jumped.

"I could have sworn you were wearing a bra tonight," I told her, reaching out to tweak one nipple with a finger and a thumb. She pushed her chest closer to me and moaned through a smile.

"It's built in to the tank top," she explained as I closed a nipple in my mouth.

"What?" I mumbled.

She laughed. "My bra. It's built in to the tank top."

A drop of precome leaked from the tip of my cock as I pictured my dick between her tits.

"Thatch!"

"What?" I said with a laugh. "Bras are blasphemous. Don't ever mention them in this house again."

"You brought it up!"

Laughing, I pushed up off the bed, sadly away from her tits, and pulled a squealing Phil from between my legs. He took off running as soon as he hit the floor, but he was the last priority on my list right now.

Making quick work of the fabric around my ankles, I shoved it all down and off at the same time as my shoes and socks, and put my knees to the bed on each side of Cassie's hips.

"I think you're forgetting something." She laughed, gesturing to her still-fastened pants with a jerk of her head. But I shook mine as I climbed to straddle her, skimming my way up her body until my dick lined up with her chest.

"Don't worry, honey," I told her. "I'll get to those eventually."

"Thatch—"

"Unbutton them, baby. Touch yourself while I fuck your tits for a minute."

Her chest heaved, and my pupils dilated. *Goddamn.*

"Do whatever you want," I instructed, the game coming to me in an instant. "Slow and steady or hard and fast, work that clit and pump that pussy however you want until you come."

Her eyes flared, and she licked her lips.

"I'll fuck your tits until you get there. It's up to you how long I get."

She reached out quickly and pumped my dick twice and hard.

I looked over my shoulder as she reached between my legs and undid her pants, shoved them and her panties to her thighs and pushed her finger into her pussy to gather moisture.

When she brought it back out and started working it, I looked back to her.

Her eyes gleamed as she grabbed my ass and pulled me to her tits. "Come on, baby. I'll go slow."

I licked a path between her tits and straight down to her pussy, where I lapped at the top to tickle her clit.

She shivered and shoved at my head, breathing heavy with exhaustion.

"I'm gonna make you touch yourself every fucking time."

She laughed and swatted at me.

"Licking your finger clean after you came on it was the hottest thing I've ever fucking done."

Her smile curved all the way to her sleepy eyes. "Okay," she admitted. "That was pretty hot."

Climbing back up her body, I pressed a soft kiss to her lips and then fell to my side beside her, settling into my palm with an elbow in my pillow.

Cassie patted affectionately at my cheek, so I grabbed her wrist, fell to my back, and pulled her over on top of me. Her eyes moved from mine like a river, curving down my jaw to my neck, and then pooling on the tattoo across my chest. "What's this one for?"

"The tattoo?" I asked, and she nodded, settling her chin on my chest and bringing her gaze back to my eyes.

"*Mi Vida Loca*," I recited. "It means 'my crazy life.' I got it when I was twenty-seven. When it first hit me that I'd done it. That I'd succeeded in all kinds of things, and I was in complete control of my destiny. I never expected any of this. The success, the drive. I'm pretty sure everyone thought I'd be doing something menial or nothing at all."

"You were that wild?"

"Yes. But it was more a lack of focus."

She laughed and looked down at my chest contemplatively, tracing each letter slowly. "Yeah, I can relate to that."

She skimmed her fingers across my chest and over to the praying Mary on my arm. "What about this one?"

"That one is for Margo. Well, it's about her, anyway. I got it a couple of years after she passed, from Frankie, right after he opened the shop. I think it was sort of cathartic for both of us to put ink to skin to embody all the things we hoped she'd found in heaven that she'd yet to find on earth."

"Like what?" she whispered.

I ran a thumb under her eye and twisted her hair between two fingers. "Peace. Contentment. She was still so young and restless. Searching for everything and coming up with nothing."

Her nod was unhurried, and her eyes studied mine. I was sure she was looking for some kind of sign that I was over it all, but to me, I never even had to think about it anymore.

I'd never be over the way it happened, but all I felt was Cassie. She didn't leave any room for anything else.

She tapped the word "Trust" on my chest. "Why trust?"

"Because it's the only thing I really need."

"The only thing you need to what?"

"To live," I answered simply. "I don't need to know what's going to happen, or how it's going to happen, or even the why. I just want to know that whoever's making it happen cares about me enough to give me that freedom."

"Mmm," she acknowledged.

She settled like she might fall asleep, so I tapped her on the nose, my heart in my throat. I wanted her to know something that I hadn't bothered to tell anyone yet. "You missed one."

She lifted her chin off of my chest, and her eyes opened again as she'd thought it over. She was convinced she'd studied my body enough to know. It hit her like a truck. "Of course!" She rolled off of me enough to free my arm and turned it over to expose the inside. "Evolve" scrolled across in fancy, rolling script.

"Okay," she said as she traced it. "So what's this one?"

I took a deep breath and blew it out. "That's the first tattoo I ever did."

Her startled gaze jerked to mine. "*You* did this one?"

I nodded. "Last fall."

"What? How? I don't get it," she rambled.

I shrugged and looked to the comforter. "I've been apprenticing with Frankie. They make you do your first real run on yourself. You know, so you don't permanently fuck somebody else's skin up."

"It doesn't look like a first tattoo," she said, excited. "It's amazing."

"Yeah?"

"Oh my God, yes. It's really good!"

My smile would have blinded an airplane. "I was really fucking nervous about that thing for a while. I actually had to go to rugby practice the day after I did it. And of course, I ended up on the skins team. I had this gut reaction that everyone would give me a hard time for how much it sucked."

She shook her head quickly and then leaned forward to touch her lips to mine. "Do you have any more stuff?"

"No more tattoos on myself, but I've got some drawings."

The sheet left me in one smooth motion as she jumped up and

wrapped it around herself, demanding, "Show me now."

Up and out of the bed and boxer briefs on, I led her out of the room and to the second bedroom. When I opened the door, she stomped her foot.

"I can't believe I hadn't snooped in here yet! What is wrong with me?"

Chuckles shook my chest as I watched her spin in a circle, taking in the room. The walls were filled with drawings I'd done, and my notebook sat right in the middle of my sketch desk. She made a bee-line for it and started flipping through the pages.

I had all sorts of different things in there. Original designs, sayings that stood out to me sketched in varying script, and even faces and places that I'd remembered vividly enough to draw.

"Holy shit, Thatcher."

I walked up behind her and put my lips to her shoulder. "Have you ever thought about getting a tattoo?"

She shook her head slowly as she flipped through the pages one a time. "No. I've never felt like there was anything I felt strongly enough about to commit to my skin for life."

I nodded there, right in the crook of her neck, until the tickle of my facial hair made her shiver.

She paused on one page, and I read it over her shoulder. One of my absolute favorite sketches filled my chest with new meaning.

> *She was crazy. Wild.*
> *Chaos & beauty.*
> *My heart.*
> *Mine.*

Vulnerable and soft, she whispered right out into the emptiness of the room. "I want to be yours."

My eyes closed and love overwhelmed me. "You fucking are."

Forever.

CHAPTER 33

Cassie

The huge motor whined as we sped up through a hole in traffic. People barely moved out of the way, but despite our slow progress toward someone's life-or-death situation, I couldn't find it in myself to get angry. It was three o'clock in the afternoon, I was sitting shotgun in a fire truck, and I was in all my motherfucking glory.

"Thatch!" I shouted into my phone over the blaring sirens in the background.

"Cass? Where are you?"

"I'm in a fire truck cruising down 5th Avenue!"

"What?" he yelled. "I'm having trouble hearing you. It sounded like you said you're in a fire truck."

"You heard me right!" The sirens increased in three loud bursts as the fire engine maneuvered through an intersection. "I'm saving lives and putting out fires for the day!"

I couldn't hear his response because the truckload of firemen started to argue around me.

"Goddammit! Move out of the way!"

"Take a left, Ronnie! It's faster!"

"Fuck off, Vin!"

A minute later, the sirens died down and we pulled up in front of an apartment building. The guys jumped out and headed inside while I stayed back in the truck. I was finding that not all emergencies were actual emergencies. Sometimes what one person might call a kitchen fire another would call, *Bullshit, just turn off your stove, moron.*

"Are you still there, T?" I asked into the receiver.

"Yeah, honey," he responded. "I thought you had a shoot today."

"I shot a charity calendar for FDNY, and we finished a little earlier than expected," I explained. "I convinced the guys to let me go on a few runs with them. Do you have any idea how cool it is riding around in the fire truck all day?" I hopped out of the truck and started to pace on the sidewalk. The adrenaline rushes from the last five runs had my body bursting with excited, nervous energy. "I think I want to change my career."

He chuckled. "Sounds like you're enjoying yourself."

"I am," I agreed and watched pedestrians mill about the building, looking for a show. I wanted to tell them to mind their own fucking business, but the last time I had done that, the lieutenant told me to zip it or else I'd get the boot.

Obviously, since boots so weren't a summer shoe, I kept my loud mouth shut.

"Are you busy tonight?" I asked Thatch, staring into the building and hoping I'd see a lick of flames burst through the window. It would probably ruin people's lives, but it would really make mine.

Yeah, I'm an asshole today.

"Just rugby practice and then I'm free."

I grinned. "Wanna meet me for a drink after?"

"Sure. Name the time and place, and I'll be there."

"Perfect. I'll ask the guys where we're going, and I'll text you."

"And by guys, you mean the firemen, right?"

"Yep." I waited for a jealous or unsure reaction most men would've have given in that kind of scenario, but it didn't come.

Thatch merely took it all in stride. Not the least bit concerned that I was paling around with a bunch of muscly firemen. "Sounds good, honey," he answered. "I'll see you tonight."

"Okay. See ya then."

"Cass?" he asked before we ended the call.

"Yeah, baby?"

"Be careful, okay?" His voice was soft around the edges.

Goddammit, this thoughtful dickhead.

If he were standing in front of me, I might have kneed him in the balls.

But instead, I answered, "Don't worry, the only time they let me out of the truck is if I'm sneaking out of it when they're running into a building. Otherwise, the protective bastards are all about proper protocols and fire safety. They're kind of a pain in my ass, to be honest."

"Good." He chuckled. "I like these guys already."

A few beers deep, I strongly encouraged Ronnie to sing karaoke with me on stage.

"No way, Cass," he said through a laugh. "I don't care how gorgeous you are, I'm not getting up there."

I fluttered my eyelashes like a lady and then spewed words that conveyed the exact opposite. "Oh, c'mon! Don't be such a ball sac!"

"I think you mean don't be such a pussy in this scenario," Ronnie retorted.

"Hell no," I scoffed. "Pussies trump balls every time. Those bitches can take a serious pounding. Balls are the sensitive little fuckers. Shit, they'd probably cry during *Titanic*."

Vin chuckled. "Yeah, Ronnie. Stop being such a ball sac."

Ronnie flipped him off in response, but he stayed resolute in his decision.

"How about a game of quarters instead?" Brian offered, and when it came to drinking games, that was one I simply could not and would not refuse.

For the next hour, I spanked the boys at quarters while the waitress kept up a steady stream of fresh beers and rounds of shots. It was a little after nine when Thatch strode through the bar doors, freshly showered and looking sexy as hell. God help me, he made jeans and a T-shirt look better than anyone I knew.

His eyes met mine, and a slow smirk crested the corners of his lips as he headed in my direction.

"Hey, Crazy," he greeted as he leaned down to kiss my cheek.

"Hi." I grinned up at him before turning back toward the table. "Guys, this is my fiancé, Thatch," I introduced him to the six guys seated around the table. "Baby, this is Vin, Ronnie, Brian, Bruce, Eddie, and Matt."

Thatch shook each guy's hand and sat down beside me. When I hopped out of my chair and made myself comfortable in his lap, his eyebrows shot up with amusement.

"I missed you today," I whispered into his ear. "I'm glad you came out."

He kissed the corner of my mouth. "I'm glad you had a good time today."

"I think tonight is going to be even better." I waggled my brows.

Thatch smirked. "Is that right?"

I nodded slowly. "Oh, yeah. That's right."

His gaze made a slow circuit down my body, taking inventory of all of his favorite places, but his eyes really lit when they landed on the flush of my cheeks. It must have been obvious that I was just buzzed enough to break out all of my dirtiest moves. His eyes dove back to my chest as soon as the thought scrolled across my open eyes. I knew I was showing every single freaky intention.

"Anyone need a beer?" Ronnie asked, pulling Thatch's attention from my tits to across the table.

"You buyin' the next round, Ronnie?" Vin questioned.

"No, he's not," Thatch interjected. Memo received. He lifted me out of his lap and placed my ass back in my seat, but not before giving the cheek of it a healthy, *meaningful* squeeze. His hands would be spending time there later. "I've got the drinks for the night, guys." He stood and motioned for the waitress, handing off his credit card with instructions to put all of the drinks for the table on his tab.

"Hell yeah! Thanks, man!" Brian held up his bottle as Thatch sat back down beside me.

"You know," Vin chimed in, "he kind of owes us for driving his girl around all day."

Thatch chuckled, but he knew better than to say anything. He had visions of my pussy in his eyes, and there wasn't any form of male camaraderie that'd make sacrificing worth it. My face scrunched up in annoyance, and my even looser than normal lips flew.

"Hey now, dickhead! Pretty sure I'm the one in control of your calendar photos, and I haven't edited them yet. Things can end up looking a lot *smaller*. Microscopic, even."

Ronnie laughed. "Yeah, but Vin has a point, Cass."

"What's that supposed to mean?"

"It means you're a handful," Bruce added. "I guarantee the city will be sending us a complaint from the old woman you told to *move the fuck along and mind her own business*."

"She was just standing there, in the middle of the sidewalk," I argued. "She was in your way."

"She wasn't standing there, sweetheart," Ronnie corrected. "She was just moving very slowly."

Vin laughed. "Yeah, she had a walker. Give the woman a break."

"Whatever." I scoffed. "That's the last time I try to help you guys out."

They all agreed enthusiastically to my permanent hiatus, and Thatch laughed.

"That will definitely be the last time you'll ever be allowed on a fire truck," Brian agreed with a smirk.

"I don't know why you're acting all high and mighty," I retorted. "You're the one who asked me to slide down your pole about fifteen minutes after I met you."

Brian choked on his beer, and both of his hands went up in the air like he was being held at gunpoint. "In my defense," he responded, meeting Thatch's curious yet markedly less easygoing stare. "That was before I knew she was engaged and that said fiancé had arms bigger than my head."

The guys chuckled around us.

"And she kneed me in the dick the second the words came out of my mouth," Brian added. "I'm honestly not sure if I should be more scared of you or of her."

"Probably her." Thatch smirked and wrapped his arm around my shoulder, tucking me into his side.

For the next two hours, we hung out with the FDNY crew, laughing, drinking, and just shooting the shit. By the end of the night, the guys were asking Thatch to join their basketball league and meet them every Friday night for darts at Maloney's.

Fucking charmer. It didn't matter if was men or women, I swear, he held some kind of conversational gene that automatically made people want to either fuck him, be friends with him, or both.

After I finished off my fifth beer of the night, I hopped back into Thatch's lap with my cell phone in my hand. "Guess what?"

"What?"

"Big Dick is hip to our game."

I held my phone up so Thatch could see my most recent text conversation with Kline.

Me: *Earn fifty free fuel points at Shell by texting "I HAVE GAS!" to this number.*

Kline: *UNSUBSCRIBE*

Me: Error. Could not process your message. Please text '123456789101111121314151617' so that our IT department can assist you with your request.

Kline: Oh, hey, Cassie.

Kline: And Thatch.

Kline: Game over, assholes.

Me: But what if the next subscription is for porn, Big Dick?

Kline: STOP TEXTING ME, CASSIE. And tell Thatch to stop searching for disfigured dicks on the internet.

Thatch laughed, and I nuzzled my face into his neck, letting the rumble run all the way through me.

"Tired?" he asked. He ran his fingers up and down my back in soft, smooth movements.

"No." I shook my head. "Just horny."

He chuckled. "What am I going to do with you, Crazy?"

I leaned back and met his amused gaze. "Take me home and fuck me?"

Thatch tapped the table with his hand and stood while still holding me in his arms. "We're calling it a night." His strong arms maneuvered my body around so that he was giving me a piggyback ride.

The guys groaned their disapproval.

"Oh, get over yourselves," I teased. "He's taking me home so I can ride his pole."

Thatch laughed and walked around the table to shake each of their hands. "I'll keep my tab open for you guys. Feel free to close the place down."

They hooted and hollered and made all the sounds of a good

time, but I'd never wanted to hang around less.

We said our good-byes, and Thatch carried me out of the bar with his hands gripping my thighs and long legs eating up the pavement in relaxed strides.

"Next stop, Thatch's Supercock!" I shouted into the night air.

"And no sleeping until we both come, honey."

CHAPTER 34

Thatch

Thoughts of the night before consumed my sleep. I dreamed about Cassie riding my cock and the feel of her tongue in my mouth and the tug of her teeth on my nipple ring. I'd never considered piercing my cock, but the things she did with the one in my nipple made me come scarily close to actually considering it.

My lips tipped up at the phantom feel of her mouth on me. God, I loved dreams like this.

I could lay here and sleep forever if Dream Cassie kept this up.

Her tongue circled the tip as she took me all the way inside her mouth and I groaned.

That's it, baby.

She started to giggle, and I wasn't sure where it was coming from, but I liked it. It made me harder, if anything.

Oh, yeah. I'm close.

She tightened her lips and increased the suction.

Oh, fuck yes.

Her hand moved up and down on the part she couldn't fit in her mouth, letting all the lubrication from her mouth drip down to ease the motion.

Faster.

Oh man, she was so good at following orders in my dreams.

Fuck yeah, touch my balls.

Her mouth left my cock, and I felt like crying.

"Okay, baby."

My eyes shot open. Cassie's knees grazed the inside of my legs, and her heels met her ass.

"Oh, fuck," I cried in excitement at the sight of a very real Cassie kneeling between my legs and running her hand up my thigh until it met my balls.

Apparently, I hadn't been dreaming at all.

Her mouth closed around me again, her eyes peeking up to meet mine, and I came right then.

Something about the mix of the surprise, her mouth, and the weight of her unabashed eyes on mine made it impossible to hold back. No doubt I sprayed the back of her throat with the strength of my orgasm, but she just swallowed, making her neck bob explicitly.

Phil snorted at the foot of the bed. Cassie wiped her mouth with the back of her hand and climbed down to the end to get him. All while I lay there trying to come back into my right mind. Good God, I was lost in her. In the way she surprised me constantly and never held back. She wasn't embarrassed to be bold, and it made me want to foster it—to constantly create an environment where she never felt the need to be anything but herself.

As soon as Phil was up on the bed, he scrambled forward, and I threw the top sheet over my slowly softening dick. "I'm glad you didn't see that, buddy."

Cassie smirked, and I rubbed at Phil's head, still a whole lot in shock.

"What's going on?"

"I just dominated that blow job."

"You did, honey," I agreed on a grin. "But what did I do to earn it?"

"Nothing yet. It's what you're going to do."

I shook my head and smiled. "And what would that be?"

"We're going camping."

The smile fell from my face just a tiny amount. I caught it before it went too far, but she noticed. "Oh, come on. I went skydiving with you."

"I had to drag you into the plane," I pointed out as I worked to close all of the thoughts of my past back in their pretty little box. *Trust.* Cassie didn't know the details of Margo's death, but right now, she didn't need to. It would only make her feel bad about something she had absolutely no reason to blame herself for. The last thing I wanted was to hold her accountable for Margo's actions. I couldn't think of anything that would piss me off more if the roles were reversed.

I forced my mind back to her, that moment, and the words coming out of her mouth.

"Yeah, that was pretty fucked up now that I think about it."

"You ended up enjoying yourself," I pointed out, picking up her hand and twisting her engagement ring with my fingers. She looked down at the gesture and smiled.

"Exactly. And you're going to have fun now. Everyone is coming. Kline, Georgia, Wes, Will. Even Frankie and Claire."

I took a deep breath and smiled for her.

Her own happiness intensified. Phil snorted.

"Oh, and Phil. Sorry, Philmore. I didn't forget you, I swear," she amended.

"So when do we leave?"

"Right now. You have time for a shower."

"Do I have time for a shower with you?"

"No."

I ran my tongue along my top lip and then bit into the bottom.

"Okay," she caved. "There's definitely time for the special shower."

The sun was at full strength, and the humidity was set to fucking mist when we pulled into the campsite that afternoon. It was a perfect recipe for severe storms, and by the way Kline jumped out of the car with Georgie like there was a fire under his ass, I wasn't the only one who'd noticed.

I glanced back to Frankie in the back seat, and his green eyes said he knew what I was thinking. "We better bust a nut, dude."

"Yep. I'm guessing we've got an hour, tops, before it pours."

"What are you guys, meteorologists?" Cassie scoffed while Phil snorted his way around the floorboard at her feet.

"It's a fucking sauna outside," I explained. "It's not like I had to calculate the atmospheric pressure and wind shear."

"What?" Claire asked.

"Don't ask, baby," Frankie advised.

"What?" I laughed. "You don't like my above-average interest in weather, Franklin?"

"Oh, my God," Cassie cried. "You're a weather geek."

I narrowed my eyes.

"I'm engaged to a fucking nerd."

Claire laughed, and Frankie gave me a pat on the shoulder. "It had to come out sometime, buddy."

"Fuck you guys."

"Aw, don't be sad, Thatcher. Come on. Turn me on. What's the force calculation for my pussy?"

The answer poured out without planning. "Your pussy is usually stationary, and since force is mass times acceleration, it's really my cock that possesses the force in our equation."

"Oh, my God," she squealed. "It's like I don't even know you."

A tiny twinge of something panicked at the thought that maybe she *didn't* know me. What if she found out something that made her decide to move on? I didn't know if I could take it.

Unhappy with that line of thinking, I shut it down completely before it could get carried away. I had enough baggage working against me on this trip. I didn't need anything extra weighing me down.

"Come on, Frankie," I grumbled. "Help me set this shit up."

The sound of Cassie's laughter finally died down as I stepped outside and shut the door. That could have been the soundproofing of my Range Rover, though.

"Why does Cassie look like she swallowed a clown?" Georgia asked from across the site. Kline had her holding one corner of their tent while he staked the one opposite. Tall trees shot up around the entire perimeter, and pine needles made a bed on the ground in between. It was big enough to hold six or seven tents, thankfully. Of course, Wes was late like always, so if we somehow managed to run out of room, the joke would be on him.

Frankie was all too eager to share the cause of Cassie's near on fit of hilarity. "Thatch just showed her his science boner."

"It was bound to happen sometime," Kline shouted. "I think it's some kind of mathematical certainty. After he showed her his other boner so many times, he was contractually obligated to show her this one."

"There!" I pointed as though there was some high court in the woods that would come down with an explanation or ruling. "Jesus. Why doesn't anyone make fun of Kline for being smart?"

Kline smirked and gave me an innocent shrug while Georgia leaned down to whisper something in his ear with a blush.

Fucking hell.

"Come on, Thatcher," Cassie called, having finally exited the car with a squirming Phil in her arms. "Come set up our tent so you can show me your thunder down under!"

Crazy.

Mine.

CHAPTER 35

Cassie

"Let's take a hike!" Georgia stood in front of my lawn chair and held out her outstretched hand. "Come on, lazy bones, let's get some fresh mountain air." Phil tugged at the leg of my chair in an attempt to go to her. *Fucking Georgia. The Animal Whisperer.*

Thatch had been right about the rain yesterday, and truth be told, I'd been impressed as hell by his plethora of random knowledge. I mean, the guy hadn't gone to school for that shit, but still, he had a real understanding of it.

After I buttered him up with some bedtime boning, he'd finally told me that late in college, he'd been restless and searching for things to drown out the white noise. When he wasn't getting Kline and Wes into all the trouble he could think up, he was studying all kinds of things until his mind started to wander again.

The result was one really fucking smart fiancé.

My face scrunched up in annoyance. "Ugh, Wheorgie," I muttered and wished I was anywhere but in the hot heat of the midafternoon sun in the middle of the goddamn wilderness. "It's hot. I'm annoyed. And you're too fucking perky."

Camping was one of those things that was a good idea in theory. But when you actually experienced it—the bugs, the heat, sleeping on the hard ground of a tent—you realized it sucked donkey dick.

She laughed. "Shut up and come with me."

"Why can't Big Dick go hiking with you?"

"Because he just walked down to the water with the guys and Claire to fish."

I slipped my sunglasses over my eyes and leaned my head back, hoping she'd eventually go away if I fell asleep.

"That's not going to work," she declared, and I heard her footsteps crunch against the gravel as she moved behind me. "Get your ass up!" she exclaimed as she gripped the top of my chair and pushed forward. Phil took off as soon as the end of his leash cleared the bottom of the leg.

I fell out of my seat, and my ass hit the ground a few seconds later.

"What the hell!" I shouted and looked up to find my asshole of a best friend grinning down at me with a hand on her hip. "My pig is on the loose now!"

"Might as well give in now. You have to go catch Phil anyway." She held her hand out again, and I eventually took it and got to my feet.

"For the record, you're my least favorite person on this camping trip."

"That's okay, Casshead." She wrapped her arm around my shoulders and all but pushed me toward the trails. "I'll win your love back before the hike is through."

I snorted. "Don't hold your breath."

For maybe the fourth time in my life, I broke into a jog before Phil could wander off to some deserted section of the woods where inbreds lived.

"Which trail do you want to take?" she asked when Phil and I came back a few minutes later.

I had two options, go up or go down, and for some insane reason, my belly didn't drop to my feet at the thought of facing a few heights.

I had a feeling this had everything to do with Thatcher and his need to desensitize me to things. I pointed toward the one that led up rather than down. "Let's see what kind of views we can catch above the water."

She grinned.

"Don't take that as me getting excited about this."

"Oh, I won't," she said but continued with her perfect fucking grin.

As we made our way up the trail, I couldn't help but get lost in the lush views of trees and nature as far as the eye could see. It was a different world from the hustle and bustle of the city. And if I was being a little honest, I was enjoying the change of pace. Besides the mosquitos buzzing and the dirt kicking up into my face and the overall sweaty quality my skin tended to take up in this heat-infested shit forest, it was really kind of nice.

We passed through a clearing and I stopped, staring in the direction of the edge of a cliff that jackknifed straight toward the lake. Slowly, I inched forward until I could peek over and catch sight of the sun glistening off the water. My head spun a bit from the abrupt drop, but I had the overwhelming urge to strip naked and jump in.

"Holy shit, this is gorgeous," Georgia said, taking in the view. "Are you okay, Cassie? I know heights aren't really your thing."

"I'm good, actually." My feet inched a little closer to the edge. "I feel like that water is calling my name right now. It's so hot out here I swear I'm going to end up choking on air."

She held her hands above her eyes to block out the bright rays. "Hey, isn't that the guys and Claire?"

I glanced toward the left and saw our group kicked back on the rocky edge, fishing poles in hand. They were definitely within yelling distance. "Yo, Thatch!" I shouted, and he glanced up in our direction. "Take off your pants!"

"Show me your tits!" he called back, and I could see his wide grin.

Georgia laughed, and I had the overwhelming urge to do something a little reckless as I continued to stare down at the water. *Fuck it, you only live once,* I thought as I toed out of my shoes and took off my T-shirt and jean shorts, leaving me in only my bra and panties, and handed Phil's leash to Georgia.

"Whoa, what are you doing, Cassie?" she questioned in confusion.

"I'm going to jump in," I told her.

Thatch's booming voice caught my attention. "Cass! What are you doing? Put your clothes back on!"

"I'm going in!" I pointed toward the water.

"Cassie!" He abruptly stood up from his spot on the rocks and waved his arms in the air frantically. "Don't jump, honey! It's not safe!"

"It's fine, Thatcher!" I responded as I moved even closer to the edge. My bare feet scraped against the dirt until they hit the final rocks that led to a possible death. Or a good time laced with an adrenaline rush.

"Cassie!" His voice grew louder as he tried like to hell to get my attention again.

"I don't think this is a good idea," Georgia said from behind me.

My heart felt like a sports car speeding from zero to sixty in three seconds flat. It had revved up to an overwhelming speed, and I slowed my quick breaths in an attempt to calm it down.

Man, that's really fucking high. Hell, I must be high to even be considering this.

I probably was high. High on life. High on Thatch. High on every insane yet amazing thing that had happened in the past few months.

Even though my stomach had taken up residence in my feet, I didn't want to walk away from this silent challenge I had given myself. I hated when something could control me, prevent me from doing something I'd probably end up loving.

Yeah, go fuck yourself, heights.

I convinced myself I wasn't a total ball sac. I could handle this. I could *do* this. Thatch had talked me through the last few accomplishments, but this one would be all my own.

"It's not that far down," I pointed out. "People cliff jump out here all the time."

"Thatch looks really upset."

I glanced back down at him and saw he was booking it up the small trail that led to their fishing spot. His eyes stayed locked in my direction the entire time.

"Shit," I muttered. "He's a man on a mission."

"Um, yeah, I'd say he doesn't want you to cliff jump," she announced, her gaze moving with Thatch as he got closer.

"Don't jump!" His voice was only several yards away now as he jogged toward us. "It's not safe!"

"I'll be fine, Thatcher," I called over my shoulder and focused on my jump.

"Please, Cass." He was right behind me now. "Trust me, honey. Don't do this."

I glanced at him over my shoulder, and then back down at our group, who were no longer fishing. They were on their feet and staring up at us.

"T, it's not a big deal."

"It *is* a big deal. To me, *it's a big fucking deal*. Don't do it, honey," he demanded with an angry yet desperate tone to his voice.

I didn't like that. Thatch thinking he had that much control over me that he could just toss out demands and tell me what I could or couldn't do.

It didn't sit well with me. Not one fucking bit. And now that we were engaged, I felt like this one simple decision could set the precedent for life.

"C'mon, Cass, let's just go back to the campsite," Georgie tried to intervene, but I ignored her.

"Don't do it," he pleaded, his brown eyes melting in the afternoon heat. "I'm begging you not to do it."

I probably should have noticed the edge of frantic desperation in his voice, but I was still too focused on his words. His demanding fucking words.

An engagement did not give someone the right to control me.

I controlled me.

And right now, *I* controlled this.

When I didn't back away from the edge, Thatch stalked toward me.

"Cassie."

I only had about ten seconds to make a decision, or else the size and determination of my caveman would make it for me.

Jump?

Or let Thatch control me?

CHAPTER 36

Thatch

H er smirk disappeared in an instant as she turned and jumped in one smooth motion.

I couldn't tell you if I screamed or if the way I followed her was by choice or a string of involuntary events meant to catch her. One minute I was staring into the eyes of the woman I was sure wouldn't put me in this position, and the next I was in the water.

Everything about Margo's death came back with vivid intensity. The argument we'd had, the stubborn lilt of her voice as she'd told me I couldn't tell her what to do—all of it. I was there again, in a place I'd left behind years ago. A place I never revisited because I didn't need to. All I needed was the tattooed reminder right under my heart.

All I needed was trust.

A woman who put her faith in me and gave me the peace of mind to do the same for her.

And now all of it was gone—the acceptance and contentment and the visions of my future.

My lungs fought for air as I grabbed Cassie and brought her struggling form to the surface.

She spat out a mouthful of water, but otherwise, she was fine. She splashed and moved with ease, while I fought to breathe. Her lips even started to turn up into a smile—until she got a look at my face.

"Thatch?"

I took her jaws in my palms and clenched, even though I knew the strength of my grip was too hard. It had to have hurt a little, but I couldn't bring myself to stop.

I looked right into her eyes and willed myself not to cry. I'd never had a harder time.

But she was there and healthy. Her hair wasn't matted with blood, and life still beat in her eyes.

I couldn't hear much outside of the thoughts in my own head, but I did hear Claire's voice even at a whisper.

"Frankie."

The way she said his name was broken, troubled—terrified and exactly how I felt. They were reliving every second of it with me, strapped to a freight train into the past with no way to break the restraints.

I squeezed my eyes shut as tight as they would go and put my head to Cassie's chest to listen to her heartbeat. The rhythm was dangerously erratic, but somehow mine still managed to follow.

"Thatch," Cassie whispered, and the sound of her voice cut through me like the sharpest of knives. She was troubled by my reaction, but I couldn't stop one thing from repeating on a never-ending course in my mind.

Too little, too late.

"I asked you not to do it. I fucking begged you," I told her raggedly, my voice a literal manifestation of my bloody heart on my sleeve.

"I know," she conceded. I willed her to stop there, but she couldn't stand to let me have the last word. She couldn't stand to admit to being wrong, and that was the crux of the issue.

"But I make my own decisions. I don't answer to you."

"I've never asked you to. There's a difference between asking you to change the way you are and asking you to *see* me."

Her eyes were stubborn, and I felt like I'd never be able to look at them the same after this moment. They weren't just passionate; they were downright violent, and it was all directed at me.

"All I see right now is an asshole!"

The cords of my throat strained with the force of my roar. "Are you kidding me? I fucking loved you!"

"Am *I* kidding?" she screamed, her limbs shaking with the effort it took to keep herself from hitting me. I could see it in her eyes. I swallowed against the burn in my throat and held my ground. "Not once have you said those words to me. Not once, and you choose now. As some part of a demonizing power trip where it's your way or nothing? *And* it's in past tense? Fuck you, Thatcher. Fuck you hard."

"You knew how I felt," I pushed, and she reciprocated physically, giving me a shove to the chest. I charged back and got right in her face. Her chest rose and fell rapidly with the fight to keep taking in air. "I fucking asked you to spend your life with me!"

"As a fucking joke!" she screamed. "A way to win at this stupid game we've been playing, a way to one-up your biggest challenge."

"That's wasn't it, and you know it. It wasn't a joke, not any fucking bit of it. You had to have felt it."

"I didn't feel a goddamn thing," she denied, and I felt my heart freeze over.

"Well, congratulations, Cassie. Looks like you finally fucking win because I'm out."

CHAPTER 37

Cassie

I watched Georgia run after Thatch as he stalked away from me and toward our campsite. And I wanted to reach out and grab those awful words that had come out of my mouth and shove them back down my throat.

Why had I said that? Why had he said that?

What in the hell just happened?

I was equal parts baffled and angry. Pissed at me. Pissed at him. And ultimately confused by his reaction. I felt like he was overreacting about this. He was making this into something I never meant for it to be.

Yeah, but your bullshit words didn't help anything.

I couldn't deny I had been an asshole. A total fucking asshole.

Not one goddamn bit of this, of us, is a joke.

My hands trembled and my knees shook as I ran barefoot after him. The skin of my feet protested in discomfort as gravel and twigs dug into the sensitive skin.

But I would gladly take the pain if it meant getting to him.

I needed to get to him. I needed him to know that I was a liar.

I was in love with him. I *did* need him.

I knew this, what had grown between us, wasn't a joke. I knew what we had was real. It might have started out on a prank, but it had grown into everything I had ever wanted, even if I never really let myself imagine those things.

"Thatch! Wait!"

But he didn't stop. He didn't listen.

He was already inside of our tent and throwing his belongings into his duffel.

I crawled into the tent and wrapped my arms around his waist. "I'm so sorry. I didn't mean any of that," I whispered into his T-shirt. "I love you." I finally found the strength to say those three words.

Three words I had never said to anyone besides my family.

Three words that should have let him know I was all in.

I wanted him. I wanted us.

But my words didn't have any effect on him.

He shrugged me off and zipped up his bag, before maneuvering around me and getting out of the tent.

I stayed frozen in my kneeling position for a good ten seconds.

Shocked. Hurt. Angry.

Why wasn't he listening to me?

I climbed out of the tent and found him throwing his bag in the trunk. Frankie and Claire had already packed up their things and were climbing inside of his car.

"Aren't you listening to me?" I shouted. "I just fucking told you I loved you! Why aren't you listening to me? Why are you freaking out? I don't understand what's happening right now!"

He walked around the front of the vehicle and toward the driver's side door.

I ran toward him at a dead sprint and crashed my body into his before he could open the door.

"Thatch!" I cried, and his eyes refused to meet mine. He just lay limp against the door, staring over my head and out into the distance.

I wrapped my arms around his body again, hugging his huge frame as tightly as I could manage. "Please, don't leave like this," I begged. "Just talk to me. Don't leave angry."

His brown eyes finally stared down into mine. They were so cold, so distant, and it was then I realized how much I had hurt him.

"Don't go," I begged again.

"Enough, Cassie." His large hands wrapped around mine as he disentangled me from his body and moved me back with a gentle shove. "I've had enough."

"Enough?"

"Yes," he snapped. "I've had enough. I can't do this right now. I need you to give me some space to process what just happened. I need time to cool down."

"So that's it?" My voice rose with my anger. "You're just going to walk away?" I stabbed a harsh finger into his chest.

He didn't budge. Didn't react. Didn't do anything but stand there and stare down at me.

His reaction made me feel crazy. This was worse than his angry words. He wasn't giving me a single fucking emotion besides indifference.

"Stop acting like that! Stop acting like you don't care!" I slapped at his chest, hard and erratic. I was desperate for him to show me something. *Anything.* "You're done with me, Thatch? I do one thing that pisses you off, and all of a sudden you need space away from me?" I screamed. "Why don't I get a say in any of this?"

"You did get a say," he corrected, his deep voice cracking in the middle. "And I heard you loud and clear when you jumped off that cliff." He opened the driver's side door, and I tried like hell to push it back closed.

But he was too strong, swinging it open with ease. I tried to climb inside with him, but he must have signaled for Kline because I was wrapped up in strong arms and pulled away from the vehicle.

"Put me down!" I yelled as Thatch shut the driver's door and started the engine.

"Calm down, sweetheart," Kline whispered in my ear. "It's going to be okay."

"No! It's not going to be okay! He's leaving!" I cried, and Georgie's sad eyes blocked the view of Thatch driving away. A few tears dripped from her lids as she wrapped me up in her arms and held me tight. "I've got you. I've got you."

I was sitting inside my shitty apartment, inside my least favorite neighborhood in New York. The only thing Chelsea and I had in common was that we both needed a goddamn shower.

It had been three days since the camping trip. Three days since Thatch lost his shit because I had decided to recreationally cliff jump, off a cliff I knew other people had been jumping off for years.

He had made no attempts to reach out to me.

I had made three attempts to reach out to him.

The responses I got revolved around the fact that Thatch wasn't ready to talk to me.

He was being a dick.

And I was fine.

No, you're not.

I. Was. Fine.

Three soft knocks on my apartment door woke me from my heart-fucked stupor. I shuffled across the redone hardwood floors in my "Classy Bitch" socks and flung it open without checking to see who it was.

I lumbered back to my home base—*the couch*—and plopped my ass back down into the cushions. With the TV remote in hand, I searched through all of the DVR'd episodes that had accumulated since I'd been living at Thatch's apartment.

"So, you look great," Georgia said as she meandered through my apartment, occasionally picking up random takeout containers and tossing them into the trash. "How are you?"

"I'm fine."

"That's great." She glanced around the apartment. "The new floors look nice...well, at least what I can see beneath the trash."

"Thanks." I pushed play on the latest episode of *Vanderpump Rules*.

Georgia walked over toward the television and turned it off.

"Hey! I was watching that!" I flipped the television back on.

She turned it off.

I glared and turned it on again.

She turned it off again.

"Okay, I think it's time for you to leave."

"I'm not leaving."

"Well, then, I'll leave." I got to my feet and trudged into my bedroom.

She followed.

"It's nap time, G," I said as I tossed a pizza box onto the floor and crawled into my bed. "I'll call you later."

She got into the bed with me.

"Go cuddle with Big Dick. I don't feel like cuddling," I whined and pulled the comforter over my head.

She yanked it off of me, and my annoyed eyes met hers. She looked concerned, and that sympathetic expression pissed me off.

"Stop it. I don't need you over here worrying about me. I'm fine."

She shook her head. "No, you're not."

"Yes. I. Am."

"Honey, your apartment looks like New York relocated the garbage dump, and you're wearing your underwear outside of your yoga pants."

I peeked under the covers to find out that she was right. Big deal, so my underwear was outside of my pants. I'd seen numerous homeless people sport that look every fucking day in the city.

"It's okay not to be fine, you know? I wouldn't be fine if I were in your shoes."

"I'm not wearing any shoes."

"Yeah," she said through a soft laugh. "But you're wearing your Classy Bitch socks, and I've only seen you bust those out on two occasions." She held up one finger. "When they canceled *Friday Night Lights*." She held up another finger. "And when you found out that Prada purse you bought in Soho was a knockoff."

I had the overwhelming urge to burst into tears. I covered my face with my hands. "I don't like feeling like this. I never feel like this. About anything or anyone."

"Yeah, but Thatch isn't just anyone."

"You got that right. He's the biggest fucking asshole I've ever met. I wish I'd never fallen into that giant ogre's trap."

"You don't mean that."

"No," I whispered, "but I wish I meant it."

Georgia sat up and rested her back against the headboard as she rearranged me so my head was resting in her lap. Her fingers ran through my hair, occasionally getting caught in the numerous knots that had taken up what I considered permanent residence. My hairbrush could suck a fucking goat scrotum.

For a few quiet moments, I let her calming energy soothe the myriad emotions I was trying so hard to avoid.

"Why did that happen, Georgie?" I asked on a whisper. "I didn't mean for things to go down like that. I wouldn't have jumped off the cliff had I known he would freak out like that."

She glanced down at me. "Are you sure about that? Because from where I was standing, he was begging you not to do it. He looked desperate, sweetheart. Distraught, even."

Honestly, I wasn't sure. And I didn't like that my gut feeling told me I was an asshole for being so fucking stubborn.

"But why would cliff jumping freak Thatcher Kelly out?" I changed the direction of the conversation. "The man took me skydiving, for fuck's sake."

She shrugged. "I'm not sure."

"Are you sure you're not sure? Because I have a feeling Kline knows something. And if he knows, then you probably know."

"Kline wouldn't give me the details, which is saying a lot considering he never keeps anything from me. But I think it had something to do with Margo."

That had my mind racing for answers I was almost a little too scared to find out.

"C'mon, Cass." Georgia nudged me up to a sitting position. "Let's get you out of this apartment and grab some lunch. I think a little fresh air will do you some good."

She walked toward my bedroom door and glanced back with a smirk. "And we're not leaving here until you shower. You literally smell like balls."

I smiled for the first time in what felt like ages. "Like that bothers you. Everyone knows you love smelling like Kline's sac."

She flipped me off and strode down the hallway. "Get your stanky ass moving! I'm hungry!"

Slowly but surely, I got out of my bed and hopped into the shower.

I told myself it had nothing to do with Georgia being right about me not being okay and me being desperate to stop the "I miss him" loop of crazy that kept circling inside my brain, and everything to with the fact I hadn't eaten since the night before.

Yeah, that's exactly what it was.

I was fine. I was hungry, but I was motherfucking fine.

Fucking liar.

CHAPTER 38

Thatch

"You didn't have to do this tonight," I said loudly while I leaned toward Kline's ear to be heard over the noise of Z Bar.

"Didn't have to do what?" he asked back innocently.

I nodded and laughed. "Give me a break. You know what." There wasn't a question in my mind he'd rather be at home with his wife than in the middle of some crowded bar with me. But Kline Brooks was a world-class individual, and I was seriously lucky to call him my friend. "But thanks."

He raised his glass in salute before taking a drink, and I desperately tried to make his effort worth it. I wanted to pretend I was okay, like I wasn't missing Cassie—like I knew how to go on. But the truth was, I didn't. She'd become ingrained in every aspect of my life, and I *liked* her there.

I battled myself, and not for the first time since it'd all gone down. Had I really given her a fair shot? Was I making the whole thing a bigger deal than it was?

Half of me, the part that missed her—and yeah, it was probably the bottom half—thought definitely. I was letting my whole traumatic history with Margo color my opinion. But the other half had a la-ser-like memory when it came to her face in the moments before she jumped.

It wasn't a decision in good fun because she couldn't see how im-portant it was to me. It was a distinct choice. A choice to hold herself away from me and everything we'd built.

A choice where she'd always put herself before me.

Everyone always speaks of selflessness in a relationship, but I ex-pected and respected a little selfishness. I never wanted her to be the person I made her. I just wanted her to trust me enough to know the difference between respecting me and giving herself up.

But the road she was on was dirty, and she hadn't yet uncovered the center line.

"Where'd you go just now?" Kline asked. The back of my neck felt tight under my palm.

He grabbed my shoulder and gave it a squeeze, and I knew no one knew what I was feeling better than he did. Still, I had to wonder if he would have ever chosen a life separate from Georgie if their cir-cumstances had been the same.

Not a chance in hell, heaven, or Manhattan.

I looked up to see Wes walk in, and I knew they'd called in the cavalry. I shook my head, and Kline looked over his shoulder to find the source of my amusement.

"Jesus. Whitney too?" I asked. "You guys went all out."

Wes came to us on an easy weave through the crowd, and Kline turned to shake his hand when he arrived.

"Thanks for coming," I said. He grabbed my shoulder and squeezed. I smiled; I knew it wasn't my normal, but I tried.

"Ah, fuck," he breathed before pulling me into a hug. Not a bro-hug either, but a full-on comforting squeeze with one arm tight around my back and the other hand on the back of my neck.

My throat felt tight, and I had to force a swallow down past the imaginary lump.

"Love you, man," he whispered in my ear. It was so opposite of everything I normally had with Wes—and all the things I knew were always there.

Fast jokes and ribbing, our relationship could look petty from the outside looking in, but that was just the way we lived our day-to-day fun. This right here was all I needed to know to have that freedom— the three of us would be there for each other forever.

Granted, none of us was immortal, so there'd be a limit on the timeline of some kind, but with modern medicine, I was hoping it'd be somewhere in the 120-year range.

"Love you too, Whitney," I murmured back. He gave me one last squeeze and then shoved me out of the way.

"Great. Now get out of my way," he said with a teasing smile. "Your fucking huge body is blocking the bar."

My face accepted the notion of a genuine smile then, and I stepped aside so he could order a rum and Coke.

"Fucking lush," I teased as he flagged down the bartender with an arm in the air.

"Better a lush than a pussy," he said with a nod toward my beer.

"I don't know," Kline interjected. "Pussies are pretty nice."

"Right?" I agreed with a laugh, and Wes smiled at the sound.

My eyes felt downright misty at my friends' effort to make me feel better. Goddamn, this breakup was turning me into a premenstrual woman.

And then Wes's face turned from a smile to something else as he stared at something over my shoulder.

I told myself not to turn around, but apparently Cassie wasn't the only one who didn't listen to me.

Kline turned too, and I knew the moment he registered Cassie's eyes because his gaze shot to the ground before glancing back at Wes surreptitiously.

It didn't upset me to see her. Fuck, it was the opposite of that.

I *missed* her.

As I turned to set my empty beer bottle on the bar, both Kline and Wes gave me assessing looks. I nodded my assurance and then walked the short distance to where Cassie stood waiting for me.

"Thatcher."

"Crazy," I whispered, and her eyes closed tight and her chin dropped toward the ground.

I picked it up with the gentlest of touches from my index finger and waited for her eyes to meet mine.

"What are you doing here, honey?"

She shook her head and looked to the side, and I turned her face toward mine once more.

"Look me in the eye," I demanded softly.

She shrugged, helpless to her own emotion as a single tear rolled down her face. Her voice was barely audible over the din, but I heard it. "I miss you."

Florida Georgia Line's "H.O.L.Y." started to play over the speakers of the bar, a low, seductive beat thrumming through my chest with each chord, so I pulled her hand into mine and said the first thing that came to mind.

"Dance with me?"

She nodded, putting her arms around my shoulders right there without moving a step and beginning a sway to the music. Cassie closed her eyes, and her head swished back and forth until I held it steady with a hand on each side of her throat.

Fierce and feeling, her eyes jerked open and held mine in their grasp until I couldn't remember anyone or anything other than her or that moment in time.

My lips sought hers of their own accord. Flesh on flesh, all of her breath left her in a rush, and a sob bucked the entirety of her upper body. I pulled her closer, sealed my lips tighter to hers, and pushed my tongue through the seam of her lips.

She met me lick for lick, lost in each other, the feel of her tongue on mine sending shock waves through every single muscle in my body.

"It's all right, baby," I told her there, directly against her mouth. I rubbed my thumbs at the line of her throat as I kissed her again, and the tips of her long hair tickled the skin of my exposed forearms.

"I'm sorry," she apologized through a whisper, and I sighed. Relief took forty pounds directly off my chest. "I hate the way everything happened between us that day," she went on. "But I don't *need* anyone, you know? I'm my own woman. I can watch out for myself. I can make my own decisions."

I had to work to stop my eyes from narrowing.

"I've been telling myself I was fine. God, for a week, every day, all I've fucking done is tell myself I'm fine."

I closed my eyes and stepped back, setting her body apart from mine with my hands on her arms.

She still didn't get it.

Here I was thinking we were over this, that I had completely overreacted, and she still didn't get it.

"Thatch?"

"It's not good enough, Cass. You have no idea how much I want it to be, but it's not. I deserve better."

"What?" she asked, and then, when she *thought* she realized what I was saying, she started to get angry.

"You deserve better?" she asked, her voice rising. "Why the hell does a woman have to *need* you to be worthy? I guess I'll never fucking understand men."

I caught her wrist as she turned away and pulled her back. I wasn't letting it go like this.

"It's not that, and you know it. You think about me, you think about the way I am with you, and then tell me you still think you *needing* me is what this is about."

"What's it about, then? Margo? I'm not her."

"I don't want you to be!" I shouted. "Margo is so fucking far out of this equation it's not even funny. This is about you and me, and you being ready to be in a real relationship."

"I was ready!"

"No, you weren't," I disagreed. "Because someone who respected me and trusted me would know that I'm not out to fucking control you or change you. I don't want a Stepford girlfriend. I don't want to stand in front of you and keep you from things, and I certainly don't want to be pushing you from behind. All I want is someone who trusts me enough to know I never ask for anything other than respect and trust. And when you jumped that day, you robbed me of both. *That's* what this is about."

I stepped past her and shoved my way through the crowd on my way out, anger blinding me to every goddamn thing other than getting outside where I could breathe.

The oppressive summer night air hit my face as I shoved through the door, and it did nothing to relieve the choking, clawing feeling in my chest.

"Goddammit!" I yelled, startling a group of scantily clad women standing next to the building, smoking.

I stood there for five minutes trying to get my thoughts together. Truthfully, I guess part of me was hoping Cassie would chase me down. Tell me I was wrong. Tell me she wanted all of the same things I wanted.

But just like the times she'd fallen asleep during sex, my satisfaction never came.

CHAPTER 39

Cassie

It had been the week from hell. Every night I had slept in my shitty Chelsea apartment and wished I were in a California King in Midtown, enveloped in the arms of the one man I couldn't get out of my head.

But I didn't have time to sulk and mope.

I had to get my head straight for a big shoot for *Cosmopolitan* this evening.

It was a huge sixteen-page spread for their November issue, and I should have been excited about it. I should have been damn near brimming with energy over the idea of getting behind the lens, but thoughts of Thatch and me and us and everything that went wrong sat at the precipice of my mind, and I was having a hell of a time thinking about anything but him.

Fuck. Get it together. This is your career you're screwing with here.

Plus, you're driving a fucking sweet-ass convertible right now...

Which I was. When *Cosmo* had made the arrangements, I had offered to pick up the cherry-red Porsche prior to the shoot. Of course, those arrangements had solely been based on selfish motives and I had made sure I had the entire afternoon to drive this pretty baby around the city.

And God, she drove like a dream—cruising through the city with a quiet purr and taking turns with ease. It was a rare and refreshing experience to drive after living in a city where people rarely owned cars. There was just something about being behind the wheel, music blaring, roof open, and wind in my hair.

My mood started to lift as I weaved in and out of traffic, making stops at random for my Monday errands. After barely missing a parking citation for parking outside of Starbucks illegally, I headed toward Midtown and stopped at the dry cleaner. I was in and out of the quaint family business before the parking meter ran out of its measly ten minutes.

Stuck at a stoplight, I glanced in the rearview mirror and caught sight of Thatch's cleanly pressed suits lying across the back seat.

"Oh, shit," I muttered.

Did I really just pick up his dry cleaning?

It was like I had completely forgotten about everything that had happened—the breakup, the other night at the bar, him not wanting to be with me anymore.

"Fuck. Why did I do that?" I said to no one in particular.

You know why, you idiot…

I mentally chastised myself and refused to let my thoughts wander back to that sad place where I had to come to terms with the fact that Thatch wasn't mine. That we weren't together. That things were over between us.

"*Fuck!*" I shouted and turned up the volume to drown out my racing thoughts.

And I forced my brain to focus on my shoot as I headed for location.

"That's perfect, Eduardo. Just tilt your head slightly up and to the right," I instructed as he leaned against the Porsche with the New York skyline resting behind him.

I snapped a few photos from a side angle before changing positions and lying on my belly to grab some shots looking up at him.

"I never get to see you anymore, Cassie," he said and hitched his hip against the car. "I don't like it." He flashed a playful smile in my camera's direction. Eduardo was a male model I had known for years. He was about as attractive as one would imagine a male model would be, and I had noticed that very fact on more than one occasion. Believe me, we had experienced our fair share of afternoon shoots and late-night sex together.

I shook my head to clear it. The thought of him and me together made me feel dirty. Wrong. Uncomfortable.

He gave his signature smirk. "I think we should change that, gorgeous. Come out with me tonight after we're done here."

I paused behind my lens for the briefest of seconds as a million emotions ran through my veins and straight to my heart.

Normally, I would have taken Eduardo up on his offer.

Obviously, I had in the past, many, many times.

But I had absolutely zero desire to do what I normally did.

The only kind of normalcy I craved revolved around Thatch and us and spending every second of our time together. I wanted *him*. I wanted what we had. I wanted our happy bubble of jokes and pranks and hot sex and flirty winks.

God, I hated him.

Liar.

Well, I *wanted* to hate him.

I pulled my camera away from my face and glanced at my watch. 7:00 p.m.

My pink diamond engagement ring winked in the fading sun. *Fucking winked.*

I had to get rid of it. Now.

Which was why I tossed my camera in the back seat of the Porsche, opened the driver's door, and told Eduardo to get out.

He stared back at me, confused.

"Get out of the car," I demanded, and lucky for him, he listened.

Like a woman deranged, I didn't waste any time or offer any explanations to the staff on set. I peeled out of the parking lot with a loud squeal of the tires and left in the middle of one of the biggest photo shoots of my career. All because a ring was fucking *winking* at me.

Fifteen minutes later, I damn near hit a few pedestrians as I parked illegally in front of the tattoo shop. I was out of the car and striding through the entrance within seconds. The bell above the door rang erratically, and Frankie looked up from behind the reception desk, his eyes wide with both recognition and shock.

"Cass?"

My mind wouldn't let me do anything other than yell over him. "Take this fucking ring back!"

I yanked at it frantically, trying to free it from my finger, but it hung like Walter had hung on to Stan's cage. At this rate, I'd be raw and bloody, but I was obviously beyond the point of caring about anything.

The one thing I cared about didn't want me, so I wanted this reminder gone. Pulling and pulling, each yank opened up some untapped well of emotion, and by the time it even came close to coming off, I was sobbing.

"Come here," Frankie said, taking me by the elbow and gently leading me to a chair in the back. He went into the bathroom and came back out with a tissue, offering it to me with a kind smile. "Take a minute and calm down," he instructed gently.

I wiped at my eyes and found myself irrationally cursing his steely ways. "Fuck you for being so steady right now."

He smiled, and it honestly surprised me how receptive I was to it.

"Feel better?" he asked softly, and I shrugged.

"A little."

"Good."

Now that I wasn't so agitated, the ring slipped free of my finger with ease. I closed it in my fist and concentrated on giving it up. Every cell in my body was shouting its refusal. I clamped the ring harder in my hand until I felt the sting of the diamond pressing into my palm.

Eventually, I took a deep breath and found the strength to shove the ring toward Frankie. "Give this to him."

He shook his head. "I think you should give it to him yourself."

A thousand emotions pulsed through my veins until my ears buzzed with the erratic pounding of my heart. Why wouldn't Frankie just take the fucking ring? Didn't he understand? If I had to be the one to hand Thatch back the ring, *my fucking ring*, it would be the final straw. Having to face him and face the truth that we were really over would destroy me.

"*I can't*," I spat. "It rips my heart out to see him, so you can take the ring or I'll flush it down the toilet!" I shouted, throwing it to the floor when he still didn't hold out his hand.

His expression remained neutral. "Do you want to hear what I think?"

"*No*," I answered obstinately. His eyebrows went up in challenge, and I folded like a poker novice. "Yes," I admitted.

"Go on, sit down," he directed, and I had no qualms with following his orders. I was dog tired from the long day, but mostly, I was exhausted from having to remind myself a million times a day, *every goddamn day*, that I couldn't call Thatch or text him or do anything that revolved around him because we weren't together anymore. Our breakup felt like a constant one-hundred-pound weight on my shoulders.

"You scared Thatch last week."

"I know. And hurting him burned a hole through my heart. But I'm really not interested in being the ghost of his ex-girlfriend."

"Well, I'm glad to know you're so sympathetic—"

I cringed. "God, I'm so sorry," I found myself apologizing. "That was a really dick thing to say."

Frankie nodded. "Yeah, it was, but it's okay," he accepted. "And this has nothing to do with Margo."

Thatch had said the same thing. I wasn't sure I believed either of them.

"Sure, that's how she died," he went on, and my eyes widened. He nodded again. "Yeah. Jumping off a cliff into a shallow pool of water, right after Thatch begged her not to."

His words hit my chest like a bullet, and I inhaled a shaky breath.

"So it is about her," I said on a whisper.

He shook his head. "No, it's not. There, that day, the moment. Yeah, he remembered. He's the one who spent thirty minutes trying to revive her, so I know he remembered."

A single tear cut down my cheek as my heart broke for them. For Thatch—the man who deserved so much better than me—and for Frankie, so willing to open his arms to me even when I was yo-yoing between manic and a Grade A bitch.

"But you scaring him was all about you."

I shook my head and wiped at my eyes. "I don't get it." But God, I wanted to. Even though, deep down, I probably already knew the answer.

"You're the exact woman he's always wanted, Cassie. *Always*. But that day made him afraid to want it. Afraid to think of what he might be putting himself through for the rest of his life. He knows you're going to be wild and untamed, and he loves it. *Until* he feels like being so accepting of it might be the reason he loses you."

"But what do I do?" My voice was barely audible.

"What you do is always up to you, Cassie. You're the one who needs to decide what's really important to you."

I already knew the answer to that.

Moving to the corner of the room, he picked up the ring and dropped it in my hand. "And if you really think it's over, you need to give him the ring back yourself. He'll be here tonight at nine."

CHAPTER 40

Thatch

Nerves fought to take over as I set up my station and pulled all the sanitary packets from the cabinet.

I was tattooing my very first client today. Frankie and some of the other artists had pretty selflessly let me practice on them a few times, and I'd obviously practiced on myself, but working on a client was different. I didn't exactly think I'd fuck it up, but unlike what I liked to spout, it wasn't an absolute certainty that I'd be good at it.

My black mood probably wasn't helping things either.

"You ready?" Frankie asked, popping into the private room I was setting up in. My first client was a woman named Kristen. She'd come into the shop a week or so ago wanting some kind of custom book quote, and Frankie insisted this was the time. While he was a guru of portrait work, he felt like I had a gift for lettering.

Go figure. My everyday handwriting was shit.

"As I'll ever be," I answered with the best smile I could manage.

His smile, however, seemed unnecessarily bright.

"What's with your face?"

"Huh?" he said.

"What's happening here?" I asked, circling a finger around my face in explanation. "You're looking a little too much like the Joker."

"Nothing. I don't know what you're talking about."

"Seriously, why am I only friends with really shitty liars?"

He flipped me off. "I'll send her back if you're done."

"I'm done for now, but I'll get to the bottom of this eventually."

His smile grew even more demented. "I have no doubts you will."

"Whatever." I rolled my stool away and got my ink cups out for the colors I knew she wanted. I'd double-check everything before we got started, though. Women had a nasty little tendency to change their minds.

What? Don't even think about pretending that's not true.

I heard a knock on the open wood door. "Come on in—"

The ability to speak left me when I saw who it was, but the smirk on her lips brought my voice right back. For the first time in our relationship, I was in no mood to be fucked with.

"What are you doing here?" I asked her.

"I'm your first appointment," Cassie said, walking into the room and jumping up on the table in front of me.

"No. My first client is a woman named Kristen."

She shook her head. "Not anymore."

CHAPTER 41

Cassie

"**I** thought you had a photo shoot."

"Screw the photo shoot," I declared. "This is more important." I pulled up the right side of my shirt, exposing my rib cage.

It hadn't taken long after leaving Frankie to come to my senses. And to realize he'd been giving me a big fucking clue by telling me to bring the ring back myself. He'd looked downright elated when I'd walked in and raised a smirking brow.

Frankie had told me to think about what was important, and I had. He was the size of an elephant and had a trunk to rival all the others. And he was everything I needed in my life. He pushed me past my comfort zones at the same time he let me soak in them.

Thatch was my person.

He was my present and my future.

He was it for me.

God, I was such an idiot. I had risked all of that, *my fucking happiness, Thatch's happiness,* because I was too bullheaded and stubborn and couldn't stand the idea of someone else having control over me. But I was done with it now.

The funny thing about when you realize you want to spend the rest of your life with someone, is you don't want to waste another second of your life without them.
You want it all. Right now.

He stared down at me. "So, you're hijacking my first client's appointment?"

"She's not your first client. *I'm* your first client."

"It's bad for business for you to pull shit like this."

I don't care about anything but you.

I shrugged. "I don't care about anything but you."

My heart and brain were finally in sync.

A giant smile spread across my face, and I watched him intake a sharp breath. He stared down at his fingers while they fiddled with sterile packaging.

"You want me to tattoo you?" he finally asked after a pregnant pause. He searched my eyes for all of the answers I was willing to give. "Do you have something in mind? Remember, it's gonna be with you for life."

"I want you to choose."

"Are you crazy?" he asked sincerely.

I smiled at the irony and nodded. "You *know* I am."

"You're trusting me to pick out your tattoo?"

I shook my head and held his eyes with my own. I needed to make sure he got it. That despite everything I'd blown hot air about, I did need him. Because he made me a better version of me. Not different. Not worse. A newer, improved model. "I'm trusting you with everything."

He searched my unrelenting gaze for another moment, and then he turned away to prepare his station. He set up the ink and set out the needles, and I watched each movement as though it was gospel. I'd missed the sound of his voice and the sound of his laugh and all the little things that only I got to know about him.

"Everything is sterile," he instructed as he opened up each needle and turned back to me. "These will only be used on you, and then they'll be disposed of."

"Well, that's fantastic fucking news because I just want a tattoo, not Hep C," I teased, but my voice didn't hold any of its usual intensity. *I want my giant back.*

He smirked and gestured toward my exposed rib cage, but he didn't pull me into his arms and tell me he loved me either. I wasn't sure what to make of any of it. "This where you want it?"

I nodded.

"And you sure about this?"

I nodded.

He cleaned off my skin with a cool cloth.

"You're one hundred percent certain you want to do this?"

"One hundred and ten percent."

Ten minutes and several more "Are you sure?" style questions from Thatch, the sketch was on my ribs, and he slipped on latex gloves.

"Do you want to see it before I start?"

I shook my head and rested my head on the table. "No. I'll want to see it for the first time when it's done."

The very edges of a smirk graced his lips as he held up the tattoo machine for my eyes. "I'm going to do a dry run so you know what the needle feels like."

"Test away," I said and shut my eyes. The initial sting of the needle made me flinch, but otherwise, it wasn't too awful bad.

"How does it feel?" he asked, the edge of his glove-covered thumb skimming softly over the surrounding skin.

"Like you're about to create something amazing for me." I peeked out of one eye and caught his tender smile. It felt like I could breathe for the first time.

"You ready, honey?" he asked on a whisper, and I had to fight the urge to burst into tears at the sounds of his sweet endearment.

Honey. I'd missed that so much.

Taking several gulps of newfound air, I nodded my head enthusiastically. "So ready."

"Okay, Crazy. Just try to sit back and relax."

His latex-covered hand rested on my side as he leaned forward and put the tattoo needle to my skin. His face was mere inches from my ribs, and I could feel his warm breaths ease in and out from his lips and brush against my skin.

The room stayed silent, only the buzzing of the gun filling the space. I winced when the needle pushed against a particularly sensitive bundle of nerves.

"Just relax. You're doing great," he encouraged.

I closed my eyes and let Thatch work his magic, and forty minutes later, he was cleaning off my skin again and announcing, "All done."

I looked up at him and smiled. "Really?"

He nodded. "Yep."

"Can I look at it now?" I asked with excitement.

He nodded, snapped off his gloves, and helped me off the table.

I walked over toward the floor-length mirror and turned to my side.

The second my gaze caught sight of the black words etched across my reddened skin, tears filled my eyes.

> *She was crazy. Wild.*
> *Chaos & beauty.*
> *My heart.*
> *Mine.*

He stood behind me, watching my reaction in the mirror.

"For most of my life, I had only been sure about one thing," I said quietly and glanced back down at the beautiful tattoo he had created for me. "*Photography* was my one sure thing. I loved the control it brought me," I admitted. "For as long as I can remember, I had always hated not having control of my choices. It's just the way I was. I needed it. I needed the freedom to go and do and be whatever I wanted."

He started to speak, but I put a finger to his lips as my gaze met his. "But then I met you.

"You're the one and only thing I'm sure about. Everything else is just details. Because you're it for me, Thatch. And I trust you with everything because I know you trust me back."

I closed the distance between us. "I'm sorry for what I did. I'm sorry for jumping off that cliff. It was selfish and cruel, and I'm so sorry I hurt you like that. When you begged me not to do it, I should have known you weren't trying to control me, you were just trying to keep me safe." I reached up and touched his cheek.

He leaned into my touch and closed his eyes. "I should have gotten over it faster."

I shook my head. "Will you forgive me?"

"Of course, I will, honey," he whispered with his heart in his eyes.

"Will you still love me?"

Both of his hands cupped my cheeks. "I never stopped. And I'm sorry I told you like that."

I inhaled a cavernous breath as relief coursed through my veins.

I wrapped my arms around his neck and stood on my tiptoes to press a soft kiss to his lips.

"I love you."

His answering smile was blinding. He lifted me up, hands putting the softest pressure at the juncture of my ass and thighs, and wrapped my legs around his waist.

"I love you too, honey."

"Enough to still marry me?" I asked against his lips.

He chuckled. "Are you asking me?"

I nodded. "Marry me, Thatcher."

His eyes changed from playful to serious in the span of a heartbeat. "You're really asking me?"

I pressed my forehead to his and locked our gazes. "Yes. Marry me. Make me the luckiest fucking girl on the planet."

"You're that sure about us, honey?"

I held up my left hand and showed him the engagement ring I now refused to take off. Funny how this afternoon I'd been one shake shy of cutting off my finger just to get it fucking gone.

"Yes. I'm that sure."

He took my lips in a hot, deep, sexy kiss.

"Is that a yes?" I asked against his persistent mouth.

He shrugged, but a soft smile graced his lips. "Maybe."

I leaned back and stared at him.

His goddamn smile grew, and I couldn't stop my lips from mimicking his.

"You're giving me a maybe? Leslie's Instagramming about this right now. Hashtag CuntResponse."

He winked.

That fucking wink.

This was a challenge. I could see it all over his face. He wasn't content to let our relationship follow the normal path, and the more I thought about it, neither was I.

All we needed was a promise. Not some over-the-top proposal.

God-fucking-dammit, I loved him.

"I'm not taking this ring off."

His response was immediate, demanding, and everything I never knew I needed it to be.

"Rule number seventy-five, never take that fucking ring off."

BIG FAT FUCKING EPILOGUE

Cassie

The early morning sun filtered in through the floor-to-ceiling window of the living room as I padded back into the kitchen to pour a fresh cup of coffee. I stirred my favorite caramel creamer into my brew while I wiped the sleep out of my eyes.

It was early. Too goddamn early. But my internal clock had been off-kilter over the past few weeks. Lately, I'd been waking up before Thatch *and* Phil, which said a lot since our little piggy tended to rise and shine before roosters crowed.

The clock on the stove glowed 6:00 a.m. and I groaned.

This morning bird bullshit was annoying.

After a few sips from my mug, I fixed Thatcher a cup of coffee and headed back into our bedroom. My eyes took in the numerous photographs I'd hung up throughout the apartment over the past two months. Black-and-white landscapes and colorful cityscapes filled the hallway, and the picture Thatch had taken of the three of us in Central Park hung proudly over the mantel.

Thatch's apartment was no longer just his place; it was *our* home now.

Sometimes, I still couldn't believe it was real. Sometimes, it was difficult to process, that at one point in time, I had almost lost him. But we *were* real. We were an *us*. And we were *forever*. That much I was resolute on. Everything else was just minor details.

Yeah, that big motherfucker had won my heart. Loving Thatch had changed me. He was my best friend, and because of his love and friendship, he made me a better version of me.

I know, I know, that's some real sappy bullshit, huh?
Well, Love is a real fucking bitch, and once she's got you in her hold, consider yourself done for. Which is why I can honestly admit that I am officially a woman who is head over heels in love with a man who loves me for me. I know, I got real fucking lucky. I almost lost him because I had been stupid and selfish and stubborn. But I swear on Thatch's Supercock that I'll never make those mistakes again. The Jolly Green Giant is stuck with me and my crazy for life.
So, I'd like to thank you guys for not killing me off before our story got its happy ending.
And I'd also like to thank Love for being a bigger bitch than me.

Loving Thatch also made me really horny. Like I needed to bone all day long.

Over the past few weeks, all I had thought about was sex with Thatch and blowing Thatch and Thatch going down on me and Thatch naked in the shower and Thatch spanking me and me spanking Thatch…

It was a never-ending list of porny thoughts. I wondered if my selfishness had filtered from my heart to my puss-ay. And to be honest, she was a bit out of control. But man, oh man, once she expressed her need to get laid, she was fucking merciless.

Which probably explained why I set our mugs on the nightstand and crawled into bed beside a sound asleep Thatch with the intent of waking him up for a morning bang.

The sheet barely covered his huge frame, and soft snores fell from his lips. My greedy eyes took in his body with the soundtrack of my pussy shouting her approval in the background. I ogled his trim hips, his sexy V muscle, his defined abs, and as I moved my eyes up his body and caught sight of his tattoos and the shimmer of his piercing, my nipples got hard.

I wanted to eat him with a spoon.

Scratch that, I didn't need a spoon when I had two hands and my mouth.

And me, my pussy purred. Fuck, she was demanding. If I wasn't so horned up, I would've considered having a come to Jesus talk with her.

I'm aware that referring to Jesus in the same sentence as my pussy is probably frowned upon by the majority of the population. But they don't have to live with her.

I do.

And fuck, she is bossy, and I'm starting to wonder if she is on a one-pussy mission to get us pregnant, even though she knows we're on the pill.

Trust me, she needs Jesus.

And possibly a tranquilizer with a side of exorcism.

I ran my hand across the smooth skin of his chest and kissed up his neck until I reached his earlobe where I bit down gently and tugged a few times. "Thatch," I whispered. "Wake up."

"No," he said without opening his eyes.

"Baby, I—"

"No," he repeated before I could finish.

"But—"

"No, Cass," he refuted. "I think you actually broke my dick. We've fucked no less than ten times in the past twenty-four hours. It's physically impossible for me to get hard right now. It's just a prop at this point."

God, his voice sounded so fucking hot all raspy and thick with sleep.

"But what if I—"

"You have literally fucked me dry. I really hope you're okay with adoption, honey, because I'm ninety-nine percent sure my balls are empty."

I grinned into the crook of his neck. "You want to have babies with me?"

"I feel like this is a trick question. Last time I told you I wanted to see you pregnant with my kid, you slapped my dick. Not that it would matter at this point. I'm numb from the waist down."

I sat back on my heels and stared down at his handsome face. His eyes were still closed, but a small smile rested on his lips. I pressed a kiss to the corner of his mouth.

"I swear, it's not a trick question, baby."

He chuckled softly. "If it isn't a trick question, then it's you trying to goad me into sex. I know your game, Crazy. And we both know you're still on the pill, so it's a moot point anyway."

I sighed in annoyance. Damn him for being so smart. Even though he couldn't see it, I flipped him off and then rested my back against the headboard in defeat. I had thought the whole baby thing would've helped plead my "let's bone" case because, despite the fact that we had yet to get married, Thatch had been bringing up the whole "let's have kids" conversation more and more these days. If he didn't have a giant snake tucked inside his pants, I'd probably wonder if he was a woman.

His biological cock is definitely ticking. Wait. Clock. Not cock.

But seriously, his cock. *His perfect, long, thick cock. I want it so fucking bad.*

I sighed again and crossed my arms over my chest. Was it really too much to ask for a little morning sex, even though I hadn't let him go to bed until two in the morning because after our first night fuck session, I had demanded a second time and a third time and then a fourth time before bed? I didn't think so.

He sensed my annoyance and finally opened his eyes, meeting my frustrated gaze. "Honey, I'm not saying no because I don't want you. I want you all the fucking time. I'm literally saying no because I can't physically get it up." He lifted up the sheet and gestured down to his boxers with a nod of his head. "You've literally fucked my morning wood away. And that's saying something considering every morning for the last twenty-plus years, I've woken up with a hard-on."

He was right. His boner wasn't giving me his usual hello, and that was very unlike him. He *always* greeted me in the morning.

I rested my head against the headboard and groaned. "I'm just so horny right now. I feel like I will go crazy if I don't come in the next five minutes. Do you want to shoulder that, Thatch? Knowing you're the one who pushed me over the edge."

He glanced over at me and smirked. "We've already established you're crazy, honey. Beautiful but crazy. Sexy as fuck but *crazy.*"

"You love my crazy."

"Obviously. I let you break my dick."

"I did not break your dick," I said, even though my eyes were now fixated on his crotch. *Did I break his dick?* I started to wonder if we needed to take him to the hospital.

He snorted. "Yeah, honey, you did."

"What if I suck on you for a little bit?"

He shut his eyes again and seemed content to fall back asleep. "My cock needs a break. You could shove your tits in my face, and I wouldn't care at this point."

Why didn't I think of that? He could *never* resist my boobs.

He peeked out of one eye and added, "That's not a challenge."

I groaned again. "You're turning into an old man."

"You weren't saying that last night when you were begging me to put my mouth on you."

"Yes, please. Do that."

Both of his eyes opened to meet my unsatisfied and sex-consumed gaze. "You're that riled, honey?"

I nodded. "I need to get off. So fucking bad."

He moved over top of me and caged me in with his thick arms. "You want my mouth?"

"Yes."

His fingers brushed aside the strap of my tank top as his tongue licked a path from my shoulder to my neck. "You need to come?" he breathed into my ear.

My nipples hardened. "More than I need to breathe."

His mouth sucked at my neck, hitting that spot below my ear that had moans slipping past my lips. He slid his fingers into my hair and tilted my head to give him more room. And God, he *used* that extra space—his lips and tongue, sucking and licking along my skin, moving down to my shoulder and then back up again.

My back arched and my hips lifted, seeking relief from the pulsing ache building below my belly. "Please," I begged. I needed more, I needed his mouth, his lips, his hands, his cock. I needed him on me, in me, all fucking over me. I wanted everything, and I wanted it all at the same time.

My nails found their way into the smooth skin of his back, leaving their mark and showing him just how desperate I was for what he had to give.

He kissed a wet, openmouthed path down my throat and between my breasts as his body slid down mine. His large hands slipped my tank down until I was bared for his heady gaze.

"Christ." He groaned when his eyes took in my hard nipples and heaving chest.

His tongue licked a hot trail across my breast until he sucked me into his mouth.

"These fucking perfect tits were made for my big fucking hands. *Fuck,* Cass. I shouldn't be hard right now, but I am. I'm so fucking hard for you." He punctuated that statement by grinding against me until I moaned.

When those words passed his lips, I was pretty sure angels started singing.

"Yes, please. I need it, baby."

"Not yet."

His hands continued to grip my breasts, and his thumbs brushed across my nipples as his mouth moved down my belly. He licked from one hip bone to the next until he descended farther and pressed his warm mouth against my clit. He sucked on me through my panties, and my eyes rolled back.

"You're soaked. I need to lick you clean before I slide my cock inside this perfect pussy."

In two quick pulls, he tore my underwear off my body and didn't waste a second after. He sucked and ate at my pussy until my legs started to shake and I gripped his hair with my fingers.

"How do you want it, honey? My mouth or my cock?"

"If you don't fuck me right now I swear—"

He had his cock out and his hands gripping my thighs before I could finish. He thrust inside me between one panting breath and the next.

I moaned, my voice echoing inside of the silent apartment.

"More?" He pushed a little deeper.

"Don't stop. Don't ever stop."

"Fuck. Fuck. *Fuck*, Cass." He damn near growled. "You always feel so good."

Four hours and a combined four orgasms later—three for me and one for Thatch—we were riding up the elevator toward the owner's suite at Paul Howard Stadium, the home of the New York Mavericks.

I was fidgety with nervous excitement, practically bouncing from foot to foot.

Thatch smirked and wrapped his arm around my shoulders, tucking me into his side. "Don't worry, honey. He's healthy. He's in the best shape of his life. Sean's going to do great."

I nodded. "I know, but I can't stop feeling so nervous. I mean, it's my baby brother's first professional football game."

"Yeah, and he's about to show the Mavericks that drafting him was the best decision they ever made."

The elevator dinged when we reached the top level, and Thatch led me out with a hand softly pressed to my lower back.

I looked up into his confident gaze and grinned. "You're right. Sean is going to kick some serious ass today."

"I'm always right, honey. We've established this numerous times."

I lifted my hand and feigned a dick slap.

He didn't even flinch, and I tilted my head in surprise.

He smirked. "We've also established that you broke my dick, honey. You could kick me in the balls right now, and I probably wouldn't feel it."

I glanced down at his crotch and then back up to him. My mouth tilted into a devious smile.

"No," he said and shook his head. "I'm not fucking you here. So go ahead and come to terms with that fact right now."

Fact? Yeah, we'd see about that. I'd thoughtfully planned my apparel ahead of time.

Thatch

"I love you so much," I told Cassie's tits through a moan. They looked fucking spectacular today in her number seventy-eight Mavericks jersey sans bra.

Maybe it was inappropriate to ogle her chest through a shirt she donned to support her brother, but fuck. They looked *so* good. Walking into the stadium, women had looked at her like she was crazy, and men had looked at me like they were considering murder for the chance to take my place.

It had been *awesome*.

"Harder, baby," Cassie ordered in between gasps as I gave into temptation and buried my face in the low V-neck of her shirt and held her up and against the owner's suite bathroom wall. She'd been relentless for the last month or so, completely sexually insatiable, and for the first time in my life, I wasn't completely sure I could keep up.

I tried to increase my tempo and force without breaking her in half or making myself come prematurely. The line I walked for both was fantastically thin.

"Fuck my pussy, Thatch," she demanded, and I closed my eyes to fight the tingle in my spine.

"I am, honey," I told her, because I was. I was giving her everything I had to give, and she still wanted more. I both loved and hated the idea that my woman could take so much.

It was hot as fuck, but it didn't do me much good if I couldn't keep up.

Sucking at the top swell of her breast, I tightened my grip on her ass, lifted her even higher, pushed her harder into the door, and set up a pounding rhythm. The hinged wood rattled, and there wasn't a doubt in my mind all of our friends could hear every single thrust.

"Fuck yeah, oh, yeah," she screamed. Moving my mouth from her chest to her lips, I worked my tongue between the seam to silence her.

She hiccupped through her pleasure and dug her fingernails into my shoulders in an attempt to climb me higher.

One hand left me to stroke her own nipple through her shirt, and I groaned.

"Careful, baby," I warned her. "You're gonna have to finish on my tongue if you keep that up."

"Uh, oh, yeah," she moaned, ignoring me completely and chasing her own pleasure like a search dog.

"Goddamn," I told her throat. "You are the sexiest fucking woman on the planet."

Using her other hand to help, she pulled the neck of her shirt down and under her tits to bare them to my eyes and make them accessible for my mouth.

"Suck on them, Thatcher." She moaned. "Fucking eat them."

"Fuuuuck."

Never in my life would I be able to deny a request like that.

Every time her pussy swallowed my dick, milking it until I could barely pull back out, her tits bounced, and I lost control a little more.

"Get there, Cass," I ordered, shifting a hand on her ass until my fingertips met the union between her wet pussy and my dick.

Her head fell back, her long hair bunching at the back where it rubbed persistently against the door. A crease formed in her lip with the force of her bite as she tried—and failed—to contain the yell of her orgasm.

The sight of her face and the feel of her coming on my dick sent me right over the edge.

I shoved my face right in the center of her tits to muffle my groan. Grabbing on to my hair, she pulled my face into her harder.

I licked a path from the center and up, over the swell of each, and around each nipple.

She cooed and mewled like she couldn't get enough.

"Still greedy for it?" I asked on a whisper. She licked her lips and nodded.

"We'll sneak away again soon," I promised, though I doubted our sneaking was anywhere near secret or sleuth in any way at this point. And I also doubted I'd be the one to suggest said sneaking away. I was about one fuck away from my dick actually falling off.

Her feet hit the floor as I set her down gently, and I kept my hands at her hips until she steadied on her feet.

The maxi skirt she had on with no panties sure made this a lot easier. She laughed as I waved good-bye to her tits before pulling her shirt back up to cover them. "I'll miss you," I told them, and I really would.

Every time I saw them was like the first time.

"You okay?" I asked her as she cleaned herself up at the sink and I buttoned and zipped my pants and buckled my belt. "You want me to wait for you to make the walk of shame together?"

Her laugh made me back into the door. I'd never ever grow weary of it either.

"It's only the walk of shame if you have some, and you and I both know that we—"

"Don't have any," I finished for her through a chuckle. Taking a giant stride, I closed the distance between us and kissed her once, softly, on the lips. "I love you."

"I know," she said with a wink. My hand shot to my chest to catch my beating heart as I backed my way to the door. She rolled her eyes at my dramatics, and then she turned back to the mirror and rubbed at her face and fluffed at her hair to fix all the things women worried about that men hardly ever noticed. I took the opportunity to duck back outside.

Every eye in the suite came immediately to me.

Wes started a slow clap, and Kline pressed his face into Georgia's neck to hide his laugh. Georgie giggled outright in his lap.

"I'll make sure the cleaning crew spends extra time in there tonight," Wes remarked, and I flipped him off with a shrug.

"The game is getting ready to start," I reminded him. "Don't you have something you could be doing other than busting my balls?"

"Nope," he answered with a smirk. "Not right this second."

I smiled at the fact that I didn't care. Since Cassie had officially become mine, I'd been fairly immune to anything that could diminish my mood. Not much had ever affected my mood negatively before, but now my happiness was at an all-time high.

I was really fucking tired, though.

Shoving around Wes, I took the seat beside Kline just as Georgia hopped off his lap.

"You don't have to leave on my account, Georgia girl."

She smiled and waved me off. "You guys can have guy time, and I'll go see if Cassie still has leg function."

I winked at her. "Barely."

Kline groaned.

"What?" I asked, looking back to see Cassie give me a little wave as she came out of the bathroom. She motioned toward the door and Georgia and, as far as I could tell, indicated they were going to go for a walk outside.

"We'll be back," Georgia called. Kline jumped up and ran over her to give her a kiss on the lips.

Now it was Wes's turn to groan. "Jesus Christ, you guys. Did anyone notice there's a football field down there? Or is a pussy all you can see anymore?" He slid into Kline's vacated seat.

"It's a *really* pretty pussy," I told him mock-seriously.

"Who's a pussy?" Kline asked as he took the seat on my other side.

"You guys are," Wes answered.

"Pussy-whipped. I'm pussy-whipped," Kline corrected. "And trust me, no matter what you think, it's a really good fucking thing to be."

The urge to close my eyes for a minute overwhelmed me, so I gave in, slouching down and leaning my head back.

I felt a poke at my knee and cracked an eye open. "What's wrong with you?" Wes asked. "Did Cassie fuck the life out of you?"

He was teasing, but fuck me, he really wasn't far off the mark.

Kline sat up and took interest when I didn't refute him.

Wes's phone rang before I could say anything.

"Yeah?" he answered, and I rolled my eyes at his lack of greeting. What a prick. "All right. Yeah. I'll be down in a few minutes."

I waggled my eyebrows at Kline. "Looks like he has to go to work after all."

"Fuck you," Wes said, having heard me as he was hanging up the phone. "I'll be back by kickoff, hopefully." He strode for the door like a man on a mission.

"All right," Kline declared in his no-nonsense voice. "What the fuck is going on with you?"

The consideration to make a joke or avoid the topic was only brief. "I'm so tired," I told him honestly.

"Tired?"

I sat up and nodded. "Cassie has been so fucking horny lately."

He rolled his eyes, thinking I was joking. I shook my head vehemently. "No, dude. I'm talking really horny. Six, seven, eight times a day she wants it, and not only is my dick not physically capable, my tongue is sore."

"Less detail," he requested with a grimace.

"She's so fucking hot, and I'd amputate my dick before saying no, but I seriously don't know if I can keep up anymore."

He started to smile, and all it did was agitate me. I pointed at him sternly. "I'm serious. This is a problem. I mean, it's a fitting way for me to die, but I really thought I'd have a little more time with her before I did."

He laughed but held his hands up in defense when my eyes narrowed. "Let's break this down. This is new behavior?"

"She's always down for a ride on the Supercock—"

"Less detail," he stressed. "I said *less* detail."

"But it's more so. Like, a lot more." I pouted. "Help me."

His smile mocked me, but his words told me he was genuinely trying to help me find a solution. "Is there anything else different?"

"Like what? Did I get sexier?" I asked, and then answered myself. "I mean, maybe."

"Not with you, idiot. With her. Is there anything else different with her?"

I searched my mind wildly, and my eyes went to the ceiling. "She's crazy."

He shook his head. "So that's the same."

I laughed because, yeah, he was half right. "Yeah, but no. She's crazier, I think."

"Any changes in her body?" Kline asked, and my eyebrows pulled together.

Her body was fucking insane like always. "Jesus. I don't know. Her body is—"

"Don't tell me," he cut in before I could tell him more things he thought he didn't want to know.

And it hit me. This fucking smart bastard. "You think she's pregnant, don't you?"

He shrugged. "Is she? Could she be?"

Well, fuck. We were fucking like animals. There was always a chance she could be pregnant. I thought back through everything until it hit me.

"Holy shit. I do think her tits are bigger." *They've been trying to tell me all along.*

Cassie was pregnant. *Probably.*

The sound of the door opening behind us pulled my gaze to the back of the room. As Cassie and Georgia giggled their way back into the suite, I couldn't take my eyes off my best friend. She radiated happiness and beauty and life and everything I'd ever wanted.

Kline leaned over to whisper in my ear, and my heart jumped in my chest when he did. "She looks good with a glow. Congratulations."

Winnie

One month ago I had resigned as St. Luke's Chief of Emergency Medicine and signed on as the New York Mavericks' head team physician. I'd made the career change in hopes that the majority of my work-weeks would cut off at fifty hours, and most importantly, that I'd have more time to spend with my daughter, Lexi.

Being a single mother was hard. Add in a full-time job, and it was damn near impossible. But I felt like I'd made the right choice. Lexi wasn't with a babysitter all of the time, and I'd started finding time for myself, time to go out with friends, time to date—although, I had yet to really accomplish that one.

But I wasn't in a rush to dive headfirst into the dating scene any-way. I just wanted to enjoy this slice of normalcy I had accomplished by taking this new job.

The bustling sounds of the stadium filled my ears as I strode through the long hallway that led to the tunnel to walk out onto the field. Today marked the opening game for the New York Mavericks, and I was excited to see the guys get out onto the field and kick some ass.

My heels tip-tapped across the concrete as I pulled my phone out of my pocket to check for what had to be a million text messages in my group chat with Georgia and Cassie.

Georgia: Go Mavericks! Good luck today, Win!

Cassie: Ditto on what G said. How's my brother? Did he look okay during warm-ups? How's his knee? Did he say anything about it?

Georgia: SEAN IS FINE, Cass. Stop bugging her about it for the millionth time today.

Cassie: Stop texting me when you're sitting right next to me.

Georgia: You totally fucked Thatch in the owner's suite bathroom.

Cassie: I know I did. I was there.

Georgia: What's going on with you? You feeling okay?

Georgia: Hello? Earth to Cassie.

Georgia: Are

Georgia: You

Georgia: Okay

The convo went on for miles. And I couldn't help but smile at their ridiculousness. Georgia and Cassie were awesome. After I had met them at lunch with Will, they had taken it upon themselves to offer their friendship. Girls' nights, coffee dates, lunches at Georgia's house—all of it had become a common occurrence in my life.

I kept reading, wondering in amusement if the texts would ever end.

Cassie: I'd be a lot better if you stopped texting me.

Georgia: Sheesh, for a woman who just screamed her way through an orgasm, you're kind of testy today.

Cassie: I'm ignoring you.

Georgia: Gnome you're not.

Cassie: Stop. It.

Georgia: Gnome what your problem is?

Cassie: You. You are my problem.

Georgia: Gnome I'm not.

I laughed when I finally reached the last text that had been sent a mere two minutes ago and typed out a quick message.

Me: Thanks, guys! And Sean is good to go, Cass. You have nothing to worry about. Your brother is ready.

Georgia: YAY! See, Cassie? I told you!

Cassie: Thanks, Win.

Cassie: Stop texting me, Wheorgie.

Georgia: Never.

Me: Are you guys watching from the Owner's Suite?

Cassie: Yes. And you're coming out for drinks with us after. We will only take YES as an answer.

Me: YES. I've got a sitter. I need a night out.

Georgia: WOOOHOOOOO!

Cassie: (She literally just shouted that into my ear as she was texting it to you.) And it should be noted that I'm more than ready to get my drink on.

Me: Hahahaha

Me: Perfect. I'll meet up with you guys after the game, then.

My phone vibrated in my hands, and I answered on the second ring. "Dr. Winslow."

"Where are you?" Eddie, one of the team trainers, asked. His voice reeked of concern.

"Heading toward the field to make sure our standby paramedics arrived. What's wrong?"

"I need you in the locker room."

I stopped in my tracks. That didn't sound good. "Why?"

"Mitchell's hurt."

I sighed. "Let me guess, left hamstring."

"Yeah. I'm pretty sure he reinjured it."

"Goddammit." I closed my eyes and inhaled a frustrated breath through my nose. "I knew he wasn't ready for those last two preseason games." I turned around on my heel and headed back down the long tunnel. "How'd he do it?"

"Warm-ups, I think."

"Bullshit. He probably did something at practice Friday but managed to sneak it under our radar. I'll be there in a minute." I hung up the phone and strode for the locker room.

The second security opened the doors and gestured me through, the loud and boisterous noises of a male locker room getting ready for a big game hit me like a wave. The sights and sounds and smells were pretty much what most would imagine, and I did my best to keep my eyes focused on the one player I needed to see. I wasn't there to check out bare asses or spot swinging dicks.

Although, the bare asses were also just as good as most would imagine.

As I headed toward Mitchell's spot, I noted he was sitting down on the bench in front of his locker, his elbows resting on his knees, and his gaze locked on the floor.

"Great," Mitchell muttered when the tips of my heels came into his view. He looked up to meet my eyes and sighed. "Eddie is overreacting. I'm good to play, Doc."

I shook my head. "You pulled your hamstring again. You're not good to play."

"I'm fucking good to play. I know my body. And I'm fucking fine. So cool it with this bullshit. I don't need a mother."

I fought the urge to roll my eyes at the "I don't need a mother" crap. I also fought the urge to respond with, *Believe me, I don't want to be your mother. I just want you to stop acting like a fucking idiot.*

He took my pregnant pause as me relenting. "So, run along now," he added, shooing me away with a flick of his wrist.

Yes, he had just *shooed* me away. I felt my claws unsheathe.

I'd learned pretty quickly that my players *really* didn't like being told they couldn't play. And I understood it. I was sympathetic to their plight as a professional athlete. The pay might have been phenomenal, but it wasn't an easy job. Every time they stepped onto the field, they had to push their bodies as hard as they possibly could with the knowledge that they could push themselves too far. They could face an injury that could end their season, or even worse, their career.

With that being said, I could only stay sympathetic to a point. It was my job to know when they weren't healthy enough to play. But my job did *not* entail tolerating being disrespected or dealing with mouthy bullshit.

Unfortunately for me, some of these men pictured me as some little woman who could be pushed around. Not all, but definitely some. And unfortunately for them, I wasn't a pushover. I grew up with four loudmouthed older brothers, so when it came to dealing with insolent men, I had no qualms. Hell, I quite enjoyed putting them in their place, especially when they were insulting my intelligence as a physician.

I didn't graduate at the top of my class from Yale Med School and work under one of the most well-respected orthopedic surgeons in the country because I wasn't good at my job. I didn't run one of the busiest Emergency Departments in the country because I wasn't good at my job. I also didn't get hired by the Mavericks because I wasn't good at my job.

I was real fucking good at my job, and I knew medicine, *especially* orthopedic medicine.

Cameron Mitchell's injury wasn't shocking. Most NFL players with hamstring injuries returned to the field before they were fully healed, which was why over sixteen percent of those players ended up reinjuring themselves. Factor in Mitchell's obstinacy and unwillingness to rest, and it wasn't a surprise he was back to square one.

But since Mitchell was being a bit of a dick, I was going to have to handle this situation a little differently than I normally would.

"So you're good?" I asked, even though I knew he wasn't.

He glanced up at me with an annoyed expression. "Yep. That's what I said."

"Oh, okay. That's great to hear."

As Mitchell started to lace up his cleats, I leaned forward and gripped his meaty thigh with both hands. I dug my fingers into the tight muscle and immediately had the proof of his injury beneath my fingertips.

"What the fuck, Doc?" He tried to pull away, but I tightened my grip and watched him school his face into a neutral expression.

"Figured I might as well check the hamstring since I'm here," I said sweetly. "You don't mind, right? I mean, it's not like it's hurting or anything."

He shook his head, but he remained silent, mouth stretched tight in a firm line.

"Perfect." I grinned. "This will only take a minute."

My fingers moved across the muscle, noting the tightness and swelling of the tendon. Yeah, he had definitely strained his hamstring. A faint bruise already peppered the top of his skin, and in a few more hours, it'd be so pronounced that the fans in the nosebleed seats wouldn't miss it.

"No pain?" I asked, but I knew what I was doing was likely causing him some serious pain. Injuring him further? No. But making his life a living hell? Definitely yes.

He shook his head again, but his jaw clenched ever so slightly at the same time.

I tightened my grip even more and noted the boisterous sounds of the locker room grew silent. "Still no pain?"

"No. Pain," he answered, but he couldn't stop himself from wincing.

No pain, my ass.

"You're still *good?*" I pushed my fingers a little harder into his skin.

A normal someone with a pulled hamstring would have been screeching in pain, but Mitchell was a hard-ass. The man could tolerate more than the average person. It's why he was a great athlete. And his ability and contribution to this team was exactly why I wasn't going to let him play. He needed to rest his leg. He needed to get healthy again, or else his next game would probably be his last.

We stared at one another for a long moment, his face hard as stone while my fingers continued their assault, my gaze unwavering in its patient challenge.

Until, finally, he broke.

"Fuck," he grimaced. "Fine. Fucking fine." It was all he said, and I didn't push further. I wasn't going to be an asshole and make him say the words.

As I let go of Mitchell's leg, Eddie came over to stand beside me. "Not good?" he asked.

"I'm not clearing him to play today. I want an MRI on his leg and get him in an ice bath," I directed. "We'll reassess our game plan with his injury once we get the results back."

Mitchell stared down at the floor, and I patted his broad shoulder. "I'm not doing this to be an asshole," I whispered for his ears only. "I'm doing this because I want you back on that field, and I want you to finish the season knowing you can look forward to future seasons."

He nodded but didn't meet my eyes.

"Dayum, Doc. You're a bit of a ballbuster," Owens said as he replaced Eddie's vacated spot beside me. He was bigger than a house and one of the offensive lineman on the team.

I glanced over at him and smirked. "Yeah, you should remember that the next time you clean the vending machine out of my favorite peanut butter M&Ms."

He grinned and rubbed both hands down his rotund belly. "You know I gotta keep my figure in tip-top shape."

"You need to switch out those M&Ms for protein," I teased. "I mean, fuck, at least switch to Snickers."

Owens grinned and then his eyes moved toward Mitchell. "You're really not playing today, Mitch?"

"Nope." Mitchell glanced up and nodded toward me. "Dr. Ballbuster won't clear me."

His lips turned up ever so slightly into a faint smile, and I grinned back.

Eddie kneeled beside Mitchell with his bag of supplies. "Just gonna wrap you up real quick," he said as he got to work.

Commotion filtered in from the front of the locker room, followed by the words, "You've got to be shitting me. You're not clearing Mitchell?"

I didn't even turn around to answer whoever was rudely questioning my judgment. "No, I'm not *shitting you*," I responded and watched Eddie cover Mitchell's leg in an ACE wrap. "He can't play if he wants to be able to actually finish the season."

"How long?" the irritated voice asked from behind me.

"Until his hamstring is strong enough to avoid reinjury," I answered.

"He needs an MRI, and for fuck's sake, get his ass in an ice bath."

"This isn't my first rodeo with a hamstring injury, so if you don't mind, *I'll* be in charge of treating *my* patient," I responded as I turned on my heels to face whoever the fuck thought they knew more about medicine than I did.

I came face-to-face with a brilliant pair of hazel eyes, a handsome face, and a tall, muscular frame clad in a sharp suit and tie. And Lord Almighty, he was *wearing* that suit.

He stared back at me, his body visibly bristling in irritation.

I knew that face. I'd never personally met that face, but I sure as hell knew that face.

Well, *shit*. It was Wes Lancaster, owner of the Mavericks and *my* boss.

Since I hadn't signed on to the organization until late in the pre-season, and Wes Lancaster spent a hell of a lot of time on the road, this was the first time I was officially meeting him in person. We'd had a brief phone chat when he welcomed me to the team, but that conversation lasted all of two minutes.

I had a feeling this was about to be the epitome of an awkward introduction.

He stopped right in front of me and briefly glanced down at Mitchell before his eyes met mine again. "You're making him sit out before you get MRI results?" he questioned with a challenge in his voice.

It pissed me off. He might be the owner—who also happened to be insanely good-looking—but he'd hired me to do a job, so he needed to back off and let me do it.

Remorseless, I continued to look him directly in the eye. "I don't need the MRI to know he's injured. I need the MRI to know just *how* injured and how long of a recovery we're going to be dealing with."

He tilted his head to the side, and a cocky smirk graced his lips. "Do you even know who I am?"

I had the urge to smack him.

Or violently kiss that cocky smirk straight off his face.

No. I definitely just wanted to smack him. I didn't care how rich or unbelievably good-looking he was, I had *zero* desire to kiss a man who provided this shitty of a first impression.

Do you even know who I am? I mean, really? Was this guy serious?

He sounded like a total prick. Well, a really hot prick. I felt like the physical version of my perfect man had been set right in front of me, and then he'd opened his mouth and shit all over the fantasy.

"Yeah. Your face is plastered down every hallway in this stadium," I answered even though it was a bit of an exaggeration. There were maybe two pictures of Wes Lancaster in the entire Mavericks' facility, but I couldn't stop myself from razzing his ego.

I held out my hand. "It's nice to finally meet you, Mr. Lancaster. I'm Dr. Winnie Winslow, and I take my job of making sure I don't let your players go on the field if they're not one hundred percent very seriously."

He took my offered hand, and the second his warm palm touched mine, I felt like lightning shot through the ceiling and zapped straight into my chest.

What in the hell kind of visceral reaction was that?

"Nice to meet you, Dr. Winslow," he said and shook my hand, but honestly, his voice sounded like I was the very last person he wanted to be touching in that moment. "And just call me Wes." His eyes searched mine for the answer to some unknown question.

I couldn't get a good read on him. He looked cocky and amused one minute and then irritated and like he couldn't stand the sight of me the next. I felt off-balance from merely being in his presence.

"Okay, Wes. And please, just call me Winnie."

Our eyes stayed locked on one another until Eddie stood from his kneeling position and cleared his throat.

It was only then that I realized we were still shaking hands.

Why were we still shaking hands?

Surprised, we both let go at the same time and put distance between each another, but our eye contact never wavered. It felt like we were both trying to figure the other out, and I didn't even really understand why.

Wes blinked and averted his eyes from mine. His jaw clenched, and he muttered an excuse about having to check on something and strode out of the locker room like someone had lit his ass on fire.

All the while, I remained frozen in my spot—far longer than would've been considered normal.

What in the hell just happened?

Wes

Sound splintered the air as I slammed the door to the suite shut behind me and stalked to the large window overlooking the field.

"Whoa. What's wrong?" Kline asked.

Pyrotechnics sparkled and flashed as the team ran out of the tunnel, and the base noise level in the stadium lifted to a roar. It was a sound I lived for, especially now, during the first game of the season. But nothing was going according to plan, and I wasn't in control of any of it.

Goddammit.

"Cameron Mitchell can't play today."

"Why the fuck not?" Thatch yelled.

I shook my head and clenched my jaw. I didn't even know if I could talk about it, I was so pissed. My dick was the only one not with the program, thinking about a pretty physician's heels and skirt and take-no-shit attitude. Who in the fuck was that woman?

"Ah, man. We are *fucked*, Whitney," Thatch whined.

I looked over my shoulder and expected to find him on his feet and distraught over some large sum of money he had riding on my team, but instead, he sat calmly in his seat, a smile on his face as he looked at his hand interlocked with Cassie's.

It was almost funny, the sight of his giant hand engulfing hers, but the smile on his face wasn't. I didn't understand it, didn't fucking want that shit for myself, but after seeing the way he was when he thought they were over, I'd take this sappy version of him every day, all day.

I followed the line of Cassie's arm up from their hands and met her vivid blue eyes. "Your brother better be good."

She scoffed. "Can a pussy take a pounding?" A smirk curved my lips at the memory of hers doing just that in my bathroom, and a pointed eyebrow inched toward my forehead. She held my eyes with absolutely no embarrassment, confirming she knew precisely what I was thinking. "Exactly. Whatever you need? He's better. Whatever you think he can do? He can do more."

I sure as fuck hoped so.

"That's right, honey," Thatch encouraged. "You tell him."

Fucking people in love.

I rolled my eyes and looked back to the field as the captains walked to the center to do the coin toss. We needed this to go in our favor. Without our best defensive end, our offense was going to have to come out blazing and set the tempo for a race up the scoreboard.

"You have any booze in this place?" Cassie asked, and I turned back to look at her. Thatch's face had turned hard.

"Yeah," I answered her while I looked at him and tried to figure out what that was about. "There's some beer in the fridge, but if you want something else, they'll bring it."

"Beer's good," she announced with a shrug, climbing from Thatch's lap. But he grabbed on to her hips and didn't let her go.

"Uh, I'm trying to walk here, Thatcher," she challenged with a smile. His face was still remarkably devoid of one.

My confusion blossomed. What happened to the happy-go-lucky guy of fifteen seconds ago?

He glanced at Kline briefly, who just smiled and shrugged, and then turned back to Cassie. With one rough yank, he pulled her down to straddle his lap and whispered something in her ear that made her eyes light up.

She moved quick, like a jack-in-the-box, jumping back off of his lap and pulling him to standing. His eyes skated briefly across mine, something in them I didn't quite understand, before going back to her as she pulled him around the seats and back toward the en suite bathroom.

Jesus Christ, again?

"Is anybody going to actually watch this game with me?" I asked Kline testily. Frankly, I sounded kind of like a whiny kid, but Winnie fucking Winslow had me all out of whack.

Kline didn't call me on it, though. He was pretty much the only real adult among us. Rising from his seat, he walked over and stood next to me at the window and both sets of our eyes went to the field.

"What's the plan?"

I shook my head, grimacing as the coin toss went in Pittsburgh's favor, and answered honestly. "Play as hard as we can for all four fucking quarters, I guess."

Kline's smirk hooked my attention from the corner of my eye. "What?" I asked.

His head shook slightly, and he smiled. "I'm just hoping Coach Bennett's plan is a little more detailed."

Two minutes left in the fourth quarter, and we were up by seven. A fucking touchdown was practically nothing, the kind of lead that could change on a dime, but it was a lot goddamn better than being behind.

I hadn't left my spot in front of the windows, my feet having practically grown roots there, and that was the way I liked it. Involved, engaged, and in tune with every second of play.

My friends didn't have the same kind of avid concentration, but I'd done my best not to notice them as they flitted and squealed all over the room. Cassie had the most attentiveness of anyone, but only when her brother was on the field, and the way she screamed in my ear every time he did something noteworthy made me wish she didn't.

The fabric of my pants pockets bunched in my hands as I worked to not scrub my hands down my face. I knew there was a camera on me at any given time, and while it wasn't actually the case at all, I'd made an outward name for myself as having nerves of steel. Commentators often made remarks about my ability to maintain so much composure.

Hell, maybe it was a bad thing. Maybe it was something everyone mocked rather than revered, but it was what I knew. What made me comfortable.

And, as my eyes scanned the sideline to see if I could catch a glimpse of the new team physician, I knew I needed as much fucking normalcy as possible.

Fourth down and three yards to go, our defense lined up without their star defensive end, with the game on the line. My lungs ached with the huge inhale of air I took, and my jaw wasn't feeling unused either. But if we stopped them from converting this fucking fourth down, the game was over. Rodeshiemer took the snap, shuffling his feet while his eyes scanned the field for an open receiver. He was one of the best fucking passers, with one of the highest completion rates in the entire league, and my balls nearly shriveled up just thinking about having him on the other side of the line in a situation like this. *"Get him, get him, get him,"* I chanted in my head. *Fucking end this.*

His offensive line held strong, but all of his receivers were covered. I saw him glance to our weak side again, the gaping hole left by Mitchell only partially filled by his replacement, Harvesty, but Ontario Williams, our defensive tackle, finally broke his hold against Dan DeLuva and took his mammoth body barreling toward their quarterback.

Fuck yes. End this.

Pittsburgh was a formidable opponent for a reason and made for a nightmare of a first game of the season, but even they weren't invincible. Williams brought Rodeshiemer down with a thud, and my hands finally shot into the air.

Cassie cheered from the rear, and Kline clapped me on the shoulder before stepping away to claim back his wife. I smiled at the feeling of my first full breath.

That is, until I realized that Winnie was still down there as pandemonium broke out. Like a word search, I scoured each group of people one by one.

"Quinn Bailey played one fuck of a game," Thatch said from somewhere beside me. I hadn't even noticed him walk up.

I glanced at him briefly, but I kept my focus on the field as a crowd covered it like a blanket. "Oh? Are you saying you actually saw the game?"

His face was a weird mix of happiness and regret and apology all in one. I wasn't sure I'd ever seen him look this way. "Sorry, dude. I know my attention was a little split today, but I swear, today of all days, I had a reason. I'll be here right beside you the whole time next game."

I wanted to focus on what he was saying, ask him about what the fuck was going on with him, but I couldn't. Not until I found her.

"What's wrong?" he asked, and I knew I wasn't doing a good job of hiding the fucking awful feeling in my chest.

"Nothing," I denied as I kept looking.

"Are you looking for someone?" he asked. It took a whole lot of effort to keep from telling him I'd find who I was looking for a hell of a lot faster if he left me to it.

"Look!" Georgia squealed from the other end of the glass. "There's Winnie!"

My eyes shot to her to see where she was looking. I followed the line of her finger and finally saw, in the center of the crowd with a security guard beside her, Winnie was jogging straight down the middle of the field for the tunnel.

I closed my eyes and ran a hand through my hair. *This is so not fucking good.*

Most of my employees were men, or in Georgia's case, married to one of my best friends, so I didn't really find myself in this situation often, but it wasn't good. *You cannot angry-fuck one of your employees.*

Long legs wrapped around me with her skirt up to her waist and her tits in my mouth, I pictured fucking her against the goalpost. *Fuck*, I told myself. *I told you, you* can't *fuck her.*

The sound of Cassie's excited voice pulled me out of my daydream. "I'm so glad she's going out with us tonight."

I couldn't even stop myself from asking. "Who?"

She looked at me like I was crazy. "Winnie."

Shit. My gaze jerked back to the field, but she'd already disappeared inside the tunnel.

"Me too," Georgia agreed. "Where do you think we should go?"

They answered in unison. "Barcelona Bar!"

Thatch jumped to attention beside me. Honest to God, I think he'd been sleeping on his feet.

"Barcelona Bar?" His face was a mask of no-fucking-way.

Cassie transformed into a woman possessed right before our eyes. "Yes, Barcelona Bar! I want some Harry Potter shots, goddammit!"

"No," Thatch denied outright, and my eyebrows jumped up in surprise. Georgia's face said Danger Will Robinson too, but Kline, the only one who seemed to understand, stood smirking in the background.

"No?" Cassie asked back in a voice that would scare anyone. "What do you mean, 'no'?"

"Cass—"

"No, Thatcher. You've been cockblocking my good time for hours now, and I want to know what the fuck is going on."

He glanced around at all of us desperately, but no one tried to help.

"Come on, baby," he tried. "Let's go have sex."

Her eyes flashed, and she started to move toward him before she caught herself. "Wait. Are you using pussy persuasion to distract me?"

Thatch tried to look innocent, but he failed spectacularly.

"Oh my God, you are!" she yelled. "You better tell me what's going on here right fucking now, or I will destroy you."

"Cass," he whispered. "Trust me, honey. Now really isn't the time."

A knock sounded on the door of the suite, and Winnie peeked her head in. Her eyes came straight to me.

"You think you can't feel your dick now, but you definitely won't be able to when I cut it off your body," Cassie retorted.

I winced at the visual, my eyes still locked with Winnie's. It was like some weird magnet that would not let go.

"Fine," Thatch yelled. "You're pregnant, okay? Are you happy now?"

Huh? My head whipped to the side to look at the lovers' spat. Apparently, that kind of news was strong enough to break the connection.

"*What?*" Cassie shrieked.

Thatch nodded.

"No." Cassie shook her head and laughed maniacally. "That's the most ridiculous thing I've ever heard in my life."

"Cassie," Thatch tried softly.

"I'm not pregnant, you lunatic. Why would you even say something like that? It's literally the craziest thing that's ever come out of your mouth." Georgia tried to step in and put a hand of comfort to Cassie's shoulder, but she tossed it off.

"Cassie."

Cassie turned to look at her. "I'm not pregnant," she repeated.

"Cassie," Thatch tried to get her attention again.

"I'm ignoring you, Thatcher. Stop telling our friends lies." She flipped him off over her shoulder. "I swear, I'm not pregnant," she said again, and I wasn't sure if she was trying to convince us or herself.

"Honey," Thatch said and moved to stand beside her. He placed both hands on her shoulders and refused to let her shrug them off. "I'm not spouting off crazy bullshit right now. I honestly think you might be pregnant."

She shook her head, and her face morphed into utter disbelief. "Do you even realize how insane you sound? I'm on birth control. There's no way I'm pregnant."

"I think you need to take a test, honey," he said, voice soft. "When was your last period?"

"Oh, for fuck's sake," she scoffed. "I'm not going to recount my ovulation cycle with you."

But even as the words flowed past her lips, her face showed that maybe she wasn't so certain.

Winnie's unyielding voice sounded from the other side of the room.

"Come on, Cass. Let's go get a test."

She looked at Winnie for a long moment until she nodded without even an attempt to argue. Winnie had undeniable authority.

I immediately pictured her bent over my desk, a red reminder of my handprint on her ass.

Goddammit.

"Fine," Cassie relented and tossed her hands in the air. She turned toward Thatch and stabbed her finger into his chest. "Get ready to be proven wrong."

Thatch smirked, but the gentleness in his eyes showed he wasn't even considering being wrong in this scenario. That was a look of a man who was certain. And he wasn't the least bit upset but the possibility.

No, he looked thrilled.

Cassie

"I'm not pregnant," I said and opened the pregnancy test package. "I'm on birth control. There's no fucking way I'm pregnant."

Right? I took the pill every day. I hadn't been on any antibiotics. There had been zero hiccups with my cycle. Shit was normal. Well, besides the constant need to bone, but I lived with a giant who could fuck like a god. I'd like to find the woman who wouldn't want to have constant sex in that scenario.

I glanced at Georgia and Winnie. They were both leaning against the bathroom counter, watching me damn near tear the package in two. And neither had expressed they were on the same page as me. The Cassie Isn't Pregnant page.

I narrowed my eyes at Georgia when I noted the soft expression on her face and her frequent glances toward my belly. "No, Wheorgie," I said and pointed the test at her. "Go ahead and get those thoughts right out of your head. I'm. Not. Pregnant."

Her expression grew softer, and she smiled.

"Seriously. Stop looking at me like that."

"Just go take the test, Cass," she finally said.

I groaned and stepped into the bathroom stall. This was about the most ridiculous situation I had ever been involved in. Taking a goddamn pregnancy test inside Duane Reade while the guys waited outside in the parking lot. Go back ten years and put us in a high school bathroom and this could've been an episode of *Teen Mom*.

Granted, it wasn't his choice that Thatcher wasn't with me.

I had refused to let him join me while I peed on a stick. With the excited expression I had witnessed on his face, I had a feeling he would've been hovering over the toilet and holding the stick while I peed.

I was in and out of the stall in less than two minutes. After I set the test down on a clean paper towel, I washed my hands while Winnie and Georgia looked down at it the entire time.

"Seriously, you guys can stop staring at it. I already told you the answer. I'm not pregnant," I said as I dried off my hands and tossed the used paper towel in the trash. I leaned against the bathroom counter, crossed my arms over my chest, and looked everywhere but at the test.

That stupid test. I *wasn't* pregnant.

Seriously, how many times did I have to tell these idiots I wasn't pregnant?

Thatch couldn't have been more wrong about this. I was sure of it.

"Cass," Georgia whispered, "You should probably look at this."

I glanced over at her and watched her eyes go wide.

"No," I refused. "I'm not looking at it. I already know the answer."

"Cassie," Winnie chimed in, "Georgia's right. You need to check the results yourself."

I rolled my eyes. "Don't be ridiculous. Just tell me what it says… Go ahead," I said, gesturing with my hand. "Just say *Not Pregnant,* and then we can all leave this bathroom and head to the bar."

Georgia shook her head. "I can't. You need to be the one to see it."

"You guys are being ridiculous." I groaned and strode to their side of the counter and snatched the pee stick off the towel. My eyes met the result window, and I laughed.

One pink line straight down the middle. *Not pregnant.*

I held the test up in the air. "See? Not pregnant. I told you guys."

Winnie's eyes went wide while Georgia's eyes filled with tears.

I honestly felt a little bad about the whole thing. I hadn't realized she wanted me to be pregnant that badly. "I'm sorry, Georgie," I said. "I promise one day I'll get pregnant and you'll be the godmother just like we talked about."

God, my best friend was so fucking sweet I could hardly stand it.

"Uh, Cassie," Winnie said as she reached forward and wrapped her hand around my hand that was still holding the test. "You're looking at the control window. You need to move your thumb to see the actual results."

I glanced down at the test and watched as her index finger slid my thumb away from the result screen. The test window doubled in size, and the pink lines had multiplied.

One.

Two.

Wait. What?

I counted them again.

One.

Two.

What?

I'm pregnant?!

I stared down at that test for who knows how long.

I was stunned.

Speechless.

I was motherfucking *knocked up.*

"That giant bastard got me pregnant!" I shouted when verbal function returned, and I strode straight out of the bathroom, piss-stained test in hand. My feet smacked across the tile floor of Duane Reade, and within seconds, I was striding through the automatic doors toward the parking lot.

Thatch leaned against the bumper of his Range Rover, arms crossed over his chest and face relaxed, while he chatted with Kline and Wes.

I took four stomping steps out of the entrance of the store and then chucked the pregnancy test across the parking lot. It nailed Thatch square in his forehead.

"Ow, what the fuck?" He glanced up to find me practically shooting laser beams from my eyes aimed in his and *only his* direction. "Cass? Honey?"

I didn't say a word. I just pointed down at the pregnancy test sitting on the pavement beside his feet.

He titled his head to the side before bending down and picking it up.

He held the test in the air. "Did you take it already?"

"Oh, yeah," I confirmed. "I took it all right."

I heard the automatic doors open behind me and knew that Winnie and Georgia had followed me out. Kline and Wes glanced at the girls, but Thatch's eyes stared down at the test.

I swear he didn't move for a full minute.

And then, his mouth morphed into the biggest smile I had ever seen.

He looked at me, then he looked at my belly, then he looked at the test.

"We're pregnant?" he asked when his eyes met mine again.

"No," I snapped. "We're not pregnant." I pointed at myself. "I'm pregnant. I'm the one who's going to get a big fat ass, and my boobs are going to be bigger than your giant fucking head. Goddammit, Thatcher. You knocked me up!"

I didn't think it was possible, but his smile got even bigger.

Thatch

I didn't even pause, one step, two, I charged right at her until she had to look straight up to see me.

"Thatch," she whispered when she saw the look on my face. I knew it was all there, everything I was feeling—wonder, love, excitement, and a whole lot of *this is the best moment of my life*.

The asphalt scraped at the denim over my knees as I dropped to them in front of her and put my forehead to her stomach.

There was a life in there made up of half of her and half of me.

Hands to her hips, I pushed the loose fabric of her shirt up until a couple inches of skin were exposed above the waist of her skirt.

My lips had a mind of their own, and my eyes closed at the feel of her warm, thrumming skin beneath them. When her small hands sank into my hair, tears threatened at the corners of my eyes.

"Thatcher," she whispered again. I opened my eyes to look up at her, but my lips never left her skin.

"We made a baby, Cassie." Her throat bobbed, and she nodded.

God, I am so in love with her.

"Are you happy?" I asked, even though part of me was scared to know the answer.

I hadn't planned on getting her pregnant, and I certainly hadn't been trying, but here, with my mouth a few inches away from *our baby*, I'd never wanted anything more.

"It's soon," she said gently, but her eyes were soft. Love and happiness were the only two things that could ever make her look that soft.

I shook my head. "Everything. You. Me. This tiny, surely out of its motherfucking mind combination of us. The timing. It's all *so* right."

"We're going to need a new set of rules," she said with a smile.

I laughed but shook my head. "I only have one."

"Just one? I'm knocked up, the two of us are going to have to figure out how to be parents, and you only have one fucking rule?"

I pushed to my feet and put my lips to her ear. "Be worthy of my family."

Her head jerked back, and her watery eyes met mine.

"And, baby, that's one rule I'll *never* fucking break."

The End

CONTACT INFORMATION

Love Cassie, Thatch, and the crew?

Stay up to date with them and us by signing up for our newsletter: http://www.authormaxmonroe.com/#!contact/c1kcz

You may live to regret much, but we promise it won't be this. Seriously. We'll make it fun.

If you're already signed up, consider sending us a message to tell us how much you love us. We really like that. ;)

And you really don't want to miss what's next for Cassie and Thatch. #BankingHer #StalkingHer

Yes, you read that right. The crazy tables have turned, but in the funniest way possible.
Banking Her (Billionaire Bad Boys Book 2.5) is coming for you on September 6th, 2016.

Get the rest of the Billionaire Bad Boys Series here: http://www. authormaxmonroe.com/#!books/cnec

Follow us online:
Facebook: www.facebook.com/authormaxmonroe
Reader Group: www.facebook.com/groups/1561640154166388
Twitter: www.twitter.com/authormaxmonroe
Instagram: www.instagram.com/authormaxmonroe
Goodreads: https://goo.gl/8VUIz2

ACKNOWLEDGEMENTS

First of all, THANK YOU for reading. That goes for anyone who's bought a copy, read an ARC, helped us beta, edited, or found time in their busy schedule just to make sure we didn't completely fuck over your favorite Billionaire Bad Boys. (Although, Thatch probably deserved an extra couple of dick slaps during his book. We love him, but he was kind of an asshole.)

Thank you for supporting us, for talking about our books, and for just being so unbelievably loving and supportive of our characters. You've made this our MOST favorite adventure thus far.

THANK YOU to each other. Monroe is thanking Max. Max is thanking Monroe. Blah. Blah. Blah. We know, we do this every book, but that's what best friends do. So we'll just keep on doing it. Hell, we'll probably do this forever. The books and the thanking. :)

THANK YOU, our fair Lisa, for being you. You're awesome and wonderful and so damn flexible. Seriously, have you been doing yoga? It's working. ;) And it goes without saying, we love you.

THANK YOU, Kristin and Murphy, for being adaptable, editing ninjas and juggling a million things at once. You both kicked some serious ass during this book. You're the best.

THANK YOU, Amy, for getting us to start watching *Vanderpump Rules* and sharing our love for Tyler from *Teen Mom*. Oh, and that whole agent thing…you're really good at it. :)

THANK YOU, JoAnna & Sandra, for being the best Counselor Feathers. You ladies have turned Camp Love Yourself into the BEST place to be on Facebook. This is us sending you a million hugs.

THANK YOU, Sommer, for tolerating our "We Need More Things" or "Hey, it's us again" emails without actually strangling us. You're the best. There's no doubting this. And, well, you know we think you're really pretty. ;)

THANK YOU to every blogger who has read, reviewed, posted, shared, and supported us. Your enthusiasm, support, and hard work does not go unnoticed. We wish we could send you your very own Thatch as thanks. We can't. And even if we could, we don't think he'd go willingly, and we're not really comfortable walking that fine a line with human trafficking.

THANK YOU, members of CLY and CLYCOG. You guys make us smile every day. Or some such bullshit.

THANK YOU to our families. They support us, motivate us, and most importantly, tolerate us. Sometimes we're not the easiest people to live with, especially during this book when our deadline was looming. #adifferentkindofghostwriter #WalkingDead #murderisastateofmind

We honestly don't know what we'd do without you guys.

As always, all our love.

CPSIA information can be obtained
at www.ICGtesting.com
Printed in the USA
LVOW04s0532251016
510159LV00014B/447/P

9 781535 434003